A. R. MORGAN

THE SOUL OF A CHAMPION

TRIA PRIMA SERIES
BOOK 2

This book is dedicated to Scott.
You have been my rock, the pillar of strength when my whole
world fell around me.
You picked me up (literally) when I have fallen and held my hand
whenever my clumsy self stumbles.
You have been the light to my darkness.
Thank you, my PLP.

A. R. Morgan

COPYRIGHT

ISBN 979-8-9873524-3-4(Ebook)
ISBN 979-8-9873524-4-1 (Paperback)
ISBN 979-8-9873524-5-8 (Hardback)
Library of Congress Control Number: 2024907142
Illustration & Published by A R Morgan Books, Envato Elements, and Meowlayn.art & Anther Art
Edited by https://getproofreader.co.uk/ & Joe Stout
armorganbooks.com

FOREWORD

Thank you for continuing to follow along with Melisandre and me on her epic and magnificent journey! I hope you enjoy it as much as I have enjoyed writing it.

As with the first book, there are many cultural and historical references, a plethora of mythologies that I have lovingly and tirelessly researched in order to portray with as much accuracy as possible. When you go through, I encourage readers to look up many of the gods and mythical creatures mentioned.

Unfortunately, there were some languages I wasn't able to seek professional assistance with, so if you do see mistakes within them, my apologies! I did my best and it never my intent to offend or misrepresent any culture. Please note: This book has Old Irish, not modern Irish.

While there is a glossary provided, I also tried to include as much translation as possible within the text.

For more information on my books and future works, visit me at armorganbooks.com

A friendly reminder as well: This book is intended for mature audiences and does depict adult themes is only meant for **mature audiences**. Read at your own discretion!

TRIGGER WARNINGS

Implied SA, gore, violence, explicit sexual scenes, cursing, implied torture, light BDSM themes.

GLOSSARY

Alchemist: A race of beings created by Mother Nature at the dawn of time, before she created humans. Each Alchemist was genetically programmed to control a singular element. Together, they could maintain and care for the balance of nature. They lived in a hidden city called The Citadel, their land extending to a great wall known as Eladaria's Wall. Their genius was renowned, their science legendary and they became hunted after the old gods fled. Yet, a little over 600 years ago, they mysteriously disappeared.

A rún: A term that means "My love" or a term used between lovers

A thoice cheanndána: Old Irish for 'stubborn wench'.

ástin mín: 'My love' a term of endearment in Icelandic Norse.

Brownie: A creature that can be found in English and Scottish folklore. The Irish equivalent is the Grogan. This industrious fairy, or also known as hobgoblins, are small creatures that can be found in homes and other dwellings. They are extremely difficult to spot, silent and rarely seen. These little house elves have a mischievous side and make excellent spies and pickpockets, their light fingers a skill most valued in the Unseelie Kingdom.

Cantre'r Gwaelod: A legendary ancient kingdom, now sunken beneath the waves of Cardigan Bay; also known as the 'Welsh Atlantis'. This is where the Great Battle took place, where the Champions conquered the gods.

Champions: Gladiators created by the gods of all mythologies, to fight in their name. Each warrior possesses some aspects of their creator/s, their magic displaying the might of their master.

Ciúnas: Old Irish for 'Silence!' (command)

Dauði: Death in Icelandic Norse.

Dauði Dróttning: 'Death Queen' in Icelandic Norse.

Det som göms i snö, kommer fram vid tö: An Old Norse saying 'What is hidden in snow, is revealed at thaw'. It means that any secrets you have, will be revealed in time.

Draconus Lingua: The language of dragons.

Fae: These magical creatures were born from the magic of the Tuatha Dé Danann. Two kingdoms, the Seelie Court and the Unseelie Court. They are each ruled by a Champion created by the gods; Queen Mab, of the Seelie Court, and King Ruarc, of the Unseelie Court.

Fènghuáng: A mythological Chinese Phoenix, though not born of fire but the light of the sun. Believed to have incredible vibrancy in colour, they are powerful and auspicious. A creature of balance, possessing both female and male qualities, they are considered harbingers of peace.

Gaeilge: Irish Gaelic

Gu leòr: Irish Gaelic for 'enough'.

Gyðja viskunnar: Icelandic Norse, meaning 'goddess of wisdom'.

Hóra: Icelandic for 'whore'.

Ingarmr: Norse Hell-hounds.

Kasa: Japanese for 'hat'.

Καλημέρα: Greek for 'Good morning'.

Kunops: Greek for 'bitch'.

Megálo Kolossaío: A massive and magical colosseum that was designed by Zues and Odin. This arena is where the original Divine Games took place.

μικρός ασβός or mikrós asvós: Little badger

Mukt karana: Completely made up word by yours truly.

Otherworld: An alternate dimension existing on earth that Mother Nature, and the gods and goddesses of nature created to give a safe haven to creatures of magic.

Otherfolk: people and creatures that live in the Otherworld.

Paláti tou Efiálti: Kingdom of Nightmares in Greek

Searbhónta ciapánta: "Annoying servant" In Gaeilge (he's insulting this person)

Theïká Paichnídia: Greek for 'Divine Games'.

Ulchabhán Mór: Old Irish for 'Great Owl'

Were-Kind: Also born from Champions, the werewolves, werebears, werelions, etc. were created by animal gods and goddesses, their forms exemplifying their creators. They gain power through hunting and eating their prey. Fierce and brutal warriors, their strength in battle is unmatched.

Yaldā Night: An ancient festival celebrating winter solstice, or the Longest Night of the Year. It is during this time that all the powers in the Otherworld come together in peace and reenact the Divine Games.

TABLE OF CONTENTS

CHAPTER I

Losing consciousness and subsequently waking up in chains, was becoming annoyingly frequent as of late. It was downright vexing. Perhaps it was the blood loss, or perhaps it was going through a magical method of transportation, but I had no memory of how I came to be here.

Alchemists do not do well with magic, after all.

The first thing of note, as I was lying prone, was how comfortable it was. Despite being met with resistance when trying to move, Instinct kicked in as I struggled against whatever limited me.

Bound and very much limited.

All of my limbs sported butter-soft leather with reinforced steel restraints, chained to the four posts of the bed. This left me in the dignified position of spread-eagle. The situation was all the more maddening with my current state of clothing as well: a black brassiere and panties.

The extensive energy my body emits when the Stone is activated has an inconvenient habit of disintegrating clothing, unless it's something I have modified specifically for its use. Thankfully, I had the foresight to at least wear the right undergarments. The covers beneath me were soft and luxurious and I virtually sank into the mattress.

Atleast my prison is more comfortable than that of Castle Fyrkat, I thought dryly.

Looking around, my eyes squinted in the darkened room. A roaring fire was the only source of light, illuminating the room in a warm glow. It was probably why, despite being nearly naked, the room's temperature was surprisingly comfortable.

Thick drapes covered the windows and there were elaborate tapestries hanging on the walls in my view. Mahogany furniture with Celtic designs dominated the area. Lifting my head up further, I was able to make out a circular marble table with what looked like a matching chess set and two stools beneath it.

Testing my bonds again, my arms pulled but there was no give. Yanking my legs, I tried to swivel but failed. Exhaustion permeated both body and soul. My heart was weary. The metal chains crawled with magic; my alchemy useless against it. For once, I didn't even have the mental capacity to painstakingly search for a breach in the magic coating so I could transmute the chains. Clenching my jaw in frustration, my eyes closed against the feeling of helplessness.

Suddenly, the bed dipped toward the end, near my legs. I snapped to attention.

The Unseelie King was before me. He was shirtless; half his torso was black as ebony, making it difficult to discern against the shadows in the room. But the monster-yellow eye on that side glowed back at me, just as the aquamarine one on the left, twinkled. His right hand possessed sharp black talons, stark against the white sheets, while the other hand was beautiful. Elegant, even. Movement had me tensing and tugging at my bonds as he began crawling slowly towards me. Closer still, I noticed his body was littered with keloidal scars. Muscles rippled and tightened as he positioned himself over me. To my ever-blessed relief, he wore pants.

"Awake at last." The grin that accompanied his statement made me frown harder. "Unlike the Vampire Court, I am not entirely ignorant of the ways of Alchemists. I know a thing or two about keeping them chained. Yet, you are still somewhat of an anomaly among your kind; a mystery I have been very much looking forward to unravelling." Those strange eyes roamed over me hungrily, igniting my rising panic. "Now, those wounds will not heal without the assistance of magic. More specifically, Fae magic. Part of the power of Nemesis is that it stops biological regeneration and nullifies immortality. Fortunately for both of us, my saliva can heal." he gave me a pointed look. "But it can also decay, so I strongly advise you to hold still and not test me." To my surprise, he had far sharper teeth than any Fae I had ever seen.

Still, the Unseelie King could rot my limbs off for all I cared.

"Don't you DARE touch me! Untie me before I show you the meaning of nuclear, Unseelie," I hissed.

His ruby-red hair slid along my thigh as he cocked his head at me, leaning back slightly.

"I will not let you go, Melisandre. Your injuries require proper care and rest. Besides, I have survived much more than explosions, little one. Threats of that nature do not frighten the likes of me."

"There are no limits to my creativity, Fae. Now get. OFF!" I barked, renewing a more violent, albeit fruitless, struggle.

It irked me to no end that he was not far off the mark in his evaluation of my needs; using the Stone took much from me and I was weak from blood loss as well. It would be a miracle if I could transmute my pillow into thread at this point.

One of my main focuses in research has been how to recycle energy used by the Stone back into myself. It was, unfortunately, still in the hypothetical phase.

Settling himself between my legs, he unlocked one arm. Taking my chances, I swiped at him. His reaction was instant. My wrist was smacked down and pinned to the mattress. That clawed hand wrapped menacingly around my throat in clear warning.

"So wonderfully feisty, my beauty. Fight me, struggle, I beg you. Give me a reason not to delay burying myself deep within this delectable body right now. Or, you can be obedient, submit to me and be healed. Possibly even released," he warned, grinning salaciously. "I know what decision I would prefer."

"Sickness take you, you son of a spineless wretch!" I spat.

Gathering saliva, I puckered my lips in order to deliver the biggest wad of spit that had ever hit this bastard's face. Ruarc's lips slammed down onto mine and I let out a surprised yelp, then a painful whimper as his teeth cut my lips, forcing my mouth open to avoid my lips being crushed. Thrusting his tongue into mine, he dominated my mouth, forcing me into submission. The moment I attempted to bite his tongue off, he ripped my head back by my hair and continued his possession. I felt him hardened against my core as he pushed and ground against me. Although my mind filled with outrage, to my absolute horror, the traitorous tendrils of desire slowly snaked through me.

Finally, he pulled away, both of us gasping.

"Now, will you behave, or do I need to finish what you have so deliciously provoked? As you can tell," Ruarc pressed his hips into mine, "I am quite in favour of continuing."

The look I burned him with was scathing and full of fury. My heart raced, out of breath from the struggle and burning indignation.

"If it will get you off of me then have done with it!" I seethed.

I looked away. I could have combusted with the amount of rage running through me, but only by the will of the Mother did my mouth remain shut.

Ruarc clearly noticed. "Good choice."

Taking my arm, he brought it to his mouth and began licking the sliced wound. Gasping at the sting, I attempted to jerk my arm away. He tightened his grip and gave me a stern look. I looked away again, forcing myself to relax.

The Champion shackled my wrist once more after he'd finished. The stinging pain from Alcaeus' sword was gone and the wound was healed. With each laceration, the Unseelie King licked them clean. His claim of his saliva having healing properties rang true, although the scientist in me couldn't help imagining the bacterial warzone his actions inflicted.

I shuddered, thanking the Mother for my own specialised biology.

Upon finally reaching the large gash at my ribs, he pushed up my bra so the swell of one breast was exposed. He laid a gentle kiss on it before going to work and I could not hold back the gasp of stinging pain and the unwelcome intimacy his touch brought.

He finished and then trailed his nose back up, caressing the underside of my exposed breast.

"That is enough! You have accomplished your task," I snapped.

Ruarc grinned, sharp teeth resting on his lower lip. Pointed ears littered with black rings poked through his hair. His hot breath skated over my nipple, causing it to harden.

"Oh Melisandre, how stubborn you are! I know you desire me," he flicked his tongue over the hardened nub, "I can *smell* it," he purred, wrapping his lips over my nipple. His hot tongue swirled around my areola, igniting the nerves. He grasped and kneaded me, causing me to helplessly squirm. "Give in, beautiful creature, for to be with a Fae Champion will be the most exquisite experience you shall ever have; once you have a taste of us, you will crave it for eternity." His magic crawled across my skin and I shivered with revulsion but it was soon replaced with white-hot lust.

That's when it dawned on me where this suspicious desire in me was coming from: he was using magic to seduce me, to make my body crave him.

"Stop it...Ah! Stop this, Ruarc," I panted, though my voice was still sharp, refusing to lose myself to his touch. The Mark from Alcaeus burned and pulsated, as if it too was angry at the attention. Closing my eyes, I fought to keep my mind filled with my real lover, while stoking the flames of outrage to burn hotter than the lust Ruarc was trying to invoke.

The feel of Ruarc's fingers slipping through the edge of my underwear was ice water on the synthetic desire coursing through me. The memory of something Alcaeus said came roaring back to me: *You cannot force a mating bond if you are already bonded to another.*

"No, Ruarc! I am not yours to defile! I am bonded to another!" I cried out in panic.

He stopped and it felt like the temperature in the room dropped twenty degrees.

Grabbing my chin, he jerked my face to his, forcing my eyes open. "No, Alchemist, you belong to me! Llyr made a deal: safe passage and rescue for him and his mate and the hybrid boy. In return, he gave me the life of the last Alchemist! To lay any mark as I see fit! Those were the terms! Your friends have betrayed you, Melisandre—by oath and blood, you are now very much bound to me!" he barked.

"I belong to Alcaeus Pallas, Champion of Athena and Prince of the Nightmare Court! I ALREADY BEAR HIS MARK!" I shouted.

The Unseelie King's eyes widened at that before he shoved my thick hair away from my shoulders and neck. I could tell the moment he saw it because his face became incensed.

"*Scaoil!*" He commanded, the chains releasing me.

Jerking me from the bed, he grabbed me by the back of the neck and drove me from the room. I desperately pulled my bra down while fighting his merciless grip but he was unfazed by my attempts.

Tripping and stumbling, we came to a halt as we entered a massive hall where great tables were placed around the room. Straight down the middle was a long, carved out fireplace, slightly lower than the floor. Black grates fenced it in. The entire length of it would cover at least four of the great tables in the room. It would have been a wonder to behold during a festival.

At the end of the room sat two thrones made of black feathers and bleached bone. The king pushed me forward and upon getting there, threw me to the black marble floor.

"Stay!" he commanded me before letting out a shrill whistle.

The ground was freezing on my bare flesh but I stayed where I was. Glancing back at the unlit logs, I shivered.

A little warmth would be bloody nice.

A humanoid creature with tentacles surrounding its face where its mouth should be, appeared before the king. Glowing yellow eyes took me in but turned to his king.

"*Yesss,* My King?"

"Bring that traitorous Seelie bastard to me!"

"At once, My King."

Within what felt like moments, the great doors to the hall burst open. Llyr and Elis, accompanied by two winged-demon-like creatures came towards us. I attempted to rise just as Elis reached for me but a hand grabbed the back of my neck, pulling me away.

"*A Seelie! A chunúis na mbréag!*" raged Ruarc. "*Thug tú bean dom a bhí ceangailte le fear eile cheana!*"

You lying piece of shit! You gave me a woman already bound to another! Is what I understood, though he spoke so fast it was difficult to make out.

Llyr's face fell but Elis looked shocked and turned to his mate.

"I beg your pardon, my Gaeilge is a little rusty—did he just say 'gave'? You gave Melisandre, my dearest friend, to the UNSEELIE KING?" yelled Elis, completely ignoring the fuming Fae royal.

Llyr shrank back, away from Elis, but turned back to the king.

"The mark is not complete, Your Highness! It is breakable is it not? I know it is not a familiar mark but neither is it a Chosen one! Surely, it can be reversed?" Llyr pleaded, his hands shaking as he tried to appease the enraged king.

"Excuse me, Llyr O'Cananach! I am speaking to you! How DARE you bargain my best friend's life for ours! I cannot believe you! Expect to be sleeping alone for the next century, you horrible man! Thank you for bringing up Mark reversal because, apparently, I just may be in need of one!" cried Elis, positively outraged on my behalf. I was relieved, knowing Elis was not in on it.

"I did it to save us, my love! You must believe me! I know the King will take much better care—"

"Don't you 'my love' me! The only care you can count on is me strangling you in your sleep, you spineless coward! Some diplomat you are. I told you before: you have the communication skills of a tongueless bear in the dead of winter! Imagine talking to me about my best friend!"

"You were incarcerated—"

"Well, isn't that convenient—"

"*Ciúnas!*" King Ruarc roared and all went quiet. Llyr fell to his knees, bowing so low his head touched the ground. Elis continued to glare down at his mate, but gave a small bow in respect toward the royal Fae. "This is no simple 'Mark', you imbecile!" My head was yanked painfully to the side as I was shoved forward. "These symbols are from an ancient and divine ritual which can only be created by the gods themselves! She is *fated* with King Alcaeus! YOU BARGAINED A FATED MATE TO ME! I cannot claim her, even if the Mark is not completed!

Her soul can only be bound to his, you damned fool!"

All of our faces mirrored each other in downright shock. It all made sense now. Ragna's reaction when she saw it. It meant that Alcaeus could never be bound to her, not even by force. Now I understood her despair.

The reason behind the king's forceful and lascivious actions also became clear: Ruarc was going to force a mating bond in order to control me and bind me for whatever ulterior motives he had. I did not know why I was 'fated' to Alcaeus; that was not something that happened to Alchemists. The Mother binding me to a Vampire Champion was even more unbelievable. For now, however, there was clearly a benefit in going along with this absurdity.

Llyr's eyes could not be wider or face any paler. "I swear to you my king, I did not know! I would have never made that bargain! I have never seen that type of seal in my 1200 years of life!"

Ruarc cursed colourfully in Gaeilge at Llyr, who almost smacked his head against the floor in reverence once more. I was released abruptly and tumbled into Elis' waiting arms. His embrace was warm, firm, and welcome. Releasing me only so he could remove his shirt, he placed it around me and wrapped me back up in his arms.

I snuggled underneath his chin and whispered, "Toby?"

"He is fine, fast asleep in the biggest bed he has ever seen," Elis whispered back, kissing the top of my head. "I am so sorry, Mels. You must know—"

"Not now, Elis," I interrupted in hushed tones, "we shall certainly speak more later."

Now that my body had some semblance of coverage, I regained my composure within my shield of linen.

The king turned slightly back toward us, his face cold and calculating. "Though she may no longer be mate-able, she still has great use to me."

"And you to me," I replied.

His eyes narrowed. "'Tis a dangerous and foolish thing to utter in the halls of the Unseelie King. You are in *my* kingdom, before *my* throne, and in *my* presence! Watch where you tread, Alchemist. The tether of my patience is far shorter than that of the *Great Owl's*."

"I simply tread upon a path set down by your own making, Your Highness," I retorted. "Might I remind you of a sworn oath you once swore to Alcaeus, one you still have yet to uphold—until he is freed from Ragna's clutches, you owe him your allegiance!"

Baring sharpened teeth, he countered "That oath was made to a whole man, not one whose soul is now split, thus rendering the agreement null! Out of respect for my previous *alliance*, as you so call it, I considered that oath fulfilled by taking you."

Undeterred, I pulled out of Elis' embrace to face Ruarc.

"How utterly *convenient*," I sneered back. Crossing my arms, I did not allow my state of undress to take away from the commanding presence I was trying to exude. "Then I would make a deal with you, Unseelie King."

His brows shot up, his body losing the aggressive stance. For a moment, Ruarc beheld me with a calculated stare before a sly smile appeared on his face's angelic side. His bright yellow eye glimmered with mischievousness.

"Oh? Be careful, little one. Making deals with the Fae, especially with the King of the Unseelie and All That Which Lives in the Deep Dark, can prove most unwise and often unhealthy. I have no doubt it is your affection for the *Godslayer* that prompts your proposal."

"Assume what you will. Either way, I am most certain you will not assist me otherwise, and..." I paused begrudgingly at having to admit this weakness. "Well, I daresay you would make it impossible to leave your realm even if I attempted a grand escape. While I am willing to do everything I can to free Alcaeus, I need...assistance."

"Do call it for what it is, my dear: you need my help. Of course, you would try to render a deal with me to rescue your fated prince. How disgustingly romantic. Let us say I do entertain this *predictable* offer. What do I gain?"

The conversation was a precarious one, so I asked, "What is it you want?"

His grin transformed into a full smile. "In return for helping you free Alcaeus, I want you to fight as my proxy in the Divine Games and declare sole allegiance to the Unseelie Court. For we true Champions are not allowed to fight, as is tradition. Also, while I cannot bind you to me, I can certainly still have you in my bed."

I shook my head. "I am no fighter, King Ruarc."

"That is not a problem; I will train you. You have the power of nature on your side and keen intelligence. I have much to work with."

"Still, I will not declare sole allegiance to any court for Alchemists take no sides! Nor will I be whoring myself to you!"

"Then no deal. You are asking me to expose my kingdom to open war by rescuing the *Great Owl* and challenging the Nightmare Queen. While I may be the Champion of The Mórrígan and rarely do I turn down the chance to wet my blade with the blood of my enemies, the

Unseelie Court has greater things to deal with than tragic lovers." He turned away.

I wanted to throw something at him in frustration, but the sight of him leaving filled me with panic. He was right; I needed him on my side. There was no leaving this place otherwise.

"Wait!" I paused, thinking quickly, "I...will agree to become your proxy and I accept your offer of training. I will also agree to an *alliance* between myself and the Unseelie Court. In return, you will do all that is within your power to assist me in freeing Alcaeus from Ragna's control. I also ask that you extend your protection to Llyr, Elis, and Toby."

He considered me then and I could see the wheels turning.

"No. No deal."

"What? Why?!"

"I told you what I wanted. I will settle for no less, as is my prerogative."

"Damn you, you lecherous, manipulative—" I stopped abruptly upon seeing the darkening look on his face, and swallowed the rest of my insult. Instead, I acquiesced to the only thing I could allow.

"I cannot agree to sleep with you but I...I will allow you the chance to...seduce me if you think you are able. However, I will not stop the Champion of Athena when he finds out your intentions and attempts towards me," I warned.

He laughed. "Let me worry about the mighty *Godslayer*, little one. I accept these terms. My skills in the way of woman flesh and my will to get what I desire, is unmatched. It is your own strength of will that will be tested." He grinned at my expression and extended his hand. "We have a deal."

I hesitated but placed my hand in his. He raised it to his lips, kissing the back of my hand in a way that had me wanting to rip it away and sanitise it immediately. With fire. Or boiling water.

Then he bade, "Welcome, Melisandre Von Boden, Alchemist and now champion of the Unseelie Court. I look forward to seeing the true power of the Great Mother's Last Warrior."

Looking back at Elis and Llyr, their faces were grave, eyes full of apprehension. In my mind, I envisioned the handsome face of the Vampire that was the reason behind this deal.

Wait for me, Alcaeus. I will see you again.

I knew deep down that the real battle was about to begin.

Finally pulling my hand back from King Ruarc, I did a double take. There, where his lips had touched, was a black Celtic circle, the top of which depicted two ravens whose beaks were touching, closing the circle.

The symbol of the Mórrígan.

The symbol of the Mórrígan.

CHAPTER 2

Castle Fyrkat

"Your Highness, Prince Alcaeus has been locked securely in the dungeons—"

"Chain him to the wall in my bedchambers. Unclothed."

"M-my Queen?"

Ragna's emerald eyes slid to the Commander of her Royal Guard. He paled and with a quick but deep bow, left to carry out her orders. The aimless dead that surrounded her also waited for instruction, but it never came.

"He dared...utter the vows of Fated Mates...in front of me." Her knuckles were bone white with rage against the leather grip of her weapons. "My dearest prince shall know, even by the smallest amount, the suffering I went through waiting for him," she whispered to no one in particular. "Perhaps he will rethink his betrayal against me... Against the Norns... BETRAYAL!" Suddenly shouting, the queen stood and began rapidly pacing, the reanimated dead and a whimpering sorcerer her only audience now.

Letting out a raging scream, Ragna threw one of her axes at the now empty space where the portal had been. Where the Alchemist had slipped through her grasp once again.

Corpses, their empty and rotting faces stared back at her. Calling her weapon back to her, the necromancer began swinging at the zombies. Body parts went flying. The queen unleashed her fury and frustrations upon the dead and they fell, unmoving, to the ground. Finally, there was none left standing, save Mage Ilirhun, who was still crouched on the ground holding his arm.

"M-my Queen, Prince Alcaeus is as you commanded it." The Royal Guard had returned and stared at the floor obediently.

Breathing hard, Ragna's arms fell limply to her sides as the fires of her anger diminished only slightly. "Bury the dead. I will have use of them soon."

With that, she turned and marched toward her chambers.

☿♄♃♀♆∨ℨℨ

Alcaeus did not fight his chains. He was not ready to start a war, despite its inevitability. Limbs cuffed at the wrist and ankles, his body formed an X on the wall. Ragna had confiscated his clothes but that was no surprise; he was all too aware of the kinds of punishments she relished in. Her living quarters reflected it as well; bars and chains were conveniently placed around the room, some discreet and others blatant.

Yet, she would not debase him in public; despite her madness, even she understood that to take power from her consort meant to diminish her own. And it was power that she lived and breathed for. Oh, their subjects knew he would be punished for this. But once it was over, he would be required to be loyal but strong by her side once more.

He just had to grit his teeth for now and bear it.

The door slammed open. Their gazes clashed as Ragna stepped further into the room and the sound of the door closing caused the tension to thicken.

"You were careless," whispered Ragna, her grip on her axes causing Alcaeus' eyes to flick to them. "How very unlike you, Alcaeus. What would your righteous Athena think of her most prized warrior being so stupid? It is almost as if you were *wanting* me to catch you."

Silence was the prince's only response.

"I have been so gracious, so considerate to you," she went on, drawing close enough to run the cold edge of her axe lightly down his torso, "and this is how you repay my generosity." The blade reached his groin and he stiffened. "Hel would have had me dismember you. Inch by traitorous inch. She would have cut off your balls and fed them to her hellhounds while you watched. Loki would have played a game to make you find them. Then she would have given you over to her dead, commanding them to fuck you until she told them to stop." The axe's blade moved upwards once more as Ragna's eyes held his. "And she rarely did. Once, I went an entire month before I heard that blessed word." Ragna blinked rapidly for a moment, pain flashing for only a moment across her face. "Consider yourself lucky to have never gone through that kind of pain. But..." her face hardened, "perhaps you should."

Whipping away, she walked to the end of the huge canopied bed

26

and turned back to him. The axe in her left hand flew from her finger-tips, straight at Alcaeus. He did not move. Not even when it cleaved into the wall a breath away from his head. Several chestnut-hairs floated to the ground.

Pointing the remaining axe at him she seethed, "Do you love her?"

A grin slowly formed on Alcaeus' face, then a dark chuckle. "Drop the act, Ragna. Do not pretend you care. Nor will I feed into your twisted sense of sadism." His eyes observed the bonds that imprisoned him. "It has never been a fair fight with you, has it? No matter how many corpses you hid behind, like the coward you are, I still tore you to pieces in the arena. I can still hear your screams."

"I am no coward!"

Alcaeus' face morphed into a wicked sneer. "Says the monster who used my own wife and child to force my submission! Or the Brownie boy to imprison Melisandre! Or Lord Elis! Even now, you know you cannot win unless I am bound, you honourless *kunops*!"

"Do not blame me for your own weakness!" Ragna snarled. "You made your choice! You chose a dead child over your own freedom! Look around you; this is where your precious ideal of love has led you. Strapped to my wall, at my mercy while your Fated now belongs to the Raven, no less!" She sliced the air with her remaining axe. "Enough! I refuse to listen to this vitriol—I won, Alcaeus. Your power is mine. You have failed to change the prophecy. Accept it!"

He smirked, giving a subtle shake of his head. "The only thing to accept, Ragna, is that your time for relishing in your self-proclaimed victory is running out. And when it does, *accept* that my face will be the last thing you ever see when Nemesis is buried to the hilt right through your shrivelled heart!"

A growling scream, full of pain and rage, ripped from Ragna and the last axe in her hands was suddenly splitting through the air. No cry came from Alcaeus as the axe buried itself into his stomach. Blood dribbled from his mouth where his fangs had pierced his own lip from the impact. It took several moments before red began to run in small streams down his body.

Ragna's face was monstrous; skin so taut her image looked skeletal. "My body was torn to pieces by Hel's undead; she kept me conscious for every shred and rip of my flesh. She gave me to Loki for fun and what *fun*," Ragna spat the word and it dripped with bitterness, "he had on my body! I have died in every imaginable way! You have never tasted death's sadistic kiss in the ways that I have, Alcaeus! And yet you DARE threaten me with death as if I should fear it!"

Even with an axe buried in his gut and a mouth full of blood, the Champion of Athena grinned a red, mocking smile at her. "No, you broken, pathetic thing—death is too mundane for either of us. No, you deserve something far more fitting for your own transgressions. You deserve to be forgotten. Like the mistake you are."

Ragna's face went slack. The tension dropped from her body. She closed the distance between them. Slowly, her long fingers caressed the handle protruding from his body.

"I loved you once, you know," her voice was a hollow yet tentative whisper. "The chance at seeing your beautiful face; to once more experience the kindness you once had shown me, was the only hope I held onto as Hel tortured and raped me." Fingers trailed his chiselled face delicately, the same way they did on the handle. "To watch you in the arena, your wings spread in countless victories, as you soared into the sky... I loved..." she swallowed the rest of her words, only to continue, "And then after you killed me over and over again... That is when I realised something."

With a swift pull, Ragna jerked the blade from his stomach, dropping the weapon just as blood splashed to the ground. Alcaeus' flesh quickly began knitting itself back together. The queen watched in rapt fascination, a haunting thirst all over her face.

"I realised the crowd loved you. And because they loved you—they worshipped you. You were untouchable," she spat the word out. "I realised how weak love for one single person truly was." A single tear slid down that pale cheek just as her lips took a sinister curve. "But obsession from hundreds of thousands turned you into a god. Your power lay within their devotion. Admiration." Alcaeus' chin was lifted to meet those emerald eyes riddled with insanity. "*The hour of Hel is at hand. Life at Death's command. The Soul Eater will tear asunder spirits two. And from their union shall power be true. Steal Athena's most beloved wings. To become a queen of kings. Swallowed in darkness, decay, and rot.* Those were the words the Norns gave me and so it has come to pass. The people's devotion is now mine. Now I am the one who is untouchable."

Ragna stalked away towards one of two huge armoires in the room. Opening it showed a plethora of tools for torture, both sexual and sadistic. It did not take her long to choose a knout with bits of bone embedded in the leather.

"I will take great joy in punishing my treacherous consort," Ragna said as she faced him once more, "and when you cry-out for mercy, and you will, I will stay my hand. For I am far more gracious than Hel and Loki ever were. And you will crawl to me and kiss me like the loyal, doting husband you should be. Tonight, we shall finally lay together, as one."

A large splatter of bloody spit hit her. "The Sickness grips you deeply if that is how you believe this night shall end," chuckled Alcaeus. "Your delusions are getting worse, Ragna; it's clear Mage Ilirhun's remedies are failing you."

The whip flailed and snapped. Blood raced down his face and chest. Yet not a sound came from him, clearly in defiance, even after several more blows.

Bathed in red, Ragna continued mercilessly. "You!" *Crack!* "Will!" *Crack!* "Submit!" *Crack! Crack!* "To me!" *Crack! Crack! Crack!* Heaving, her hands shook and she raised the hand that held the whip to her mouth, licking the saturated blood. "I will have you this night, *ástin mín.*"

Then she froze.

A wet, guttural laugh erupted from Alcaeus. His rich baritone voice filled the room, yet its depths were filled with icy horror. Darkness crept into the room, flames going out.

"You have imprisoned the Prince of Nightmares, whore of Hel; let us see who will end the night screaming."

CHAPTER 3

Nine months later...

"*Get out of here! Go! You do not belong here, mutant!*" *The woman screeched, pulling her child away. A knobby-kneed, skinny girl covered in bruises, dodged out of the way of kicks and slaps from the surrounding people. Deeply regretting not having taken the back roads home, she darted across the small bridge and into an alleyway.*

Great golden spires seemed to touch the clouds, moulded into intricately carved white gothic towers. Beautiful stained glass could be seen from miles away, depicting stories of the greatest philosophers among them.

The ragged girl flew across the stone streets, a black blur sticking to the shadows. Each district was reminiscent of the clan that lived there; the earth clans had beautiful wooden and clay homes that spiralled up massive trees. The water clans lived in floating houses that sat on the crystal-clear waters of the Blytheheim Sea. Air clans dominated many of the spires seen around the capital, of course. The Fire clans lived in the centre, their dwellings stacked like small mountains, beautifully coloured. All the smithing trades could be found there.

With her feet kicking up dirt as she ran, she finally arrived at the outskirts of the city when finally, a rundown cottage came into view. It was still part of the earth clan district but noticeably stood apart.

Bursting through the door the girl cried out, "Mama? Mama! I tried to get the bread but they would not give it to me..."

A thin, dark-haired woman turned, placing the vegetables she was washing, down. Her kind eyes filled with warmth at seeing her daughter but then a frown quickly replaced it.

"Daughter, why then do you hold several loaves? Did you steal it?"

"Well... I... Mama, they kicked and slapped me when I tried to go into the shop. So...I had to become creative and wait until the baker took his normal smoking break..."

The mother let out a weary sigh, rubbing her temples. "Melisandre... you cannot steal."

"I left the money on the table! I didn't technically steal..." Kicking a small stone on the floor, the girl dared to look at her only parent.

With a small shake of her head and a defeated chuckle, the mother replied, "No, I suppose you did not. Are you alright?"

Melisandre nodded, slightly scoffing at the question so as to not worry her mother. She was used to this kind of treatment and her mother had enough to worry about.

"I will finish cooking dinner and then we can go into the forest and try transmuting some wood again. Were you able to sneak into the conservatory for some lessons?"

Melisandre nodded and with a sly grin, said, "I did! I found the perfect spot too, up in the rafters. They'll never see me."

Her mother grinned and turned back to the food she was preparing. "If you fall to your demise, tell the Great Mother I am not responsible for your absolutely foolish amount of courage and genius."

The girl laughed and rolled her eyes as she climbed the steps to her room.

☿☉♃♄Ψ♀♈♈

I awoke with a start. Flopping back into my pillows, I rubbed the sleep from my face. The smell of the vanilla-lavender perfume my mother wore still lingered potently in my memories, as did her kind gold and silver eyes. The way she clapped her hands together whenever she laughed, cute dimples appearing on either side of her cheeks.

Nostalgia hit me as fiercely as the cold did.

It hadn't been but three hours since I nodded off but sleep was elusive here. Despite the chill, I slipped from the cosy bed and shrugged a shawl over my shoulders, making my way to the large window that overlooked the Darkling City below. Unlike Fyrkat Castle, the Unseelie Fortress held no balconies that I had seen so far which, sadly, had been very little of it.

Bright moonlight illuminated the land. Yet, with it came a bittersweet loneliness. Hugging myself harder, my thoughts drifted back to my mother for a moment. Feelings of failure stabbed at me; the memory of her kindness was merely a reminder at my own maternal shortcomings with Toby. I had barely seen him since we'd arrived; mostly because his Brownie side declared him a ward of the Unseelie Court, but a part of me couldn't help wondering if he was avoiding me.

Shaking my head, my thoughts turned to other matters.

I worried about Zephyr and Ares. That wolf was so mysterious. It wasn't until now that I realised he seemed to come and go as he pleased, the Vampires and staff never uttering a word. It was as if he was visible only to me. As for Zeph, I could only hope he kept his nasty habit of biting people he didn't like to himself. And that they had not killed him for belonging to me.

Leaning my forehead against the glass, I let thoughts of the Nightmare Prince fill my mind. Our last encounter had left me shaken, though no feelings of resentment were borne from it. The haunting green fire that continued to stalk my dreams was the only thing to blame for Alcaeus' actions.

Still, I could not feel his presence there no matter how hard I tried mentally to reach out. After being subjected to Ruarc's perverse healing, all I desired was Alcaeus' comforting presence in my mind. Emptiness and disappointment were all that answered my call.

When have I ever sought comfort with a man so readily before? Why is it his arms, his presence, I immediately seek in the darkness? Rolling my eyes at my weakness, I rallied myself. *Come on Melisandre, you're stronger than this. You've lived your entire life without this man, don't lose yourself now. There are those seeking exactly this kind of exploit; for both your sakes, focus.*

My unfinished Mark was a constant dull ache, however, seeming to worsen each day in his absence. Sometimes, the overwhelming desire to be near him, to touch him, left me horribly shaken and in painful need. Other times, it burned with agony, almost angrily before coming to an instant stop. It was an onslaught to my resolve. Yet, we had been cooped up in this cold and unforgiving realm for months; even my dreams remained empty of him. Only nightmares of me trying to reach him, only for a black hound, engulfed in green flame, to swallow him whole in front of me.

What could this silence mean? Was he alright?

I saw his release from Ragna's grasp right as we went through the portal; why did he not reach out to me? Was he back under her control?

Did she...touch him? Was he with her...right now?

With a frustrated growl, I whipped away from the window as anger exploded in my chest at the thought. It was not jealousy, no, but the idea she toyed with him against his will. That he was helpless against her while she...

I threw my robe down abruptly just as I silenced that thought.

"Alcaeus is far from helpless, and you know it. Don't insult him with your doubts. Besides, thinking these things will get you nowhere. Dwelling on that which you cannot change is futile." Even as I whispered these words aloud to myself, the piercing hurt at the echoing images those questions stirred, stabbed at me.

Pulling on warmer attire, I quickly strode from the room. In the last couple of weeks, we had been here, I had gotten to know some of the layouts of this monstrosity of a castle. Unfortunately, this place was literally made of magic; hallways seemed never-ending, never changing. Nothing stirred yet it always felt as if you were being watched from the shadows. It was downright eerie. Ruarc had told me to just hold the image of the place I desired to go and, if it was allowed, the Fortress would make sure I arrived. Having never seen the damn place, I could come up with vague images of the only places I'd want to go—the library and anywhere but *here*.

Naturally, the latter was more appealing so my first experiment was to see how far out of the castle I could get. That failed miserably when it led me straight to the Unseelie King himself. Which, of course, gave him the horribly mistaken impression I was accepting his advances.

I grimaced but couldn't contain the emerging smirk at the memory—him trying to pin me into a small table against the wall while I, taking the silver candelabra from said table, proceeded to smash in the side of his face with it. The pretty half, too. Accelerating the molecules of the wax until boiling was a nice touch as well.

The black marble floors had veins of gold slicing through the stone and they sparkled in the torchlight as I made my way to the athenaeum. My long, black fur-lined jacket trailed behind me as I briskly walked down the echoing hallway. Arched ceilings held large braziers but they gave little in way of warmth. This entire place seemed to be devoid of warmth; if I didn't know any different, I would have believed this place was the Nightmare Court. It certainly had the scenery.

Suddenly, a movement in the shadows had me coming to a halt, my senses skyrocketing.

"Who's there? Show yourself!" I commanded, challenging the darkness.

For a moment, nothing happened. Then the inky blackness moved. A tall figure shrouded in black robes, like a hooded wraith, emerged.

"Lady Von Boden," the deep voice greeted me.

My eyes widened in recognition.

"You're...you're the lich! Alcaeus—"

"Yes, I am he who serves the Nightmare Prince."

Serves, implying he still does. I frowned at this, anger bubbling up in my belly.

"You serve him still?" I asked, suspicion thick in my voice.

"He *is* my master." There was no wavering, no hesitation to be found in that voice that went deeper than any well.

I clenched my fists. "And yet you abandoned him when he needed you most." Only silence answered my accusation. A frustrated growl slipped from me. "Where were you when Sotiris' last breath was sucked out by Ragna? Where were you when your master's soul was manipulated by green fire, turned into nothing more than a dancing puppet? Your loyalties are as suspicious as your presence before me now, instead of protecting your liege!"

The lich raised a black-gloved hand. "Patience, Alchemist. All will be revealed to you. Your anger is not without merit but there is much you do not know. Come," he gestured past him, "lets us adjourn where the walls will not whisper back to their own master."

I crossed my arms as I gave the outstretched hand a searing glare.

"If only to trap me, I imagine. Truly, your devotion must certainly lie with the queen; it stands to reason as to why you were able to leave alive," I growled, "and unscathed."

"The queen cannot kill me, nor do I have a soul she can consume; my very existence makes a mockery out of her powers. It is understandable, your lack of trust, and thus why Prince Alcaeus gave me the orders he did. Here, a show of good faith."

Out of thin air, a tungsten and platinum staff with an iron band snaking around it appeared. A feeling of home struck me.

"My staff," I whispered in awe. With a shaking hand, I took it. The cold metals against my hand, how the elements sang to me, brought tremendous relief. "How in the Mother's name did you get this? I left it in the throne room..."

"When you and the prince were away in the prince's cottage, I was finishing laying the protection wards upon your chamber and discovered it on the floor. At the prince's command, I took the liberty of placing a finder's spell upon it, leaving it in the safekeeping of Lord Elis LeGervase before he was imprisoned. With your permission, I can place an answering mark upon your hand; it will never be lost to you."

I ran my hands over it with familiarity, finding the feeling of home with it in my grasp.

"Unfortunately, magic is a lost cause with me. Even so, placing that mark must mean it would never be lost to you, either," I replied, suspicion still prevalent in my tone.

"I have little use for those metals, Alchemist. My interests lie purely in the arcane and the soul. My own functions perfectly for my needs. Now please, we are wasting moonlight."

Wariness settled deep but my insatiable curiosity got the better of me as I took a hesitant step forward. His candid honesty only created more concern. A million questions sped around in my mind but they all led me to the memory of midnight eyes, firm lips on mine, and the whisper of leather and spices. I bit my tongue in the face of my impatience, forcing my focus on being hyper-aware of the being that was leading me to an unknown location.

My footsteps echoed as we continued on but the lich made no sound as he moved. Perhaps magic muffled his own floating-steps. The strange orb with the sapphire shards at the top of his staff glowed in the darkness. It was made of gnarled wood, with streaks of white and mahogany, wrapping and twisting its way up. At a stand, its height was as tall as the lich. I wanted to study it further but kept my curiosity in check.

After a few minutes, the walls began to shudder. The lich raised his staff and spoke something, quiet enough that I couldn't quite make out his words. The ground shook and suddenly all stopped. That's when I saw an arched door frame with spiral stone stairs ahead of us.

Groaning mentally, I reluctantly trudged up behind him. It didn't take long for my thighs to start burning and my glutes to remind me how much I neglect their exercise. In what felt like an eternity, we finally reached the top. I held onto the wall, wheezing as if I had breathed nothing but pipe smoke for the last century.

"Please, Lady Von Boden, come inside. We were much slower in getting here than I had anticipated."

"Look..." *gasp*, "Some of us," *wheeze*, "were not made for this level," *gasp*, "of extraneous..." I took a deep breath, my heart finally slowing pace, "exercise. I'm not like," I waved my hand sloppily in his direction, "like you. I certainly was not... Oh gods, my legs...anticipating climbing stairs up to stratospheric heights."

"If you are to be a Champion, fighting in the Megálo Kolossaío, you will need to—"

"Yes, yes," I grumped, stumbling past him and through the open door, "I am quite aware."

I stopped a few feet inside, taking in my surroundings. It was how I would expect a lich's tower to look; lots of books piled in precarious stacks, wax candles burned low, and random taxidermized creatures pinned to plaques. The smell of dust, parchment, and tallow filled my nose. Even the three ravens in bird-cages were not surprising. What stopped me in my tracks were the hundreds of papers, some with symbols, some with strange writing, literally stabbed all over the walls. A few were spread across the floor as if they'd fallen. The markings were written in... I reached out with my senses; blood.

"What—"

"Research," interrupted the lich. His abruptness snapped me back to him, which made me realise something.

"I'm sorry but I don't recall your name."

"Cillian."

"Ah, yes. Cillian." I looked around again, noticing there was nowhere to sit save for the rickety chair facing the large desk. Placing my hands on my hips, I squared away at him, eager for answers. "Now will you explain your suspiciously timed absence while your prince was in dire need of you? I take it Ruarc cannot hear us here? Does he know you're here? Even more dubious if he does."

"Do Alchemists often ask questions with obvious answers?" He didn't turn to me but was rifling through papers and shelves and drawers, clearly looking for something. "Of course the Raven King knows of my presence—he knows of everything and anything that moves within his realm. He created The Fortress. Magic flows like water within him; thus, my own power is limited to this single room. We have a reprieve from his omniscience."

"Alright, fine. Then tell me why are you here? I will not ask again." I warned him. My patience was at an end.

Cillian paused, stopping his search for a moment, his head inclined in my direction.

"The first thing you must realise and accept, Alchemist, is that there were plans laid down far before your entrance; the prince has been planning this for over a thousand years. You were and are the *key*. I remember the day Prince Alcaeus became aware of your presence. At your first breath, my king called upon me and my scrying mirror, though we failed to find you with it. Even under the queen's watchful eye, he scoured the land, searching for you. It still took several hundred years, as you were most elusive."

Confused, I took in his words. "Why? The key to what, exactly?"

"Are you Alchemists always so blind to the ways of the heart? The soul? The gods bound you! From the wheel of life, so your soul-threads were weaved, destined to find each other in life and fated mates would you become! Just as The Fates foretold the great goddess."

"Foretold what? What is this prophecy?"

Cillian stopped for a moment, turning to her.

> *"The hour of Hel is at hand*
> *Life at Death's command*
> *The Soul Eater will tear asunder spirits two*
> *And from their union shall power be true*
> *Steal Athena's most beloved wings*
> *To become a queen of kings*
> *Swallowed in darkness, decay and rot*
> *Should threads once woven, be bound anew*
> *Spirits of one in the ancient Yew*
> *Roots break and the earth will shake*
> *Into the sky, so shall the Owl fly*

When Prince Alcaeus surmised that the threads meant he had a Fated Mate, we began the search. Then we found you. Sotiris refused to believe it but I had no such doubts."

My head shook at the impossibility of what he suggested, still reeling over the supposed prophecy.

"That's ridiculous! I am not born of the gods! You challenge my ignorance but I challenge your absurd hypothesis! You have the wrong person! No gods had a hand in my making other than the Mother herself!" I argued. "That is why Alchemists have no magic nor can we really sense it well. We are better seen as enemies of the old gods; they sought to exterminate us when they first arrived on these earthly planes. Surely you know this?"

"As anyone does when they have been around as long as I have. Yet even among her enemies, surely Mother Nature had allies? Was it not Gaia who split the planes to keep humans safe? Did not Izanagi have the blessing of the Mother to create the islands of Japan? Or Viracocha in the creation of lands for his people? When the great giant Ymir came, bringing chaos to the Mother, was it not his own children, born of his flesh, that stopped him? The great All-Father who created a place where they could battle against the giants looking to consume the Mother? Her gratitude to them was the creation of Yggdrasil—so that they may be connected to their previous realms. Is it so hard to believe that the Mother may have designed your life with one of the gods?"

"No...that...your path of logic is flawed," I replied, shaking my head. "She guarded us, protected us from the old gods. That was not in any of the literature... Master Kian told me we were at war with them. That was why it was forbidden to leave the Citadel! I read everything in The Great Library, the Forbidden Texts—it was all the same!"

Cillian sighed as if my answers were that of a child.

"Your master was not entirely wrong, but war, as you should know, was never so binary in 'earth versus the gods'. Many deities of agriculture, fertility, and nature were against those desiring to conquer Mother Nature and enslave her children."

"Are you implying that you believe the Mother agreed with another god to bind my soul with a Champion? With Alcaeus?"

"Not any god, but with none other than the daughter of Zeus."

"Athena," I whispered, stating the obvious, but my mind was in a thousand other places with a million other questions. "But...why?"

"That is the question my Master and I have been trying to answer. Athena only gave my prince the prophecy before she too left the earthly realm. All of our working theories believe it has something to do with the Sickness, or perhaps they saw the destruction—"

"If you do not know then let's not waste our breath contemplating what you could not solve for hundreds of years. I am far more disturbed that it appears to me Alcaeus has known of my existence, of my purpose," I spat, "assuming Athena and the Mother did truly predestine this, for far longer than before we had met!"

"My lady, I had hoped—"

"No, no more. At this point, only Alcaeus can answer for his actions. Right now, it's your turn. So, you are going to tell me right now: Why. Weren't. You. There?"

CHAPTER 4

"I was absent by Prince Alcaeus' command. It was he who foretold the queen's rage and even warned Sotiris of his own demise if he did not heed my Master's warning. His owls have seen the fragments of Ragna's dissolution into her madness but Sotiris believed he could protect our liege by taking the necklace; the captain's arrogance cost him much!" Cillian spat the last bit as if the very words were a bitter acid. "Prince Alcaeus knew it was only a matter of time before Ragna grew impatient, eager to see her part of the prophecy complete. What none had anticipated was how quickly the fated-bond would demand completion," he floated toward me but stopped after a few steps. "With each completed stage of the Mark, the energy and magic between you grew. A familiar mark would have only elevated the prince's powers, which was exactly what Ragna was hoping for as she too would then feed from that power, but the magic buzzed around you two like a bonfire burning in the darkest of nights, inaccessible to her. Thus, I was sent to find the Unseelie King, in hopes to gain an alliance before... Well, it matters not. I was too late. Lord O'Cananach's message held a far more convincing offer; Prince Alcaeus would never have bartered you for his freedom."

My eyebrows shot up. While I had felt the changes between us, it was strictly that: between him and me. The burning, aching need when we are apart; the song that echoed between our hearts had only become more evident. But I was an Alchemist; I could not sense magic the same way those created by the old gods could. Only if the user was extremely powerful, or through bursts of magical power could I feel it, like a thousand insects crawling across my skin. Although, now that I thought about it, Alcaeus' power felt...*good.*

"Surely Ragna realised this after the first Mark? Why did she not immediately put a stop to it? Instead, she played games, pushing and pushing for me to react, always trying to control me. A childish bully."

Cillian shook his head. "She never dreamed the bond between you and my Master was a divine one for they are more of a legend, a romantic myth. All Marks look the same after the first bite. The Seelie ambassador believed you possessed a Chosen Mates bite at first, which can be altered if not completed. The second bite, unfortunately, was incriminating but only to those who know it for what it is. Had you completed it..." His hooded head shook slowly.

I frowned at this revelation, not entirely sure what to make of that. Yet, what continued to bother me the most was that Alcaeus seemed to have known all this and did not think to warn me. My lip curled as the bitter taste of anger consumed me. Doubt also crept its slimy tentacles into the recesses of my mind.

After all that was said, he still did not trust me... He led me to believe... and why would he do that? He knew we were fated, assuming that is true, and did not act until now. Perhaps it is me who truly was the fool. There is clearly more here than meets the eye. What am I missing?!

As if sensing my turmoil, Cillian appeared before me, taking my focus away from my thoughts.

"Do not doubt Prince Alcaeus, my lady. You must know all he has done; all he has sacrificed has been for you."

I stared up into the faceless hood of the lich.

"Such...pretty words," I whispered. Taking a step back, my voice hardened. "You've made it clear you think me an ignorant fool, Cillian, and if what you say is true, consider me guilty of the crime. Even if he developed an affection for me, I was still a means to an end in Alcaeus' eyes," I ground my teeth and slammed my staff on the ground in anger. "VAMPIRES AND THEIR GAMES!" I shouted. I swivelled and pointed my staff at Cillian. "If he truly knew this would come to pass, who I was to him, and yet still kept me in the dark, then there is a greater goal, beyond just the heart. Speak truly, *lich*!" I seethed. "If we were to complete the Mark, what would happen?"

"In theory, we believe it will release the part of his soul imprisoned by Ragna, for the power of the gods is far superior to any soul-tethering magic the Nightmare Queen possesses."

"Would he not then be free to exact his revenge upon Ragna and reclaim his throne? Is it not his true purpose, his true desire, to become king and rule once more?! How convenient, now that Ragna has done all the work for him, all Vampires subject to one dominion! The more I think on it, the bigger the possibility that I am but a part of a larger political scheme."

He hesitated, remaining perfectly still. After a moment of silence, I shook my head. Turning away, I made for the door.

As I turned the knob, Cillian said, "Do you wish to see him?"

I froze.

Swallowing, I turned slightly, though my hand remained on the door. "What?"

His dark shadowy form floated across the room, to a mahogany cabinet that was covered in cobwebs and melted candle wax. It opened surprisingly easily.

My heart thumped in my chest. Why did I always feel myself at war with Alcaeus? I was torn between my rage at him using me and yet every part of me awakened like a live wire at the possibility of seeing him again.

Cillian approached me, holding something small in his gloved hand.

"This is a soul-stone; already you and my Master have begun re-binding your souls together through the mating bond. Place it upon your Mark and say '*Ubi est, sic ego sum*'. You shall meet where your bond connects the strongest. The power within is limited so use it with discretion and do not linger. You can only use it once."

Ubi est, sic ego sum... Where he is, so am I.

Shaking my head, I countered, "I cannot use magic. It will not work."

"For this, it shall. I promise you."

For a moment longer I hesitated before reaching my hand out. Cillian placed the stone gently in my waiting palm. It was pure white with gold markings etched into the smooth surface. The magic within blocked my ability to see what the rock was made of; I sneered at it. How I longed to be in a place without magic.

I looked back up at the lich once more before I opened the door and made my way out.

Going down the stairs brought nothing but mental relief and I quickly imagined my bedroom as I reached the end of the winding staircase. The hallway shuddered like a mirage and my door peeked out at the end of it. The Unseelie Fortress always remained eerily empty and for that I was grateful.

Rushing to my door, I quickly went in. Slamming it behind me, I pressed my back against it. The hearth still burned brightly, the light dancing along the angled, blackwood bed resting against the opposite wall. Taking in the empty room, I finally lifted the stone up to the firelight.

It truly was beautiful. Still, my lip curled.

Fucking magic.

I grumbled and pushed away from the door, going to stand near the fireplace.

Does it physically transport me? Or...he said that we would 'meet where our bond connects the strongest', which must mean...spiritually?

"Bollocks and metaphysics!" I pinched the bridge of my nose in irritation. "What a waste of time. Bloody pseudoscience!" I went to toss the stone on the side table nearby.

But if I could see him... I stopped, gripping the stone to me.

"Fuck!" Letting out a growl, I jerked my shirt down over my shoulder, smacking the stone onto my unfinished Mark.

"Ubi est, sic ego sum!"

My vision went white. All went silent.

Birds chirping. Water running. I inhaled deeply, summer grasses, pine, and earth filled my nostrils. Cracking my eyes open, I stared up into a sky filled with the reds and oranges of a sunset, peeking through the trees. Slowly sitting up, I took in the surrounding forest. A forest I knew. Looking behind me, my eyes widened.

Alcaeus' cottage.

Coming to a stand, I dusted myself off, taking cautious steps toward the little house. Just as I was about to call out his name, the door swung open and there he was.

His face, that warm masculine face, looked back at me in disbelief. "*Mikrós asvós*? Is it... is it really you? How?"

"Cillian gave me a soul stone. He—Mmph!" Lips captured mine as strong arms enveloped me in his embrace. His tongue plunged into my mouth greedily, dominating any contrary thoughts that would have me pushing him away. Desire exploded from every nerve, and I grabbed onto him, desperately slipping my hands up to his face and through his thick chestnut hair.

"Alcaeus," I gasped between kisses. I let out a sound of surprise as he swiftly laid me on the soft grass. I melted into his weight, revelling in it. His hands seemed to be everywhere, desperate for the feel of me. Wrapping my legs around his waist, I pushed our hips together, suddenly desperate to feel the ridges and hardness of him. The evidence of his desire only inflamed my own. He felt so tangible, so real.

Yet my dilemma with him hung like stale air between us, needing to be addressed.

"Mmm...wait..." I said breathlessly, trying to remember the reason I was so cross with him. He buried his head in my neck and breathed deeply as if to calm himself, his arms coming up on either side of my face. Cradling my head, the prince pulled away.

A look came over his face, one that brought me back to that fateful day.

A day that Ruarc saved me from, I thought begrudgingly.

Reaching one hand down until his palm found my wrist, Alcaeus lifted my arm into his view. A flicker of anger danced in his eyes as he stared at long-healed wounds.

"The last thing I remember that day was you. In the arms of King Ruarc. Covered in blood. You reached for me..." He stopped himself, concern and regret flickering across his face. "These wounds... I caused them. I hurt you." It wasn't a question. Alcaeus stated it as fact.

Shaking my head, I corrected, "No! I mean yes, you did but that was Ragna controlling you. Neither of us expected the true power she has over you, or how it manifests itself. I do not begrudge actions outside of your control."

"Nevertheless, what happened just showed how powerless I am—"

I pushed a finger against his lips. "No. Not how powerless you are. Only how powerful Ragna is."

His eyes narrowed slightly, but I still did not remove my finger, silencing him. Then, very slowly, he opened his mouth. White canines peeked through, extending menacingly as his teeth continued to part. Keeping the same captivating pace, he wrapped his teeth around my finger, firm enough to trap me but not painful. A hot, wet tongue pressed against the tip, just as his lips encased my finger. Warmth shot up my arm and through my body. Tongue swirling, he sucked. My breath gave out. Eyes flicking up to his, I was instantly ensnared.

The heat in his gaze bewitched me.

I slipped my finger from his mouth, immediately replacing it with a heated kiss. He answered back. Relishing in it, taking greedily. Yet, the residual tendrils of anger and doubt remained, not to be ignored.

Focus.

I broke away, letting the memory of what had transpired between Cillian and myself re-fuel my purpose.

Alcaeus gave me a small smile. "My wise little Fated. How I have longed to look upon your face. Are you well?" Alcaeus asked as he studied me with tenderness, swirling circles along my temple and cheek. I beheld his own visage, those beautiful midnight eyes and proud cheekbones. The sharp line of his brow and the scar that marked one.

"Fated..." I reached up and took his face in my hands. Emotions surged as I whispered, "Liar. You are a liar, Alcaeus."

He did not seem surprised, or shocked. I could not even identify remorse. His expression was almost as if he had been waiting for me to come to that conclusion.

"You lied to me. Even by omission, you knew all of this would happen and still you *lied*." Shaking my head, I released his face. "How you have spoken to me about being a light in the darkness and yet it is in the darkness you continue to scheme. Why do you treat me as a means to an end, Alcaeus? Just as I am about to believe the sincerity of your intentions, suddenly the rug is pulled from under me. Be true: your real goal is to take Ragna's place, isn't it? And you need me to do it." I swallowed hard, trying to tamp down my hurt. "*Fated Mates...* How long have you known?"

I pushed against him but he didn't budge.

"I will not patronise you by denying your accusations; we do not have much time if you are using a soul stone. So, let me only explain my intentions surrounding my actions." I opened my mouth to push the issue, my anger rising, but he silenced me with a hard, quick kiss. "Please, hear me, Melisandre, please." I glared at him but held my tongue. He gave me a gentle kiss on the corner of my mouth and continued. "First and foremost; never refer to yourself as a means to an end! My love, if anything is a lie, then those words are! You are the means for which I breathe, the means I fight for. Never mistake that. Without you, all of this means nothing; without the reason from which my contentment stems, my existence is pointless," His eyes bore into mine so intensely, it left no room for doubt. "Everything that has led up to this has been thousands of years in the making. Yes, you are the key to this. Only with you can I—"

"Exact your revenge and take the throne," I interrupted bitterly.

He shook his head. "My revenge, yes, but also to gain our freedom, the freedom of the people of Khaviel. Bringing balance back to the kingdoms. You know not what my people have suffered these past thousand years, mikrós asvós. I have done what I can in the limited capacity I was able. Hope is not lost—there is a prophecy, one that foretold the age of gods coming to an end, that sickness would spread through the lands and death would rule over life—"

"I know. Cillian told me."

He gave me a smile of relief. "So he did. Good. Then you also know that my creator, Athena, prepared for it. She was the one who warned me of the prophecy, that there was a way—" He grimaced, his body tensing.

I reached back up to him, holding him.

"What's wrong?" I asked, worried.

He shook his head as if shaking off pervasive thoughts.

"We are in the realm where our souls meet, my love. Ragna has imprisoned my conscience here because, even imprisoned, she cannot control me any other way. Come Yaldā, I expect her to release me, for appearance's sake but—argh!" He clenched his teeth and his hold on me tightened.

I placed my hands on his head. Images slammed into my mind. As if I saw through Alcaeus' eyes. Bound. Feminine laughter. Torturous screams. A woman's hands slid up his naked torso. Lush lips kissing a path down, down, down...her head bobbing up and down. She glanced up. Glittering emerald eyes stared back at me. An evil smile in her eyes emerged as she pulled her blood-red lips off him. Suddenly her face curled into an ugly snarl.

"*He is mine!*" she hissed.

Her face morphed into a black hound, flesh rotting and falling from bone. Razor-sharp teeth dripped with saliva. Her eyes burned with green flame as a deep guttural growl rumbled and it was the only warning I had before her jaws snapped at my face. I jerked back, landing with a thud on the ground.

Bolting upright, my bedroom surroundings came rushing at me. The stone lay a foot away from me. Other than my harsh breaths, the crackle of the fire was the only other sound in the room.

Alcaeus...

"It hurts." My voice cracked as I held my chest, taking heaving breaths.

Is that what is happening to him? Is she using his body...?

Pale hands with blood-red nails, sliding down his skin. Blonde head moving...

I felt my eyes water as nausea punched me in the gut like a mule kick and my body broke out into a cold sweat. A torrent of emotions blew through me and suddenly I couldn't breathe. I needed air.

I was almost hyperventilating when I ripped my door open and ran out. Picturing outside, anywhere as long as it was outside, I bolted down the endless corridor. Every moment, images crept into my mind, always followed by terrible words that slithered like snakes across my mind.

She's touching him...using him...kissing him...sucking—

I smacked the side of my head, violently shaking it to dispel the thoughts.

"Stop it! Stop thinking!" I desperately snapped at myself.

Finally, the walls morphed into arches with railings, revealing foliage and trees. Cold fresh air hit me in the face like a wet blanket and I sucked it in, gasping. I turned sharply at the entrance and burst through the path only to come to a sudden stop. I had thought it was an outside entrance to a forest but, as I took in the gleaming fountains and glowing plants in the night, I realised it was actually a massive garden.

Small waterfalls moulded into small streams, the gentle sound of them trickling throughout gave this place a calming and gentle atmosphere. Some could be seen peeking out through thick bushes and flowers. All the plants had this strange luminescence as if created by magic.

The feel of the garden was not natural, their atomic structures I could not sense. Nevertheless, I slowly walked deeper into this wondrous place. A much larger stream ran through the middle of the garden, weaving and winding to other undiscovered parts. Beautiful glowing flowers of purples, greens, and pinks, lined the banks. The sounds of water and the chirping of nightlife calmed me only slightly.

I spotted a granite bench overlooking the main stream and eagerly made my way over to it. Letting out a dramatic exhale, I forced myself to release the tension in my body. Looking up, the massive white-barked trees loomed over me but even through their red and purple leaves, I could see the night sky. The darkness held so many glittering stars, one could get lost searching them.

It was then that I took note of my trembling limbs; not because of the chill, but because of the helpless rage within that had nowhere to go. Always that helpless. Trapped.

"What troubles my little Alchemist this eve?"

I snapped my head up to the intruding sound. Ruarc emerged from the foliage, from a path I had not seen before.

"Whatever it is, it must be dire, to have flushed you out from the burrow of your rooms from which, I have noticed, you are stubbornly remiss in leaving."

He was once again shirtless, although he had a leather harness that holstered knives along his chest, wrists, and waistband. Black pants and boots were difficult to make out in the glowing night but an ornate scabbard strapped to his side glistened like starlight.

"I am in no mood for your games Ruarc," I bit out, "or was ruining your beautiful face not enough?"

He raised a brow. "You find me beautiful then? Fear not, I have flawlessly recovered. You are free to gaze upon my perfection once more."

"How *regrettable* that I did not melt the metal of the candelabra over your face instead of the wax," I snapped back. "Leave me alone."

Ruarc's face settled into mysteriousness, a talent I was rather quite envious of. I've long accepted my face to be capable of two emotions, those of which I'm sure you could guess.

The king was across from me, standing imperiously on the other side of the stream. Taking several deliberate steps forward, he came to a stop before trampling on the lush flowers resting there. Entire buds, petals and all, suddenly extended towards him as if in greeting.

A Champion of the great Celtic battle goddess, the very one who is said to drink the blood of slain kings at victory celebrations, whom flowers reach for as if he was a ray of sunshine in this dark place? I shook my head, snorting; I would never understand them.

As if seeing my thoughts, Ruarc said, "It is foolish to believe that you can understand the complexities of Champions purely on the limited knowledge of their creator, Alchemist. Or from whatever tall tales humans have spun." He rested a hand on his hips and cocked his head at me. "Mother Nature, while one of the most powerful entities, is also one of the most predictable—she abides by her own cyclic laws, always in constant motion. In the presence of unbalance, she creates chaos only to bring homeostasis in its wake. Down to the last atom, she is, and forever will be, comprehensible. The old gods counter her in almost every aspect. To be sure, divine powers were always meant to balance each other but that is not always so, is it? Otherwise, why else would we have the stories, the myths, that even mankind now regales?"

Rolling my eyes, I retorted, "Yet for all their confusing and mysterious ways, they are still as hopelessly flawed as the humans that worship them. That is why the Mother remains and the old gods do not. Get to your point. I grow weary of this conversation."

Ruarc's eyes sharpened. "Your oversimplification of Champions, your constant hiding and simpering behind books will cost you everything! Are not the great Alchemists known for having insatiable curiosity? The greediest bastards for knowledge over any lich or sorcerer in the magical world—even Sages bow to the intellectual prowess of the legendary philosophers! Your stubbornness in possessing such a linear opinion of us, your lack of passion in understanding anything different to you, will *cost* you Alcaeus!"

Indignation spread through me like wildfire. I shot to my feet, squaring off with the Unseelie King.

"You know nothing about us! Do you not think I did not scour Ragna's own libraries for every last morsel of information on that evil, conniving bitch?! I needed more time—"

"Gah!" Ruarc hissed, cutting me off with a wave of his hand. "You are thousands of years too young to tell me what I do and do not know of the Alchemist race! They were not always hidden away, a trait you desperately need to be broken of! You are so very young, like a baby bird believing its world is but the perimeter of its nest, unable to perceive the vastness of the sky! Enough of your damn excuses! Come!" He barked, opening his arms wide. "It is time for you to learn how to fly."

CHAPTER 5

Before I could protest, run, or do anything to avoid this man, black shadow swirled around us like a tornado. My hair whipped across my face so hard, the strands hitting my skin stung. I went to grab onto the bench but my hand hit nothing, wind threading through my fingers. The centrifugal force kept me upright but I curled into myself, wrapping my arms around my head. I rocked to and fro, the whistling of the vortex the only thing I could hear.

Suddenly, it stopped.

Even as silence descended, I waited a few moments before unfolding myself to look around. Ruarc still stood in front of me but my attention was immediately on the barren wasteland we now stood upon. Dead tree stumps littered the ground, their bark dried and cracked. Dead animal bones could be found here and there, yet nothing but desolation as far as the eye could see. The sky was overcast, the clouds almost having a reddish hue. Even the air felt thick with the memory of the devastation this place had gone through.

"This was once a great forest in my kingdom. Brocéliande was my greatest treasure and my people loved it well." His voice became wistful, softer, as he also turned to look out at the ruin of what was left. "Before the Great Divide, when humans and Fae mingled, many legends were created here."

"You mean those such as Merlin and the Lady of the Lake?"

Ruarc nodded slowly, sadly. "Just so."

I frowned, trying to remember my Fae history. "Forgive me but I was under the impression that Brocéliande belonged to the Seelie?"

He shook his head and with a derisive snort, countered, "Mab would claim, and continues to do so, that anything of beauty and glory belongs to the Shining Court. Yet, that is not so." He bent down, running his black-clawed hand through the equally blackened soil. "A banshee has many monstrous forms for she is grief personified. Or the Oilliphéist—a great sea serpent who guards all creatures within his waters. These creatures of the Unseelie, whom the Seelie Queen would call ugly and vile, needing to be destroyed, are far from that. The scales of the Oilliphéist are more beautiful than any sirens, and if you are lucky enough to gain its loyalty, never will your ship capsize or be raided or perish by drowning. The banshee? She only came to be because she truly loved and lost, her keening a warning so that others may avoid the same fate. Even with monsters, there can be found exceptional beauty, among other virtues."

My eyes widened at this new side of the Unseelie King and I felt as if I was seeing an entirely different man altogether. Maybe he was right. Maybe I was being too linear in my thinking.

"Beauty is, and always will be, subjective to the beholder. Environment, collective and individual values, and oftentimes that which we lack, all shape and form our preference in defining our personal versions of beauty," I replied.

"Ah, there is the philosopher." Ruarc grinned, turning back to me. "But it is not the philosopher I intend to bring out today, it is the warrior. Come, Alchemist. Show me what you can do."

I frowned and snapped, "I have no weapon! My staff is back—shit!" Jerking back, I narrowly dodged a knife sailing past my head. Stumbling backward, I landed with an ungraceful thud in the dirt.

Ruarc drew his sword. The sound made the fine hairs on my body stand straight up. It was not the black obsidian one he drew when he took me from the Nightmare Court but it was impressively terrifying nonetheless.

"You still do not understand what. You. Are! Now, get up!"

"I know EXACTLY what I am! I—Ah!" I was already coming to a stand when the Unseelie King charged me. I scrambled back, eyes darting everywhere for something to transmute, all senses still tuned into the threat coming at me with great speed. In but a moment, his sword was swinging down; my runes brightened as I transmuted the incoming energy of his movement, redirecting it back at him into a concussive force. As if he'd been kicked by a horse, Ruarc flew backwards. Black shadows erupted around him and slowed his movement until he came to a stop.

He glared at me. "Running away. Always. Running. Away."

"I'm not running!" I spat back.

He came flying at me again but now the black smoky shadows that surrounded him chased me as well.

I clenched my teeth as my mind raced, backing up and dodging as he continued to put me on the defensive. My runes began to glow as I shifted my senses to a molecular view. Before I had time to think of something, Ruarc was on me again and I took a solid kick to the chest. Instinctively, I tried transmuting the force back into his leg, in hopes to break the bone but all I managed was to cause him to swing away.

Swiftly coming to a stand once more, I tried to put space between us. The air shifted and I turned to face Ruarc but he was far closer than I had realised. Unfortunately, I was too slow against his incredible speed and felt my sternum crack at the weight of his boot once more. I went flying backward yet again. Sharp pain speared through me and my eyes watered at the pain as I gasped, hitting the ground with a thud, barely missing a spiked tree stump. My entire ribcage burned and it took everything I could to hold back the scream but I quickly transmuted the crack back into solid bone.

He was already on me before I could get off the ground. Instinct took over when I saw both sword and smoky shadow nearly at my throat. I triggered my earth runes and two transmutation circles appeared where my fingers pierced the ground. Carbon spikes shot out like bullets, spearing into Ruarc. Imperceptibly fast, the Unseelie was there one moment and a fraction of a second later, just out of reach. The sudden sound of slicing and the points of the carbon spikes fell to the ground.

I scrambled up, backing up a few steps. Through the sharp carbon pikes, Ruarc stood staring at me. Slowly he looked down at himself. Pinpricks of blood showed where the tips of the spikes touched him. Taking his hand, he wiped his chest. It was a devious smirk that greeted me and then he was on me again. The shadows raced for me, reaching their insidious tendrils toward my face.

Bending down, I grabbed a fistful of earth. With a thought, I activated my silicon dioxide rune on my right hip. Shadows swallowed me, wrapping around every part of me like a straightjacket. So tightly did it grip me I could scarcely breathe. Pulling the protons around me, I shoved them through the object in my hand, just as my electrical rune on my chest activated. Laser red lights pierced through the shadow, slicing through it. The black inky prison released me abruptly, disappearing altogether.

Stumbling as I gasped for breath, tossing the glass prism in my hand at Ruarc's feet.

"There could be so much more..." He seemed to whisper, although I heard it clearly. He stared at the prism on the ground, the glass still reflecting small rainbows around it. "Tell me, Alchemist: why do you withhold your greatness? What shackles of fear and guilt imprison you so that you would watch your loved ones murdered in front of you before using this magnificent power?"

Shifting his attention back to me, his gaze pierced mine so intensely it felt visceral. Anger rushed through me. He did not understand. No one did.

"So...*ignorant*. You all think that I am this," I wave a hand in the air, "this powerful being, as if there are no consequences for what I do! You don't understand. Not you. Not Ragna. Not Alcaeus. No one fucking understands!" I snapped back. "This isn't magic, Ruarc! Magic can be reversed, curses broken. Magic defies logic, physics, in so many *irritating* ways but even it has its own laws!" I smacked a hand to my chest. "The stone is of creation, master of time manipulation. It is what CREATES the laws! I can manipulate the very atoms that formulate our existence; one wrong calculation and the earth as we know it, this realm, becomes nothing but a black hole. I will not be the cause of that!"

He studied me so intensely that I half expected him to attack me. He pointed a black-clawed finger at me.

"Your lack of faith in yourself is the only thing to blame for your ineptitude, Alchemist. You will die in the arena with a spine so weak! Where is the woman who would become Alcaeus' queen?! Reveal her to me!"

"An Alchemist should NEVER be able to do what I can do! That was not our intended design! What do you think happens when you seek your own *greatness*, believe in yourself so much you come up with this delusion that you can be more?!" I retaliated. Smacking a hand to my chest, I took a step toward him. "I *murdered* the entire race of Alchemists for this power, destroyed everything I held dear, and I will NOT do it again!" I screamed back, only to take a sharp breath as my guilt came roaring from deep within. Breathing heavily, I couldn't contain the emotion on my face.

"Never again," I finished hoarsely. This was the closest I had ever been to revealing the details of my greatest sin, but I would be damned if Ruarc was the one to hear it. So, I remained silent.

The smoky magic that surrounded the king did not disappear but only seemed to grow thicker and denser around him. I slowly backed up, shaking my head.

Narrowing his eyes at me, he continued to study me for a moment before finally saying, "It is clear to me that lack of fighting skill is not what tethers you from reaching your true potential. Just as your mind is your greatest weapon, so too is it your greatest weakness. Come," the Fae king demanded, holding out his monstrous right hand, "we have far too much to resolve in too short of a time to linger pointlessly."

Still breathing hard, I looked back at him warily before I made my way to his side. Taking his hand, I let him pull me forward into waiting arms.

Then darkness.

ꘛꙩꙅꘓꚕ꙽V⹅

We arrived in a sitting room, simple but elegant. The large fireplace, with its hand-carved Celtic patterns that wound their way up to the ceiling, was the focal point of the vicinity. The dark mahogany furniture was large and plush, giving the room a warm and cosy atmosphere. Books and ornaments filled the little alcoves in the walls and a small refreshments area could be seen across from where they stood, to the right of the seating area.

Ruarc stepped away from me and towards the hearth. He stopped in front of it, half-turning to face my direction. With a wave of his clawed hand, two tumblers, filled with amber liquid and a single ball of ice in each, appeared on the small table between the two stuffed chairs facing the fireplace.

"Come, sit."

Seeing no way out of this, I did so, my normal perpetual frown stuck on my face. Plopping into the chair, I swung one leg over the other as I took the glass in hand. It was a beautiful, ornate crystal. Already the fumes of scotch filled my nose, the peaty notes giving me a modicum of comfort. Sensing the beginnings of a lecture, my jaw tensed. My gaze fixed on the burning licks of flame, the heat welcome against the cold.

"Now, tell me," Began Ruarc, his voice a quiet rumble against the crackling of the fire, "Does Alcaeus know the reason you hold yourself back? Does he know how you became the Philosopher's Stone?"

His question, while I knew it was coming, still stirred the feelings of betrayal I had initially felt when we were taken to this realm.

"Llyr, that traitorous bastard," I grumbled, taking a bitter sip of whiskey. I made no move to answer him further.

"While Llyr may not be of my court, he is Fae and I am the king of such—I am the sovereign he called upon and so thus answers to me. I would have ripped the truth from him either way; hearing it in screams would have been so much more satisfying as that is the only sound a Seelie should make." The monstrous side of his face held a devious smirk. "And being that as he is Fae, he did what any desperate Fae facing death and torture would do: he made a deal. So do not begrudge him for doing exactly what is in his nature."

"It was not his secret to tell."

"At least he had the courage to tell it."

I smacked the empty glass down on the table. Folding my hands on my lap, I cocked my head to the side.

"You know what I am, Ruarc. I already told you it was mass genocide of an entire race culminating into what I am now. That is your answer. I will not say more about it. As for Alcaeus – yes, he knows what I am. As for the specifics of how the Stone came into creation, I've given him enough information that the rest he can piece together, if he hasn't already. I tried to stay hidden because imprisonment and slavery were the only outcomes I could logically see as my future, as I knew it was only a matter of time before I was discovered. Does that answer your question? Are we done here?" I asked snappily, eager for this conversation to be over.

"You insufferably obdurate creature," growled Ruarc. In a sudden movement, he surrounded me, trapping me in my chair with his clawed hands gripping the armrests. I tried to sink back as far as I could but he came nose to nose with me and I froze. A hand gripped my chin harshly and I went to jerk my head away but the look on the Darkling King's face kept me still.

"If I did not need you for the Divine Games and if you were not the soulmate of the *Great Owl*, your insolence would be paid for in blood and flesh. This beautiful and uncivil tongue," Ruarc focused on my mouth, the claw at his thumb pressing into my lips painfully, "would be punished and used to serve me in any way I desire. Tread carefully with how you speak to a Champion and king, Alchemist, for I have a mind to forget who you belong to and thoroughly enjoy testing how often the Stone would bring you back from the dead."

For a horrifying moment, it looked as if he was about to either kiss me or make good on his threat but then he gave a final frustrated sound, flashing sharp teeth before disappearing. I stared into the empty space, unseeing. As per usual, the only emotions I seemed to possess were anger and annoyance.

I got up with a huff, making a beeline for the bottles of liquor.

CHAPTER 6

A bottle and a half later, I was sprawled in the chair, the glass resting on my stomach, held loosely in one hand and my legs were fully extended towards the hearth. Unfortunately, we Alchemists have decidedly effective livers so I was only slightly sloshed. I had hoped the whiskey, while comforting and warming as it was, would dull the rage inside me. The constant frustration. The fear. I felt as if those were the only emotions I'd experienced these last six months.

No, you did have a reprieve, I thought to myself. For a moment in time, you were content in the arms of him. My Nightmare Prince...

In my less-than-sober state, I let myself live in that memory. In the cottage. The weight and warmth of him. The intoxicated smell that was succinctly Alcaeus. His deep but gentle voice. The smile that made the rest of the world stop. The way he looked at me, both in wonder and tenderness; a way no one had ever looked at me in all my years.

My eyes misted over and I struggled to swallow down the lump in my throat. Knowing what he might be suffering through at Ragna's hands only fed my sorrow. Taking a large swig, I let the burn of the single malt overpower my sadness, clinging to the warmth that curled in my chest as it went down. I hid my face in my free hand, elbow resting against the armrest.

"King Ruarc said I would find you here, my little troll," said Elis, his voice breaking through my hazy pensiveness.

I didn't turn to look at him or move from my position, rather, I waited until I heard his boots move against the hardwood, telling me he'd come around the empty chair next to me. I snuck a peek at him; for Elis, he wore rather simple clothes, black trousers, and an ornate creme shirt. The normal vibrant energy that he always exuded seemed duller.

"Oh, my darling, I leave you alone for a few days and now look at the state of you," he joked, although it was tinged with a bit of sadness.

I shook my finger at him with the hand that held the glass, my head still in my hand.

"Nuh-uh, there'll be noooo judgment here, I shall be free from criticism for once," I said, my words only slightly slurred.

"Give me that." Elis swiped the empty glass from my hand.

"Hey, give it—"

"Calm down, you lush. You need a refill and I myself am in dire need of strong spirits." He took a sniff of my empty glass. "Single malt it is. We're going to need it, methinks."

After a moment, I felt his presence in front of me once more. I looked up as he waved the now-filled tumbler in my face. After it was securely in hand, my friend sat gracefully into the opposite empty chair with a big sigh. We sat in silence, letting the weight of all that had transpired sit between us.

Finally, I asked, "Where is Llyr? Toby?"

Elis took a sip of a clear liquid in an elegant crystal goblet. "I thought it best that Llyr steer clear of you until I knew you wouldn't murder him. Not that he doesn't deserve it; I am still appalled. Man can suck his own cock while he thinks about his abhorrent decision-making," he said grumpily. "As for Toby, there are a lot more hybrid brownies here but the King has put him in the care of the third in command, his lead tactician. His Highness seems to believe the boy has a future as a spy."

I sat up at that. "And you let him? Elis! He is MY ward! He can't do that!"

He turned suddenly, leaning forward, and stared me down. "No, Melisandre, he is not any longer and the king absolutely can. Toby is half Fae and we are in Fae lands which are ruled by a Fae king – he answers to the sovereign of the Unseelie now and it is *he* who determines our boy's fate. He even bears the Unseelie king's sigil on his right hand."

I glanced at my own hand that bore the king's seal—Ruarc's words about Llyr came flying back to me. Elis was right. I was in *Ruarc's* kingdom now and I had brought him one of his own kind, albeit unwittingly. I had no authority over anything except myself and a small portion of the cosmos. I had no kingdom; I was no queen. In this realm and in all of the Otherworld, I had nothing. Was...nothing.

Slumping back, I took a healthy gulp, trying to chase away the desperate feeling of emptiness. The feelings of watching those I cared about slipping away, unable to stop it. The powerlessness.

In a rare moment of vulnerability, I decided to open up for once.

Perhaps I was tired of all the secrets and, now that mine was out, continuing to hide just seemed futile.

"I'm tired, Elis. I'm just...done. I'm sick of being hunted, manipulated, pulled, and twisted from one powerful tyrant to the next like a damn bone between a pack of starving wolves! Tired of being the centrepiece in everyone's sadistic game of control. Everyone wants me to be this powerful, fantastical weapon to wield. For all his proclamations of love, a small part of me even wonders if Alcaeus' use for me isn't only to warm his bed," I said bitterly. "All my life, I just wanted to live peacefully, away from any society. After what I...what I *caused*, my only goal was merely to live alone with my guilt and avoid hurting anyone else. For as long as I can remember, someone else has always determined my own fate. The one time I tried taking control, everyone I ever knew ended up dying. I'm done hurting people. I have taken so fucking much and I-I," a sob caught in my throat, "I just want to be left alone...I miss my home. I miss Zephyr. Even that damn wolf..." Tears tracked down my face and I didn't bother to hide them.

Elis didn't answer right away, nor did he kneel before me to comfort me as he normally would have. He allowed me a moment to compose myself, which meant downing the rest of the scotch in my hand.

"You will be happy to know," he said slowly, "that Zephyr is in the care of the stable master here. Kelpies are protected by contract and belong to the Unseelie; he was summoned easily enough. As for Ares, I have not seen him. That may be a better question for the lich, Cillian."

I heard a clink of glass and turned my head to look at Elis. He'd placed his drink down and folded his hands in his lap. Lavender eyes looked back at me thoughtfully.

"My dear, you and I have been friends for quite a time. You have saved my life twice now. I am living proof you are capable of more than pain and death. I am...young compared to those around me; even Llyr has hundreds of years on me. I understand that there is much of this world I still do not understand. My father, may a thousand devils curse his soul, would be the first to tell you I have no mind for wielding political power. Oh, I am a horrible gossip and I enjoy social machinations as well as any courtier does. Yet I play the game because it is expected, no, *required* of me. So, I do understand what it means to be under the authority of a tyrant, my dove, you know this.

"Nevertheless, and please don't fillet me for saying this but..." he took a deep breath as if to steady himself. "You clearly have a power more threatening than anything the Otherworld has seen for a very long time. While your complaints are understandable, my dear, I daresay you very much allow it to happen. Instead of hiding—"

I laughed.

A crazy, hysterical laugh bubbled out of me. I laughed with full-bellied insanity. Then, without warning, a ball of frustrated anger burst forth and I responded by hurling my whiskey glass into the stone of the hearth.

The silence that followed was deafening.

I knew Elis was staring at me as if I'd lost it. Maybe I had. I leaned forward, head in hands, my elbows resting on my knees.

From there, I said, "It is amazing what ignorance will say in the face of power it cannot even begin to understand. No, it's not magic. It's something far more ancient and unfathomable I wield and everyone just thinks they're as safe as silly human magic tricks."

"Then make me understand, Mels! Help me, please! Tell me why it took Toby and I getting skewered like a damn boar before you unleashed yourself on Ragna?!" Elis cried; the emotion thick in his voice. "Please, my dearest friend, of which you are! Never doubt it. Please let me be yours too..."

I had said something so similar to Alcaeus once when Sophie died. How many times have I gotten angry with my lover and all his secrets? Oh, how little room I had to talk.

"What a hypocrite I am..." I whispered.

Leaning backward again into my chair, I stared back at the flames once more. "Fine, Elis. I'll tell you. Perhaps I have lived in my head and with my truth for far too long. I will try to shorten it as best I can but prepare yourself—tis a long and sad tale."

"At your leisure, my dear." Elis picked up his glass as he sat back, readying himself for my story.

With a deep breath, I began.

CHAPTER 7

618 Years ago, near the border of Eladaria's Wall

"Come child! I haven't got all bloody day! Once you're done sharpening those tools, you must fix the fence; Gertrude broke it earlier. Damn bovine, more trouble than that stingy meat is worth," muttered the old Alchemist, bent over a small trinket he was attempting to fix.

"Master Kian, I just don't understand! When you have three elements to call, all of which could be used in fixing that fence, mind you, why you can't just transmute it—" Melisandre glanced up from the whetstone to meet her mentor's steely glare. Wisely, she stopped and finished with, "Yes, Master."

Her days were usually filled with mundane tasks, much to her utter frustration. She had come to Kian Ardahvans' at her mother's last request, shortly after she was murdered by the Council's guard, by the command of the Elders. It was her hope that Melisandre would find answers to her divergence, the reason behind the mysterious deaths of her people.

Alchemists of different clans had been dying mysteriously and at a rapid rate. New runes had also been appearing on Melisandre's skin in the wake of their death, something she did not think was a coincidence.

Neither did the Elders.

Accidentally murdering the father of her closest friend, the only person to ever show her kindness, inevitably led to the hunt and subsequent banishment of Melisandre.

Since the day the Mother gave her Life's Breath, she was always different. Many believed it was because her mother was not bound to anyone when she became pregnant; it was unheard of. No one knew who

Melisandre's father was and her mother never revealed the truth to her.

For Melisandre was born with a symbol no one had ever witnessed in all of their histories – an image that held all of the primary elements in a circle in the centre of her chest.

Unfortunately, as with anything too young to hold such power, it led to deadly and horrible things. Ignorance was the Achilles heel of an Alchemist, thus why education began as soon as verbal words were recognized. Which was why this little divergent was now hounding poor Master Kian.

"Sir, I've finished fixing the fence. Only took me three attempts since Gertrude kept wanting pets," she announced, grinning at the silly old cow's antics. Seeing the old hermit bent over his books, quill scribbling furiously, she had a moment to look around. Master Kian rarely let her linger long in his cosy little library, always finding something for her to do that put her out of his way.

She enviously eyed the Alchemist Staff that leaned on the desk next to the crotchety old man. The metals forming the staff gleamed as if taunting her with a carrot she could never have. Dust and cobwebs were ever present but the smell of old books and parchment filled Melisandre with a yearning so fierce she could no longer hold her desires back.

"I... Um... M-master Kian," she began, nervously rubbing her hands, "Look, I came to you because of my mother's last instruction—"

"So you have said on countless occasions and continuing to repeat yourself is wasting my time. There are dishes to be done and hares to catch if we are to eat anything for supper," grouched the old man, never once looking up from his writing.

Melisandre had been here for months and she was done with playing housemaid.

"Sir! I am not your servant! Enough already!"

"Enough of what? Taking advantage of my generosity and my time?" snapped Master Kian. "Thank goodness for that! There is the door, you are free to leave. Quickly too, if you'd be so inclined. I have things to do!" He pointed to the door with a feathered quill, still staring at his work, then continued writing.

Fury boomed through the young Alchemist. She stomped over to the old oak desk and slammed her fists down. The staff slid from its perch, falling to the ground with a loud clatter. Kian glared up at her through bushy grey eyebrows that matched his impressively long beard. His lips pursed into a thin line as he leaned back in his chair.

"Now you listen to me, you old crab! There are people, OUR PEOPLE, dying! And every time they do, new symbols, THEIR symbols, show up on my skin! The Council BLAMES ME! I have the Four Elements on my chest and no knowledge of how to control it let alone use it! I *vaporized* a man trying to save my dearest friend, almost killing her too in the process!" Melisandre cried, voice thick with emotion as her fury turned to sorrow. "Please... please help me. I-I don't want to hurt anyone, sir..." Tears filled her eyes, illuminating her silver and gold irises. "I can't keep being idle when.... when..." She couldn't finish, instead covering her face with her hands.

Master Kian studied the emotional little thing in front of him, taking in the small stature of the young woman. He was silent for several minutes, allowing her to calm down.

"Take a seat, Melisandre," he instructed, his voice gravelly but oddly gentle. "And wipe those tears; emotions have no business when we are in the sanctity of learning. That is actually our first lesson - controlling your overactive amygdala. Never met such a dramatic one in my life."

Melisandre bit back her snappy retort, not wanting to stop the very thing she'd been requesting since she had arrived.

"Now, in memory of my beautiful garden, you so thoroughly destroyed—"

"The begonias are still there," interrupted Melisandre but quickly shut her mouth at her teacher's glare.

"As I was saying, in memory of my garden, I will...teach you what I can. But understand this, Miss Von Boden—you are an anomaly of which I have never seen. Even with all my years, I have an inkling I will only be able to impart the fundamentals. The rest will be up to you." Pushing back his rickety chair, he stood, adjusting his black robe over the basic cotton tunic underneath. Standing in front of the books, he reached for one. "Now, tell me what exactly is a 'transmutation'?"

"Uh, it's um..." Horrified, Melisandre scrambled for an answer.

Master Kian turned around, his long grey beard whipping past him from the movement.

"Did they not teach you this in school?" he asked, flabbergasted. "You should know this answer by 4 years of age!"

"I wasn't allowed to attend, Master. Though I did sneak into some! But it was hard to hear from where I was." She looked down, shame pinkening her cheeks.

He stared at her in shock. "What in all the Mother's Creation was the Council thinking, banning an Alchemist from education when she bears all the symbols?! Bah! Let the rot take them! Useless idiots!" He leaned over to pick up the fallen staff and Melisandre went to help but he waved her away. His silver hair, braided and only slightly longer than his beard, fell to one side. Placing his staff back where it had been, Kian then leaned over his desk, staring at his new student pointedly. "Well, girl, we have our work cut out for us then. I refuse to put up with the snivelling daughter of mayhem and chaos incarnate one moment longer." He stuck out a gnarled finger, pointing at her. "You better be damn ready to get your arse whipped by the devil of education. No whining. No laziness. No arguing. And, so help me, NO transmutations of any kind without my express permission! Is that understood!?"

"Y-yes! Yes, I understand."

"Good. Now, where were we... Ah! Yes, what is a transmutation." Grabbing the book he had intended previously, he opened it and flipped through several pages. "The changing of one element to another is caused by *radioactive decay*. An Alchemist's symbol gives you the sight and ability to change the structure of your element's atomic nuclei. A proper restructure should result in a nuclear reaction by changing the neutrons or protons, depending on your desired outcome. Here," he handed her a piece of parchment and a quill, "write this down. Alpha decay and beta decay..."

And so, Melisandre spent her evenings under Master Kian's militant tutelage, her daytime spent running around the small cottage with all of her mentor's menial demands.

Time passed, and months grew into years. Melisandre continued gaining new symbols, much to her dismay and horror. Initially, they had been one maybe every 6 months. Now, they were appearing every couple of weeks. Small, faint symbols. She began to get desperate, begging the old Alchemist for answers, but no matter how many hypotheses they had or experiments they performed, no solution was to be found. There was only one option Melisandre could think of, that might hold the key to success.

So, there she stood once again before her mentor, nervously squeezing her hands.

"Master Kian?" A grunt was her only reply.

Trying again, she began, "Master Kian, you made mention that the Forbidden Texts may contain the answers about my *condition* at the Great Library in the Citadel..."

"Yes, and?" he asked, suspicion clear in his gaze, one thick eyebrow raised as if in warning.

"Well, I-uh I think maybe I should try to—"

"Do not even *think* about finishing that sentence," growled Kian.

"But sir, we are out of options! There must be something that could tell us anything about me or maybe why people keep dying and I suddenly have new symbols! I can just sneak in there, find what we need and get out—"

"No! Even if you managed to slip past their security, even reading the text is strictly forbidden! If you were to be caught, they would kill you on sight, you stupid girl!"

"I won't be caught," Melisandre responded confidently, undeterred by Kian's vehemence.

"Your ego, child, will be the death of you!"

"I know the backways and alleys and even hidden passageways better than anyone! I know how to survive there!"

"Absolutely not!"

"I know what I'm doing!"

"You—! Why—! Oh, confound it all! Fine," snapped Master Kian, throwing up his hands and papers alike. "I refuse to argue with a foolish ingrate intent on dying! Stubborn, bull-headed, injudicious halfwit!"

Angrily grabbing this and that, he slammed all manner of odds and ends down, tossing objects, letting out his frustration and disapproval. Melisandre swallowed hard at the sight, only slightly second-guessing herself before stubbornly lifting her chin as she turned to leave. She knew she could do this and was damn sure the key to everything lay in the vault of Forbidden Texts.

Grabbing her things, she made her way to the door. The voice that followed her exit almost made her give up her decision.

"And if you DO somehow manage to make it out alive, do not DARE show up at my doorstep! Don't even think it!"

A lump caught in her throat and she stared hard at the worn floor beneath her feet.

I can do this. Too long have we gone without solutions. I MUST do this!

And thus, her journey began, back to the Citadel of Creat

CHAPTER 8

Citadel of Creation, Three Years Later

She had found it. The solution to the mysterious deaths and how to possibly prevent them.

Sneaking into the Great Library had been unbelievably harder than she had anticipated. Four months it took, obsessively studying the Council Guard's shift routine and blind spots. Her years of study with Master Kian had thankfully given her the discipline she needed to control her manipulation of atoms and molecular structures. When she'd finally breached the secured vault, Melisandre was in awe of what she had found.

Books on all the transmutations that went against the Mother's Natural law; human transmutation, chimaera creation, and transmuting elements to be used for purposes of war. Alchemists were supposed to be peaceful people, who lived solely on the concept of balance; to be at odds or be involved in conflict meant to choose a side and that was not something any child of nature did.

Written reports of those Alchemists who had attempted the forbidden, those who had witnessed it, and their subsequent execution, were also found. There was so much knowledge here, Melisandre realised that to take the texts would be too much and so decided to sneak her way in, time and time again. Finally, after six months of research, she stumbled upon an incredible piece of information – an entire grid of creation circles, circles that held all the elemental symbols, encompassed the city, one for each element district. Even the water clans, the circles to be found in the design of their floating walkways and docks.

She also discovered the autopsy reports of those who died mysteriously, their element nowhere to be found. Melisandre could see why they had hidden them away; the bodies appeared to have been rendered human, their irises left colourless. If this got out to the public, it would cause absolute chaos and terror. The idea that your element could be stripped from them was every Alchemist's worse nightmare, as it was the equivalent of having their very soul taken away.

So, she went to work.

She theorised that if perhaps by connecting herself, as she carried the Four Primary Elements, to the transmutation grid while also incorporating aspects of the circle of human transmutation, perhaps she could reset all Alchemists' cellular structure to prevent any and all diseases and that she might also be able to bring back those who passed within a few days of the circle once activated, and give them back their symbols.

It was a fantastical theory and a mad one at that. Nevertheless, she had spent countless weeks developing formulas, making sure every circle was perfect in her blueprints of the city and of her master plan, checking and rechecking as needed. So confident in her work that with the final blueprint in hand, she went back to old Master Kian's, ignoring his last warning when she had left.

When she arrived at the old man's cottage, it was dark and no candles were lit. Coming to a stop at the door, she raised her hand to knock.

The door burst open and a thick stack of papers, wadded into a cylinder, came flying towards her face.

With a loud smack, Melisandre staggered backward. Before she could recover, another whack had her flailing and she landed in the dirt with a loud thud.

"How DARE you show your face again!" raged the old Alchemist. "I told you never to come back! Now look at you, idiot girl, once again before me!"

Throwing down her knapsack, she stood. "Of course I would, you old crusty curmudgeon! I found the ans—Oh!"

Arms wrapped around her, the smell of his library and candle wax filled her nose as the other Alchemist embraced her. She was so shocked that all she could do was stand there silently.

"I thought you were dead, child," whispered Kian, as he squeezed her harder.

Emotion welled up within her and she hugged him back. They stood like that for several moments before Master Kian gruffly pulled away and turned back toward the front door of his cottage.

"Now that I know you're safe, you can leave." Opening his door, he stepped through.

"Wait! Master Kian, please wait! I think I found the answer," begged Melisandre.

He turned only slightly to look at her although he didn't respond.

"Please," she grabbed her knapsack and pulled out her folded blueprint, "it's here, I have my plan laid out. I discovered that the whole city is standing on every transmutation circle for every element! What I thought were cobbled-coloured stones, were actually the circles themselves! I also found that the people that died have been quite literally rendered human! I still haven't quite calculated the reason...but, I think I can solve it nonetheless! See, here, if I just had an adjusted human transmutation circle—Hey! What are you doing!" Melisandre cried as Master Kian swiped the blueprint from her hand, tearing it to shreds as he transmuted it to confetti.

Horrified, she watched the pieces flutter to the ground. Suddenly her mentor grabbed her by the shoulders, his crinkly face mere inches from her.

"Now you listen to me, you will NOT do this! Human transmutation is FORBIDDEN for a reason, Melisandre Von Boden! No one was ever meant to bring back the dead and none have ever succeeded! The circles encompassing that city are NEVER to be used by ANYONE, for they are what connect all Alchemists to the earth! You will not do it! DO YOU UNDERSTAND ME?!" His voice boomed as he shook her violently.

"But I can do this! I can—"

"THIS IS BLASPHEMY! SACRILEGE! I will not STAND FOR IT! Be done with it, girl, or it will be the death of you and countless others!" He released her with enough momentum it had her sprawling back on the ground.

She bolted back upright and angrily grabbed her bag. Jogging a few feet away she turned back around and shouted, "You just watch old man! I know I am right! Just watch while I save the people from this sickness and then *you'll* be THANKING ME!" With that, she bolted away, back towards the citadel.

She did not see the old man turn back to the shredded pieces of paper and transmute it to its former glory. As he studied it closer, he paled, dropping it.

"Mother save us! She will kill us all!"

ÿʘ⅃Ⴙψᐯℨℨ

Cloaked and hooded, in the dead of night, Melisandre finished the final adjustment to her circles with her chalk. All were asleep and the quiet only helped her focus. Having placed human transmutation circles within each large elemental circle, she adjusted it only slightly, removing the symbols that would take from others and replacing them with her own elemental symbol. Once finished, she made her way to the very centre.

Once there, she stood in the middle with her hands out. She was shaking.

"Deep breaths, Melisandre, just like Master Kian said," she whispered, only just calming herself.

"Hey! You! What are you doing over there!" The guard's voice startled her and she whipped around to face them.

"No no no! Dammit all!" Thrusting her hands out, she closed her eyes, sensing the molecules all around her, and activated the symbols on her chest. The circles instantly reacted, energy blasting forward causing them to brighten with purple light.

"Stop! IN THE NAME OF THE MOTHER, STOP WHAT YOU'RE DOING!" screamed the guards, pointing their Alchemists' staffs at her. Their armoured footsteps were getting closer.

Melisandre ignored them.

She pushed algorithms through her mind, out through the symbol on her chest, and into the massive circles below her. Energy like none she had ever felt seared through her and she cried out. Lights in the buildings around her began turning on and people began looking out their windows and opening their doors. Still, she held on, continuing to push the changes through the circles. A hand reached for her in her periphery.

The touch never came.

A blood-curdling scream sounded and her head swivelled toward it. The guards were on the ground, one holding his arm, the other reaching for his back as if it was actively burning. Another scream joined, and then another. The clang of metal on stone echoed all around her, as people's staffs hit the ground.

"I'm sorry!" cried Melisandre, "It will all be over soon! Just a little more...!"

Only several more formulas...

"STOP CHILD, NO!"

She jerked up, staring at the figure leaning heavily upon his own staff.

"MELISANDRE! WHAT HAVE YOU DONE?! STOP THIS NOW!" demanded Master Kian.

"I cannot! I MUST fix this! I can heal you! I can heal you all!" she cried.

He dropped to his knees, letting go of his staff as he began clawing at his side where his element symbol was. The old man screamed through gritted teeth, one hand reaching up and holding the side of his head. "YOU KNOW NOT WHAT YOU DO! YOU HAVE BROUGHT DOOM UPON US! DO YOU NOT HEAR HER? MOTHER EARTH SCREAMS CHILD!"

Indeed, the earth did tremble. Buildings began breaking and dust was filling the air. The screams!

"I CAN DO THIS," she screamed. "I WILL SAVE YOU! I MUST MAKE IT RIGHT!"

With that, she pushed the last of the equations through her own symbol and into the circle. The energy burned through her like a thousand lightning bolts and she screamed, collapsing. It felt as though she was about to split into a million pieces, all the while being suffocated by the immense pressure building within her.

Just as suddenly, everything went quiet. The pain stopped. When she opened her eyes, she was in a white space. Nothing was there except for the kneeling form of her teacher, whose head was slumped, arms limp at his sides. She got up and ran to him but her steps made no noise. She did not feel the ground and it was as if she floated to him. Slowly, he looked up at her, an aged face filled with sorrow and grief.

Regret.

She went to touch him but stopped when he slowly shook his head. "No, child. You shall walk the earth alone and bear the sins for what you have done."

"What? Master?"

He closed his eyes and vanished, the world going black once again.

When she awoke once more, the screams of her people still fresh in her memory, there was nothing but silence. Her body felt as though it had been rendered apart but then put back together. Slowly, and with great difficulty, she sat up and looked around.

"Hello?" she croaked.

Her master's staff lay on the ground, a pile of clothes next to it. Her eyes slid to the next pile of clothes, then the next. To the piles resting in open doorways and the hundreds of Alchemists' staffs lying all around.

Horror sank deep into her gut.

Everyone had disappeared.

CHAPTER 9

"For a hundred years, I stayed locked up in that Great Library, trying to understand what I had done," I pointed to the symbol underneath my silver left eye, "This is the symbol for death, and this here," I pointed to my gold right eye, "is life."

Finally, I put my finger on the symbol right above my brows, in the middle of my forehead, "This is the Philosopher's Stone. It mocked me, that answer staring back at me every time I looked into a mirror but for so many years, I refused to believe it. I scoured and scoured the texts, begging the Mother for it to mean anything else," my voice broke and I looked back at Elis. "He tried to warn me, Elis. He tried so hard and I didn't fucking listen. I was so damn stubborn and arrogant and everyone died because of it!"

Tears streamed down my face, the guilt and shame as fresh and destructive as it was the day I committed the atrocious crime.

"So that's what happened, that's why I am the way I am." I drunkenly motioned up and down my body before letting my hands flop to the side. "To be honest, I have never uttered that story out loud...but I guess it's time to face the music if you will." When I went to wipe away the rest of my tears, white-laced linen flapped in front of my face. With a grateful smile, I took the proffered handkerchief. "When I finally accepted what I was and what exactly I had actually done, I ran. Been running ever since." With a shuddering sigh, I whispered, "Yet, no matter how much time has passed, I can still hear their screams..."

Dwelling on that thought too much became overwhelming, so I got up and wobbled to where the liquor was, snagging a bottle, and made my way back to the chair. I uncorked it with my mouth, spit it on the floor, and took a long and healthy swig.

"My god woman, a one-legged pirate has more manners than—no," Elis took a breath, "Let me stop myself. I'll ignore your barbarous act of drinking from the bottle with *no* glass since you just laid all your sins bare... Actually, I'm going to need my own bottle," Elis said hurriedly, snapping up quickly and grabbing the nearest bottle of vodka.

Sitting back down, he poured until his goblet was full and downed it, repeating it twice more before saying, "Well all of this explains quite a lot. Although, I still think your grumpy nature is inherent." I snorted but he continued. "So, what exactly is the Philosopher's Stone? Did you figure out how you...hmm." He cleared his throat and made a motion with his hand.

"Killed everyone? It's alright Elis. We can both agree that I have had enough time to accept what I did." Taking one last swig, I set the bottle down on the small table between us. "The elementary answer is this: the Philosopher's Stone is a vessel of energy. With the ability to control all of the elements and with the ability to manipulate atoms, the stone stole all of the potential energy an Alchemist will exude throughout their lifetime. Essentially, I manipulated time; both present, past, and future. The Stone is, quite simply, made from all of the Alchemists' time and energy, their elements transmuted into my very DNA. My own cellular structure was restructured so that they are immune to the normal damage cells endure from all the radioactive waves that cause ageing. We Alchemists typically only live to around 400 years.

"Now, normally I would need to take energy from one source and transmute it into another, which allows a change to happen. With the stone, all of the energy is here," I placed my hand on my chest, "an endless pool to draw from. I'm injured? My cells now have all the energy and speed they need to regenerate. With one split atom, I can wipe out an entire city, even a province. But I can also create one. The forest surrounding my home is one of my own making.

"However, what still baffles me is that if I do use exceptional amounts of energy from the stone, like when I used the life transfer transmutation for you and Toby, my physical capacity is still left in a weakened state; I still have to recover. My calculations are still off as to why—"

"Ah, well, how about I nod my pretty head and pretend I know all of what you just said," Elis replied teasingly, his interruption making it clear that my tangent was not fully comprehended. "But I must address your fear of becoming the big bad villain. I tell you this: all power, no matter if it is based in magic or not, will always have a dark side. You and I both know that the outcome of the power used is all dependent on the heart of whoever wields it. I truly believe that, despite your very legitimate concerns, I know you will not render this world into oblivion."

Smirking, I picked up my bottle of whiskey for another drink. "I will certainly try not to, although I can't promise Castle Fyrkat won't meet that end."

"Ha! Fair enough," Elis grinned, "Speaking of which, did you end up reading about the transmutations for warfare?"

I gave him an incredulous look. "Of course I did."

"Good. Based on my previous experiences with levels of brutality that I have personally witnessed in the games, you're going to need it," he replied, downing another glass and quickly refilling it. "You know though, I just can't make this out... I don't really understand i."

I frowned. "What?"

"Well, why not tell Alcaeus all of this? I know in the beginning you didn't trust him; I mean, I certainly had my doubts as well—"

"Elis, you would have stripped naked, put a collar around your neck, and slapped your own ass for him if he told you to, with that damnable seductive voice of his. Doubts, my ass."

He gasped. "I would never—well...no...I... Perhaps if he was naked f-first." he stuttered, "He is my liege, you know. It's my duty to obey." His conviction was getting weaker with each word and the playful twinkle in his eyes told me he knew it too. I gave him the look, and he laughed and said, "I refuse to be shamed by someone who is as much of a hussy as I am for my dearest and most blessed prince! You two were certainly getting on well enough before we left. I daresay you were on the verge of professing a very specific, dreaded type of emotion that never in a million years would I have believed you were susceptible to."

I looked down, as bittersweet sadness and yearning took over. My Mark began to ache, as it always did, but especially when the subject of Alcaeus was even mentioned.

"I...didn't know him, Elis," I said softly. "Hell, we still barely know each other, all things considered. We've spent so little time with one another." Glancing at Elis and seeing his exasperated look, I quickly countered, "Come now, we've both lived long enough to know, especially in the environment you were in, that a beautiful face can hide the darkest evil. I was justified in not trusting him, even after he revealed to me his own imprisonment. Even more so, I was worried Ragna would manipulate him when she knew just how powerful I was. She almost did. For Alcaeus' own sake too, I did not think it wise to reveal all so soon. If it was up to me and had Ragna not forced my hand, all would still be ignorant of what I am."

He frowned in a disagreeing way and rubbed his forehead, trying to visibly formulate his response.

"I understand your position on this Mels, I truly do. After hearing your devastating tale, so much now makes sense. However," he paused slightly before giving a rather large sigh, "I would imagine you could stand up to any Champion if you embrace your true potential. Maybe even one of the gods."

Frowning, I replied, "I truly wouldn't know since that is the very thing I have sought to avoid. However, you're sounding far too much like Ruarc, Elis. I don't like it."

He huffed but sat forward, resting his elbows on his knees. "I am your best friend, my little troll, and I will never do anything to jeopardise that; even cursing my own Chosen to a cold bed for months on end as punishment for what he did to you. Truly, my life became yours to command when you saved it that fateful night two hundred years past—no," he held out his hand, "don't argue with me on this, for it is true. We Vampires have a code of honour about these things. That being said, I happen to *agree* with the Unseelie King on this one—I think it might be time for the last Alchemist to make her own mark on the world. I truly believe that you could do so much for the dying Otherworld, my dove."

Giving him a long look, I processed his words. It would be easy to get angry and tell him off and perhaps I would have, before everything happened. I certainly would have then. So filled with shame and guilt, so fearful of being discovered and imprisoned, that any attempt at uncovering my dark secret had me lashing out like an angry viper intent on striking.

Now? Now, the reality was that all the effort I put into guarding that very secret was ultimately in vain; the truth so bare to the world that it made me question why indeed I continued to hide. Especially when all it seemed to lead to was more people ending up hurt.

Or dead.

"Perhaps you're right. Perhaps it's time to stop trying to protect you, Toby... My own peace of mind. Quite so, I believe it *is* time I began fighting..." I whispered, staring off into the dancing flames in the hearth. After a moment, I took a breath and said "Not tonight though, I could barely fight my way out of a paper bag after all the whiskey."

Elis giggled, "Yes, well, the occasion certainly called for it!" He took another drink, his mood becoming more serious as he reached out and took my hand. "Thank you, my darling, for trusting me with your not-so-secret secret. That must have been a terribly heavy thing to carry for so long, I cannot imagine," he said softly, running his thumb along the back of my hand soothingly. "Now, I know why you didn't tell Alcaeus your secrets but...he is your Fated, my love, there is nothing he would not do for you or against you. It is my sincere belief he feels far too deeply to be considered a threat at this point."

The corner of my mouth lifted slightly, although my heart ached once more. "Right before Ragna forced us into the throne room, I went on a rampage to Alcaeus' study, fuming that he, once again, deceived me into believing the mark he gave me was a familiar's mark. You must understand, Elis: marking and binding rituals that are founded in magic, are as foreign to us Alchemists as peace seems to be among humans," I sighed, shaking my head. "Kevyn helped me research many different marks, including the one you and Llyr share. Nevertheless, upon my blustering entry, Alcaeus did what he does best: splashed cold water onto the fires of my temper, swept me up into his arms, and... told me he loved me."

Visions of his face and the tenderness in his eyes filled my mind. His adamant refusal as I implored him to take back his feelings. To destroy them. Most of all, the living proof of his sentiments in the gentle and steady thump against the palm of my hand upon his chest.

My heart beats only for you...

My own heart clenched, the alcohol completely obliterating whatever emotional control I usually sustained. I squeezed my eyes shut, hiding my face in my hand as my elbow rested on the armrest, away from Elis.

"Oh, my dove," exhaled Elis, and I could just imagine his face, filled with pity. A moment of silence passed before he said tentatively, "That... that is quite the thing to say, especially to you. Our stoic and mysterious king, his heart felled by our little grump; never doubted you for a second!" he teased and only laughed harder at the look I gave him. "No! I refuse to let you be sad when you've told me something so wonderful! Anyways, being your Fated, love would come expediently, I imagine. Oh, pray-tell, what did he call you? Oh yes...what does the *little badger* think of this?"

"Oh Elis, I am going to need another bottle before I answer that."

"Rubbish! You've already revealed your skeletons, what's a little revealing of the heart, eh?"

Groaning, I let out an exasperated sound. "You're a pushy-nosy-busybody and worse than any mother in existence, you know that?" He smiled back at me shamelessly, staring at me expectantly. "Ugh, I don't know Elis, I truly don't. Yes, I care for him. *Deeply*, I might add. I veritably ache for the man because of this damn Mark." I shook my head.

"But every time I think I am starting to know him, begin to trust him, I come to find the proverbial rug pulled from me, landing on my ass in a pile of intrigue and ulterior motives. Besides, the concept of 'fated mates' was never within any realm of possibility for Alchemists until...well...me. Love is..." I snorted, shaking my head. "I would probably be the first Alchemist to ever consider such an emotion."

My best friend rolled his eyes. "Melly, love is not just an emotion! I would argue that is very much a verb, an action, which you are very much taking. Honestly, your emotional constipation never ceases to amaze!" He leaned forward pointing his glass at me. "You've contracted the Unseelie King for his help with Ragna. You're fighting in the games. Since we've been here, you've holed up in the library every chance you get. For what? As much as we all know I would be a worthy reason, it's not because of me or Toby; it's because of Alcaeus. And he would do the same. I would bet there is much he has done we are still unaware of."

"Emotional constipation? Really, Elis? Well, according to your very clear description, love is a verb, and thus my *emotional ineptness* may continue, as it were," I shot back, grinning as he threw up a hand in defeat, muttering how hopeless I was. "Either way, let it be enough for now that I want to free him and that I will fight for him. I spilled my worst sins to you; I have nothing left to face that reality right now. Whether I accept that I am in love with him—"

"Better chance of getting a werewolf to turn vegan..."

"—or not, will not change my course of actions either way. Let it be enough that I have deep feelings for him and that I will do all I can to free him. For now, I'm going to go sleep off the near-fatal amount of liquor I have imbibed and so should you."

The martini glass made a *clinking* sound as Elis set it gracefully down on the table as he rose. Making a valiant effort to maintain my balance as I also stood, his hand grasped my wrist and pulled me into his embrace. I sloppily smacked against him and the only sign my friend was inebriated as well was the flop of his cheek against the top of my head.

"Hey, Elis?"

"Hmm?"

"You think Toby would see me yet?"

"Oh aye, soon enough. King Ruarc has kept the little bugger busy, busy, busy. Look, Mels, I know your relationship with him has been rocky—"

"More like blown to oblivion, shattered beyond repair," I lamented, my voice muffled against the fabric of his shirt.

He sighed. "Yet, I believe it is repairable. Give it time. He loves you,

Mels; you're the only real mother-figure that boy has had and I think he knows you gave everything you could to protect him. He asks about you whenever he visits us, which has been pretty rare as of late. While he still has his reservations, watching Prince Alcaeus attack you did something to him. He was beside himself. Nevertheless, give it time as he is, as I said, very busy with training. I'm pretty sure he's also being educated academically as well. Alas, I do believe we've been made redundant in that regard."

I gave a weak chuckle and nodded.

Give him time.

Perhaps that was part of being a parental figure - letting a child come to you instead of always trying to force a solution before they're ready. No matter how badly I wanted to find a modicum of normalcy again with Toby, he had been through pure hell in his life; something I related to so very strongly. The least I could do was allow him to set his own pace.

Elis and I parted ways. Somehow, I managed to make it to my quarters without crashing into anything. As the swirling drunken darkness sucked me into unconsciousness, my last thoughts were that Cillian and I needed to talk once more as I believe Elis was quite right about one thing:

We didn't know all that which Alcaeus had done for me or about me, and I was damned if I was going to remain in the dark about it.

CHAPTER 10

The smell of linen, deep forest, and the distinct scent of Alcaeus had me slowly opening my eyes. I was naked, snuggled tightly around the sleeping warrior. Ever so slowly, so as to not wake him, the sheets slid off of my shoulders as I propped myself up on my elbow. The fabric had slid down past his waist, barely covering the rest of him, one muscular leg free of the bedding. Gentle light from the setting sun peeked softly through the quaint window above us, casting him in a romantic glow.

My eyes roamed over my lover as I soaked up the opportunity to secretly admire him. Golden skin, smooth in some parts, ragged and slightly discoloured in others where the memory of past battles fought still lingered on his body. Dark hair covered him in all the right places, not too thick but the roughness of it ignited sensuality. In a state of rest, the definition of his strength was more subtle, only small shadows on the muscled areas, yet the flash of memory of them tightening with each thrust, how his biceps and forearms flexed and moved as they held me tight against him, made me feel as if I knew the truth to a secret no one else did.

I smiled deviously, desire building up in me the more I drank him in.

"My face, a rather glorious sight I might add, is a bit further north of your gaze, mikrós asvós." Alcaeus' voice was rich and husky from sleep.

Grinning fully now, I replied, "Ah but truly, I was saving the best for last."

His full smile answered my teasing and I felt his large hand slide up my back in a gentle caress. Rough fingers slipped around my neck, softly treading up and around my ear. He grabbed me suddenly, pulling me up his body while turning on his side so we faced one another. He let go of my neck only to slide his hand down my hip and onto my thigh, hiking it up over his own.

I gasped as I felt the hardness of his desire against me, warm and throbbing. Lips encased mine, his tongue dipping inside, demanding a dance of oral pleasure. He moaned into my mouth as I danced back, my tongue mimicking the motions I wanted from him and he gently, leisurely, pushed his hips against me. With one arm snaking around his neck, I buried my hand in his thick chestnut hair, my other sliding down his chest. My fingers rippled along the curves of his abdominal muscles, relishing the feel of his velvet-smooth skin. Upon reaching the head of his cock, I curled my fingers around his thickness, my thumb rubbing back and forth, gently swiping up the built-up fluid.

His moan was darker this time, filled with need. His hand holding onto my thigh, slid down to grip my cheek and pressed himself harder against me. I could take it no longer and lifted my hips up slightly. Alcaeus noticed immediately, aligning himself with me and sank slowly inside, both of us holding our breath and then exhaling the moment we were completely connected. Burying his face in my neck, his hand reached up and cupped my breast, kneading it as he lightly pinched and rolled the hardened nipple. I arched into him and he took that opportunity to push into the depths of me still. I cried out then, the sensation immeasurable.

"Yes, agápi mu, feel me. Feel all of me. This is what you do to me," he whispered hoarsely as he began to slowly move inside of me, pressing deep each time.

So much so, I had to squeeze my eyes closed as I held my breath every time his hips came flush against mine. He kissed me again, harder this time. Pulling back slightly, he then thoroughly showered my face and neck with kisses and nips. Hot breath and the musky scent of sex were oil to the fire burning through me. Pushing me to my back, Alcaeus rose above me, hooking underneath my knees as he spread my thighs wide, hands grasped around my legs. Kneeling, he looked down at me, those midnight blue eyes, half-lidded with lust.

"Perfect," he whispered, moving in and out of me gently, in order to keep himself slick while he took his fill of me.

My mouth made an 'O' at the sensation and I slid my hands up and cupped my breasts, undulating my hips against him.

He let out a growling groan and thrust back hard in answer to my seductive teasing. A small cry of pleasure and surprise escaped me.

"To look down at you and know you, all of you, belongs to me, fills my mind with wonderful and dangerous things, my teasing little fox."

I grinned, "That is quickly becoming unbelievable if you don't cease your chatter and start moving, Alcaeus. This 'fox' is getting impatient."

He thrust against me harder still, in response, "You say this now but we both know that within minutes, you shall scream my name, begging me to stop."

"Try me."

He grinned but began thrusting hard against me, unforgiving. The smack of flesh against flesh, the wet sounds of his explosive movement, echoed in the room. My cries joined and I raised my hands up to grab onto the pillows beneath my head for support.

"Oh god, oh god," I chanted, barely even able to catch a breath. The winding pressure built inside of me and I felt my muscles beginning to tighten. So close!

"Oh, oh! I'm so—"

"Ride it, Melisandre, come for me!"

"Alcaeus!" I cried out, snapping awake. Gasping, blinking rapidly as I jerked my hand from my folds. "A...a dream. Just a...a dream."

Coming down from bliss, an overwhelming ache filled me within. Not with passion nor desire but a terrible emptiness, a devastating hollowness. My body shivered in the cold empty room; a resounding reminder of Alcaeus' absence. The memory of the warmth of his touch was nothing but a cruel ghost, come to haunt me. He wasn't dead but, in that moment, it felt like it. The Mark amplified everything: my thoughts, feelings, memories. Some days I didn't know what was real anymore.

That is all I have of him, I realised. My face crumpled in despair. Curling in on myself, my shoulders shook. Mentally, I reached out, though I knew it would be in vain.

I miss you...so much.

Silence greeted me.

A distinct whine had my head snapping towards its direction, right as the mattress swayed and dipped from the large creature that had jumped up.

"Ares...? How?"

Shocked, I stared at the massive black wolf with his signature odd white marking on his head, crawling toward me.

He reached for my hands, gently licking them several times before curling into my arms. Amber eyes studied my face before that pink tongue slipped out, swiping away at my tear-streaked cheek. I buried my face into his fur, squeezing him against me. He didn't growl or complain, just let me hold him.

I pulled back a little. "I am so confused. How on earth did you get here?" Of course, he didn't respond, just made a few whining sounds and sniffed. I shook my head. "Without a doubt, truly you are the strangest and most mysterious wolf in all of the Otherworld. Are you a phantom wolf? Come to haunt me?"

"Not haunt you; guard you."

I jumped up and out of the bed with a squeal. Ares sat up, though he didn't growl. He knew the intruder standing at the foot of my bed.

"Cillian! What—"

The cloaked lich held up a shrouded hand, interrupting the beginning of a sound tongue-lashing.

"I apologise for my intrusion, Alchemist, but your presence is sorely needed and demanded by King Ruarc. I am here to collect you."

I shook my head. "Why? What's the matter? And what do you mean guarding me?"

"My lady, we do not have time—"

"Answers! Now lich!"

He held his hand out to me in supplication. "I will give them to you, but please come with me. We are needed in the city; the Sickness has broken out and the King of Darklings needs your help."

Giving him a long-measured look, I replied, "Fine, but leave me so that I can dress." He inclined his head and turned to leave but I stopped him, asking, "But answer me this: what do you mean by *guarding* me? Ares has been mine for several years and lived with me in my home."

He stopped and looked back at me. "His name is Lycaon, and he was once a man. Now he is cursed in the form of a wolf by Zeus himself, after feeding the god the sacrificed remains of a child." Ares, or rather Lycaon, growled deep and Cillian inclined his head toward the wolf. "Indeed, my friend, we both know the imprudence of angering the gods. King Alcaeus protected him from the wrath of Zeus and gave him sanctuary on the condition of his undying loyalty. At my king's request, I bequeathed a spell upon Lycaon that allows him to leave a place without the need for doors and can be unseen if he so chooses for short periods of time. This was so that Lycaon could protect you in secret if he needed to. He has actually been with you for far longer than several years, though, clearly, he did not make himself known."

I felt my eyebrows hit my hairline as all the pieces began to fall together about Ares' weird comings and goings, how no one ever remarked too much on his presence save a few guards, how he 'conveniently' disappeared whenever Alcaeus was with me.

Before I could probe further, Cillian made his way to the door. He stopped before going through and leaned on his staff to look at me once more. "I beg you to hurry, my lady. The situation requires expediency."

Then he was gone. I stared at the door for half a second and then at the wolf still lying on my bed.

Pointing an accusatory finger at him, I said, "Oh, you and I have so much to discuss you mangy, flea-bitten—" He growled and grumbled and I could almost hear the words. "No, no, you're right. I'm sorry Ares, the fault lies with Alcaeus." I rubbed my face in exasperation. "I have so many questions! Ugh... Sacrificed remains of a child? That's disgusting and low, even for you. We would not have been friends, you and I. That's all I will say on the matter."

With a growly huff, he looked away, laying his huge head on his paws.

Shaking my head, I made my way to the wardrobe. I began to pull my shirt off when it hit me and I gasped. Swivelling to the wolf on the bed who was now staring at me.

"Ares! You peeping Tom! Look away! No, actually, you get out too! Do not argue with me, I know now there is a man underneath all that fur. Shoo!"

He grumbled but jumped off my bed and went to the door. I opened it and he looked up at me with a whine.

"Absolutely not, you pervert. You've already seen enough of me. Out!" I pointed to the hallway.

He huffed and trotted out.

Quickly changing, I grabbed my staff and walked out to the corridor. Cillian appeared instantly before me.

"Alchemist, this shall feel strange but do not fear."

I frowned and opened my mouth to respond but my world dropped from beneath me and I was free-falling. At least, I thought I was. My stomach was in my throat when I felt the firm ground underneath my feet once more. However, my brain believed we were still falling so my knees gave out, my face becoming one with the dirt. I heard my staff clank and begin to roll away, but it stopped suddenly. Lifting my throbbing head up slightly, I saw a leather boot had stopped it.

Groaning, I pushed myself up, glaring at the shrouded lich. The chaos around me, however, kept me from speaking. People and creatures alike were running and screaming, although the sound was muffled as if I was listening through a pillow.

We were in what appeared to be a town square, with a beautiful and massive fountain in the middle. Torches and lanterns lit the area, though the brightness of the moon gave enough light to illuminate the horror that surrounded me.

I had never seen the Sickness up close; only once did I encounter it but I had pushed through the Veil into the human realm just before a maddened creature could even get close.

The sounds of metal upon flesh and bone had me turning to see Unseelie soldiers fighting monstrous creatures, some humanoid, some pure animal. That's when I realised our arrival had been completely ignored.

"Can they not see us? Why are they not attacking?" I asked, turning to Cillian who bent over to pick up my staff, and handed it to me.

"I have shrouded our presence and created a barrier to protect us, all of which I will release when you are ready."

I looked around again, seeing no immediate solution to the chaos around me. Suddenly, a massively horrifying creature on two legs emerged. On its head, an impressive set of antlers on either side jutted out, several feet in length. It had the skull of an elk but the sharp teeth of a bear. Disproportionately long arms with hands that ended in spear-like claws swiped at the swarm of the crazed Sick that seemed to attack him in endless waves. It stood at least twelve feet tall, ancient, and utterly terrifying.

I had read of a creature like this once in a book of legends: a leshy. An ancient forest spirit, who protected its inhabitants while hunting those that intend harm. As it belonged to Slavic gods, its presence here was baffling for it did not belong to the Unseelie.

Then it spoke.

"Lich of Ebroriath! I know you are here! Release the Alchemist! We must rid this place of Sick! Now!"

My jaw dropped.

"Ruarc?!"

CHAPTER 11

Having no time to react to this discovery, the creature in question went back to his slaughter as the lich behind me spoke.

"I am releasing the barrier, my lady. Prepare yourself!" Cillian raised his staff, shouting, *"Mukt karana!"* With a flash of light, the barrier dropped and a cacophony of sound pierced my eardrums.

A blood-curdling scream behind me had me twisting, barely reacting in time as a Sickling came flying in my direction. Out of pure reflex, I turned and thrust my staff right through it. The flesh was rotting away from its body, the smell of death and decay assaulting my senses. It was bipedal and jaws snapped frantically, trying to get to me. Long incisors dripped with blackened saliva.

It was a Vampire. Or used to be.

Its eyes were fully black with no pupils. With a flash of alchemical runes, the creature burst into flames. I shoved it from my staff. Swivelling around, I noted the absolute chaos and swarm around us. Most of the Unseelie citizens had fled, but the few that remained were fighting valiantly but quickly being cut down.

Where are Ruarc's armies? His guards? The Wild Hunt?!

With no time to find those answers, we needed an immediate course of action.

"Ruarc!" I called out. "We must lead them away from here! There are too many innocents that will be caught up in a transmutation! Find something that will bait them away!"

The Unseelie king roared in answer, ripping apart the dozen or so

Sicklings in his claws.

Hearing my name behind me, I turned to Cillian.

"I will create barriers for the city, but I will need to hold my position or it will fall," cautioned the sorcerer.

Fully facing him, I asked, "How long? How long can you give us?"

The hooded wraith thrust his staff out behind me, just as I felt the air shift. I jerked away just as the Sickling exploded into ash.

"I can give you three hours."

Nodding, I replied, "That is enough."

Cillian disappeared but within a few moments a huge boom sounded and, while I could not see it, the tell-tale sign of magic crawled over my skin.

Another screech behind me but this time I was too slow to react, getting knocked to the ground by another zombified creature. My breath whooshed out of me as whatever Sickling that tackled me, now pinned me down with its body. Claws pierced through my clothing, into my flesh, dragging down my back. I screamed, my runes already coming to life. Pulling the kinetic energy from all of the movement around us, I transmuted it, syphoning it through my body as I activated a redistribution transmutation circle above us. Using my own body as a mirroring circle, I sent the massive surge of electricity through the Sickling and immediately felt the creature stiffen. To keep myself from also being burned, I redirected the energy back into my body and straight into the Stone.

Suddenly the weight was lifted from me, the creature had fallen to the ground at my side. Incinerated, one could not even begin to guess what it had been, as it was now nothing but a husk, blackened and charred.

I pushed myself up, my back screaming and burning with pain. When I came to a stand, I froze.

It was quiet, too quiet.

The swarm of Sick surrounded me, staring, fixated. The sounds of cracking bone had me swerving my gaze to Ruarc in his leshy form, depositing the remnants of the Sick on the ground. By the sudden stillness in his own form, the king also realised the Sicklings were hyper-focused on me. Several lifted their noses in the air, in a sniffing motion. They growled and hissed, taking a step in my direction. Stinging wetness dripped down my back and that's when a sudden understanding came to me.

My blood. They smell my blood!

They charged. Before I was swallowed by the mass, huge talons wrapped around my legs, flipping me upside down, and lifting me into the air. I snagged my staff off the ground just in time. Fumbling, I almost dropped it, but held on for dear life.

Dangling upside down, I watched the Sick overflow where I had just been, my blood dripping down my arms, the back of my neck, and onto the ground. Only a few feet above them, I flinched when several tried to jump at me.

"We shall lead them away! I know of a place where we can eliminate them!" shouted Ruarc, his voice a strange growling screech. I tried looking up but I could only catch glimpses of fur, feathers, and a massive beak. The talons that held me looked like an eagle's, though his back legs were lion's feet.

He had transformed into a gryphon. The Champion of the Mórrígan was a true shapeshifter. Not a Were. Not a Changeling, but a legendary shapeshifter. The mirror image of the goddess that created him.

The Darkling King took off and I desperately gripped my staff to my chest with both arms, squeezing my eyes shut.

"Let your arm hang, Alchemist! We need to give them a blood trail!"

So I did.

Still holding my staff in a death grip against my chest, I hung my left arm and watched the blood begin to drip down my fingertips. The horde below us moved like a tidal wave of rotting, moving corpses. Buildings turned into trees, a blur flying past me as we left the city.

Blood rushed to my head and the swinging back and forth was doing nothing to curb the nausea that was beginning to crawl up my throat. I shut my eyes again, trying to stop the feeling of my stomach rolling.

"Are we there yet!? I believe... I am about to...hmph!" I slapped a hand over my mouth trying to fight, unsuccessfully, my gag reflex.

"Almost there, Melisandre! Get ready!"

The ground was getting closer at an alarming rate.

"Ruarc, slow down! Shit!" I curled around myself, feeling his grip around my legs tightens.

That's when I realised he was beginning to swing me back and forth. This bastard.

"Don't you DARE!" I yelled.

He let go when I was parallel to him. Screaming, I hit the ground and went rolling. The breath was knocked from me and my body eventually came to a stop, sprawling and gasping. I felt the earth shudder and I turned my head to see that the Unseelie King was no longer a gryphon, but a full-blown fire wyvern. Black and blood-red wings billowed, stretching out as they held his weight. Scales that glimmered red ran up his long neck, revealing a black underbelly. A horned head that resembled a prehistoric predator, held the king's tell-tale bright yellow eye and his aquamarine one. Deep rumbling came from the winged-beast beside me, and a burst of flame erupted from his mouth, straight into the horde of infected now running at us.

We were in a huge clearing although the forest line could be seen from where we were. A quick glance upwards showed me dark clouds, and threatening rain.

This should work nicely.

I began jogging toward the horde but shouted in Ruarc's direction. "I need to capture one so I can examine it! Keep them back!"

The wyvern roared as the horde came closer, his long neck reached out and grabbed one, throwing it in my direction. It flew, landing a few feet from me. Wasting no time, I transmuted the ground, stone bands appearing around the neck, arms, and legs of the Sickling.

Leaving it there and with staff in hand, I ran even closer to the horde which was attempting to reach the Darkling king but his impressive flames held them back.

I lifted my staff up to the clouds, and transmutation circles appeared within them. At the same time, more appeared as large, bright purple circles underneath the horde. Feeding energy into the clouds, I built up their charge while increasing the oxygen around us. Just as Ruarc released another stream of flame, I activated the circles, tethering the energy of his fire. Lightning struck repeatedly within the circle, the sound of thunder deafening. Ruarc's continued streams of fire helped continue the energy transfer until there was nothing but torched flesh and ash.

The air was so charged I felt all the hairs on my body stand on end; I had no doubt my hair looked a right mess.

Walking over to the imprisoned Sick, it screamed and spat at me. Its rotting flesh was putrid in the humid atmosphere and I covered my nose for a moment, trying to hold back my dry heaving. The creature seemed to have no awareness of its skeleton peeking out from its limbs, or the flesh falling from its face.

"It is Unseelie...a boggart." Ruarc's human form appeared next to me, his expression dark.

I looked back at the struggling creature. Going up to it, I knelt down next to its arm. Locating an open wound, I adjusted my senses, using the Stone's inner sight to break down the flesh to a molecular level so that I might see the infection for myself.

My eyebrows hit my hairline as I gasped at what I was seeing. Shaking my head, I sat back on my heels, processing.

"What? What did you find, Alchemist?" Ruarc asked impatiently.

Slowly shaking my head, I didn't answer right away, trying to think of how to explain it. Coming to a stand, I faced Ruarc.

"I have not spent much time studying otherworldly creatures so their molecular structures aren't as familiar to me as those of humans or animals. Most living things are quite similar, however. I saw two things: cells with an ogive shape, with small spikes surrounding them. I also found acylopolyamine toxin and cytolytic peptide molecules. I've only ever found something similar in animals. Which would mean...necrosis..." I trailed off, still testing my hypotheses against all the information in my mind.

"Necrosis? Well, that is rather obvious from both stench and sight, Alchemist! What else!" demanded the king, impatience vibrant in his tone.

I took in the drooling, decaying face of the boggart. Placing a hand toward the sky, a circle appeared in the cloud. I transmuted the cloud to release the moisture and it came raining down upon us.

The creature screamed and struggled violently, trying to get away.

Shaking my head I began to laugh. Not a humorous one, no. In disbelief.

"It's rabies! Necrotic rabies!"

CHAPTER 12

A hand went around my throat, squeezing with rage. I grabbed onto Ruarc's forearm instinctively. He brought me within inches of his face.

"You discovered this, simply by looking at it?"

"Let...let go...I can't bre—"

"ANSWER ME!"

"Y-yesss."

He cursed, releasing me suddenly and I fell to my knees coughing and sputtering. Black shadow surrounded us, and the telltale sign of the wind flying past me told me we were teleporting. I reached for my staff, wrapping my fingers around the metal before everything went black. Within moments, a cold granite floor was beneath me, and the abrupt sounds of the clattering of dishware and chairs that were being shoved backward.

Just as I was coming to a stand, a rough hand grabbed the back of my head, fingers fisting my hair. My staff clattered to the ground and I was once again in the face of a very angry monarch.

"You mean to tell me that you could have taken ONE LOOK at the Sick and would have KNOWN what this is? Can you find a cure? IS IT POSSIBLE?" Ruarc screamed at me, his face so close that spit sprayed me with every word.

"Yes, but I don't know if I can find a cure! The humans have a vaccine I might be able to study- Ow! Let go Ruarc! You're hurting me, you bast-Ah!" His grip tightened on me and he slammed me onto the table.

"Knowing this, KNOWING you could have done something about this, for hundreds of years! Thousands upon thousands have died and what were you doing?! HIDING! LIKE THE COWARD YOU ARE! WORTHLESS! MAY THE SICKNESS TAKE YOU!" He let go, shoving away from me, and darkness swirled around him. In a blink, he was gone.

I was panting, so confused at what had just transpired, staring blankly at the space the king had just been in.

"Ms...Ms. Melly? Are you alright?"

I blinked several times, finally becoming aware of my surroundings. Toby had moved toward my right, tentatively creeping closer. He looked...older. There was an air of ageing around him.

After all he had been through, I wasn't surprised in the least.

"I'm fine," I whispered, standing upright, reaching my blood-stained hand out to him. Seeing how dirty I was, I jerked my hand back but he snagged it, pulling me into a hug.

Turning my head, Llyr and Elis were staring at me, wide-eyed and just as confused. The dinnerware was all skewed, some having fallen and broken from my back being slammed onto the table.

Elis cleared his throat and motioned to the rest of the table that had been spared. "Would you care to join us? I'm sure we can get an extra place..." He trailed off, looking for a servant of any kind but the room was empty. "Actually, you can have mine, my dove. I wasn't terribly hungry anyways."

"No, no, it's alright, Elis," I replied as Toby released me but didn't move away. "I should get cleaned up; we destroyed the horde of Sick that attacked the town. I...I believe I discovered what the Sickness actually is."

Surprise painted both of their faces but it was Llyr who spoke.

"Ah, then it is no wonder King Ruarc is in a fit." All of our attention snapped to him as he continued. "I am sure it's not quite my place to say but... King Ruarc lost his lover to the Sickness. There was a rumour they would eventually become Chosen but she..." he trailed off, though there was little need to continue.

I understood.

A moment of silence passed and I nodded in empathy. My back was throbbing as I carefully made my way toward the door.

"Ms. Melly?"

I turned. "Yes, Toby?"

"Might I...come to see you?" He looked nervous, cheeks with a pinch of colour on them.

"Of course, Toby. Always." I replied gently, giving him a reassuring smile.

I began making my way out of the room once more but was, once again, interrupted.

"Melisandre! Please, wait!" I turned to see Llyr rushing at me, his pale green and cream shirt and pants making his burnished ginger locks vibrant against the dark interior of the room.

Elis made a move to stop him but I quickly shook my head, letting him know it was okay. Upon reaching me, Llyr went down on one knee. The sight was such a surprise, I couldn't help but grin and tease him.

"I'm sorry, Llyr, but I must turn down your proposal; you're already taken and, apparently, so am I," I joked, trying to lighten the mood. His sombre look prepared me for a lengthy apology and I wanted him to understand I held no ill will toward him.

He did crack a smile at that, saying, "I fear Elis would behead me if I knelt for you when I did not for him."

The man in question scoffed. "Pft, I would certainly break your kneecaps if she got you on one knee when I could not. Beheading is far too messy and rendering you immobile and at my mercy would be far more exciting," he retorted, examining his delicate nail beds.

We all grinned but Llyr's face fell serious once more as he looked up at me.

"Please, Melisandre, I know that words alone cannot express how sorry I am–"

"I know, Llyr. I know," I interrupted, putting a hand out reassuringly. "It worked out for the best and that is all that matters. Do not fear - our friendship is still intact." I patted his shoulder and a meaningful look passed between us as he came to a stand. Turning back to leave, I caught his words as I was closing the door.

"Melisandre, you are a far better person than I think even you know."

A small smile lit my face, but deep down I truly just did not have social energy to expend on needless quarrels. It wasn't in my nature to hold grudges, let alone waste energy on unnecessary conflict.

The doors closed quietly behind me and I imagined my quarters. As I began walking, the corridor moved, shifting in the night. The torch at the end of the hall illuminated, revealing the door to my room. I went in and closed it gently, then promptly slammed my back against it in surprise.

"R-Ruarc?" I asked hesitantly.

He was sitting at the edge of my bed, booted heels propped on the bottom wooden frame, elbows resting on his knees. Long tapered fingers were steepled against his monstrous one and the reflection of flames from the lit hearth danced over his face. He was weaponless, and I was beginning to truly believe this man did not own a single shirt in his wardrobe.

Blood-red hair cascaded around him giving him an ethereal look. One would think it would make him appear softer and feminine, but I would tell you it only emphasised every angle of the deadly creature he was.

He did not look at me but continued to stare off into the fire, clearly lost in his thoughts.

Taking a hesitant step toward him, I cautiously walked a bit further into the room, my eyes never leaving the figure on my bed.

I waited.

"If the Fae should be known for anything, it's their proclivity for gossip." Ruarc's voice was more speculative than threatening, giving me a bit of courage to respond.

"You heard? About what Llyr said about your lov—"

"My lover, yes." His eyes slid toward me, accentuating the last syllable so the word slithered out of his lips. The sharp furrow of his brow and the tensing of his jaw let me know that Llyr was probably correct in his assumption.

"Is that why you were so angry with me? Because of her?" I asked, crossing my arms over my chest. The Darkling King might make me wary for he was as predictable as the wind, but cowering in the face of his random outbursts would get us nowhere.

"My Viviane. My beautiful, fierce enchantress," whispered Ruarc, his face softening as he recalled her name. "She was the lone candle in the darkest room. So incandescent her flame, I was naught but a moth destined to be burned, so consumed by the fire of her soul. Truly, she would have made a most wondrous queen." He looked down at his hands, now open as if to show their emptiness. Grimacing, the king curled his fingers into fists. "That Seelie *rat* was correct—she was struck down by the

Sickness. It was imperceptible at first, memory loss...random outbursts of anger. Nothing uncommon, for I was surely known to drive her to such a state on occasion. But then the screaming started. Agony as I had never heard from her before." Unclenching his hands, he lifted up his right arm as if to examine it, the animalistic claws almost blending in with the shadows of the room. "For weeks, she screamed. Her flesh began to rot. She had to be chained so as to not attack anyone, for it was as if her magic left her and all that she could do was thrash around like a wild beast caught in a snare.

"I could not bear to see her suffer. My Viviane, once so full of life, now a raging corpse chained to our bed." Curling his hand into a fist once again, he let his arm drop onto his knee. "So, I killed her. Ended her misery. Had I known that each day I was losing her, little by little, I would have killed her sooner; for at least she would still be my Viviane when she met her end. I could have said goodbye. That the last words she would have *understood* was the love I bore her. What I killed was not her."

I swallowed hard in the silence that followed after; out of all of my faults, offering comfort to someone who grieved was up there in all that I lacked. So, whatever condolences I may have had were kept to myself. He would not appreciate them anyways, judging from how it appeared he held me responsible to some extent. Instead, I offered the truth.

"Whether I had been here sooner, may or may not have mattered; rabies in humans and animals, once infected, is always fatal. They have vaccinations, to prevent the continuous spread, but I fear that it would have been far too late for your lover. Who knows how long it will take me to come up with an equivalent vaccination to what the humans have? Even then, I theorise that magic and immortal cellular structure would not be receptive to medication. I'd have to work with someone like Cillian..." I shook my head, rubbing my forehead. "I cannot do that while also trying to prepare for the Divine Games during Yaldā. Look, Ruarc, I understand why you might be angry with me –"

He scoffed. "You sat and hid away while the rest of the Others were suffering and dying—"

"I had just cause to and you know it!" I snapped back. "Do not ignore the reality of that which has already come to pass! I now see that you would have bound me to yourself, against my will might I add, in an effort to find a cure for the Sickness. Yet, regardless of any noble intentions you might have had, your actions not only prove my point but also justify my own for hiding. I will not be controlled, chained, or enslaved! Why is that so hard to understand?"

Ruby-red hair whipped around as Ruarc came to a stand, swerving toward me. Coming to a stop just a foot away, he stared down at me.

"How are you still so ignorant of your own capacities?" Eyes incredulous, he took me by the shoulders and pulled me closer. "You ARE the Philosopher's Stone! You have more power in your being than any Champion ever created. If you are enslaved, bound, it would be by your own allowance!"

Reaching up to grab his arms, I made no effort to push them away but rather squeezed them in earnest.

"I know that now," I pleaded, "I am guilty of so many things, and being a coward in regards to the power I wield can certainly be counted among them. But no more. I am here now. I will not run nor hide, nor allow those in power to hurt those I love. Not even you. So, save your anger at that which cannot be undone. Understand that my actions were justified in their own manner, but I now recognize that my current path straightens anew, in a direction that contains a purpose. Let that be enough."

Studying me, he didn't let go, though he did loosen his grip. Then he slid his arm around my waist, pulling me against him. A hand went to my face to cup my cheek, his thumb caressing it. A memory of Alcaeus holding me just like this shot to my mind and my Mark burned. My breath hitched.

Just as I was about to push him away, he whispered, "So much of your spirit reminds me of her...sometimes it's as if it is she who shouts back at me." He closed his eyes, as if relishing this moment. Then he said, "You will not be able to beat your opponents in pure combat; we both know this. So, your battle must be fought by the sword of intellect, the strategy of cunning, well before the physical fight begins. We have three weeks, Alchemist. Waste not a moment of it."

What I was not prepared for was the gentle kiss he laid on my forehead. He pulled away, though his hand cupping my face still lingered.

"There is hope for you yet, daughter of Danu."

Then he was gone.

CHAPTER 13

The hot bath felt glorious. So much so, I nearly drowned myself twice as the beckoning of slumber teased me. My back ached, though the wound had healed. Worries about getting the Sickness were low on my priorities; I would have known immediately if I had been infected.

Actually, can the Sickness affect Alchemists? But I have the power of the Stone...

Or does it only target immortal cellular structures? If that were the case, I'd be at risk, potentially...biologically, my structure does not quite match theirs, so...

"That would be worth researching, actually," I surmised out loud. The desire to learn, understand and find solutions was so strong that I almost left my watery haven.

Almost.

The bathroom was attached to my room, although the panelled door was hidden.

When I had first arrived, I had to track down the ever-invisible and elusive servants of the Fortress. It took shouting 'I NEED ASSIS-TANCE' before the tentacle-faced steward appeared before me. His appendages *wriggled* and it was hard not to assume it was in annoyance. After showing me where and how to open it. I tried asking his name and all I was met with were menacing golden eyes before he disappeared silently. It would be outright hypocrisy if I, of all people, begrudged him of such an unsociable nature.

Just like the staff, my meals were always magically appearing where

I was and disappearing in the same manner. Sometimes before I was finished. Most of the time it was wildly convenient but it did make me curious as to how Elis, Llyr, and Toby managed to always dine together.

After I was acceptably pruney, I finally emerged from the tub. Slipping into some silk nightclothes, I tied the matching royal blue silk robe around me. Ruarc had been most generous indeed, providing an entire wardrobe of clothing for me to use. Most of which were far more revealing than my introversion allowed. So, I stuck with the few pieces that wouldn't make even the least experienced harlot blush.

My room was warm and cosy. It reminded me a bit of home, something I yearned for sharply. As I walked closer to the bed, amber eyes greeted me.

"Hello, friend," I greeted, taking Ares' big head in both my hands. "You must know that you will and forever will be, Ares to me. And, while I know now that you are not entirely all wolf, that a man lurks beneath this fur, well...it is awfully cold tonight...I hope you stay." A warm tongue licked my forearm and I could not stop myself from giving him a kiss on his forehead.

Alcaeus, you may be sly, sneaking in this overgrown wolf-man puppy but I am so very grateful for his presence.

"I knew he would be far more successful at getting you to accept him than you would me. Do not fault me for being rather devious in my efforts to keep you safe."

I gasped, my hands coming to cover my mouth. Ares reacted, coming to a stand with a whine as he cocked his head at me.

Shutting my eyes, overwhelming relief spilled through me upon hearing the rich timbre of Alcaeus' voice in my head. My Mark came to life, pulsating at the same rate as my heart.

"Alcaeus! You're free," I whispered out loud. "Are you...? Did she..." I could not finish my thought as it hurt to even think it. I felt a sadness in my mind though it was quickly swept away.

"Do not worry about me, Melisandre. Trust that I am yours. Solely. My mind is free of Ragna's control for now. Though, I will not hide that my body is imprisoned. Come Yaldā, Ragna will release me fully. Now tell me, how do you fare? Is the Darkling King treating my Fated well?"

I hesitated, uncertain of all I should reveal. Clearly, I took too long as the feeling of his anger crossed my mind.

"Melisandre. Tell me."

"Well... he certainly struggles with keeping his hands to himself," I admitted, "but I am just as quick to remind him how unwelcome it is. Overall, I cannot complain too much."

Silence.

"...Alcaeus?" I asked hesitantly.

"Did you agree to allow him to seduce you, *mikrós asvós*?"

"How did you...?" I crossed my arms, my face morphing into a deep frown. My indignance flared at the question, as it was reminiscent of a child being scolded.

"I absolutely did! Ruarc was refusing my terms in helping me save you, demanding I 'warm his bed', were the exact words, I believe, he used! That does not mean I would acquiesce to it in reality! To be clear, it was the chance to seduce me - which yes, he has tried and almost lost half his face. So don't you dare get angry with me, doing what I must to save you." I ended my tirade with a finger pointing to empty air.

Feeling his humour, he chuckled, saying, **"Oh, my sweet little badger, not for a moment would I hold you at fault for Ruarc's licentious ways. No, not at all."** Then his voice turned dark, a deep kind of possessive, in a way that was different from when he defended me against Ragna. **"I have every intention of relieving the Unseelie King of the use of any part of that which has touched you. For you are mine and mine alone. Now, tell me, what do you mean by 'terms'? Did you make a deal with the Unseelie, Melisandre?"** Alcaeus demanded, his voice sharp.

Swallowing audibly, I sighed. Not used to being under censure, I began to pace, hands on my hips.

"Yes. I did. We both know he would not allow me out of his kingdom. While I doubt he could imprison me for long, Elis and Toby are here. I refuse to have a repeat of the last several months. Besides, we need his help, Alcaeus. We need him. Even with my level of pride can I admit that."

He neither agreed nor disagreed with me, instead saying, **"Making deals with Fae is a dangerous gamble, especially King Ruarc, and they are not. Without. Consequences."** I glared into the dark corners of the room but he continued on before I could snap a retort. **"His cunning is as legendary as his prowess in battle. What did you prom-**

ise him? All of it, *mikrós asvós*. **I would know what he has cost you so that I might repay him in kind."**

At this I stop pacing, my head tilting back as I stared at the ceiling, frustrated. With a big exhale, I spilled it all.

"After an irritating amount of negotiation, I agreed to an alliance with the Unseelie kingdom. As we've already discussed, the opportunity to seduce me and that I would be his champion and fight in the upcoming games—"

"You WHAT?! Tell me it is not so, Melisandre! You cannot be serious!"

"Do not doubt my determination, let alone my courage, in doing what I must to free you or myself, for that matter! If duelling immortal creatures gets me that much closer to freeing you, to destroying Ragna, then by the Mother, I will do it!" I snapped. Shoulders slumping, my vitriol cooled. "Please, Alcaeus, believe in me. Too long have I hid in the shadows, only using the Stone in desperate times of survival. Too long have I done nothing. Believe me, I most of all, understand that I am no warrior. But neither am I powerless. No... quite the opposite."

"My love, it is not just a duel. It is a battle to the death! I will not—"

"Yes. You will," I interrupted, my voice strong and even. "A battle to the death, you say? If that is the case, then know that Lord Cyto's gruesome end was only a preview of how creative a scientist I can be. So, it is not me you should worry about, my owl." I smiled at my new nickname for him, though it turned slightly sinister at my implication.

I heard his audible sigh and felt the defeat in my mind. Weariness coloured his voice, having lost its edge of anger, panic, and protectiveness.

"This was not at all what I had intended nor wanted. It was my sincere hope that you would remain safe and guarded by King Ruarc until I devised a workable plan to escape Ragna, coming to you to complete the Mark so that she would not pursue us and we would be free. I do not want this for you, Melisandre, my love." His voice ended in a whisper, making my heart twinge at his distress.

"That has never been, nor ever will be, an option now, Alcaeus," I responded gently.

"When my owls delivered their observations of the interac-

tions between you and King Ruarc, your faux battle, your slaying of the Sicklings, I refused to believe what I saw through my servants' eyes. Now, I hope to convince you otherwise. Knowing my former ally has tried to seduce you away from me as well... as I stand here chained; my failing attempts in keeping the world away from you were utterly in vain, exposing me as pathetic and rendered so completely redundant, it seems."

"How did you...? What do you mean 'owls?' Do not tell me you have me under surveillance using owls." I grouched, confused. Stepping close to my windows, I did a quick scan which revealed no owls spying in. Shaking my head at his silence, I rebuked, "I know you are worried about me, but spying is beneath you, Alcaeus. It's patronising to be treated so incapable. I am the Philosopher's Stone, for the Great Mother's sake!" Sighing, I rested my head against the carved wooden column of the four-poster bed. "Rest assured though, you have neither failed me nor do I believe for one moment you are pathetic... possibly a little redundant, given your current state," I gently teased. "Besides, I am very aware neither of our bodies are our own, at this moment. I saw what... what she was doing. Know that our situations, in their own ways, aren't that different," I finished, my voice having softened in sadness.

Silence slipped in between the lines of thought, the atmosphere tinged with despair. Using it to gather my thoughts, truth demanded presence upon my lips.

"It hurts me," I whispered into the dark, "knowing she is touching you. That pain slices through me, down to the bone. It eats at me like an incessant grind. So, if that is the symptom of my heart possessing yours, then I suppose I cannot find fault with your own jealous possession of mine. But no one, not even the Champion of the Mórrígan, will have me without my full cooperation. Which stands to mean only you have a right to it. To me. Trust me as much as I am trusting you."

Warmth filled my mind, trickling down my body. The sensation grew and I swear I could feel Alcaeus' arms around me. Closing my eyes, I melted into it, basking in it.

"Nothing, not man, woman, nor the divine, could tear asunder what the Fates have determined us to be. For our souls were rendered from the same fabric, my love, sewn together by the gods themselves. I will always watch over you. Be your shelter

from the storm. No chains, bars, not even the possession of half of my soul will prevent me from being by your side. I am your shield, Melisandre, just as much as I am seeing you become mine." Pride filled his voice at the end and I found myself blushing all over. **"Come what may, little warrior, together we will conquer whatever the future holds for us. Damnit! Ragna comes! I must go. I will be waiting for you, mikrós asvós,"** he said hurriedly. Feeling him pause, he did take his time in saying, **"I love you."**

My face fell at those words, my eyes watering with emotion.

Perhaps I should try it. Try saying it.

"I...I lo—" His presence was no longer in my mind. "Alcaeus?" I let out a frustrated cry, pacing angrily before flopping down next to Ares, who wagged his tail hesitantly as his warm nose touched my arm. Scooting to the middle of the bed, the large wolf followed and laid down beside me.

Curling into his thick, warm fur, I held Ares so tightly I was surprised he didn't growl. Battling against anxiety and intrusive thoughts on what Ragna could possibly be doing, I decided to let only anger burn within.

For her days are numbered, I reminded myself. As she will soon be forced to accept her chains are temporary, a symbol of her delusion and false sense of power over him. I will rip the metaphorical cloth from over her eyes and she will see the truth.

That Alcaeus is mine.

CHAPTER 14

"My lady, the Massster callsssss."

I jerked my head up from the text I was studying.

"You are to meet him in the War Room."

"Where is the—Wait! Hello?! Oh, for fuck's sake," I swore, grumbling as I watched him vanish. The tentacled steward only stayed long enough to confirm I had heard his message before disappearing.

Slamming the massive tome of *Creatures of Sluagh & Their Origins* closed, I unfurled from my cross-legged position atop the large oak table I had been sitting on. Knocking several books over as I got down, I cursed and bent over to pick them up, as several had landed underneath the table.

"It would be my pleasure to escort you, my lady," resounded a deep voice from behind, startling me.

A loud ***thunk*** reverberated in the massive athenaeum as my head smacked into the solid underside of the table.

Yelping and letting out an impressive string of curses that would do any sailor proud, I stood up. My hand rubbed the back of my head where a bump was now forming. Turning, I gave another undignified squeak, my lower back smacking into the table as I jerked backward.

Cillian, in all his eerie wraith-like glory, was close enough that my legs had almost tangled in his robes, the cloth still swaying slightly.

"Is there some sort of sick, twisted inside joke I'm unaware of? Let's all sneak up on the Alchemist and see who can terrify her the most?" I snapped, glaring up at him.

"I was not aware of any comedic agreement, though there is no denying the amusement that comes with your reactions to my presence," he replied, humour surprisingly obvious in his deep voice.

Rolling my eyes, I snorted. "Your amusement is my undying annoyance." Pushing away, I walked around him, grabbing a few texts to place back on the shelves. "What does Ruarc want?"

"Yaldā is nigh. We will leave soon for Khaviel. It is within reason to assume we must discuss a course of action, primarily regarding the Divine Games. This is the first celebration you are attending, is it not?"

"You know it is," I murmured as I reached up to place a book on a higher shelf. It slipped from my fingers, falling to the ground with a loud thud. "Rats," I cursed, picking it up and trying again. "You know, I'd hardly call slaughtering other creatures in an areee—" I jumped slightly, almost getting the book on the shelf, "—na a cause for celebration—oh bloody hell!" I snapped when the book almost tumbled from my grip yet again. My fumbling fingers were suddenly grabbed by a large, gloved black one as the lich took the book from my hand and placed it on the shelf with ease.

Feeling his presence against my back, I stared directly up and into the blackened hood where Cillian's face should be. Only endless darkness was to be seen. Not a nose, lips, or any defining facial feature that might have belayed any humanoid characteristics.

Before I realised what I was doing, my hand was reaching upwards as I whispered, "What is in there, I wonder...?"

Quick as the strike of a snake, his hand snapped around my wrist, a mere inch from touching his hood.

"Not all of us are born with the privilege of knowledge being spoon-fed to us since birth, Lady Von Boden. The acquisition of such came at great cost in both body and soul." Cillian's haunting voice held no trace of irritation or annoyance, always the pragmatic and direct tone. "From previous experiences, I find it best for one's curiosities to remain as such. With knowledge gained, so too does it come with consequences."

Gently, he released my wrist, floating away. In a rare moment of humour, I just could not resist teasing him. "Oh, come now, lich. Surely you know words such as those are the equivalent of dangling the proverbial carrot in front of me. Now I must know. I've never dissected a lich before; I can only imagine what I could discover in the name of science," I grinned slightly, walking toward him.

He was already getting close to the door but stopped, turning slightly to me.

"If I come upon another, then your wish is my command, my lady. However, I would advise against seeking intimate knowledge of me as that would undoubtedly disrupt the emotional equilibrium between yourself and that of my prince."

My lips parted and I blushed at his implication.

"Intimate knowledge, how very presump—" My retort ended just as soon as it began when it dawned on me that he had just responded to my teasing in kind. I couldn't help it. I laughed. "My, you are full of surprises Cillian. I'll give you that. Well, best not to keep the Unseelie King waiting much longer. Lead the way."

Inclining his head, he took the lead.

ᚢᚲᚱᚻᚹᚢ

"...won't happen that way."

"How many times must I repeat myself? That's exactly what our scouts have seen! My best spies have confirmed it!"

Loud masculine voices could be heard just as Cillian and I approached the double doors of the seeming base of operations. War flags bearing Mórrígan's sigil stood proudly on either side of the doorway. The doors themselves opened without assistance upon our reaching them.

"That could mean a million different things! Most likely, it was just a horde of Sicklings!"

"A bloody army of them?! Are you daft—"

"Regardless of what may or may not have been seen, Queen Ragna is planning something- why else do you believe she adamantly insisted on hosting Yaldā? It was supposed to be held by the Kings and Queens of Were this year!"

"Some kind of insidious leverage, blackmail, is no doubt in play—"

"That would match her typical *modus operandi*, as it were..."

"This is absurd! It's a trap, I tell you!"

Cillian and I had walked into a full debate, not a single person acknowledging our arrival. The Unseelie King was seated at the far end, one ankle resting atop his knee. His head leaned apathetically on the tips of his fingers and his face held that unreadable mysteriousness I have become accustomed to seeing on him. My attention was diverted, however, to the heated exchange dominating the room.

Three men I'd never seen before were huddled toward the end of a sizable oval table. It could easily seat twelve people, its dark wood glossy despite evidence of being well used. Yet, the wood framed the real showcase. As we drew closer, I noticed that the surface moved like a quicksilver liquid, with thunderous clouds behind it, lighting up different spots at random.

Tearing my attention away, I noticed one man sat on the right side, an empty chair between him and the king. Another man, slight of frame with long brown hair that was tied back, stood holding the back of said empty chair, in a heated debate with the man standing across from him.

The room itself was large enough to hold hanging braziers and the walls were lined with bookshelves, though small compared to other headquarters I had been in. However, the wall directly behind Ruarc was littered with weapons of all kinds, a display that would impress any museum.

As we came to a stop directly in front of the table, Ruarc held up a hand and the verbal chaos ceased.

"Enough," the king said, his voice almost quiet compared to the loud snapping of the others. "Alchemist. Lich. Do join this rather un-productive discussion." He elegantly motioned to the empty seats but continued speaking. "Now, I believe we can all agree on the painfully obvious reality that Ragna does indeed have ulterior motives for which will undoubtedly serve her insatiable need for power and control. While it may inconvenience the rest of the world—"

"Sire, *inconvenience* is…it's not—" The man interrupting was to the right of Ruarc, looking positively flabbergasted.

"A nightmare for anyone not created a Champion, to be sure," the king interrupted, "but I am not afraid of the Soul-Eater; there is nothing she can do to me that I cannot return to her in kind, ten-fold."

The one man seated was running a finger gently over his bottom lip, as if speculating. His fair hair blocked some of his face from my angle. "With utmost respect, Your Highness, your own gifts would only feed her undead armies."

Ruarc narrowed his eyes at the man. "Just as her own would feed The Wild Hunt; spirits filled with vengeance and an insatiable desire for blood and death are far superior to that of an army of reanimated flesh. In no reality would the Necromancer Queen ever conquer the Unseelie, let alone strike fear into the heart of its king! This topic is concluded. We must now focus on the most difficult task at hand - preparing this young Alchemist in the art of politics and diplomacy, assuming it is possible." His bi-coloured eyes rolled to me, one sardonic brow lifted in lieu of his smirk.

Crossing my arms, I retorted, "I am adept when I need to be, thank you."

"Ha!" laughed Ruarc. Gesturing to the man standing to his right, he said "Cú Chulainn, General of The Wild Hunt. And," motioning to-wards the opposite man standing, "this here is his lieutenant, Láeg." The man sitting finally turned to me and I was met with piercing blue eyes and a fair face. "This is my Second in Command, Master of Intrigue and lead Tactician, Fionn Mac Cumhaill. You all know Cillian, the Lich of Ebriorath. This is Melisandre Von Boden; the last of her kind and soon to be the chosen champion of the Unseelie Court in the Divine Games. Let it also be known that she is the embodiment of the Philosopher's Stone. Though, that fact shall and will remain confidential among only those in this room." All heads in the room gave affirmative nods, silently acknowledging the undercurrent of warning in the Darkling King's voice.

Both standing men turned to me, assessing frowns marking their faces. The one he called Cú Chulainn was simply striking. A man one might call beautifully masculine in every sense of the word. Spun-gold hair was luscious and thick, the top half braided to keep it out of his face, the rest running past his impressive shoulders. He had a good height on him, only slightly shorter than the Unseelie King.

Yet for one so aesthetically pleasing, there was something hiding behind those deep blue eyes; something dangerous. A look I see in all who lived by the sword but have yet to be felled by it.

His lieutenant's build reminded me of Elis', though slightly more muscular. Gentle eyes and a kind smile, Láeg looked almost out of place amongst these warriors. However, I knew of his story: the most skilled charioteer and driver, this man had a way with steeds that would give Poseidon a run for his money.

Láeg nodded his dark brown head at me politely in silent greeting and took a seat next to Fionn. Cillian and I split off, him taking a place beside the empty chair in front of Cú. I stood opposite him, leaning my hip against the table, my arms folded as I faced Ruarc, though my attention was turned to the General that was greeting me.

"Welcome, Lady Von Boden. It is an *immense* honour to meet someone so legendary. Hauntingly beautiful, I might add. Those eyes... never have I seen the like. Your feminine presence will be a refreshing divergence among these primitive beasts," Cú teased charmingly.

I never trusted a man with a sugared tongue.

"Of all traits one might use to praise a woman, I would hardly consider 'femininity' counted among mine," I replied, my voice a bored monotone. "As legends go, you are far more earning of that title, *Hound of Ulster*. Never without his ever-faithful companion, I might add." Looking at Láeg, I gave him a polite nod. My eyes slid to the man sitting directly in front of me. "My goodness, to have the fearless leader of the *Fianna*, whose wisdom is unmatched among men, as your Master of Intrigue..." Shaking my head, my gaze was placed once more on Ruarc.

"Well, let's just say I don't envy your enemies, Ruarc."

What I was not expecting was the glare the king returned my way.

"You will address me accordingly, Melisandre, and show the respect due when we are amongst others," Ruarc commanded, "especially once we arrive at Castle Fyrkat. What I may tolerate here in my own domain, I will not amongst those very enemies you do not envy."

Raising a challenging brow, I snapped back, "I am not your subject, Ruarc, but your *ally*, per our agreement. Do not try to flex your dominion over me as if it were otherwise."

He stood suddenly, leaning over the table menacingly. A slight movement in my periphery had my eyes darting over to Cú, who was now grinning wide with a glint of admiration in his eyes. Yet the feel of magic suddenly crawling over my skin had my attention back on Ruarc.

"Thank you for so adequately proving my point at the overwhelmingly impossible task of teaching you diplomacy, especially when we have so little time!" His presence became bigger, darker. Then he vanished, only to suddenly be pressing me into the table, hip to hip. My back curved away as far as it could go without me actually laying down and yet we were nearly chest to chest.

Damn magic.

"Are you so socially inept that you do not understand the necessity for political pretence in a dance of power dynamics!? One weak link in the chain, one show of dissension among us, and Ragna, being the fucking hellhound that she is, will smell it and sink her teeth right into the heart of us!" The Unseelie King's breath was hot against my face and my back was starting to pinch in discomfort.

Attempting to shove him off, he snatched my wrists, just as Fionn's steady voice interrupted us.

"I do believe I side with the lady."

Both of our faces whipped to him, surprise on mine and outrage on Ruarc's.

"Allow me to explain, my liege."

"Please. Do." Said liege bit out. "Quickly."

Bowing his head, Fionn continued, "Queen Ragna is expecting Lady Von Boden to be returning for the sake of her lover, *The Great Owl*. It is known that the Necromancer Queen has long desired her consort; is desperate to have him, possess him. Just look at the means by which she initially captured him. She also possesses the truth of the Alchemist's secret. Our enemy's jealousy and paranoia will afford us no opportunity to execute our plans and she will be scheming accordingly. We must find a way to lower her guard if we have any chance of finding an opening.

Devise a way to redirect her focus. Aye, there is only one way I, myself, have concocted that may work."

Ruarc shifted away from me enough that I could stand straight, though still had a hold of my wrists.

"Well? What is it?" I asked impatiently, pulling at his iron grip.

"When you next see Alcaeus, deny him. Treat him as but a stranger. When we arrive in Khaviel, we must show them your emotional ties with him have been severed. That your feelings for the Nightmare Prince have been replaced. That—"

"Absolutely n—"

"—you and the Unseelie King have become lovers instead."

CHAPTER 15

"I beg your pardon?" My whole body went still and the feeling of horror was hard to ignore.

"It would only be a pretence, nothing more. Yet, in order for it to work," Fionn switched his attention to Ruarc, "the lady would need to be familiar with you, Sire, and you with her. Make Queen Ragna believe Lady Von Boden is no longer interested in Prince Alcaeus, now that she has had a taste of sidhe flesh. Royal, no less. The Raven of the Mórrígan is well known to be unsurpassed in his skills as a lover; it is not so unbelievable."

I couldn't contain the sigh of relief as I exhaled. Ruarc had finally loosened his grip but still did not let go and my irritation was rising. Instead, I felt his normal thumb caress the sensitive part of my wrist. Looking into his face, my concern grew; not because he looked pleased or put off, but because I could not tell what he was thinking.

"So," Ruarc finally responded. "Let Ragna believe the Alchemist is truly mine so that her vigilance in keeping them apart, lessens. Possibly giving us an opening to allow them to finish the Mark. The idea certainly has merit but there is still a problem—"

"We're Fated, Alcaeus and I. Ragna knows this. She'll see right through our plans." Quick to interrupt, I did not believe for one moment this plan could work. The Mark alone made being apart agonising. Not only that, while Alcaeus and I might be able to pretend indifference, there was no way I was agreeing to play Ruarc's lover when I knew he would take full advantage.

"Hmm," murmured Fionn, scratching his beard. Both Láeg and Cú's jaws dropped in shock. Cillian still said nothing, sitting like a ghost as only his head moved when someone was speaking.

"Perhaps," Fionn began after a moment, "it may only result in complicating yours and the prince's self-discipline, my lady. Ignorance in the way of Fated Mates will be in our favour; not much is known beyond the gods being responsible for creating the bond. King Ruarc is far older than Queen Ragna, and was privy to many of the god's dealings. The queen was not. Chances of her knowing about the Fated Mark—"

"She does! Before Ruarc took me, she saw the Mark and was, well, devastated by it. It won't work."

He held up a pointed finger, "Ah, but then that also means she knows it is not completed. She is also aware that King Ruarc is unmated and her spies have undoubtedly told her of Llyr's deal, I am sure of it. So let me correct myself: you must become *intended*. One can still be hand-fasted without mating. As it stands, we must gamble on what we know as much as the unknown. We have no other choice. United we must be in front of The Gathering, so that is how we shall appear."

My frown deepened. I knew Fionn's plan was good, very sound. Already he lived up to the stories regaling his wisdom.

Oh, how badly I did not want to do it.

The licentious lout holding me lifted one hand to his face, making a move to kiss it. I struggled, my voice slightly higher in panic.

"Wait! I still don't believe it can work! Alcaeus won't stand for his former ally being so familiar with me! We have to tell him or he'll ruin whatever plans we have."

Despite my attempts at pulling away, Ruarc finally got his kiss on the inside of my wrist. Just as I started curling my fingers into claws to try and scratch his face, I was swung around, my back pressed firmly to Ruarc's chest. My arms were crossed over my body, as he gripped my forearms like a straight-jacket.

His lips pressed against my temple. The moment his tongue flicked out, tracing the top line of my ear, all of my runes began to glow threateningly. No one made a move to stop him. Not even Cillian.

He chuckled into the shell of my ear. "Ragna will release her hold on him for Yaldā, of that I have no doubt. She needs him for diplomatic purposes and it would raise suspicion amongst his allies if she maintained his mental prison. Fret not—you will get your opportunity to relay our plans. The lich will succeed if you fail. No," his voice darkened, "I think you just might enjoy this charade as much as I will and that's why you are fighting my Tactician's plan."

I did not trust myself to speak. Transmutation circles appeared throughout the room. Chairs scraped back as the others stood, and even Cillian got to his feet quickly, a pleading hand going out toward us.

"I do not think it wise, Your Highness, to taunt the Alchemist," he warned.

Ruarc just laughed, leaning far enough down to kiss my shoulder, then my cheek.

"I am not afraid of you, my little spitfire, nor your Fated. Ruin my table or any of the furniture in this room, and I will punish you like the insolent, *a thoice cheanndána* that you are and I will enjoy it. Thoroughly. Accept it," his voice now a velvet whisper against my face, "Until you complete the Mark, you are mine to play with, *wife*." Once again, I felt the heat of his tongue.

I snapped.

A wooden spike appeared so fast, Ruarc could not react. It pierced through his face, impaling him against the wall behind me. Not even his men had the time to make a move toward him.

Calm and collected, I turned to see the lance had gone right through his mouth.

Blood dripped from him, down the lance and I watched it for a moment before saying, "Remember, *husband*: it is only a pretence." I transmuted the chair, which I had also connected to the table for support, back to normal before the Unseelie King could snap the wood. I watched as he dropped to his knees with a hand over his face. Already, I could see his wounds healing at an astonishing rate. "No furniture ruined, thus no punishment deserved. If I have learned anything about you, Ruarc, it is that the only form of boundaries you seem to understand are those written in violence." I turned towards the rest of the room, noting the shocked and wary faces aimed at me. Cillian had his hooded head buried in his hand which could only be interpreted as exasperation. "Consider the plan a go, only to commence once we reach Castle Fyrkat. I'll be in the athenaeum if you need me. Gentleman." I gave a single nod at them as I took my leave, not sparing Ruarc a single glance.

Only the sound of menacing, blood-wet laughter followed me out.

ਠᕲੁħΨ∨ӠӠ

"Are you ready, Ms. Melly?" Toby's voice surprised me and I looked up from my packing to see him standing in the doorway.

"Toby, what a pleasant surprise. I'd hoped I would see you before we left," I told him, patting the top of my clothes before shutting and locking the trunk. It was small, as I had packed light, only bringing the few pieces of clothing I thought were appropriate and not too revealing. "Please, come in."

Gesturing to the single chair in the room by the hearth, I transmuted the floor, bring it up to create a stool-like sitting place for myself.

Toby's face lit up. "Wow, that's really cool Ms. Melly. I wish you'd done that more often back home."

As we took our seats, I shook my head. "I couldn't risk being caught, by either Otherworld creatures sneaking past or by humans and their aerial technology. Certainly would have been convenient at times. It's not like I hid from you, though. Like when you broke your bicycle that one summer. You cried so loud I thought old man Pete was going to file a noise complaint, so I transmuted it back to its original state."

"Well, yeah! That was the first gift I'd ever gotten, just for me. Not some bloody hand-me-down," the boy scoffed. "I loved that bike."

There was a difference in him, I noticed the moment he started speaking.

"Your speech has changed quite a bit."

"Yeah, Master Fionn started my education immediately. I'd had no time to recover before he had me hitting the books. 'A master spy's best weapons are competency and sharp wit—both are born from knowledge,' he told me. I sounded like an 'uneducated human buffoon' he'd say. So, I'd get a wack on my hands every time I didn't pronounce something 'properly'." He lifted up his fingers, only two of which were bandaged. "They all used to look like these two but, as you can see, I'm learning." It was nice to see the cheeky grin I loved so much, appearing on his face once more.

"Well, the Master of Intrigue and I shall have to heartily disagree. Familial ties aside, I think you should be proud of your Birmingham origins; it is rich in history and culture. A lovely place, known for its industry and highly skilled craftsmen. No one should shame you for it. Besides, the dialect makes you, you."

Brown eyes studied me then and we were both silent for a handful of moments.

Toby shifted in his seat to face me more directly. "Ms. Melly, I'm sorry. No - please. Let me say this." He looked down at his hands briefly, clearly gathering his thoughts. "It took me a long time to accept what you did to Sophie and why ya did it. Being here, among other Fae, it was like being thrown into an ice cold bath; my whole world got turned upside down. But...I do feel more at home here, like I finally belong among my own kind. Yet, I still sometimes feel like I'm drownin'," he confessed, laughing lightly but I saw the sorrow in his eyes. "But I get it now. I get what you did for me..." he took a deep breath, "only a parent would do. Only someone who loves their kid would do it. I'm not yours, I know but...you've treated me like one for these past three, almost four years. So, for that: thank you. You, Mister Elis and Mister Llyr—you're my family. Because of that, I forgive you for taking away Sophie. I know it...i-it was t-the only way." His voice broke at the end of that, shoulders curling around himself and slightly shaking.

Normally I'd freeze and scramble with what to do or say in this situation. So, I took a page out of Elis' book and slid to my knees in front of him, grabbing his hands in mine. I said nothing, just held his hands like that while allowing him this moment.

"I still...gods, I fuckin' miss 'er," choked my ward, his accent coming back thick. "Me own siblings could kiss a dead rat's arse compared to my Soph. I've never had anyone I cared about that much before. Only fer 'er to die! She was my first friend...my best friend. I should have protected her. Should have told her to ditch, hide in our spot—"

"Toby, shhh. Look at me," I interrupted, refusing to allow him to go down that dark rabbit hole. My hands cupped his face as I stared deeply into those chocolate brown eyes welling with tears. "Dwelling on the 'what ifs' or the 'should haves' will not change what has already come to pass. I'm telling you now: there is not a single thing you could have done to protect her. You are grieving—your mind will naturally speculate but when it does, maybe think of Sophie in this way: ask yourself what she would want. Would she rather see you trapped in the moment of her death or live in the memories you had together? If you are going to go back in time with your mind, go where Sophie would want you to be."

His face crumpled and I stood, pulling him in for a hug. Toby had grown, now reaching up to my shoulder. Those little arms were not so little anymore and they wrapped around me firmly.

Rubbing his back in gentle circles, I held him. The weight of guilt I'd been carrying since that fateful night finally lifted, my heart lightening.

He'll be alright, Sophie. Rest in peace, sweet girl, I thought, in honour of her.

After only a few minutes, we released each other and I couldn't resist giving him a gentle chuck under the chin, changing the subject.

"In no time, you'll be as tall as I am." I went to go and grab my staff, putting on the black riding gloves and fur-lined coat. "So, will you continue your studies while we're away? Has Master Fionn helped you with your kleptomania at all?"

"Yes, I've learned to completely control it now. He did some kind of magic that helps with it too. As far as what I'll be doing..." He hesitated so long I stopped what I was doing to look at him. His eyes were only slightly red, though clear of the previous emotion. Clearing his throat, he confessed, "Well, I'm going with you."

"No, you are not."

"Yes, Ms. Melly. I am. Those are my orders."

I slammed my staff onto the floor in protest. "I will not have a repeat of the goddamn nightmare that was these last ten months! Is Ruarc insane!? Where the hell is he? I'm going to—"

"Please Ms. Melly! Stop!" Toby stepped in front of me before I could leave, gripping my shoulders. "My king said you would say that and he told me to tell you this: I am under his rule now. If Queen Ragna were to make a move against you, using me, it would ignite a war. For it goes against the *The Kingdoms of Old's Peace Treaty,* signed at the first Divine Games after the Uprising. I am immune!" He gave a sharp shake to my frame before holding up the back of his hand to my face. "See? I bear his mark now! She cannot hurt me. Not like last time. I swear it."

Taking a breath, I stared at the black marking that Elis had previously warned me about. The Celtic knot was far more elaborate than my own, the two black ravens whose beaks touched to finish the circle. A stark reminder of whom he answered to.

'My king', he had said.

I took his smaller hand gently, running my thumb over the haunting declaration that he was no longer my ward.

"I see," I whispered. Clearing my throat, I let go of his hand. "Well, in that case, what exactly is your mission?"

Toby gave me a look of relief and responded, "Everyone attending has spies of their own. King Ruarc said the Alchemist should have one as well."

My eyebrows shot up.

"You are to be my spy?" I asked in disbelief.

Toby frowned. "Well, I know I just started but I know that castle better than anyone else going. Plus, Master Fionn is going with us so it's not like I'll be on me own. My own, sorry." He looked down and scuffed the floor with his shoe.

Letting out a frustrated sound, I said, "Fine. We'll talk on the way about what that is going to look like." I shoved my pointer finger into his chest. "But you stay out of sight, understood? You will live in the shadows and do exactly. As. I. Say!" Poking a little harder with each word, my new little spy yelped, letting out a giggling 'ow' with each shove.

"Understood, Ms. Melly. Let me get your bags."

He grabbed my trunk, and with the grace of a newborn foal, stumbled through the doorway, banging it on everything within reach. I followed him resolutely. My mind immediately went to the Nightmare Prince.

I'm coming, Alcaeus. Wait for me.

Always.

CHAPTER 16

What I would not give for a road. Even a muddy one, riddled with potholes. Our path out of the Unseelie kingdom began with eight large portals in a line; strange black holes carved into space, like standing mirrors. When I asked why we did not create a singular portal for our entire retinue, Cillian explained that it was best to only have two portals per ley-line; each individual going through, pulls magic. Too many people through one portal and the ley-line can drain. Having a sizable company of almost twenty, guards and personal attendants included, that many portals made sense.

So, flying steeds and all, we went through. Elis and Toby caught me before I face-planted coming out. Snickers and giggles followed me as I stumbled against Zephyr, grabbing onto his mane to steady myself. The vertigo was something awful and I squeezed my eyes shut as my stomach rolled like a boat on the choppy seas.

"Here," Llyr said, coming up beside me, "this should help with the dizziness. Lemon oil usually works best but, alas, all I can summon are lemon verbena leaves. Rub them and hold them to your nose, like this."

I took them, rubbing the leaves desperately and smacking them to my nose. I gave a pained smile in thanks. Taking in my surroundings, the numerous smells of conifer and deciduous trees, and earthy freshness bombarded my nose. The area around the small clearing we had ended up in was surrounded by thick forest. Looking up, I took in the position of the stars and moons.

This is the western border of Khaviel, I surmised.

As we all began orienting ourselves, the Unseelie King addressed the group.

"The Alchemist, Lord Fionn, and I shall fly the rest of the way to

Castle Fyrkat! I will keep the skies clear while General Cú Chulainn and the Lieutenant take to the ground. The rest of you will join them. Tobias!" he called, and my former ward quickly appeared by his side. The king grabbed him by the shoulder. "You will ride with your former guardian. Stay with her at all times. When we reach the castle, you shall remain hidden, unseen. Do you remember your training?"

"Yes, Sire."

"Good," replied the king, patting him on the shoulder. "Be her ears and eyes; we cannot trust the Great Owl's reach while he remains tied to the Necromancer." Turning away, he walked away from the group and let out a screeching whistle. With a hand in the air, he motioned for us to begin our journey.

My gaze searched for where I had last seen Elis and Llyr. Carriages and chariots began appearing out of thin air, and the guards and attendants began hitching the horses to them.

Zephyr curled his wings tight against his body and bent one leg, extending the other. It was a trick that took me 20 years to teach the stubborn beast but I'd be damned if I looked like a buffoon trying to hop onto his gigantic frame.

Settling into my seat, I reached for Toby and he swung his leg over the saddle, getting comfortable behind me. Giving him a click, Zeph obeyed and came to a stand.

Feeling the continued squirming of my passenger, I swivelled around to see him grinning ear to ear.

"Well, ain't this the bees' knees! Oh—I mean, isn't it wonderful?" Toby laughed nervously at the sliding look Fionn gave him before the Master of Intrigue hopped on his own winged steed.

I had lost sight of Ruarc but I noticed Llyr and Elis climbing into a carriage. Ares was sitting next to the carriage wheel, waiting. Then I noticed Elis had stopped and looked back at me, giving a little wave. A sudden floral scent filled my nose and I looked down to see a deep red snapdragon woven within my lapel. Smiling, his meaning was clear: *Protection.*

I looked up just in time to see Elis giving me a wink before disappearing into the carriage. I still didn't see Ruarc, but I led Zephyr away from the company so that we had room to take flight.

As soon as he had the room, Zeph took flight. Used to his excited antics, I was prepared for my Kelpie-Pegasus to bolt but my passenger was not. Strength I didn't know Toby was capable of was felt in the suffocating band his arms made around my waist. The girlish-squealing scream that followed us into the air told everyone he was no longer excited about his first Pegasus ride.

When we cleared the trees, Zephyr reared back with a sharp whinny. It was then I realised there was no need for concern in not being able to find The Unseelie King of the Sluagh. For he seemed to take up most of the sky. A great winged monster sliced the air with wings big enough to engulf half a village. Three heads snapped and growled. Though, even from this distance, I could see all three seemed to have Ruarc's monster yellow and aquamarine eyes. The massive body of the dragon didn't get its size from girth but rather the length of his bones and the long, hefty tail. Visually, this legendary monster looked just as swift as it was powerful. If I didn't know that it was Ruarc underneath those scales, I would either have to wipe out half of Khaviel to kill it or make a run for it.

I was betting on the latter.

"Ellén Trechend," whispered Toby in awe.

Getting a scared Kelpie-Pegasus to calm down while also keeping one's seat in midair was no easy feat but I managed with a little help by transmuting the neurons in the raphe nuclei of his brain, stimulating more serotonin.

Having avoided nearly falling to our deaths, Zephyr eased and drew slightly closer to his King. Ruarc let out a roar that was an unmistakable call to move forward. His large body turned and began to make its way in the direction of Castle Fyrkat.

Glancing around, I finally caught the Master of Intrigue on his own flying steed, slightly ahead of us and to my right. The bright moons and stars made it easy to see him, despite his shrouded appearance and the black coat of his own horse.

With nothing but the cool breeze on our faces and the quiet flapping wings, the night was peaceful. We travelled swiftly, and the view up above was breathtaking.

I should really take Zephyr out at night more... I thought to myself, basking in starlight. If there weren't risks of wyverns and griffins, or other aerial predators, I probably would do this more often.

So far on this trip, only the occasional wyvern was spotted in the distance, which kept their space from us after seeing the Ellén Trechend.

Toby's voice broke through the silence.

"I would never have expected King Ruarc to become Ellén Trechend. I read in a book once that it had been killed by some poet. But then... many of the people from myths and legends I've met, should be dead. Yet they're here, alive. Were they all lies, Ms. Melly?"

Adjusting my hips in the saddle slightly, I couldn't resist reaching down and scratching Zephyr's neck as I answered.

"I have found that many legends were horrific and brutal, two adjectives humans abhor as they are typically on the losing side of those tales. So, creating heroes is necessary to give hope to a species that is utterly finite. I have also found that magic very much displays the same properties as the principles of energy: it cannot be destroyed, but simply transferred. All creatures made by the old gods were made by magic, not energy. Only those created by the Mother were created using energy. Yet, unlike those made of pure energy, magical deaths do not seem to adhere to the same principles of natural science. Simply put, Toby: perhaps they did slay these creatures or perhaps they did not; it hardly matters since the result was never permanent, because magic was involved. One does not simply slay magic; if it was possible, I would be back in our home still throwing books at my thieving little ward," I teased, shooting him a grin over my shoulder.

He gave me an affectionate squeeze. Feeling his head rest against my back brought the protective surge of emotion and I could no longer hold back my concern.

"I really don't think this is a good idea," I said aloud.

"What? Me comin' with you?"

My silence was answer enough for him.

"Well, I can see why you'd think that Ms. Melly. You're always trying to protect everyone. Which I am quite grateful for, no bones about that. But," he hesitated, clearly searching for the right words, "with all due respect mum, I think maybe you want to protect so badly that you can't see why it's a good thing I'm going..."

My brows shot up in surprise; this was the first time I'd ever taken criticism from him. His bravery intrigued me.

"Oh? Do explain."

He gulped. "W-well, you see 'ere, um...that's just it right? I know the castle. The servants trust me. I can stay out of sight. And, believe you me, I have no problems avoiding that rightful bi—I mean, the queen. So, it makes sense I can be a great asset to you."

Unable to withhold my grin, I replied, "Asset, is it? My, Fionn has really pushed your studies, hasn't he?"

"It was a good word, ain't it? I'll be right posh in no time," Toby laughed.

Sighing, I begrudgingly agreed with him. "It would go against Nature itself to not want to protect you, Toby. You are a youngling and it's the job of your elders to see to your maturation. However, you are not wrong; it's hard to differentiate the benefits of having you here, over the cost and risk if you were caught. Nevertheless, if it was up to me, you'd be still studying in the library back at The Fortress. So, I'm sure you're grateful I'm no longer in charge. Also," I turned around to look at him, "I think you've earned the right to curse that woman till the end of time, so don't hold back on my account."

Toby let out a chuckle, saying, "Yeah, just a bit." With a quick squeeze, he continued, "Just so you know, though, I'll always look up to you, Ms. Melly. He might be my new king, but you'll always be my guardian. Besides, I bet you'd still win in a fight against 'im."

I snorted. "I don't know, that creature ahead would make even me think twice. Clearly, Ruarc is going for shock-value upon our arrival."

"Yeah, like watching a nightmare come to life, that. What do you think everyone will think when they see us?"

I didn't respond right away, looking ahead instead. My frown deepened. Tell-tale spires, the great stone bridge, and glittering water shone like a beacon in the night. My nerves started to tingle.

Alcaeus, I don't know if you can hear my thoughts but until I know our communication is not compromised by Ragna, I will try not to communicate this way. However, I must warn you to not react to whatever you hear or see when we arrive. I will explain all, once we find a safe place. Please... just trust me.

No response came. My stomach quickly turned to wriggling worms in apprehension.

"I think we're about to find out, Toby. We're here."

CHAPTER 17

The Unseelie King made sure his entrance was as dramatic as he was, circling the city twice to make his presence known. The grand finale was his epic landing atop the largest and highest towers with a roar before jumping down into the entry courtyard. Our entourage was already coming through the gates when I landed Zephyr next to the now bipedal form of the Fae king. Lord Fionn followed, his steed dancing in agitation after he touched the ground, but a calming hand from his owner helped lessen the tension.

Before I could dismount, the Master of Intrigue was at my side. I saw him place one hand on Toby's knee, whispering to him. Stepping away, Toby got down and I quickly followed suit. Turning to him, I gave a slight jump.

"T-Toby? What—"

"Shhh! Glamour, Ms. Melly," he whispered. Even his voice was raspier, slightly deeper. "Also, it's Ollie, my lady."

The boy in front of me had deep blue eyes and ink-black hair, long, with half of it braided away from his face. One eye had a milk-whiteness to it that indicated blindness. I reached out reflexively but stopped myself at his panicked look.

"Right...Ollie," I side-eyed him before glancing up at the team of liveried groomsmen coming toward us. "Why don't you...make sure to go with the servants and put away my things once we go inside."

"Yes, my lady."

A groomsman came up to us, offering his hand. "My lady, if I may?"

Giving over Zephyr's reins, I walked around him to go to Ruarc, who was fully clothed for once. Dressed in all black with blood red accents, a long cloak dragged behind him. His back was to me but at the sound of my approach, he turned, blasting me with a brilliant smile. I stumbled, shocked at the sight of him; gone was the monstrous form, now two aquamarine eyes stared back at me. He looked...perfect.

Someone clearing their throat loudly had me looking up at the waiting steward. A look of disgust crossed my face when I saw that pompous worm, Oweyn. If I didn't know the depth of my own hatred for the slimy Vampire, I would say the queen's seneschal's expression at my presence was even more disgusted.

Remember, you and Ruarc have to appear romantic.

I gave the Darkling King a tight smile, holding out my hand to his outstretched one. Pulling me into him, he laid a gentle kiss on my forehead before facing Oweyn. The steward's face showed an obvious struggle between shock, confusion, then apathy, but managed to regain his composure.

"Glamour, I take it?" I asked under my breath.

"Well, it would be poor form to scare people before even the drinks are served," he joked.

The movement of Oweyn bowing deeply, had us turning to him as he addressed Ruarc.

"Welcome, King Ruarc Ó Ceallaigh and his Court, to Castle Fyrkat. Home to the Nightmare Queen, the Champion of Hel, the protector of all Vamp –"

"Silence, *searbhónta ciapánta*," Ruarc interrupted, with every ounce of arrogance that is a monarch's prerogative. "We have travelled far and are too weary for your drivel. Have we missed the Welcoming Banquet?"

"M-my apologies, Your majesty. No, actually, you're just in time—"

"Excellent. Lead the way."

Oweyn gave a curt bow, his face stone. Satisfaction curled within me. Unfortunately, it was short lived. As we began up the steps, déjà vu hit me and the weight of so much happening in such a short time had me pausing for a moment.

Ruarc tightened his arm around me then let go, grabbing my hand instead, pulling me along. With every step, that feeling of butterflies frantically flying around in my stomach got worse. My heart pounded. Dread, anticipation, the desire to flee, all fought for dominance in my head. Yet, as we were led further in, only one face in my mind was left.

Alcaeus...

Mikrós asvós, I am here.

I took in a breath at the sound of his voice in my mind, instinctively squeezing Ruarc's hand, to which he responded by raising the back of my hand to his lips. Trying not to shrink back, I failed at filtering my thoughts.

I felt Alcaeus' apprehension.

Never have I wanted to explain myself more, but fear of Ragna's monitoring kept me silent. Then I felt his presence leave me, and my Mark burned, throbbing to the point of pain. Yet, as we drew closer to the doors to the Great Hall, the pain began to turn warm and soothing. He was in there, just beyond the doors.

Stopping just outside, Oweyn turned to us, although only addressing Ruarc.

"We shall wait for the rest of your court to join you before I announce your presence to the Nightmare Court, Your Majesty. Queen Ragna and Prince Alcaeus have already been informed of your arrival."

"Oh, I made sure of it, my simple little Vampire," replied the Unseelie King and I was positively tickled at the blatant struggle of emotions on Oweyn's stoic demeanour.

Oh, how he hated this.

"Wait," I said to Ruarc and he turned to me, "Will we not have time to...to, I don't know, freshen up? I'm still in my travel clothes –"

A finger to my lips silenced me. "We are but presenting ourselves. Afterward, we will have time to prepare for the Welcoming Feast. Do not worry, a rún, I will make sure you outshine them all," he grinned, tapping my lips. Magic crawled over me and I couldn't help but look down.

Everything seemed clean, my black boots shiny. Nothing wrinkled. I sniffed my arm.

Clean, although...wait. I sniffed myself again, instantly glaring up at him.

"I reek of you!" My accusation came out as a seething whisper, trying to keep it down. Instantly his arms came around me, lifting me up until my ear was against his lips.

"Of course, sweet one, after all those nights of pleasure? You should smell like no one else," Ruarc whispered back, giving me a quick kiss on the cheek before letting me go. "Ah, there they are."

Turning, I saw Ruarc's advisors and, behind them, came Llyr and Elis. My best friend was fussing over his cuffs and I could see how flustered he was in his jerky movements as they walked. He began fussing over his mate's cravat before Llyr made them stop walking, firmly grabbing Elis' hands.

Making a move to greet them, Ruarc's hand grabbed mine, preventing me.

Elis was still talking a mile a minute but was quickly silenced by Llyr, who dipped down and planted a firm kiss. My best friend stilled and I almost looked away, fearing I was intruding on their intimate moment but Llyr pulled away from my now dreamy-eyed friend, tugging him toward the party.

"My lords and ladies, they are ready to receive you," announced Oweyn, which meant I would not get the encouragement I had hoped for from Elis.

I made a move to release Ruarc's hand, but he held on tighter, saying, "No, Melisandre, you shall remain at my side. Chin high, Alchemist. You represent the Unseelie now."

Before I could argue, the doors opened followed by a booming voice announcing us to the crowd.

The loud sounds of chatter and socialising dominated the room and you could hear the faint sound of music in the background. The queen's colours of gold and red still filled the room, her banners with the green-flamed hellhounds, Hel's sigil, waving proudly. Yet, this time, the flags of all the participating kingdoms hung on the walls as well.

The carpet leading to the thrones was clear of nobles and courtiers, save for the guards standing at attention. We were far enough away I could not make out the faces of Ragna and Alcaeus but just seeing his outline shot my heart rate up, its pounding blocking out all the noise.

My Mark tingled and buzzed.

Ruarc seemed to catch on and squeezed my hand firmly. Swallowing hard, I switched my gaze to look at those around us as we walked, seeking distraction, but I was blind to them. Only Alcaeus filled my mind.

We finally came to a stop, and the room quieted. I looked up at Ruarc, whose full attention was now on my enemy in front of us. Slowly, my gaze slid to Ragna. Those glittering emerald eyes mirrored my own hatred, but there was that unforgettable glint of insanity and cunning there as well. Of promises executed in the dark only ending in unheard screams of pain.

Surprisingly, the one who I expected to be by her side but wasn't—Mage Ilirhun. Perhaps the sickness had finally got to him. Good riddance.

I tried to keep my face as stoic as possible which meant avoiding looking at Alcaeus at all.

Remember, Ruarc is your lover now... He's my lover now.... My lover now... I chanted in my mind.

"Greetings, King of the Unseelie, Champion of the Mórrígan. We welcome you to Idrisid. While our last encounter left us in a rather distasteful conflict of interest, I do hope your unfortunate moment of trespassing on my lands can be all but forgotten so that we may celebrate Yaldā in its true spirit of peace and prosperity." Ragna's voice was as smooth as the gold throne she sat upon; her words as sweet as they were supplicating.

Ruarc nodded his head at her. "Indeed, it is the time to put *bygones* aside. The Unseelie Court extends its gratitude toward Queen Ragna and Prince Alcaeus' hospitality and we look forward to participating in the Divine Games. Good fortune be upon you both." He slipped his arm around my waist, pulling me close.

It was then I could no longer keep myself from looking at Alcaeus.

His face was a stone mask. Yet, my heart clenched as our eyes met. Time stood still. A flicker of warmth. That siren's call from inside my chest beckoned me, aching to get closer to him. All the world seemed right.

Then his eyes flicked down to where Ruarc held me and, for a split second, I saw the whites of his knuckles gripping his throne and reality set it.

"Come, *a rún*," the Unseelie King said to me. Turning to the royals in front of us, he gave them a graceful nod, saying, "Until the banquet this eve."

Risking one last glance at Alcaeus, an apathetic face stared back but his stare on the Unseelie King was so intense, my doubts about our success only worsened. Ruarc turned us away, walking back the way we came. I passed Elis and concern marred his face.

"We'll speak later," I whispered to him as we passed.

Once we approached the huge double doors leading out, Ruarc said under his breath, "You did well, Melisandre. Once we reach our rooms, we will discuss our next steps." His arm released me, hand sliding easily into mine.

It took everything in me not to look back but I felt the burn of my Nightmare Prince's glare long after we had left the throne room

CHAPTER 18

A small part of me held out a sliver of hope our rooms would be close to the Royal Consort's tower but that was not to be. My time here left me unable to know the entire layout of the castle, as I was restricted to only Alcaeus' tower and the library, but I knew we were nowhere close to him.

The living arrangements we had been given were no less impressive, however, having sitting rooms and an even larger wash area than what had been in my previous chambers. A second door from the sitting room revealed a quaint study. A matching balcony from my old rooms was overlooking the southeast side of Idrisid.

As soon as we walked in, I did a quick check of the area. Eager to wash, I walked into the bedroom and immediately recognized my Alchemist's staff resting against the wardrobe. Next to it was a sword.

I narrowed my eyes at it. And boots. Men's boots. Striding over to the wardrobe, I ripped it open. My clothes were neatly hanging. So was the men's clothing right next to it.

Cursing, I made a beeline for the door. Before I could open it, however, Ruarc was standing before me.

Hands on my hips, I snapped, "We are not staying in the same room!"

Lifting a quizzical brow, he folded his arms across his chest. "Of course we are. We are lovers. Where else would we sleep?"

Letting out a growl of frustration, I replied, "Fine, but we are still not sleeping," I waved at the bed, "together, on that!"

To make my point, I walked over and grabbed one of the pillows off the bed, then walked toward the rug in front of the hearth.

Ruarc grabbed a corner of the pillow and I tried to jerk it back.

"Melisandre," he groaned my name in frustration, "please, for once in your life stop being such a prude!" A quick step into me, he went nose to nose, the pillow the only thing separating us. "We are on Queen Ragna's land now. We are in Queen Ragna's castle. We are *breathing* Queen Ragna's fucking air! Did you not learn the first time the dangers of assuming you are alone when you are walking amongst Vampires? Magic, being all around us mind you, is capable of speaking to those with power, as clear as we are conversing now."

He managed to rip the pillow from my grasp. I tried to grab it back but he stopped me by snatching my wrist and bringing it to his chest.

"Let go!" I snapped, struggling to pull free.

"A compromise, if you will," he replied.

Glaring up at him, I waited for his proposal.

Letting me go, he put his hand up slowly as if in surrender. "Sleep. When we are both in that bed, we will only sleep. No sex. But we must be in that bed. Together."

I frowned harder, sticking a finger into his chest. "Sleep. Only." I proceeded to walk around him, snatching the pillow back. "And no cuddling either!" Was my final demand as I left the room and stalked into the washroom, locking the door firmly behind me.

"*Toice cheanndána!*" Ruarc's muffled exasperated curse could be heard, shortly followed by the slamming of a door.

Looking down at the cushion in my hands, I sighed.

"I don't know why I took the pillow," I murmured into the silence, giving it a squeeze before tossing it aside. The large space gave my voice some reverb, making me sound louder. My mind was in shambles and there was nothing more I wanted to do than burst through Alcaeus' doors and hide away in his arms. Memories of the cottage flooded my mind and I ached for that reality once more.

Then, realizing what I just thought had me rolling my eyes as I came to stand in front of the mirror above the washbasin. I pointed a finger at my reflection.

"When did you become such a sap?" I chastised, "Losing yourself to idealism. Come off it, Mel..."

Starting the bath, I ripped my clothes off, folding them and placing them to the side. Just as I reached for the edge of the tub, I stumbled, grabbing on.

I let go just as quickly.

Blood covered my hands. It dripped slowly off the side of the tub. The water inside was red and opaque. The water pouring out of the faucet was like a throat that was slashed abruptly. A sharp pain pierced my abdomen, exactly where Lord Cyto had stabbed me. I dropped to one knee, hugging myself.

What...? What is happening?

Gasping in pain, I shook my head violently, desperately trying to expel what I knew to be an illusion. Opening my eyes, I lifted my hand to my face. Blood dripped from it, slow at first but then began to pour.

"Ms. Melly... Why... Why did you kill me? I was an Alchemist too..." A voice I never thought to hear again echoed all around me, that sweet tone that could only belong to Sophie.

"No...stop," I whispered in horror.

"Murderer...you are a MURDERER! KILLER OF CHILDREN!"

I slapped my hands over my ears. "Stop, stop, stop! This isn't real!"

"Toby will NEVER be safe! HE WILL DIE BY YOUR HANDS! YOU WILL SLAY ALL THOSE YOU LO—"

A high-pitched bird call pierced through the voice; it wasn't a screech but a bunch of short calls that I could hear even through covered ears. Opening my eyes, I turned toward the sound coming from the direction of the balcony.

The smallest owl I had ever seen flew toward me, landing on the edge of the tub that was now free of blood. Sophie's echoing voice had also stopped as well as the phantom pain of my old wound.

Shaking slightly, a few deep breaths had my racing heart calm once more and I was able to study my little rescuer.

The little bird's colours were a mixture of delicate browns, golds, and blacks and it couldn't be more than five and half inches tall. Large, pale-yellow eyes blinked back at me, its white brows stark against the rest of its colouring.

I recognized the breed.

"Well, aren't you the cutest thing, my little elf owl," I cooed at it. Sighing, I gently touched its tiny belly with the back of my knuckle, and it allowed me to do so. "Thank you for coming to my rescue. You must belong to Alcaeus." The little owl reached down with his beak, gently mouthing and tasting my finger as birds do to get to know you.

Something had dropped from its grasp when it had perched on the side of the tub, landing on the ground in front of me.

Reaching down I grabbed the item. It was a necklace. A leather band held a small gold emblem: a sword with outstretched wings at the top and two snakes weaving and slithering up the blade.

"This is a symbol for Athena," I whispered. "Oh, Alcaeus..."

He sent this to me.

This was no coincidence, the owl's presence and the waking nightmare disappearing. My Mark, always making its presence known, throbbed. My heart hurt. I hugged the emblem to my chest. Oh, how badly I wanted to reach out, just to speak with him. Tell him 'Thank you'. But I couldn't risk it. Everything rested on Ragna believing I now belonged to Ruarc.

Even so...

Coming to a stand, I tied the necklace around my neck. It hung low, deeply nestled between my breasts. Easy to hide.

I smiled at that, stepping into the water that was, thankfully, still warm. The little owl, surprisingly, only hopped to the side instead of flying off.

"Hmm, I would wager you are a..." I gently touched it again, then crept my fingers along its little body until I found his wings, spreading them gently, "...boy, by the looks of it. Your wings are on the short side, my dear friend. But we'll keep that between us." I released his wings and he ruffled them out a bit. "So that means there is only one name for you: Maximus! Yes, I think Maximus fits you well," I grinned as 'Maximus' chirped at me.

"This is the Nightmare Court; the magic here will play on your darkest fears, your most hidden secrets. Also, I forbid you to wear that." I whipped around in the tub so fast, water sloshed out.

Ruarc leaned against the bathroom counter, arms crossed. He was shirtless once more.

"How the hell did you...? Nevermind, get out!" I snapped, covering my chest with one hand as I pointed to the door. Maximus had flapped his wings in agitation, flying up slightly to avoid getting splashed but settled back close to me.

The Unseelie King glared at the bird.

"Begone, servant!" he commanded, rising and walking toward us. "And tell your master to take care around Melisandre—she belongs to me now."

Maximus darted into the air, flapping away through the balcony and disappeared into the night sky.

Ready to give him a piece of my mind, Ruarc stopped me by saying, "If I can feel the presence of the Royal Consort, then so can Ragna." He shook his head as he pinched the bridge of his nose. "We must find a way to reach Alcaeus quickly, or you two will be the end of each other and all of our plans will be for naught!"

"Then why hasn't Cillian spoken with him yet?" I asked, pulling my knees up in a feeble attempt to cover myself. "Besides, how on earth am

I supposed to communicate to Alcaeus when you keep scaring off all of the possibilities?!"

"The Lich has been tied up trying to break through many of the wards Queen Ragna's mages have placed on the Great Owl's rooms. She is desperate to keep you two apart. That plays into our favour but only if you do your part!"

"I..." Scrambling for a retort, I couldn't think of one. He was right. Clenching my jaw in hopeless frustration, I gave him the response he was looking for, "Fine. But no sex. That's non-negotiable."

Ruarc gave me a good long stare before nodding slowly. Then he began to undo his trousers.

"Hey," I barked, "I said no se—"

A knock at the door.

Trousers were on the floor and Ruarc was already stepping into the bath opposite of me, dragging me to his naked chest just as a second knock sounded.

His arms snaked around my middle, one hand then sliding up to cup my neck. "Relax," he whispered.

I tried. I really did. That was until I felt him rock-hard against my lower back.

"Are you serious?" I growled softly.

"Here, let me help you," he replied a little sultry, and I felt his seduction magic crawl over my skin. "A moment!" Ruarc shouted, giving me time to adjust.

Desire pooled within me and I closed my eyes, letting it happen. My mark began to burn aggressively and not in a good way.

"Ahh," I whimpered, my hand covering it, but I finally managed to relax my body into his.

"Come in!" He yelled before whispering to me once more, "That's it, relax. Just enjoy the feeling of desire, little grumpy one."

If I wasn't so focused on trying to play a role, I would have snorted at the endearment but couldn't stop the eyeroll.

The door opened.

"Your Highness, my lady, the Welcome Feast will begin in one hour. Is there anything I can assist you with?" I turned at the familiar voice.

Ada.

Keeping my mouth shut, I shot her a glare. She paled, quickly looking away but continued to wait for further instruction like the good little, back-stabbing, servant that she was.

"No, just some privacy, if you will," replied Ruarc, making a show of physical affection.

Ada didn't move right away, her eyes widening at the both of us. Ruarc noticed as well.

"Unless you'd prefer to watch? Or is disobeying a king a suicidal hobby of yours?" The underlying threat in his voice was clear enough.

"M-my most humble...a-apologies...my l-lor-lady-Your Highnesses!" she stuttered, bowing dramatically before quickly disappearing with the click of the door.

"*Your Highnesses*, hmm? Certainly has a nice ring to it, does it not?" Ruarc's hot breath was a caress against my skin as his magic continued to play me like a fiddle. The angry burning of my mark didn't feel so worrisome any more as his touch began to consume me. He cupped my breasts, thumbs flicking over my hard nipples, teasing them expertly. I gasped, pushing against him in reaction as my hands came up to cup his. Teeth nipped at my sensitive skin as he pushed back at me, promising satisfaction if I just continued to give in. A niggling feeling warned me this was not okay but...it felt so good. I hadn't felt this relaxed since, well...

The cottage. With Alcaeus.

My eyes shot open as my lust cooled like a cold front in the night. My mind felt like it was waking from a long slumber, groggy and slow. I struggled to stand but Ruarc still held me by my chest, not letting go.

"Shhh, sweet one, you were enjoying yourself so much," he encouraged, trying to tempt me once more. However, the voice that once fed into the magic now sounded fake, his spell broken.

"St-stop it...let me out." I struggled, his powers sliding along my skin.

Just before I fell victim to his touch once more, a deep guttural growl interrupted us. We both turned to see Ares' huge head low, ears pinned back as his golden eyes glowed menacingly. Sharp teeth were bared, dripping as if he was rabid. The wolf snapped his jaws, guaranteeing a violent fight if Ruarc did not let go of me.

I used the distraction to quickly hop out, but not before transmuting the water to freezing. As Ruarc gasped at the temperature change, cursing colourfully in Gaeilge, I grabbed a towel and hurried out of the room.

Although, it was impossible to discern if I was running from the guilt at almost succumbing, the fury at his trickery, or the desperate loneliness that reared its ugly head.

CHAPTER 19

"There she is!" Elis called out to me from where he and Llyr were standing outside of the great hall. Dressed impeccably, the Lord of Flowers dazzled in golds, creams, and pale lavenders while his mate wore darker tones to bring out his beautiful ginger hair.

However, Elis' expression did not match his finery as he took in my oversized black velvet cloak that hid my outfit for the evening.

"I begged King Ruarc to let me dress you but that stubborn asshoof," Llyr elbowed him and Elis shot him a glare before continuing, "Mels, for goodness' sake, take that damn cloak off—oh. Oh, my." As my cloak slipped off, both men's eyes went wide.

My 'dress' was two pieces of black cloth wrapped around my breasts crisscrossed, coming around my waist. The fabric was thin enough that if you looked close enough, you could make out my darker areolas. It melted into a solid black, body-forming sheath that flared out into black lace dragging behind me. Except, there was a slit that went all the way to my hip and slightly past that. I wore four inch, strappy, open-toed stilettos that still put me shorter than Elis. Unfortunately, I was far too busty for this dress and it showed by the bulging flesh on either side of the fabric.

Elis leaned forward and whispered with a hiss, "Mels, your *blossoms* are about to fall *out* of the bouquet! You can't go in like this! You look more like...uh...well..."

"The dress is, um, it is certainly..." attempted Llyr.

"Like Ruarc's sexually deviant mistress. Yes. I am aware." I bit out, choking over every word with embarrassment. "Suffice to say that, from now on, no man may choose my clothing."

"Well, I wouldn't go that far," muttered Elis.

I turned to Llyr. "I cannot transmute this fabric since it is drenched in magic, undoubtedly Ruarc's doing. Can you remove it somehow?"

The Fae lord tapped a finger to his lips in consideration, an elegant hand on his hip while looking me up and down. His moss green eyes lit up. "Ah! I have just the solution." Turning to Elis, he asked, "My love, I need several clusters of buds. Any flower will do."

His mate raised a questioning brow but acquiesced, his hand hovering over Llyr's open one. Several bunches of green stems with unopened bulbs at the end, appeared in his hand.

"Perfect," replied Llyr. He began saying something in Gaeilge, running the buds down my dress, like a human metal detector or scanner. As he went, the buds began to open into beautiful white stargazer lilies. Llyr walked around me, chanting until he was once again before me. The flowers were not only fully blossomed but now glowing. They were breathtaking.

I looked down, noticing the lack of magic on my dress now. Wasting no time, I transmuted part of my cloak into the dress. The velvet now moulded over my chest, the gauzy fabric that used to cover my breasts now a sexy halter wrapped delicately around my neck. Black-velvet gloves now encased my arms up to the elbow. I kept the slit. Why? Perhaps because some deep part of me wanted to be a feast for a certain someone's eyes tonight.

Elis clapped his hands together in approval. "Ah, there. Beautiful. Edgy, too. Wouldn't be you without it! Now, the finishing touch." He took one of the smaller lilies and fitted it into the side of my soft French-braided hair. The flower rested in such a way it appeared to be tucked behind my ear. Pulling a few curling tendrils to frame my face, he gave me a gentle smile. "You're perfect, my dear friend. The Prince will not be able to keep his eyes off you—oh, Your Highness!"

We all turned to see Ruarc and even I found myself admiring how stunning he was. Looking sharp in a leine-croich, a traditional long-sleeved tunic that hung just above his knees. It was black as night and matched his knee-high boots. It was belted with a sterling silver leather belt, with rubies and black diamonds peeking out. Breeches that mirrored the red of his braided hair. A matching fly plaid was wrapped around him, pinned at the right shoulder with a platinum raven brooch. A ruby sparkled in the place of the bird's eye.

The Unseelie King looked me up and down, then turned an annoyed eye to Llyr, who simply bowed, bringing the lilies behind his back.

"I knew it was unlikely you would keep the dress as is, but—"

"That was not a dress, Ruarc," I interrupted, "that was a flimsy piece of fabric meant only for your entertainment and my humiliation.

Don't pretend otherwise. Now, can we get this over with?" Readjusting my gloves, I gestured to the closed doors where the sounds of drinking and merriment could be heard. The lighting was warm for once, adding to the festive mood.

"So impatient, *a rún*," chastised Ruarc but he signalled to the footman that we were ready. He grabbed my hand firmly and tucked it into the crook of his arm.

Leaning down, he whispered, "Remember. We are lovers, engaged to be handfasted. This all relies on you. Do not fail."

I clenched my jaw at the reminder but snapped, "I won't."

Kissing my temple, he replied, "That's my—"

"No." I snapped, cutting off his praise then immediately schooled my features just in time for the doors to open.

The festivities were in full swing. Ribbon and fire dancers were the first to fill my vision as they danced the same tempo as all the flames from the braziers above. There were also pedestals with massive copper bowls filled with lit coal blazing throughout the room. Music and drums set the mood and all the conversation and laughter made focusing difficult. Rows of tables and benches filled the sides of the hall, leaving the middle open for entertainment.

As we walked further into the room, brownie servants, maids with jugs or heavy-ladened with food, scurried past. Cupbearers stood at the ready and it was clear the wine or whatever was being served, flowed steadily. The variety of creatures that filled the room were mostly humanoid in presence. Different religions of mythological beings could be found in every direction. Despite the bipedal shape of many, their dress and appearance indicated their true form.

Several nixies, shapeshifting water-beings that appeared to humans as horses, laughed at the antics of a tengu demon as he used his long nose to tickle the nearest one. A group of bugbears were making short work of an entire roasted pig, their terrifying and misshapen bodies clearly showing their relation to the goblin family.

Once past the tables and dancers, a huge raised crescent-shaped table dominated the end of the room, where the high table would normally be. While Queen Ragna's place and the seat of her consort in the middle of the table were raised, the rest of the chairs resembled lesser thrones, each bearing the sigil and colours of the Champions that sat in them. Next to Ragna, a fearsome man sat beside her, a shining golden laurel stark against his black curls.

This must be the previous winner of the games, I concluded.

The proud Mórrígan sigil and colours stood stark among the smaller thrones toward the end. However, only one seat was available. Seeing this, I began to pull away as we came to a stop near it but Ruarc held fast.

"There's only one—" I attempted but Ruarc shushed me by taking his seat and pulled me into his lap, my back tucked into his right shoulder and chest. Trying not to act rigid, I draped both of my legs over his left thigh. Unfortunately, this also put me in direct line of sight with Alcaeus and Ragna.

Across from us was Ajani, the Champion of the Ethiopian god Medr, who had two beautiful creatures fawning over him. Ruarc was quietly whispering to me the identities of all those who sat around us, his lips tickling my ear. Taking my cue, I pulled away slightly, smiling as I gently cupped his face.

Running my thumb over his full lips, I whispered back, "Do all of these Champions have proxies fighting in the games?"

"Some, not all," Ruarc replied, kissing the pad of my thumb, "but we will find out who is participating on the morrow, when the Naming Ceremony begins. There, the proxies will be announced and then approved or denied by the Great Council."

"The Great Council?" I asked.

"Yes, all the remaining original Champions will hold court these next twelve days. There will be many meetings; although I would argue it is more verbal warfare than anything. Yet, somehow, peace and trading agreements come out of it. It has always been a mystery to me." At my look of annoyance, he chuckled, "Worry not, I will not force your attendance for the most part. You have enough to prepare for. I would much rather have you waiting for me, naked—"

"Raven of the Mórrígan," a voice I was both relieved and anxious to hear, "you are quite late to the festivities. Some things certainly do not change." My eyes locked with Alcaeus' for a brief, unreadable moment before his attention was turned to the man whose lap I sat on.

The Royal Consort, too, was a master at holding a mysterious edge but I could see the slight lowering of his brow, the tightness in his posture.

"My sincerest apologies, Great Owl, I was quite preoccupied," Ruarc replied, then gave a slow and deliberate kiss to my neck. "I am sure you can understand, having such a breathtaking woman by your side as well."

For once, I didn't know what to do. I'm a terrible liar. My acting abilities were non-existent. Looking at Alcaeus any longer would surely reveal this as a sham. So, I stared at Ruarc's chest, fiddling with his plaid. His large hand suddenly engulfed mine and I curled my hand into a fist.

He wants me to look.

The queen was busy speaking with the person to her left but I had no doubt she was paying attention.

Alcaeus gave a nod in agreement, "Indeed I do. She can be quite *consuming*."

Ragna turned to him then, giving a warm smile as she slipped her hand in his, giving it a squeeze. He squeezed it back.

My stomach clenched.

"Well, well, your former familiar has been chosen by another it would seem," purred the queen. "If I had known you were bringing your new mistress, King Ruarc, I would have included a seat. Most prefer our toys on their knees. On the floor."

He sniffed, cocking his head at her. "If she was that, you would be correct, but Melisandre is my intended. We are to be handfasted," replied Ruarc, holding my hand up, and even I had to try not to act surprised at the sudden piece of jewellery that appeared.

A huge teardrop-shaped ruby sat encased by black diamonds and, set in a platinum band, glittered in the light. It sat heavy on my finger and I bit my lip from reacting to it.

Surprise was stark on Ragna's face as her eyes darted between us before it melted seamlessly into genuine happiness. "Then congratulations are in order. Which reminds me…"

Oweyn appeared instantly as she whispered something to him. The feel of power filled the room and the sounds died down. All attention turned toward the now standing Queen and her consort.

She raised her arms in welcome revealing her dark emerald green gown. "I bid you welcome, Champions of the old gods, kings and queens of the Otherworld and all of their subjects. It is my great honour to host this year's Divine Games, an epic tournament that will showcase the power of each kingdom and give all of you the entertainment of a lifetime. On the morrow, we shall have the Naming Ceremony in which each Champion participating will call forth their proxy.

"Thereon, our festivities include the Yule Ball, Royal Garden Party, a Gathering, and many activities before and after the great tournament! As always, the winner of the Divine Games shall wear the laurel of victory and be declared high champion until the next Yaldā!" She raised her golden chalice to the royalty to her left and then to her right, finally lifting it to the crowd in front. "May the Norns smile upon you and may the best champion win!" All raised their glasses and as Queen Ragna drank, a cry went up and all cheered. Just as I assumed she would retake her seat, she raised her hand once more and the crowd went silent. "Pray thee, one more moment for I have one more announcement to make." Our gazes locked, and I held my breath. "On the first day, after Yaldā has ended, I am most pleased to announce that all of you are hereby invited to stay and attend the royal wedding of the Royal Consort, Prince Alcaeus Pallas, and myself." The crowd let out a cheer and applause filled the room.

Ragna's eyes still had not left mine, like a tunnel with only her emerald eyes staring back. The feeling of suffocating was getting stronger.

Ruarc's hold on me tightened but I did not flinch.

"Let the festivities commence!" Music once more filled the room as Ragna sat back down, a satisfied smirk on her face.

Knowing it was foolish, I tried to read Alcaeus' face as he stared back at me but Ruarc distracted me, saying, "My congratulations to the happy couple! That shall soon be us as well, *a rún*." He nuzzled my ear and neck. The Unseelie King was trying to distract me and I desperately needed to let him take the lead.

Many were offering their congratulations, Ragna's beautiful smile beaming. Yet Alcaeus still stared back at me, and for a moment I thought I saw sorrow. My own emotions were brimming so close to the surface. If I could just mentally...

I gasped in a pleasurable moan as Ruarc's sensual magic hit me like a boulder at full speed, my head whipping backward as my body stiffened with lust. The Unseelie king took his opportunity to plunge his tongue into my mouth, kissing me deeply and capturing my moan with his onslaught.

For once, I let him.

CHAPTER 20

"That was foolish," snapped Ruarc as he followed behind me, slamming the door to our room shut.

"I know," I whispered back.

"You almost ruined everything!"

"I know..."

"The *Great Owl* saw it as well! If we are to make Ragna believe it, we cannot have her Consort believing otherwise! How many damn times must we go over this—"

"I know!" I shouted back, breathing heavily. "Whatever happened to getting word to Alcaeus? I know we just got here; I know we haven't had time but I cannot just walk around letting him believe—"

"Believe what? That you are mine? That you want him no longer? Why can you not make him believe that if it is our only chance at saving his soul? Is that not why we are here, woman?!" He demanded, arms splaying wide in question.

"I..." Shutting my mouth, I looked down as my reply died in the face of his logic. I wasn't even remotely angry that he kissed me or manipulated me with magic. If he hadn't, all of this would have been for naught. Yet, because of Ruarc's fast thinking and his inherent lecherous ways, the seeds of doubt we planted may yet have a chance to grow.

Getting myself under control, I beheld his exasperated face as I replied softly, "You are correct. I lost sight of the...goal. You saved us back there so believe me when I say I am most grateful." I placed a hand on my Mark, turning more fully to him. "But hear me, Ruarc," I said firmly, "you need to understand that this bond that we have is so much deeper and stronger than even I can understand. Never has my connection to someone been so, so...vibrant. My Mark aches when he is gone. It burns with a frenzied passion when he is close. It has been the siren's call between us since the moment we met. So, we can play our games, pretending in front of Ragna, but he will see right through the charade. I'm sure he already suspects. He will find a way to me and demand answers, since I know he feels it too."

"Oh, he most certainly does," Ruarc smirked, "for I have not seen the look of my death upon his face since our last battle, before the Uprising. Tonight, I saw it once more." Letting out a long breath, he pushed his hand through his hair in defeat. Then all of his movement froze. He grinned slowly.

Mischievously.

"You are positively brilliant, my young one! Ha! Ah, but that is precisely what we shall do."

Confused, I asked, "What? What are *we* doing?"

Tapping a finger in the air, he answered, "We bait him to us. Give him hints, a call for help, if you will. King Alcaeus loves to be the hero just as much as I enjoy playing the villain. So, we shall use that to our advantage. Which means, my grumpy goblin, that you can be exactly as you are. No acting. Well, to an extent. I will scout out the grounds to see where the festivities are to be held. If we can draw him away from Ragna, even for a moment, perhaps we can give you two a few moments to explain our plan. He should also be able to give us vital information in weakening her defences. Hmm," ruminated Ruarc, "I need to speak with Cillian on this. I shall be back. Do not wait up, a rún." With a cheeky wink, he strode out of our quarters.

"I am not a goblin, wretched man," I grumped under my breath.

It was a good plan. Certainly made it easier for me. Anything that would give us a chance to catch him alone. Honestly, anything for me to stop this bloody charade.

Running my hands down my black velvet gown, the reality of how uncomfortable I was hit me. Checking to see if Ares wasn't sneaking around invisible somewhere, I quickly changed into more comfortable clothing and grabbed my staff. After the recent events, I was far too wired to sleep. Besides, there was one particular Sage I was eager to see again.

The door creaked slightly as my head peeked through, looking left and right to see the hallway empty. Shutting the door quietly behind me I followed the long stretch to the stairs that led to the second level. The sun was not quite up yet, about an hour off but the halls were silent. A perfect time to mull over all of the information and memories of the last twenty-four hours.

One thought kept preoccupying the forefront of my mind.

What DO you know of Alcaeus Pallas?

Based on the information present, he was my Fated Mate. Which means The Mother and Athena had some girl time and decided to create us.

But why? There was a piece to this puzzle I was missing but for now, I set it aside. Alcaeus knew of me for a long time before I even knew he existed.

But for how long? How long has he watched me from the shadows? It was this very fact that had me grinding my teeth. While I might be able to sense things down to an atomic level, I have to focus, purposefully look for it. Never did I sense him. Another problem only Alcaeus could answer.

The cold breeze hit me as I stepped outside to look around. The courtyard was vast and a few people still lingered, some sitting at quaint tables and others walking as they chatted. Recognising the top of the library's roof, I headed towards it. Nearing the edge of the yard, I picked up on gossip that was most certainly about me.

"...his intended?! Her?! After our Royal Consort cast her off? Alchemists are quite the greedy creatures, are they not?"

A group of nobles were playing a board game but their attention was clearly on me. They knew I could hear them and it was clear they didn't care.

"Imagine trying to compete with the beautiful Queen Ragna. Another Champion, no less. Rumours also have it that *she* was the one who killed Lord Cyto! The ego on that one, no shame whatsoever."

"No wonder they're extinct. Trying to have not one but TWO Champions in her bed, the murdering slut. They're better off dead."

I walked by, paying them no mind. If foul mouths and poisonous words got under my skin at this age, well, let's just say Ruarc would be correct in his belief in my inabilities in diplomacy and we can't have that now, can we?

Once past the courtyard, I entered a covered walkway, my staff making a pleasing **clunk** against the stone. It was quiet once more and the fresh air was addicting. Coming back to my previous thoughts, I continued to question what I knew of Alcaeus.

He was thoughtful, gentle, kind. Always looking for solutions, as I do, though I have noticed he will find the answer but not always let on that he knows. He likes being in control, that's obvious from his constant planning and...bedroom activities. Not surprising as he is a king, used to leading. I still know so little about the power he wields other than his sword, Nemesis, which seems to suck the magic out of its victims and Alcaeus absorbs it. Oh,

I must interrogate him when I have the chance; I would love to know how that works. Hmm... He makes me smile, laugh even. Grinning stupidly, I could at least admit it. Seeing the lights of the library, my smile widened as I drew closer to the massive building. *He is very easy to talk to. A dangerous thing, really. Unlike this psychopathic queen, empathy seems to come naturally to him. Also—*

My thoughts abruptly cut off as a hand grabbed my throat and slammed me to the ground. The sound of my staff hitting stones resounded in the open space, rolling away. Something wrapped around my limbs, rendering me immobile. Instantly, my runes came to life in defence, waiting for my command.

Emerald eyes glared back at me, trapping my gaze.

"Alchemist," hissed Ragna, "I knew you would come back. You are so very predictable. For one with such a genius, you are *terrible* at political strategy." Her grip was like steel around my neck and just as cold. "Did you think I would believe your marriage to Ruarc? Do you take me for a fool?!" Ragna's bony fingers squeezed harder as she spat out the last words.

"It's the truth," I wheezed, glaring back at her, "we are to be handfasted."

Wrath consumed all the lines of her face but then it relaxed, morphing into a grin. She giggled. That giggle turned into a shout as she lifted up my head, whatever bound me released me long enough for her to slam me to the ground. White dots speckled my vision.

"Lies! You and Alcaeus are Fated! You are here to finish the Mark, damn you!"

Ragna was right about one thing—I was a terrible liar. But I could wield the truth like the sword it was.

"Why would I want to remain with half a man!? You could take his soul at any point!"

She stopped, narrowing her eyes at me, her nails digging into my skin. "Why should I believe you?

"Why? Because it's the truth, goddammit!" I spat, "Why the fuck would I want a man with half a soul, tied to another, when the Raven of the Mórrígan has offered me protection, a place at his side, and my freedom? Alcaeus can give me none of that. Only imprisonment and having to deal with a fucking cunt of a queen!"

Her teeth snapped so close to my face I was surprised they did not graze my skin. I did not flinch. "Perhaps my advisors are right—you are a greedy little slut. But I can acknowledge your thirst for survival." She released my neck with a shove, standing above me. I took that opportunity to glance at what bound me.

Hands. Bones. Rotted flesh sticking up through the ground. The dead obeying their master.

"While I am still not entirely inclined to believe your lying whore-mouth, it matters not. Come tomorrow, we shall see how weak your bond is with the Unseelie King," She put her foot on my chest, "and just how strong your loyalty and affections are to my Consort."

"I do believe the lady has gotten the message, Queen Ragna," interrupted a warm but gruff voice. "Kindly let her up so that she and I might have our planned reunion." I heard Sage Kevyn's hobbling gait come down the stairs above me.

Queen Ragna gave the Sage a long look before vanishing into the dawn. The hands released me, sinking back into the ground. Coughing and sputtering, I stood and dusted myself off. Picking up my staff, I made my way over to Sage Kevyn who was already walking back up the stairs. Our walk back to his office was brisk and silent. The library was warm and safe, void of anyone else. Upon arriving at his door, he placed a hand in the middle and it unlocked with a click.

He closed the door softly behind him once we were both inside his private study.

Letting out a sigh, he said, "Ah, well, I should say I was surprised to see you but I had a feeling you would be back—oof!" Dropping my staff, I wrapped my arms around the old man, my momentum rocking us slightly. He had been my oasis when I had been here. A good friend. Perhaps it was also that he reminded me so much of Master Kian that I couldn't stop myself from embracing him.

Warm and surprisingly sturdy arms came around me in a bear-hug. It had been so long since I had felt truly safe, so I held on a little longer. He must have realised this because he chuckled, saying, "Ah, I've missed you too, sweetie. It does this old Sage good to see you. Are you well, my dear?" Pulling back slightly, he took my chin and inspected my face.

Giving him a tender smile, I replied, "I am well, Kevyn. Thank you for obliging my moment of affection. You are truly a sight for sore eyes around here."

Kevyn's robin's egg blue eyes sparkled with warmth as he looked down at me. "You are always welcome here, Melisandre. Your 'moment of affection' is what we like to call a 'hug' around here and you merely beat me to it. My apologies for not reaching you sooner, before Ragna pounced on you, that feral cat. Not like she would hurt you; you're under the protection of King Ruarc, at least that is the word around here." Giving me an inquiring look, he gestured to the two chairs in front of the fireplace.

I violently shoved intimate memories with Alcaeus aside as I sat rather stiffly in the high-backed chair. Two steaming cups of tea magically appeared before us, along with some biscuits on dainty china.

"How quaint," I said, reaching towards the coffee table and snagging a biscuit.

"And convenient!" grinned Kevyn, lifting his cup for a sip. "While many use magic to justify their slothful ways, my bum-knee is grateful for it!" Patting the afflicted joint, he gave it a good rub.

"What happened, if I may ask?"

He waved me off saying, "Oh, it was a very long time ago, back when I was human. An unfortunate case of polio."

Surprised, I replied, "You were human once? How?"

Setting his tea down, the Old Sage pulled his gold-rimmed glasses from their perch, inspecting them. Finding some dirt, he took a cloth from his robe and began to clean them while saying, "Oh yes, that is how Sages come to be. People are a flawed folk, no doubt, but sometimes there are those who are born with not just a thirst for knowledge but a thirst for wisdom. Knowledge is easy to come by," he gestured to all the books around us, "this room is filled with it. But wisdom?" he asked, pointing a finger at me, "wisdom is the product of overcoming adversity over and over again. It requires suffering. Pain. Perseverance!" His eyes lit up at the last word and I was but a student awaiting her mentor once more. "There are some people who go through unimaginable things and gain so much wisdom throughout their life that even the universe takes notice of them. There are sacred things in this brutal world that even the Powers That Be will protect. When I died, or rather, *thought* I died, the great Mysteries offered me the life of a Sage; to take all that I had gained from life and be a keeper of knowledge and wisdom to all realms. To live thousands upon thousands of lives, all the while afforded all of the mistakes in order to learn from them so others might not have to."

Filled with a bit of awe, I relaxed into my chair a little more. "That is fascinating, Kevyn. I would never have guessed, although, it makes sense. Humans," I smiled fondly, "I quite enjoy their company, prefer it even, when they're not trying to annihilate or self-destruct. I spent most of my life in the human realm, save for a few trips to the Otherworld here and there. Quite fond of their music."

Kevyn's eyes lit up. "Ah! I almost forgot!" He stood, hobbling over to a beautiful standing cabinet to the right of his desk. Taking out some keys, he fiddled with them until he found the right one, inserting it. Reaching in he pulled out a case, something I recognized instantly.

"The violin that Elis gave me! How did you get it?"

"This was actually my violin, before I gave it to Elis to give to you since King Alcaeus informed me you played," he informed me, coming back over to his seat.

"Oh! I didn't know—" My protests were silenced at the wave of his hand as he handed it over.

"Nonsense, it was a gift. I haven't played in over 175 years. It is too exceptional an instrument to merely gather dust in this library. You can do me a favour though, if it is not too much trouble?"

Sliding my hands over the cognac-brown, Tuscany leather cover of the case, I replied, "Of course, what can I do for you?"

"Would you entertain this old Sage in a song or two?"

Grinning, I bowed my head graciously. "I certainly can and it would be my pleasure to do so. Although, I must warn you—it has been almost 9 months since I've played. So, forgive any weak fingered notes."

I moved the stack of books on the coffee table to the side so I could set the case down but then stopped when one of the titles caught my eye.

Gingerly touching the spine I whispered, "Hamlet..." Not able to resist, I picked up and flipped through it. "You know, I met William Shakespeare on several occasions. Many believed he was a hopeless romantic but it was truly born from cynicism. He had an uncanny ability to see right through people's blustering and frequently made fun of the rich. Even in this book, he displays how easily humans can be swayed, blinded. The fact that Hamlet had to pretend madness to such an extreme that even Ophelia, his love, believed him...wait." An idea burst forth. I held up the book to Kevyn. "Has Alcaeus read this?"

He nodded. "Oh, several times. You both have similar tastes."

"Can you please give this to him? I need to write a note within." A pen and paper appeared and I wrote *Act 2*. Glancing at Kevyn before I proceeded, I asked, "May I write in the book?"

He frowned but replied, "If you must. I can remove it later. Never did I think I would say yes to that. Hmph."

Flipping open to *Act II*, I drew a small symbol of the water element. Then, scaling down the text, I found *Scene 2*, writing the symbol for air. From there, I scrolled down to line *115*, drawing the symbol for fire next to the word. Finally, I drew the symbol for earth at line *119*. Closing the book with a **clap**, I handed it over to Sage Kevyn. "Please ensure this gets to him and only him." I held his gaze for several moments, conveying how essential it was that it was not intercepted.

He nodded. "You have my word. It shall be done."

A sudden banging on the door had us both jumping in our seats.

"Blast it all, one moment please! One moment!" Kevyn called out, quickly hobbling over to the door while mumbling irritably under his breath. Coming to a stand, I was surprised to see a very out of breath Toby leaning against the door.

"Ms. Melly. Come quick!"

"What's wrong?"

"King Ruarc calls for you. I know what Ragna has planned for tomorrow and it ain't good!"

CHAPTER 21

Badgering Toby for answers on our rushed walk back only proved how stubborn my former ward had become. There was a time one severe look from me and he crumbled. Now, he was immoveable. He insisted all would be revealed when we arrived.

He led me back to the tower, although we went into a new room that was more of a common room. Fionn, Láeg, and Cú were already there. Muscled arms crossed over his chest, the shirtless Ruarc stood legs apart, gazing out to the balcony. For once, his emotions were clear. He was not happy.

"What is it?" I asked, resting my staff against the back of one of the chairs. "Toby said he discovered Ragna's plan but refused to tell me until we got here. So?"

All three men near me became tight-lipped, refusing to look at me and apprehension was ice crawling up my neck. Walking over to the Unseelie King's side, I touched his arm lightly.

"Ruarc...?"

He didn't turn to me but his voice commanded the area. "Queen Ragna plots to put Alcaeus in the Divine Games. Against you."

I froze. "She what?"

"How did we not see this coming? Of course she would do this," mumbled Cú. "Did you not calculate this, Fionn?"

The man in question shook his head. "I considered it, but the probability of the Great Council agreeing to this was low enough to not even consider it a threat. It has never been done."

"That is because it goes against the laws of the Divine Games," interjected Ruarc. "After the gods fled, we Champions put an end to competing but recognized the importance of having its tradition in both remembrance and a reminder of all that we had overcome. *No Champion rendered by the gods, shall compete in the Divine Games for the chains of enslavement were thus broken in the great Battle of Cantre'r Gwaelod. Instead, let he who possesses the powers of the divine call upon a proxy to fight in his stead, so that their victory is remembered till the end of time,"* he quoted.

"So, then, there is nothing to worry over, right?" Toby asked, confused.

Fionn laced his hands together, deep in thought. Láeg stood off to the side, leaning a shoulder against the empty hearth. He observed the room, making no move to add to the conversation. Cú stood suddenly, walking over to Ruarc.

"My king, you have the gift of sight on the battlefield. Do you see them fighting?"

Blood-red hair fell gently down his back as he turned to look at his general. A moment of silence passed between them.

A moment I did not like.

"You saw it," I declared. When he did not respond, I marched right up to him. "You saw us fighting. You know how it is going to end."

Ruarc looked down at me, the glamour that had been covering his monstrous side having been lifted so that the yellow eye was stark against the blackened skin. "Yes."

I didn't need to try to psychoanalyse his features to discern how that fight would end. However, Ruarc refused to let me dwell on it, as he said, "My visions are merely glimpses into potential outcomes. Choices can always be made to unweave the threads that Badb, Macha, and Nemain have weaved. The sisters that make-up The Mórrígan only weave that which has the most likely outcome but that does not mean another pattern cannot lie within," he said, running a knuckle down my cheek. Facing those in the room, he ordered, "Come, let us retire. We have enough to concern ourselves with, especially with the Naming Ceremony. The conclusion of which will be a deciding factor in much."

All the men bowed and took their leave, although Cú took the opportunity to give me a wink before he disappeared through the door. Toby bid me goodnight and disappeared entirely, leaving me wide-eyed and wondering where the hell he had learned that.

"The boy has proven most gifted in glamour and we discovered he actually comes from a gifted line of *séansaí*, Brownies who are particularly skilled in the power of *fading*. That is why they can become invisible to the naked eye, even a magical one," Ruarc informed me as he led us out of the room and toward our rooms. "It is unfortunate his human side will prohibit him to reach his full potential, but I believe he will make a loyal and talented spy." Seeing my darting eyes to make sure we were alone, he added, "Worry not; I can assure us *some* privacy in our conversations."

Taking a moment to consider his words, I replied, "I beg to differ. His human side will serve him well, I think. In my time living among them, I met several who had a great ability to read others as if they were words on a page. Toby came from a large but abusive household; this forced him into being hyper-vigilant, noting every small detail, every shift in people's emotions. He misses nothing. While his beginnings fill me with anger to no end, it is because of this that I believe he will do quite well."

He looked down at me, a perfect brow arched. "Hyper-vigilance. A trait you two seem to share; were your beginnings just as violent then?"

Rolling my eyes over to him in annoyance, I retorted, "Don't feign that deep of an interest in me, Ruarc. Anyone who has seen combat and conflict possesses the trait. Regardless, I am uncomfortable with Toby being used by you in such a manner; he's just a child."

"A child that will grow into a man, Melisandre; the sooner he is guided towards embracing his true potential, the more likely he will survive. His path should be evidence enough of the necessity of what he is training for."

"Perhaps," I relented, "but if anyone deserves a happy childhood, it's Toby."

"Sounding like seasoned parents, deciding the fates of their offspring. Who is this Toby, I wonder?"

Both of us came to an abrupt stop. Our eavesdropper was a beautiful woman, skin kissed by glistening ebony. Rich amber and gold-flecked eyes held curiosity and the reflection of one who had seen a thousand years of life. A long skirt shifted at the slightest of movements, her upper torso was bare. Delicate gold chains hung down her neck, draping across her pert breasts. Thick black hair was her crowning glory, long and braided with gold and ivory beads.

"Toby was Melisandre's ward. Sadly, he is no longer with us," Ruarc replied smoothly, "You are looking quite well, Unatti." Turning to me, he introduced us. "*A rún*, this is the legendary Werelioness, Unatti, Champion of the Nubian lion-god, Apedemak. She stands as one of the High Queens of the Were Kingdom. Unatti, this is my intended, Melisandre Von Boden. She is—"

"The last Alchemist," Unatti interjected, her warm gaze assessing me, "Oh yes, I am well aware. You are quite the popular topic among the Champions, Lady Von Boden. I have wanted to see for myself if all the talk was merited."

"And was it?" I asked, already wanting this meeting to be over.

She smiled, the whiteness of her teeth stark against her complexion. "Oh, but we just met so I have yet to decide. Your eyes, though– it is no wonder the gods waged war with The Mother just to see her most beloved creations, for they are a fearsome thing to behold." Unatti walked towards me, then rounded her steps so she was to my right, as if preparing to pass by.

Reaching out, she grasped the hand with Ruarc's ring, taking a moment to admire it. Her hands were so very warm, smooth, but had a rough quality to it. The hand of a warrior.

"We shall see more of one another, Alchemist. I will not let the Raven keep you all to himself." Her face held mysterious promises and a fascination that only true predators show. "My mate calls, otherwise I would stay longer. I bid both of you a good night."

With a regal nod of her head, she left us. I watched her saunter down the hallway, hips swaying seductively.

"She, herself, was a *fearsome* thing to fight against in the arena," murmured Ruarc, repeating Unatti's words, "A greater lioness, there is none. Unatti has certainly earned her place among royalty. She would be a worthwhile ally."

"You trust her, then?" I asked in disbelief.

"Trust has nothing to do with it. You would be wise to not trust anyone, little Alchemist. This you should know already. Come, to bed," he commanded, pulling me towards our door.

Once inside, I escaped into the washroom to change, procrastinating until I heard a gentle knock. Nervousness ran up my skin like ants; I had not slept with anyone since Alcaeus. To do so felt like a betrayal to the intimacy we had shared. Clutching the pendant my owl had given me, I paced.

"Melisandre, I know you are stalling. Sleep only," he reassured me.

Hiding behind the only emotion I could wield like a sword, I jerked the door open, glaring up at the shirtless and barefoot king.

"And no cuddling," I snapped back, darting past him. Marching over to the bed, I shoved the covers back and climbed in, curling around the edge of the mattress. Feeling the mattress dip behind me, I tightened my hold on the duvet around me. A masculine chuckle was all that greeted me before even breathing took its place.

The dawn's reaching fingers of light caused my eyes to become heavy. A sound whispered in my mind. Then another and another until a delicate tune began to play.

Piano. Alcaeus'Alcaues' piano. The notes called to me, beckoning me to get lost in its colours that spoke of warmth and affection, with an underlying bittersweet note that I felt too deeply. My thoughts drifted.

You saw us fighting. You know how this is going to end.

Yes.

CHAPTER 22

The vastness of Fyrkat Castle continued to surprise me. Queen Ragna seemed to have absconded with the Roman Senate's chambers, which I now stood in the shrouded entryway of. Made up of an outer circle and an inner circle, the building was large and parliamentary in presentation. The inner chamber was rounded, built like an amphitheatre with huge stone steps as seating. The outer circle was really a long corridor of stone walls and arched ceilings, reminding me of a cathedral undercroft. Doors to the inner-chamber were opened but the darkness hid us waiting proxies well.

I stood alone, the other contestants giving me a wide berth and wary looks. Hairs on the back of my neck stood up in warning and my eyes found the cause - the former champion from last year's games. He still had the golden laurel on his head, his black beard braided and hanging down to mid chest. Black eyes stared me down with an intensity that spoke only one thing: I was a threat.

Wanting to pay more attention to what was in front of me, I leaned against the doorframe. Gripping my staff tightly, I continued to study the crowded room. The flags of all the Champions stood proudly throughout. Rather austere in gold-veined white marble, the decorations were minimal, aside from the flags. It was incredible, really, seeing the enormity of diversity of the world's cultures gathered in a single area.

The dull roar of talking made it difficult to pick up any one conversation. It was only the Champions and their ministers and advisors who were seated. Ragna and Alcaeus were not on the forefront for once, instead sitting several rows up and to the left. They were surrounded by black-robed advisors and councilmen who spoke among themselves.

The slimy mage, Ilirhun is once more absent. I wonder if the Sickness got him.

Alcaeus was in conversation, as was Ragna, and he had yet to notice my presence. Though my position in the darkened entryway gave me a clear view of him. In that moment, weakness conquered me and I studied him. My affection for him was a light locked inside my heart, its beams stubbornly peeking through. Memorising every line of his broad form, the way his hands moved as he spoke. The moving cords and tendons in his neck and shoulders. Perfect sharp lines in the profile of his face. The memory of his skin beneath my fingertips had me tingling.

Suddenly, his eyes snapped around, searching. A ruffling caught my attention above me, and I spotted a great horned owl up in the rafters, staring back down at me. My gaze immediately went to Alcaeus, who was now staring straight at me. My hand instinctively went to my throat where his necklace lay hidden behind the layers.

He noticed.

The way his look softened made my heart clench and I had to turn away. Ceasing conversations and utter silence had me turning back once more, however. A familiar figure was standing in the empty centre, with her strong arms raised.

"Good evening, brothers and sisters, fellow Champions. I, Unatti, chosen by all of you to act as Speaker for the Great Council, bid you welcome and am here as a reminder to keep the peace." Her rich alto voice resonated as her last words held an edge of warning. "Let the first meeting of Champions this Yaldā commence!" Applause went around the room before Unatti lowered her arms and the room was quiet once more. "We shall begin with the Naming Ceremony. Afterward, as is custom, each of you will be granted the opportunity to either state a grievance or challenge another's proxy. If stating a grievance, the choice of first *blood, submission*, or *to the death* will be given."

Raising her hand to her right, she called, "I call upon those who have brought proxies. Name them!"

An ornately clad woman stood immediately, her clothes boasting both ceremonial and warrior aspects. Of the Korean style, I would wager.

"I, Nammo, Champion of Ungnyeo and Were-Queen of the Seoraksan Mountain, name my proxy - Chumo the Holy!"

The man called pushed through us, walking the long stretch to the middle of the amphitheatre. A beautiful bow in his right hand, a full quiver at his back, the man bowed to his master once he came to a stop. Then, guided by Unatti, he went to stand to the side of the circle. More Champions stood, calling their proxies. After four Champions had announced their fighters, it was my turn.

"I, Ruarc Ó Ceallaigh, Champion of The Mórrígan, Unseelie King of the Sluagh, name my proxy - The Alchemist, Melisandre Von Boden!"

Furious hushed whispers coursed all around, everyone clearly eager to see a creature in the flesh that had only been a legend to them. But when I moved, all went quiet.

A deep breath started off my walk to the centre of the room, my staff echoing off the chamber floor. Not a sound could be heard beyond metal on stone and my confident steps. All eyes were on me. Eyes that had once hunted my people. Eyes that would see me in chains, the Stone's power under their control. Eyes that now looked at me with a hunger that made my skin crawl.

Coming to a stop in the middle, I slammed my staff down a little harder. The underlying message was there: See me. Underestimate me at your own downfall.

Not letting my gaze falter, I met Ruarc's proud stare. Bowing my head slightly, he returned the gesture and I was then led to an empty space on the side. Finally, I let attention flicker to Alcaeus. The mark warmed, almost vibrating against me. By the look on his face, I know he felt it too. I quickly averted my attention.

"I, Anyas, Champion of Illapu—"

The slam of a door had us all turning to the entrance as the sound of footsteps followed suit. As if someone had let in the sun itself, a breathtakingly beautiful woman glided at the head of her entourage, tall and lithe. A crown, seemingly made of sunlight and flowers, rested upon straight black hair that flowed behind her like a wedding veil. Her sun yellow and white gown glittered with every graceful step, rendering the gold veins in the marble floor, mute.

"My most sincere apologies at my rather late and untimely arrival; the journey was far longer and more strenuous because of the Sickness. As I have so rudely interrupted, shall I continue?"

The look on the Speaker's face was not a happy one. "Queen Mab, there is protocol to be followed. While we can forgive your tardiness, you must wait until the former Champion has named their proxy."

The Seelie queen bowed her head graciously, "I completely understand and my apologies to Anyas for stealing the spotlight." No part of Mab's demeanour belayed remorse and the Champion in question glared back at her before whispering furiously to the man beside them. Mab smiled wider. "But, as to not further the interruption, does it not make the most sense for me to state my proxy quickly and be done with it?"

After a quick glance to Anyas, who gave an annoyed wave, Unatti let out a frustrated sigh. "Be quick about it. But any further interruptions will not be tolerated."

Queen Mab beamed. "You are most gracious, Queen Unatti. Anyas." With a flourish of her elegant arms, she announced, "I, Mab, Champion of Áine, Queen of the Seelie Kingdom, name my proxy..."

Tension unfurled itself within the room.

"The Beithir!"

A collective gasp moulded into hushed whispers, which evolved to angry and shocked voices. Champions alike refused her champion of choice as was evident in the bits of shouting and finger pointing.

"A proxy cannot be a mindless beast!"

"She bends the rules! A serpent cannot be a proxy!"

Unatti held her hand up and the room quieted. "There are no rules pertaining to the physical composition of a proxy. Only that it is not an original Champion."

A wave of furious grumbling washed over the crowded room. I caught snippets of comments from those closest to me.

"Queen Unatti speaks true."

"But it means Queen Mab will have the upper hand in any battle."

"No one will agree to this—"

"I will agree to it." The golden and sultry voice of Ragna slithered through the barrage of shouting. All attention turned to her in mutual surprise. There were some, however, who were not.

Ruarc's steely gaze met mine and understanding passed between us. This time, though, I did not hesitate in also meeting Alcaeus' midnight stare. His face betrayed nothing. Or so I thought.

There. I saw it.

Sorrow.

"I will agree to it!" Ragna started again, coming to a stand.

The room went silent with collective shock. The rivalry between the two queens was legendary so for Ragna to agree could only mean she had an ulterior motive. My heart sank because I knew exactly what it was.

"I believe Queen Mab's choice in proxy opens the door for necessary diversity in the Divine Games. We have been stuck in tradition for far too long. The winds of change are upon us." She smiled down at the Seelie Queen in challenge. "I, Ragna Valdis Heldóttir, Champion of Hel, Queen of Khaviel and all Vampire-kind, name my proxy..." Pausing, her eyes slowly making their way around the room. "Alcaeus Pallas!"

The room erupted. Unatti tried to bring order but even her great voice was lost among the cacophony of chaos.

"How dare you, Queen Ragna!"

"This is against everything the treaty was made for!"

"Champions cannot fight!"

"This is an insult to all those who died to prevent exactly this!"

"PREPOSTEROUS!"

"He is a Champion! Undefeated at that! Proxies stand no chance!"

"Alcaeus, you can't possibly agree to this!"

Suddenly the whole room went bright and people yelled and screamed, hiding themselves away from the burning light. Yet just as quickly as it appeared, like a lone candle in the night, it was snuffed out.

"My apologies, my fellow Champions, this is most unbecoming. Let us all calm ourselves." chastised Queen Mab, her voice a gentle water on a hot day. The light had most certainly come from her. "Now, Queen Ragna, praytell what your reasoning is by submitting your own fiancé into the arena? Indeed, Prince Alcaeus, once king, what say you?"

My eyes narrowed at her saccharin tone and her angelic grace. I couldn't quite put my finger on why but looking at her made me want to spit in her tea just to wipe that bloody sunshine off her face.

"While abrasive as always, Queen Mab, you are most efficient in handling a crowd," Ragna smiled back insincerely, "but I appreciate you giving me a chance to state my case." The answering queen bowed her head in acknowledgement. "Now, I proposed my fiancé as my proxy for he is mine in both body and soul already. He is a Champion without wings, his elementary power from Athena no longer usable. One could consider him... no longer a Champion." She put forth slyly. Alcaeus' head was bowed, hands resting on the tops of his knees.

The room had gone quiet, the dawning horror of Ragna's implication had many easing back into their seats in fear. This was the *Great Owl*, the undefeated Champion of the original Divine Games. The mighty *Godslayer*, now merely a broken immortal.

Mab cleared her throat delicately, braving the question no one wanted to ask but everyone wanted to know.

"And... how might that be?"

With an arched brow, her grin grew into the evil one that I had become so familiar with. Alcaeus' hands clenched and he curled into himself. Then, he relaxed, sitting up straight. Tell-tale green flames danced across his body as Ragna met the gasps of horror with glee, unremorseful at her heinous crime.

My face held nothing but hatred of which I did not bother to hide. Inside, my heart clenched in fury, seeing Alcaeus' chains flaunted so publicly. The cold metal of my staff was my strongest anchor to not completely tear her apart, atom by atom.

"Essentially, he is my thrall," she replied proudly, "which, I do believe, makes him most qualified to be my proxy."

"What have you done, Queen Ragna?" growled Unatti. "He is to be your mate yet you have defiled him!"

Ragna quickly put up a hand in warning. "Careful, Queen Unatti - we are naming proxies, not discussing my intimate dealings with my consort. Let us not be distracted."

"I quite agree," said Queen Mab, much to everyone's surprise. "What Queen Ragna does between her and her consort is of no concern to us Champions."

"Even if it includes one of us? She has ruined him!" Someone shouted.

The Seelie Queen shook her head, her black hair falling forward slightly. "What is done is done. As long as Queen Ragna does not attempt this with another one of us, I see no reason to dwell on the past." Her intense stare with the Vampire Queen held an electrifying tension and hidden meaning. When Ragna raised a dismissive brow, Mab asked,

"Tell me, has Prince Alcaeus expressed his unwillingness to this arrangement?"

The room fell silent yet again, discomfort and apprehension rippling through the congregation. Grinding my teeth, I glared at all those around. Surely they knew this was not his consent! How could they stand there seeing his very chains!

I stepped forward.

Do not, *mikrós asvós*. Be still.

The sound of his rich baritone froze every cell of me for a brief moment before I glanced up to see his gaze. Absent were the green flames. Yearning, raw yearning, stared back at me.

A burning on my hand with the mark of The Mórrígan had me glaring up at Ruarc who glared back, shaking his head.

To my horror, Queen Mab suddenly focused those brilliant aquamarine eyes on me, my movements having drawn her attention. She drew closer and I cringed internally at the brightness of her presence.

"This is the Alchemist, then? The one they say is the Mother's Elixir of Life? The Philosopher's Stone?" I simply glowered back at her, making no move to answer. She smiled gently but a shift in her face gave me pause. Turning to the room, she said, "The Alchemist is the product of the earth goddess, of nature herself. Could the argument not be made that she is also a Champion, if not in power alone? If you are allowing my Fae counterpart to have a Champion in the fight, is it not also fair for Ragna to have hers?"

She spoke the truth and everyone knew it. No one liked it, that much was clear. But nor did anyone continue to dispute it.

"Ah," Mab continued, "well, then. That settles it." Turning to Unatti, she asked, "While I am a staunch advocate for following tradition, my party is quite tired. Might I call my challenge?"

Queen Unatti glared at her, stalking her like the lioness she was beneath her velvet dark skin.

"You will do this once, and only once, Seelie Queen of the Light Court. No more will I afford you the chance to bend the rules, otherwise I shall be the one you will be fighting in the arena!" Unatti snapped.

I was beginning to like Unatti more and more.

"I, Queen Mab, desire a fight between my proxy and that of Queen Ragna's."

"State your intent - challenge or grievance?" demanded Unatti.

Queen Mab lifted her chin. "Grievance."

Ragna folded her arms, waiting.

"State the reason behind your grievance!" shouted Unatti.

This time, Queen Mab's angelic face filled with anger. With rage.

"I have just cause to believe Queen Ragna kidnapped and murdered my Chosen Mate - King Oberon. So, as you have now put your mate's life in the hands of the games, so too shall I take this opportunity the fates have bestowed upon me and pay in kind!"

Shock and anger rippled throughout, the disgust and disdain toward Ragna growing monumentally.

Unatti held up a hand for silence. "And how would you see justice fulfilled, Queen Mab?"

The sunlight Fae's face morphed into an insidious smile. "To the death."

"Do you accept this grievance challenge, Queen Ragna?" Asked Unatti.

"I do." Ragna replied, her satisfied smirk absolutely slappable.

I closed my eyes. The cold tendrils of anxiety seeped into my veins.

"As you were first challenged, Queen Ragna, as is custom, you have the floor," said Unatti.

"I, Queen Ragna, desire a fight between my proxy and that of King Ruarc's."

There it is.

Now her eyes were on me, not Ruarc. I met her gaze unflinchingly, hoping she saw how much of a cunt she really was.

"State your –"

"Grievance." Interrupted Ragna, unfazed by Unatti's deep growl that even had the fine hairs on my neck standing to attention.

"State the reason behind your grievance!"

"My grievance is with King Ruarc, invading my kingdom and stealing *my* property," Ragna accused, pointing a finger at me, "*property* which was guilty of treason for conspiring against me! I demand justice!"

All eyes went to Ruarc, who calmly stood.

"How would you see justice fulfilled, Queen Ragna?"

She smirked. A look I could only interpret as victory came over her face. "To the death."

"Do you accept this grievance challenge, King Ruarc?"

"Oh, I've been *waiting* for this. I accept your challenge Ragna," he responded, the arrogant smirk matching Ragna's. He would not be outdone when it came to confidence.

My eyes once again found Alcaeus'. I found reassurance, warmth, comfort, and hope in that hauntingly beautiful stare. But Ruarc's words continued to haunt me like an unforgivable sin.

You saw us fighting. You know how this is going to end.

Yes.

CHAPTER 23

One more had challenged me to fight during the Naming Ceremony. My challenger? The Japanese Tengu from the banquet. His Champion was eager to see my abilities, according to Ruarc. A fight to submission.

The events from the ceremony had left me stressed and rattled. The moment it was dismissed, I escaped to Sage Kevyn's study.

The window was cool against my brow, a blissful comfort, while I stared into the moonlit night. Soft beams of light illuminated the grass below, disappearing in the density of trees in the distance. My finger continued to trace the pendant Alcaeus gave me, now on full display in the safety of the Sage's office. Knees raised, I had my other arm tucked across my body as I rested against the floor-to-ceiling window in this literary sanctuary.

A deep sigh did nothing to relieve my heart of the ache that struck during the horrific events of the day. My thoughts should have been filled with trying to devise a way to defeat the Tengu; I knew so little about them. Yet, no amount of self-discipline could keep me away from the image of Alcaeus' face when the challenge between us was struck. Every emotion I could see was a strike in my memory like a pickaxe against stone. Watching Ragna so callously flaunt her control over his body in front of all of his peers, sickened me.

Rustling had me turning and then giving a little jump in surprise when my new little owl friend, Maximus, flew to me and settled on the top of my knee.

"How did you get in here?" I asked, smiling at him.

"It was flapping around out here and I figured it would be nice to have an audience while I give my bestie a piece of my mind." Elis' voice was sharp and heated with anger. I knew why. Honestly, I couldn't blame him.

After coaxing Maximus onto my fingers, I stood, shifting him to my shoulder.

"Elis," I greeted, "Look, I know—"

"You know you have so much explaining to do!" he snapped. "How DARE you keep your relationship to King Ruarc from me! Tell me, Melisandre, who am I? What is my name? Hmm? Oh yes, that's right! Elis FUCKING LeGervase - greatest and most faithful ally of Melisandre NEGLECTFUL Von Boden! I cannot believe—Ahhh!" Elis gasped, snatching my hand with Ruarc's gaudy engagement ring. His saucer wide eyes began to mist over. "You..ah...uhuh...ehhh," he squeaked, incoherent voice breaking. He whipped away with a desperate sob.

I rolled my eyes. Elis and his damned theatrics.

"By all the gods, Elis! It's not real!" I began to explain but Elis snapped me a look over his shoulder.

"Those are rubies from the mountains of Le Mont Doré! They are most certainly real! And don't even get me started on those diamonds!" He sassed, sniffing dramatically as he returned to giving me the bright side of his stiffened back.

I rubbed my temples in deliberate circles while taking a deep breath. "Elis, for fuck's sake—this is me we're talking about."

"Exactly! You and your weakness for hot men!"

My deadpan stare into his back should have burned a hole through his maroon silk shirt.

"I am not the only one in this room that has been guilty of falling for a pretty face but you seem to remain faithful to your Chosen—why would you doubt I would be the same?"

He didn't respond, just continued to fill the room with pathetic sniffles. So I stomped over to him, mumbled curses following me until I was almost nose to chest with him. My pendant almost made him cross-eyed as I shoved it in his face.

"I. Am. True. To. Him!" I spoke every word sharply, emphasising my point. "I needed a way to get Ragna to lower her guard so I can find a way to meet with Alcaeus so we can complete the mark! Fionn devised a plan that Ruarc and I would *pose* as... as..."

"A couple," Elis provided, "*Intended.*"

"Yes," I sighed, "exactly. We couldn't very well demand a private audience, now could we? Silly vampire."

Elis glared down at me. "Don't you 'silly vampire' me! Put yourself in my shoes with your tiny and unmanicured feet! How was I supposed to know any of this! You didn't even try to see me!" His voice broke at the last part.

"Ahh," I said, realising that *this* was the real reason behind my sensitive friend's demeanour. "I see. Well... I'm sorry. Life has been horrifically complicated since we got here, Elis. You and I both know how much Ruarc tries to dominate my time. Please, for once, I ask you for understanding."

A lift of a chin and angry sniff told me I'd have to try a little harder to convince this delicate flower to open up. Maximus sensed my movement and flew off to a nearby perch.

Swallowing my grumblings, I let out a sigh and awkwardly opened my arms. Elis didn't move. Another begrudging breath and my arms stiffly came around his waist. I didn't quite let our bodies touch but gave him a stiff pat on the back to finalise my attempts at a hug. Bastard made me stand there for an uncomfortable length of time before he snorted and crushed me against him.

"You're the worst hug-giver this side of the Veil. It's like embracing plywood when you initiate."

"Wow. Ow!" Yelping, Elis gave me several hard smacks on the back before releasing me. Rolling my shoulders did nothing to help the sting. "Alright, alright—I deserve that, but...I am truly sorry, Elis."

My sincerity seemed to break through as his brow lessened its severity, lavender eyes drying.

"Well," began Elis, shaking his head a little as if to regain composure, "just know you're not leaving here until I am satisfied with all the missing pieces of information." A slender finger jabbed at me. "And no more avoiding me! I am an invaluable asset!"

Crossing my arms, I tilted my head at him. "I can deal with that."

We sat in the two chairs facing the hearth, my little owl coming back for more affection. I spilled all the drama surrounding the situation. It was an unexpected relief, really, sharing it all with Elis. He sat quietly and listened, only occasionally asking questions to fill in any voids.

"So," he finally replied after a healthy bout of silence, "do you really believe King Ruarc is only doing all of this out of the goodness of his heart?"

"Well—"

"Well nothing, my dove, you can't possibly be that obtuse."

Glaring at him, I snapped, "Of course I don't! I'm sure he has his own twisted reasons but our options are severely limited at this moment. By the looks of things, the only opportunity to get time with Alcaeus is in the arena."

His eyes went wide. "The arena?! Tell me Ragna did not- No...of course she would." Lavender eyes filled with fear. "Oh, my little troll... How will you fight him?"

Breaking away from his heartfelt gaze, I stared into the dancing flames in the hearth. That was not a question I was prepared to answer.

"I don't know, Elis," I responded quietly after a time. "Truly, I haven't a clue. The one time I tried to hurt him, my mark immobilised me with pain. Why it did not affect him that way, well, I can only surmise that it has something to do with Ragna's control over him." Moving Maximus to my knee, I pet the front of him as he nibbled at me affectionately. "It appears I shall be going up against the Tengu first, so I will concern myself with that."

"Are you worried you will lose?"

I gave him a hard stare, then shook my head before replying, "No. I am far more worried about bringing down the entire arena. I'm afraid of hurting people. I have never done transmutations of this scale for the sake of combat. The process of manipulating molecular structures to this scale, rapidly at that, can have devastating consequences if I make even a single mistake. I've said it a million times - Alchemists are not fighters. We're philosophers, scientists."

Elis ran a contemplative finger across his full lips. "But... Alcaeus is not your enemy."

"No," I agreed, "but I'm not really fighting Alcaeus. I'm fighting Ragna."

The sound of the door opening took us both by surprise. Maximus took flight, finding a perch up on one of the bookshelves. Sage Kevyn came through, arms full of books and scrolls. Quickly coming to his aid, I grabbed a stack from him and he smiled his thanks.

"I am surprised to not see you at this evening's feast—"

A gasp to my right, and Elis shot up from his seat. "Oh we are so very late! King Ruarc asked me to fetch you but I was so angry! Gods' teeth! Come, troll, we're late. You'll have to just go in this." Distaste marred his face but he waltzed past Kevyn, who rolled his eyes at my friend, both of us watching him make a grand exit out the door.

"Dramatic, that one," murmured Kevyn. "You would have thought mathematics and science physically tortured Lord LeGervase during his studies. Never have I had a student who sobbed so loudly at the sight of a new formula."

Snorting, I broke down in laughter as I made my way to the door. "It's truly a wonder how he and I became friends."

"Let alone stayed friends since you always make us late! Really, Melisandre, the feast will be over!" interrupted Elis with a huff.

Mirroring Sage Kevyn's eye roll, I bid him farewell and followed my indignant diva to the Great Hall.

After enduring Elis' chastising for my outfit choices for court, we walked through the open doors and into the middle of the active festivities. Most had already eaten, many standing in small groups laughing and talking. Some had taken to dancing, the music merry and upbeat.

Instantly, I was aware of Alcaeus' attention on me, predatory eyes watching me from his place at the high table as we moved through the room slowly.

"Llyr is waiting for us—Ah! There he is!" He waved, although I was too short to see his mate through the crowded room. "Yes, if we could just squeeze there, pardon—Oh. Camille." The mask of nobility slipped onto my friend's face with expertise, his voice now pleasant but with a tone of guarded boredom.

A tall woman sporting a willowy figure, wore a beautiful dress that left little to the imagination. Gold jewellery sparkled in the ambiance of the room. She looked down at Elis, her slender hand placed lightly on his chest.

"Lord LeGervase, Elis, you have yet to come to call," she purred, strawberry locks coiled atop her head. They were unmoving as she changed her attention to me. Disdain wrinkled her pert nose. "Surely, in your absence from court, you have not resorted to frolicking with the peasantry, my lord. With such an ugly little thing, too."

With a sassy cock of his honey-blond head, Elis smoothly retorted, "Ah, sweet Camille, how little I have missed the vapidity of the nobility our beloved Queen surrounds herself with. The only peasantry here is your complete lack of self-awareness to your own acquired station which, I do believe, began on your knees. Now, if you'll excuse me." Grabbing my arm, Elis pulled us around the outraged Camille.

He snuck a glance back at me. "My apologies, my dear, this room is nothing but pompous whores and back-stabbing vipers. You know this, of course, but allow me to provide what little verbal protection I can."

Trying to hold back my smile, I shook my head. "No, Elis, when it comes to you, I am but a bystander awaiting the inevitable entertainment. Do carry on."

A light laugh escaped him as we continued toward where Llyr was sitting. Suddenly, a steel grip ripped me away from Elis, who looked back with alarm. Ruarc dragged me away from him and though he glared at the Fae king, my friend made no move to stop him.

"Ruarc! What is the matter with you?" I demanded, tugging back but failing as he continued to pull me towards the edge of the Great Hall. When we reached a less crowded space, I was flung against the wall by momentum alone.

Grunting, I flexed my neck so my head didn't whiplash against the stone. Rubbing my forearm where his grip had bruised, I glared up at him.

Red hair filled my vision before his lips shoved against mine, bruisingly. The kiss was all teeth and violence, and I pushed him away.

"Slap me," He growled, pulling back.

He didn't have to ask me twice. Happy to oblige, I lifted my hand as I generated all of my pent up frustration. My palm struck his cheek with a resounding **CRACK** that left him visibly stunned.

"Wha—ugh!" I began but Ruarc's hand slammed into my throat, raising me against the wall until my toes barely touched the floor. Grabbing his muscled forearm, I struggled.

"Now," He said darkly, "Take a look at your lover. LOOK AT HIM."

I realised what he was trying to do.

"Let the fear crawl up your belly."

My eyes darted over to the dais. Ragna was not present, surprisingly, but Alcaeus was. With rapt attention. He leaned forward, staring us down. Ruarc pulled me forward slightly, only to be shoved against the wall once more.

Alcaeus stood.

"Reach out to him with your mind. Let him *feel* your fear," commanded the Unseelie King, squeezing my neck harder. The monster was before me and no amount of glamour could hide it.

Squeezing my eyes shut when Ruarc's hot tongue snaked up the side of my face, I imagined what it would be like to truly be at the mercy of The Mórrígan's creation.

Please... Alcaeus!

CHAPTER 24

Ruarc released me abruptly and grabbed me by the hair, eliciting a yelp as he dragged me to the double doors. I could barely keep up as we marched across the castle grounds, my eyes watering from the tension and pain. For a moment, I wondered if this wasn't the ploy I thought it was.

He didn't stop until we reached the quiet garden behind the library. Huge oaks towered over us, the only light from the night sky, the brilliant moon and stars, keeping us from total darkness. Once completely under the cover of foliage, he released the punishing hold on my hair.

"Damnit Ruarc, you're going to render me bald!" I spat, spinning around to face this lunatic.

He didn't react, instead the maniacal gleam in his eye burned brighter.

"This is going to hurt," he warned.

Before I could question the ominous statement, he grabbed the back of my neck with his right hand, spinning me around. His monster-hand came around to my font and my eyes followed the movement in horror as a single clawed finger elongated. The tip which then came closer, brushing the skin above my mark.

"Wait! No—" The needle sharp point pierced my Mating mark.

I screamed.

Trying to get away, the pain was excruciating, as if my very soul was being stabbed. Runes came to life, the Stone awakening at the assault.

"He *comes*," Ruarc said, a smile clear in his voice.

The temperature dropped, an indication of new magic entering the vicinity. A whoosh, a painful grunt, and the Unseelie King's presence was ripped away. My knees gave out but I was able to twist my body to watch the ordeal unfold.

Ruarc was airborne before a large blur grabbed him by the neck and slammed him into one of the massive oak trunks. Alcaeus' presence was bigger and darker than anything I had ever experienced from him, his magic a tangible vibration around us. Magic that felt like the deep cold of midnight and impending nightmares.

Why can I see it so clearly? Feel it like it came from my own hand?

I walked toward them cautiously but stopped, Alcaeus' back still to me, when I heard their exchange.

"*A Ulchabháin Mhóir,*" spat the Unseelie King, addressing him as *The Great Owl* in Gaelic, blood trickling from the side of his mouth. "Took you long enough."

Alcaeus let out a growl before slamming Ruarc against the tree once more. The old oak trunk groaned.

"You DARE put your filthy raven claws on MY Fated? Do you wish death upon your kingdom, *old friend*? Touch her like that again and I promise no amount of magic will save you from me!" The Nightmare Prince raged, gritted teeth so exposed, as if prepared to rip Ruarc's throat out. "How I regret the mercy I showed you in the arena!"

The Mórrígan's Champion smiled back in challenge. "*Lá de na laethanta seo, cuirfimid críoch leis an gcath sin na cinniúna san airéine, agus feicfimid ansin cé a bhéarfaidh an chraobh leis.*"

Someday we will finish that fateful battle in the arena and then we shall see who the victor truly is, was what I understood. Curiosity piqued within me at his reference.

"But," Ruarc continued, his voice raspy from the strangling grip Alcaeus still had on him, "for now, we needed to get you away from Ragna, even for a moment. This was the only way."

Alcaeus released him, slightly relaxing his stance. "I know now," he replied, "that this is a fallacy between you both. I received Melisandre's message."

Ruarc raised a brow at that. Then a pointed look at me. "Oh? I was unaware she reached out to you."

When the Nightmare Prince swivelled to me, his gaze was an intense black fury, the geometric pattern defining his eyes. A curtain of inky blackness erupted from Alcaeus, veiling us from the world.

Ruarc could neither be seen nor heard.

It was just us.

Then my Vampire's demeanour morphed, the fury turning into a dark swirling desire that instantly lit me aflame. So intense, I reflexively stepped back. Despite the darkness, I could see him as clear as day.

"Oh yes," he said, his voice a dark promise full of wicked and delicious things. "She did."

He stepped toward me.

"Doubt thou the stars are fire," another step, his voice a silky intimacy stroking my emotions.

"Doubt that the sun doth move." Closer he came, continuing to recite Hamlet with each step.

"Doubt truth to be a liar." Now in front of me, staring down as he cupped my face with both hands.

"But never doubt I love." He kissed me and my nerves exploded.

His hot tongue felt like home and longing. Pushing against him, my mouth dancing with his. Everything in that moment, I wanted to devour and never let go. One warm, rough hand slid to the back of my neck to hold me firmly against him. His presence filled my head, and his thoughts melded with mine. For just a time, all the world stopped, and the only thing that mattered was him here with me.

Alcaeus finally pulled away, both of us breathless. His gaze flickered to the small trail of blood stemming from my mark where Ruarc had pierced. Dipping down, the heat of his tongue slid up and to where the small hole was, pressing it slightly. The pain disappeared. Lifting his head, Alcaeus took in my face, studying it tenderly.

"Oh, how I have missed you. The moment you walked into the Great Hall, all I could think of was trying to find a way to you," he whispered to me. "I will never let him or anyone touch you again like that, *mikrós asvós.*" His thumbs caressed my cheeks and my face softened in light of his protectiveness.

Oh, how beautifully empty those words were. We both knew how little power he would have over that in the coming days. Yet, they still filled me with comfort. My own hands rested on his forearms, relishing in the feel of him.

"It was all an act, Alcaeus," I replied, my voice still breathy from his kiss. "We needed Ragna to believe we are here for the Divine Games and only that."

"I know, my love," his gentle voice tinted with sadness, having lost the raging and wrathful turbulence at the sight of seeing Ruarc hurt me. The sphere of darkness receded, revealing the Unseelie King once more.

"Alcaeus," said Ruarc, his raspy voice recovering from the brutal attack he had just endured, "we must discuss you completing the mark."

The hands that held me so tenderly dropped, the lines on Alcaeus' face sharpening as he became withdrawn.

"I do not know if that will be possible. Even now, Ragna searches for me. More than a few moments, it seems, and I feel her powers crawling into my soul. Half an hour was the longest I have gone without her haunting my thoughts. I am still waiting upon Zhenbai and Cillian to complete the task I have appointed them. It was potentially a fool's errand, but we had to try."

"What errand?" asked Ruarc.

A silent look passed between them before Alcaeus said only, "*Paláti tou Efiálti.*"

Slowly, Ruarc's brows travelled up his face in surprise. "You cannot mean... but I thought it was sealed?"

"Zhenbai and Cillian have found a way," replied Alcaeus, "I am but waiting on their confirmation. I cannot make my move otherwise. Completing the mark any time before then would end in failure."

"Palace of Nightmare? I don't understand," I asked in confusion. "I thought this was the Nightmare Court?"

My Fated's expression was weighted, the many truths I was desperate to hear were clearly on the tip of his tongue. He was considering it. I silently implored him for those answers, my fingers curling around the front of his black-vested shirt.

With a heart-dropping shake of his head, he said, "That is something I must leave to Ruarc's discretion as I do not have the time you deserve to tell it. Until I have word from either of them—"

"Zhenbai would be your only point of contact," interjected Ruarc. "Cillian has all but vanished. I tasked him with bringing down any wards that may keep you from Melisandre, any spells that could prevent you both from completing the mark. Alas, he has not been answering my call. Your lich has betrayed us both, Alcaeus."

"No," said Alcaeus sharply, resigned demeanour stiffening. "Cillian must have found something, or Ragna got to him." Then he shook his head, as if dismissing the idea. "No... Her ego would not permit her to keep his capture a secret. She jumps at any chance to flaunt her twisted sense of power over others, most especially me. Which means he is most certainly on to something that is keeping him silent. The Lich of Ebror-iath is loyal to me and will remain so, doubt it not."

There was no room for argument and the twitch of muscles and hard stare from Ruarc told me he knew it too.

"Then you must find a way, *A Ulchabháin Mhóir*, to complete the mark. Before—" Ruarc paused, looking away sharply.

Alcaeus gave him a look of confusion before looking at me. Whatever he saw in my face disturbed him.

"You are the Mórrígan's Raven; you have her gift of sight in the outcome of battles," stated Alcaeus. "What did you see?"

Ruarc finally turned to him, staring. The slight shake of his head was all the answer he gave.

The moment was sombre, words having no place in it.

"We shall speak of this later," said Alcaeus, breaking the silence. "For now, I must return. Melisandre," I wrapped my arms around myself as he continued, "our fate was written in the stars. Do not lose hope. But also–our mark is only going to get stronger the nearer we are to each other. So keep that pendant on at all times. It will protect you from my magic of nightmares and fear."

Then he was gone.

A dancing breeze picked up, causing my hair to tickle my skin. I stared at the blank space, confused, his last words echoing as if he was still there.

"Nightmares?" I whispered, as the memory of the bathroom incident came flooding back.

"Did you think that the nightmares, the tendrils of fear and anxiety when you stepped into this castle were from Ragna? Oh, no, my dear. Many make that mistake," chuckled Ruarc, breaking me from my trance. "That is because they never knew a time when Alcaeus was his true self. Yes, he was created by Athena, but she sought the power of others in his making. Many of us, in fact, were not created by a single maker. Ragna herself was created by both Hel and Loki. My own creator was in fact three separate deities."

Absorbing this new information, I needed to ask, "Then who else made Alcaeus?"

Before answering, he took my hand and laid it in the crook of his arm, leading us out of the garden. "It was Athena, to be sure, but in her wisdom, she sought to capture the power of none other than the primordials. Or, more specifically, Nyx. Athena somehow convinced the great goddess to give but a drop of her blood to her beloved creation. So, too, did the goddess of darkness' two sons. Morpheus, the god of dreams, gave first. Then, Epiales, the very spirit of nightmares." Too stunned to speak, I just followed quietly behind him as he led us back to our rooms. "Many of the gods created Champions purely to resolve their conflicts with others without shedding the blood of innocents or their own. Yet, for some reason that I cannot fathom, Athena desired a Champion who represented the Greek Gods in their entirety." A thought made Ruarc grin slightly. "Although, it has been suggested that Epiales did not prick his finger, like his mother or brother, but rather slit his wrist so that his powers would supersede and become Alcaeus' greatest weapon."

"So," I began, "*Paláti tou Efiálti*... The Palace of Nightmare, what did he mean by that?"

Several guards walked by and Ruarc waited a few moments before responding, "That was his kingdom. Ragna had it and all its occupants magically sealed within the day she conquered him. Some say it is frozen in time. But who knows," he said as he opened the door to our room for me, "if what he said was true about his lich and Lord Zhenbai finding a way to break the seal, well..."

Walking further into the room, I relished the cosy warmth.

"Well? Well what?"

"Well, then, if you two are able to complete the mark, the coming days are only going to get much darker, little Alchemist," he sighed, though there was a faint enthusiasm in his tone that made me think he was rather looking forward to it.

I made my way toward the bathroom before pausing at the door, turning to where Ruarc now stood by the fire.

"You said 'Alcaeus' true form. What did you mean by that?" I asked.

"He is the real King of Nightmares, my dear. His true form is what you should fear the most."

CHAPTER 25

350 Years Ago...

Large ferns gently swayed in the evening breeze as the setting sun shone its last rays of light through the Scottish forest. Though the trees were many, the distance between them made them look like lone soldiers. Their gnarled bark was a testament to their age, giving the forest an ambience of history and mystics. Coverage was minimal but it did not stop the predator that walked through it all soundlessly. Owls perched above, watching their master; their flight from tree to tree just as silent as him.

He commanded several to scout up ahead. Once one crossed the Veil, there was little to be concerned with; humans posed no threat to one such as himself. No, impending threats did not motivate the excitement that filled each step. It was the news of a creature he had waited over a thousand years to find. The Lich's scrying had led him here, but that was all the sorcerer was able to provide. Farther and farther he prowled through the forest, never once slipping on the wet stones covered in rich green moss.

The smell of petrichor was strong, yet underneath the layers of rain and decay, lay her scent. She smelled of...home. Of warmth. Of life.

He quickened his steps. Cloaked in darkness, the night welcomed him as the sun finally set.

"Lycaon," he called, and the black wolf appeared in front of him. "If you see her, do not alert her to our presence. It is reconnaissance only. We must find her."

The massive wolf bowed his head low and then disappeared. Alcaeus could still feel the wolf's presence up ahead as he continued following the alluring scent he'd caught wind of just moments ago.

"She is close," he whispered into the night.

The forest opened up to reveal a massive ancient oak, its regal branches impressive yet comforting. It sheltered a huge black horse, its hooves tucked around it as it lay plucking at the grass. A human would not have been able to see what rested against it in this darkness; but he was no human and the sudden awakening of the last piece of his soul stopped him mid-step.

An opened book was draped over the face of the person resting against the horse. Dark clothing left much to the imagination but it could not hide the sensual curves of her body. Nor did it hide her petite stature, though, it did not help that lying next to the massive equine only emphasised it. A silver staff lay haphazardly over her lap, one gloved hand resting on it. Shallow breaths indicated she slept.

"There you are," he whispered. "And she dreams."

Alcaeus reached forward, sending out tendrils of his magic to caress her dream. He wanted to know. He must know.

Equations flew by at an incomprehensible speed, scenes of experiments, both failures and successes flashed in his sight. Food. Flaky, buttery pastry filled with gravy, chunks of beef, potatoes, and spices. Whiskey. Books. So many books. More food. An old man. Flowers. Strange circles. Panic. Fear. Death–

The woman shot up, the book tumbling to the ground. She yelped and cursed, as the corner of the spine must have landed on her hand, which she was shaking and rubbing in jerky motions.

"Confound it all!" She snapped out loud. "Sweet Mother, look at the hour!" Letting out a groan, she came to her feet, dusting off the back of her gown. "Damnit, Zeph, why did you not wake me? Normally, you would be stomping on me for an apple by now! Ah, I am famished. Let's go home." Grabbing her staff off the ground, she waited while the large horse got to its feet.

Alcaeus watched her silently, completely enthralled. When she turned her head his way, the breath caught in his throat. Gold and silver eyes glowed in the darkness, so beautiful and haunting, nothing could compare to it. Revealing her to be a species he would never have expected. One that made it imperative he protect.

The Champion knew she could not see him, but when her gaze rested upon him unknowingly, his soul ached to be with her. His magic flared at the instinct to mark her, demanding to fuse his soul with hers.

For two thousand years he had waited. For over a thousand he had searched. Now she stood before him, breathtaking and beautiful.

Perfect.

She seemed to sense him but shook her head and began walking east of where he hid in the shadows. Long black hair with large bouncing curls was a wild mane around her. Untameable.

Like her, I wonder? Alcaeus thought to himself.

He followed her silently from a distance. She was talking rather animatedly to her large companion, who followed obediently. The Nightmare Prince could see her small, slender hand making motions in the air while the other used the staff as a walking stick. Her voice was not high pitched or grating, but a warmer, deeper resonance that he wanted to listen to endlessly.

Eventually, the structure of a nicely sized cottage came into view. After getting the beast of a horse settled, she made her way to the door. She stopped abruptly, swinging around to peer into the darkened trees to his left.

Alcaeus tensed. A flash in his vision. One of his owls had seen something. No, someone. Entering the vicinity. Taking hold of his owl's consciousness, he saw a smaller Vampire wearing a hood over his head, crouched as he observed the cottage. With a swift movement, the stranger looked straight into the eyes of his owl. The stranger's eyes widened in fear. He stepped back, inching away from the house before breaking into a run.

But it was too late.

Alcaeus caught the smaller Vampire by the neck with a single hand, who let out a strangled groan, and lifted him up in the air. Feet dangled and kicked as the spy quickly dropped the dagger he had pulled. The prince's magic shrouded them, swallowing any sounds that could be made.

"One of Ragna's rats," Alcaeus sneered. "Why are you here?"

"Q-Queen Ragna tasked me with watching over you," he wheezed, "she was concerned for your health, Your Highness."

Eyes narrowing, an insidious grin crawled up his handsome features. "How thoughtful."

Placing Ragna's spy carefully on his feet, he let go of its skinny neck. The spy stumbled back, rubbing the area. Then it happened. A slash of light, and the spy's head rolled. Nemesis glowed brightly in the inky black-

ness, only to be muted when Alcaeus just as quickly sheathed it. He called for the wolf once more, who appeared in an instant.

"I will take the body back to the Veil; Cillian has been whining for new specimens for some time now. Stay here and watch over the woman. Do not reveal yourself to her unless I command it. Kill anyone from the Otherworld. Protect her at all costs, Lycaon. She is everything. Do you understand?"

The wolf looked at him curiously, but after a moment, bowed his head low. Then he vanished.

Alcaeus was still wrapped in the cocoon of his magic when he felt her there. Right there. So close.

Placing a hand to the swirling black wall, his heart pounded as he felt her fingertips brush his. She could not see him, nor hear him, let alone feel what he had just felt. Yet, for the first time in over a thousand years, a flicker of hope and longing filled him.

"Soon, sweet one," he whispered to her. "I will protect you from the Otherworld for as long as I can. Soon, I will find a way to you and we shall be as our Creators have intended it. Together. As one."

Present day...

Hazy smoke curled around Alcaeus, the embers of his pipe glowing. A long pause before letting out a whoosh of an aromatic cloud from his exhale. The moment he had first laid eyes on his Fated was one he would replay in his mind in the many dark days to come. He had observed her from a respectful distance, slaying all who discovered her sweet little haven. Unfortunately, Alcaeus was unable to watch over her as often as he would have liked; drawing Ragna's attention to her was what he wanted to avoid the most.

Yet, all his efforts were in vain.

Resting against the stone pillar of his balcony, the Nightmare Prince sat on the ultra-wide granite balustrade. With an elbow resting on a raised knee, he willed himself to get lost in the memories of her once more.

"Your Highness," Tomwyl's soft voice cut through his focus, "King Ruarc insisted on speaking with you. I tried to tell him—"

"Come, come, Alcaeus. It's about time we discussed things without having women around trying to pull at our strings like the puppets we are, hmm?" The Unseelie king interrupted and the poor steward went pale.

"My apologies, Your High—"

Alcaeus shook his head. "It is quite alright, Tomwyl. Thank you. Leave us, please."

Tomwyl gave a curt nod and, with one last wary look at Ruarc, he left them.

Alcaeus did not bother to look at his old rival, instead watching the city below him. It teemed with life, the market a busy and buzzing place. He could hear the haggling, the laughter, the shouts of irritation as young ones knocked over wares as they raced by in their play. So many different species of creatures down there, a melting pot of cultures from around the world. The city was booming, untouched by the Sickness. An oasis for hybrids and the outcasts. All because of him.

"I wondered when you would snake your way in here, old friend," Alcaeus said quietly, though he knew the Fae had heard him. "You have never been one to wait."

An indelicate snort caught his attention. King Ruarc's hair was always the first thing one noticed about him. It hung like small rivers of blood down his body, a striking colour against the porcelain skin on one side. Against the monstrous black side, the red hair was war paint on one of the deadliest foes Alcaeus had ever faced. The yellow eye that had once burned with bloodthirsty challenge, now assessed him.

"And you wait too long, *friend*," chastised Ruarc. "Time is of the essence and you are the last person I should have to remind. Queen Ragna is most persistent in keeping you out of reach of everyone, let alone Melisandre." His tone relayed his annoyance. The Fae sported his usual shirtless fashion. A kilt and black boot his only form of clothing.

"You cannot fault her for not wanting me to plot and scheme with my allies, for that is surely her conviction. I am at her mercy, which she enjoys flaunting at every turn. In any case, control is Ragna's only expression of affection," Alcaeus replied sardonically.

Ruarc grimaced. "Wenches on power trips have never been to my taste. Oh, I enjoy a woman with spirit. Even a powerful one." His demeanour turned wistful, clearly thinking of someone specific. After a moment, he dropped the teasing façade. "You had every opportunity to complete the Mark. Why wait for *Paláti tou Efiálti* to be released? I would have given you shelter if that was the cause of your delayed decision. For a price, of course."

Fae could never hide their true nature.

"If the only consequences solely impacted Melisandre and myself then, certainly, I would have finished the Mark the moment I saw her over three hundred years ago. Yet, both you and I know that is not the privilege of a king now, is it?" He continued his leisurely attention to the simple pipe. "With leadership, with power, so thus are we bound by the shackles of a greater responsibility. I will not subject my people here to slaughter. Ragna went on a genocide mission the first time she decided to conquer the kingdoms. Her armies were manifested from the flesh and bones of her own people. People who worshipped her. I cannot allow that to happen again."

"Ah." Ruarc leaned against the opposite pillar, crossing his arms. "Always the martyr, aren't we? After all these years, the thought of innocents dying for you still pricks at your honour. Come off it, old boy. No one has that luxury. Especially now."

"The gods may have gone but it does not mean the rest of us should not abide in their wisdom; Ragna is a perfect example of what happens when you stray from order, justice, and reason." Alcaeus' last words were tight with anger. "The defining line between a monster and a king, or queen for that matter, can be found in the manner in which he rules his people, is it not? I will not leave them to slaughter for my own gain. Ruling corpses is Ragna's game."

Ruarc let out a snort of laughter. "Alcaeus, who do you think you are speaking to? You speak of the very type of monster I am king of! My entire court is made up of all that which people fear in the darkness, of the evil that lurks in their stories. Besides, a powerless king deserves not the title if he cannot help himself first." He waved his hand in the air dismissively. "I did not come here to banter philosophy, especially with the Champion of Athena. What a horrible waste of time when we have so little of it. No, we must discuss a plan—"

"There is no plan, Ruarc," interrupted Alcaeus, putting out his pipe as he uncurled from his sitting position. "Rather, what plans that are already in place cannot move forward until Paláti tou Efiálti has been freed. Nor would I bring the war to your kingdom when it has already been decimated by the Sickness." At Ruarc's stiffening form and wary look, Alcaeus faced him. "Yes, Raven, I am well aware of the reason behind your absence. The losses your kingdom has taken has been most... devastating, to be sure."

A darkness came over Ruarc's face and Alcaeus was careful to not goad him with any show of pity. "Unseelie magic is so close to death magic that... it seems to attract the Sickness far greater than others," mumbled Ruarc. "My thanks in sending Cillian to our aid. His barriers saved many. Your Fated as well..." He paused as a look of intimate wonder passed over his face that Alcaeus decidedly did not like. "She was magnificent. It took Melisandre less than fifteen minutes to see the molecular structure of the Sickness and discover its nefarious design." Unfurling his arms, he took several deliberate steps toward Alcaeus. "How can you wait to claim such a creature, when her potential is at your beckoning fingertips? The power of nature at your command, of life, if you would only take it! Yes, she hides in her mental fortress, her idiotic moral compass nothing but a shackling hindrance. But with every wall I destroy, every push and pull, she emerges more powerful, more breathtaking—"

"Watch. Your. Next. Words," snapped Alcaeus, dark suspicion dripping from him like melted wax. "You overstep yourself, Unseelie—she is not yours to wield. To break. Nor to mould ."

A sharp brow curved in challenge as Ruarc countered, "Oh, but she very much is, *Great Owl*. While she is under my protection, she is mine. She bears the mark of our agreement." He took another meaningful step forward. "If you care for her at all, then coddling her, allowing her to hide away from her true potential, is a crime against her!"

"My Fated is an innocent in all of this! Her only crime was caring far too much for those around her and having it wielded against her! This is not her fight; you know it isn't." Alcaeus closed more distance between them, every step measured. "The substance of your mark only goes insofar as your bargain with her. Do not even try to suggest otherwise."

"*Innocent?*" Ruarc sneered. "Your precious Fated is no white lamb; the truth of her actions gives her every right to stand among the Champions as an equal. Surely you realise now that her becoming the Elixir of Life came at a blood price?"

"Not for a moment do I believe that was Melisandre's intent. She is not a killer. Alchemists are a peaceful people—"

"Were!" the Fae king interjected. "They were until Melisandre Von Boden destroyed her entire species in her desire for power! She is no different to any Champion or god that has walked the Otherworld!" He snorted in derision, "You speak of Ragna being queen of corpses when your own Fated has just as many bodies under her."

"No!" Alcaeus shouted back, his arm swinging outward to cut off the conversation.

Jerking away, he paced to the large desk, leaning on the top with both hands. Memories of Melisandre in the cottage; the way she had curled around his lower body, determined to sleep in the middle of the bed. Her soft snoring and delicate face, lost in sleep. The way she hovered over books and manuscripts, her passionate focus only made him want to show her everything he knew. Her perpetual frown and the scrunch of that adorably pert nose. Gentle hands and soothing tone with every animal she encountered. But mostly, he would never forget the determination and grief on her face at witnessing the brutal murder of her ward and Lord LeGervase.

But it wasn't vengeance that followed. It was the power of life. And that said everything.

Alcaeus let go of a weighted breath, the tension within evaporating. Instead, a condescending laugh bubbled out of him. "No. All this time with her and you have missed the mark, old friend. You do not know her at all."

The smirking chuckle that sounded to the right of him made Alcaeus wary, as Ruarc leaned closer in. "I know how she moans when her nipples are tweaked just right. I know how she writhes when she finally lets go. I know how badly she would rip Ragna apart if she only had the right encouragement—ugh!" The groaning of wood and a loud **smack** resounded as the Raven's head was slammed down onto the desk, the other warrior's hand on the back of his neck like a metal vice.

"Save your psychological games for Ragna," growled Alcaeus in the Raven's ear as he leaned over him. "Your manipulations are useless here!" Met with an arrogant laugh, Alcaeus pushed him down harder.

"Oh, but I do believe the *Great Owl* has had his feathers ruffled, nevertheless." The man in question shoved away from him and Ruarc stumbled back, straightening with that wicked grin on his face.

The tension was thick as Alcaeus tried to bring the conversation back to the topic at hand, deflecting away from the carnal knowledge Ruarc claimed to have. "While you and I may relish in the rush of battle and spilling the blood of those who cross us, Melisandre laments. She mourns. My little Alchemist only accepts death as a natural course of life, but she cannot stand it when said life is taken prematurely or unjustly. Far from it." He looked away, back out toward the veranda. He too wished for Melisandre's potential, but for far different reasons. If only to see her free and untouchable by all those seeking her enslavement. Her destruction. "The only plan is this–Melisandre will fight in two days' time. All I can do is try to protect her when I can. Even if it is from me."

Ruarc looked down, idly stroking the plaid of his kilt as he mulled over the Nightmare King's words. "Love is a wretched thing. Even *The Great Owl* falls victim to its idealistic clutches." He sauntered closer, coming to a stop with his arms crossed and in a spread-legged stance. "She is rather soft-hearted, I'll give you that. Been a damned annoyance. I will do what I can to prepare her for the fight. But you must do the same. The coming battle between you two—"

The abrupt shake of Alcaeus' head stopped the continuation. "No, do not bring those words into existence. Do not give it power. Not yet. There is still hope."

Ruarc gave a frustrated growl but did not press the issue. "Fine. We will proceed as planned. Ragna must continue thinking Melisandre and I are to be hand-fasted. So do not come for my balls when I publicly enjoy the privileges that status comes with."

Alcaeus slid him a dangerous look. "Then I suggest you make your exit quickly before I take the opportunity Fate has given me at this moment."

A hearty laugh followed the Unseelie King as he did exactly that.

CHAPTER 26

"Shhh! Get Ada in here now! The Queen is having one of her fits! Night terrors all this morn!" cried the older minister to the group of terrified Brownie maids huddled in the corner. They shook, several having pulled out their handkerchiefs to wipe away their fearful tears.

"*NOOOOO! PLEASE MISTRESS! DO NOT LET HIM—AHH-HHH!*" The screams pierced through the air, sending the servants and ministers fleeing.

"I'm here, Councillor Malcom, I'm here!" panted Ada, out of breath for having rushed up the winding steps to Ragna's private tower. "Councillor?" Everyone had fled.

"GET OFF ME! *Við axarblað mitt munt þú mæta dauða þínum! Ég sver það við hamar Þórs! LOKI!*" (*You will meet your death by the blade of my axe! By Thor's Hammer, I swear it! Loki*)

Trembling hands clenched her apron and skirts as the small Brownie woman stared at the door that barred her from the mad queen. Nervously chewing her lips, Ada put a shaking hand on the handle. Its creaking could barely be heard over the agonised moan that met the lady's maid as it swung open.

Ada let out a gasp, smacking her tiny hands over her mouth.

The room was a sea of blood and death.

So many bodies. Some, just the parts, flung across the room. Slaves the queen had demanded the night before. Stale sanguineous apparitions filled the air. The stinking stench of iron and dead flesh was so overwhelming, Ada quickly covered her nose with the corner of her apron. Finally, her eyes settled on her monarch.

Ragna sat back on her heels in the middle of the great bed, her spine hunched forward. The normally proud shoulders shook, her form rocking back and forth ever so slightly. Her blonde tresses hung around her, though the colour barely peeked through the bright stain of red. The sheets were so drenched in blood that they dragged slowly, making wet squelching sounds, as the mad queen clenched them to her chest.

Incoherent, rapid mumbling was all that came from Ragna now, and Ada took that opportunity to get closer.

"M-my Queen?" asked Ada, her voice barely above a whisper. "My Queen? You are safe now. It's me, Ada." She reached out one hand to steady herself as she used the other to lift her skirts, carefully avoiding the dead.

"Hann mun deyja... Hann mun deyja..." (He will die... He will die)

"It's alright, My Queen, it's alright. Ada's here," Her hand met the cold, clammy skin of Ragna's clenched fist. "You're alright now—Ah!"

A wet hand shot out, slamming into Ada's neck with a crushing grip. Crazed emerald eyes that shone through bloody locks of hair, were filled with the fear and rage of a cornered animal

"You will not take me, *hóra Loka! Þú munt ekki taka mig! (whore of Loki! You will not take me!)"* screamed Ragna.

The maid struggled against the choking vice, desperate to break her queen of the horrifying memory that had imprisoned her reality. "My Queen! Awaken! Please! Remember—Ah! Remember your...ugh—consort. Prince Alcaeus!"

"Alcaeus... Alcaeus...*ástin mín.*" mumbled Ragna, a mere whisper compared to her previous scream. "I... I... Ada? My poor sweet Ada." The queen quickly loosened her grip, running her bloody hands along Ada's small face.

She did not flinch away, instead gently placed her small hands over Ragna's, ceasing the movement. "Yes, My Queen, it is I. You are safe now. It's alright. Come, let us get you into the bath. Nothing a nice hot bath can't fix. I shall even use your favourite scents; lily of the valley, patchouli, and maybe some orange oil?"

"Yes... Yes, water," whispered Ragna, her face vacant. Lost.

Ada gently dragged the bloody sheets away, careful not to startle her queen. Taking the queen's hand, she coaxed her off the bed, holding strong when Ragna stumbled slightly.

"Where is he?" croaked the queen. "Where is he!" Now at a scream, the queen's eyes became wild and enraged. "ALCAEUS!" Green flames burst from her, crawling down her body.

The fingers of flame reached for the dead bodies around her and the dead fleshed jerked. Muscles spasmed, joints reflexing. Even the severed limbs began to dance to her tune of death.

"My Queen! Please!" pleaded Ada, her tiny hands out in front of her. "I will bring Alcaeus!"

Suddenly, the queen collapsed to her knees on the floor, leaning forward on her two hands. Ada put her hand out to touch her shoulder, but froze at the sinister giggle coming from the bloody figure. A severed forearm and hand grasped its way to the Necromancer, desperate to reach its master.

"You... You are not Alcaeus!" Ragna screamed, grabbing it only to tear the hand at the wrist from the forearm in one motion.

Ada smacked her hands over her mouth, unable to contain her horror. She squelched her nauseous reaction. Just as quickly, she let her hands fall to her side. The last thing she wanted was Ragna to smell her fear. When she was in the grip of her madness, the queen could not recognize friend from foe and Ada very much enjoyed living.

"A moment, My Queen. I will go and fetch your beloved." But before she could move a few feet from the queen, the door opened.

Councillor Malcom, one of the queen's closest advisors, walked through. Behind him was Prince Alcaeus, followed by four of the Queen's Guard.

"My Queen! I brought him! I knew you would want him—"

"OUT! GET OUT!" Ragna screamed. Everyone jumped, save for the Consort who remained unmoving and unreadable. Even the guards flinched in the face of their queen. They quickly made their exit, although Councillor Malcom hesitated as he stared at the small Brownie woman. She gave him a reassuring nod and, with a curt one of his own, the counsellor made his escape.

"I-I'll get the bath ready," said Ada. She stopped at the door, turning to the Royal Consort. "My Prince, would you please assist the Queen?" Normally, Ada would have never dared speak to Prince Alcaeus in such a manner, but the queen's hold on him had eliminated any consequences the little maid would have normally feared.

As Ada disappeared into the washroom, Ragna put a bloody hand in the air.

"Yes, be a good little puppet and help your Queen."

The prince's face was stone as he obeyed, stiffly taking her hand in his. Ragna climbed up his body, staining his clothes in sticky blood. At full height, she rested her head against his shoulder, her arms wound tightly around his waist. Alcaeus did not return the embrace.

"Oh, my sweet prince," cooed Ragna, "The Norns gave you me. Only you. My mistress promised me the power. Promised me you'd be mine if I just let Loki... Let the men... let the dead... have me... so I could have you. My sweet, sweet reward." She pulled away, gazing longingly up at him. In an instant, rage contorted her features. Flesh against flesh, a resounding slap echoed throughout the room. Alcaeus made no move to block her, his face snapping to the side. His hair covered whatever expression he had as he remained unmoving. "Then you had to go and marry *her*! The Unseelie bitch! She touched you! When you were mine! MINE!" she screamed. Ragna's face fell, almost as if in remorse. "Oh but, my Alcaeus, do not worry, I made it right! Now you're mine." She laid her head back against his firm shoulder once more.

"My Queen, your bath is ready," interrupted Ada, her sweet voice cutting through the chaos.

An uncharacteristic giggle erupted from Ragna as she took the prince's hand, leading them to her private bathing room.

It was not a tub or open shower area that were standard in other washrooms throughout Castle Fyrkat; it was a massive pool centred in a huge chamber that rivalled the size of her bedroom.

Letting go of Alcaeus' hand, she stepped in front of the pool's steps. Waving away Ada's helping hand, Ragna let her nightgown drop to the ground in a wet heap. She stepped into the glassy water, her movements causing soft ripples throughout. She turned, hand in the Royal Consort's direction.

"Come, *ástin mín*, join me," she beckoned.

Alcaeus shook his head, his posture becoming rigid. "I've already bathed, Your Majesty. I still need to meet with the Council—"

"I said, come!" snapped Ragna. "Obey me."

The prince's face was determined. "No. I will not join you willingly, Ragna."

Queen Ragna's eyes glittered at his defiance. In a flash, she was before him, water dripping from her naked body. "That can be arranged." The necklace holding his soul appeared. Just as Alcaeus attempted to snag it from her grasp, green flames erupted between both of them. Then it receded, leaving Alcaeus in a glow. Only his eyes held her flame, empty of all emotion or life.

Ragna grinned, satisfied.

"Ada, help the Consort undress. Cut the clothes if you have to." The Brownie maid quickly went to do her queen's bidding. Ragna watched as Ada cut away the prince's shirt, watching eagerly as it fell to the ground. Once his boots were removed, the maid went to undo his belt.

"Slowly, Ada, slowly. I want to enjoy this." said Ragna. Doing as she was commanded, slowly the prince's trousers fell to the floor. "Wonderful. Now, *ástin mín*, come."

CHAPTER 27

My Mark burned so badly, I woke with a yelp. Inexplicable rage coursed through me with a vengeance. I fisted the sheet, one hand slapping against it, when a fresh wave of burning coursed through it.

"Fuck!" I cried. "Ahhh!" Shaking, my breaths came in shallow gulps.

Ruarc responded quickly, on his knees next to me. "Melisandre, what is the matter? Are you hurt?"

"The Mark!" I wheezed in agony. "It's burning!"

"Shit," he cursed. "Ragna must be...hold on. Trust me, Alchemist!" Pinning me down, he yanked my head to the side and removed my hand from the magical symbol where my neck met my shoulder. My body fought him despite knowing he was trying to help.

"W-why? What's happening?" I cried, desperately confused.

"Your prince is in trouble." Ruarc slapped his hand to my Mark, gripping it violently. The buzz of magic hit me like a freight train. I dry-heaved, thankful my stomach was empty.

The Unseelie King began chanting in such an ancient form of Gaelic, it was indecipherable. My Mark responded by shooting searing pain throughout my body. My whole form stiffened against the onslaught; if it wasn't for Ruarc pinning me down, I would have come off the bed.

Consciousness became fuzzy, disorienting. Then, it happened. Just like when Alcaeus and I had done the second Mark, I felt my consciousness slip through a vortex, except this time, I went past where we had met with our souls and straight into the Nightmare Prince's mind.

I gasped. I was naked. Wet. Staring into Ragna's closed eyes. She was kissing me.

No, not me. Alcaeus.

Wrath rushed through me and I felt the Philosopher's Stone answer my call.

"Wait, Melisandre! Don't let Ragna know it's you. Let me!" Ruarc was with me, his mental call as if his thoughts were right beside mine.

Yes.

I felt it then. Raw primordial magic crashing through my mind. A thousand ravens swarmed to the surface and through our connection; eyes glowing red, their beaks and talons razor sharp, past the barriers of Alcaeus' eyes. The cacophony of their squawks tested the limits of hearing. The black cloud of birds hit Ragna so hard her naked body catapulted out of the water and smacked into the far stone wall. Landing with a sickening crack, she crumpled to the ground. The ravens gave one last circle before extinguishing like a puff of smoke.

*"**Mikrós asvós?**"* Alcaeus' voice was broken, noticing my presence in his mind.

Alcaeus! I—

Before I could continue the thought, his own black cloud surrounded him just as I felt myself being thrown from his mind. Suddenly, I was staring into Ruarc's intense face, his hair a curtain around us.

"Get off," I snapped, pushing myself up and away from him, desperate to get out of the bed.

"What are you doing? Wait!" demanded Ruarc, rolling off to the other side.

Only in my black silk nightie, I snagged the matching black dressing robe and slipped my arms through. Tying the sash in mid-step for the door, my body was swung about when Ruarc grabbed my arm.

"Where are you going? It's midday!" he blustered.

"I need to go to him. I need to see him!" I said, determination and desperation of equal measure in my voice. Jerking my arm from him, he continued to try to dissuade me.

"He is a Champion, Melisandre! Prince Alcaeus will live. You saw it. Ragna is an unconscious lump on the floor. Your lover is fine—"

"No! He is not fine, Ruarc. I know he's not," I insisted. "I don't care if you're the strongest gladiator demi-god there is, capable of wiping entire armies—I will not allow him to face this kind of darkness alone."

"Alchemist, he *is* the darkness—"

"Then I shall be his light!" I snapped back. Jaw clenching, I fought my frustration. "He needs me, Ruarc. Let me go."

Our stare-down held many things; Ruarc's concern, annoyance, pleading. Mine, immoveable, pain, truth.

My heart hurt so badly. Yes, I could skin Ragna alive, among many other creative forms of torture, for the unimaginable pain she had caused Alcaeus. But I could not bear the thought of him being alone. There was a short glimpse of a thought before he had shut me out. One of holding me. Of our bodies tangled together, his head in my arms as I held him against my heart. No one would stop me from being that for him. Even for just a moment.

"Don't follow me. Don't try to stop me. You will fail." Were my final words as I slipped into the corridor, the door shutting behind me.

It was silent in the castle, only guards and the occasional servant scurrying to and fro. Bare feet slapping against the rugs and marble, I headed straight for the Library. Something told me he would not be in his rooms, where Ragna could easily find him. No, there was only one place I knew he would go.

Making haste across the courtyard, the sun's heat barely touched me against the protection of the cold December. Bursting through the great library doors, the lights were low, but still present. My heart raced and my sides burned, mentally kicking myself for neglecting my anaerobic fitness. But there was no time to rest. Sprinting to Sage Kevyn's office, I didn't bother knocking; just swinging the door open.

My heart plummeted. Empty.

"Damnit," I whispered. "Damnit!" I swung the door closed in frustration, although it was too heavy to slam. All the air went out of me and my shoulders slumped. "You were supposed to be here..."

Catching sight of the chair, the one that held such delicious memories, I trudged over to it, plopping down. My hands skimmed the armrests as my heart clenched at the memories pouring through me. Tears began to gather in my eyes and I hung my head in my hands.

Then I heard it. Soft notes below me. Piano. Shooting up out of the seat, I began to look for a hatch, or anything resembling a door. Frantically pulling aside rugs and furniture showed nothing.

The playing stopped.

"Fuck! Where is it? Where is it!" I cried, slipping into my Alchemist's Vision. There. The desk!

I rushed over to it, pulling out drawers, lifting items perched on top. Nothing. Pushing against it did nothing. Nothing. Frustratingly, the desk was coated in magic; transmutation would likely fail.

Collapsing to my knees, ready to concede defeat, my eyes caught a symbol underneath the desk. Crawling closer, the black markings stood out–Alcaeus' symbol. I touched it. Clicks, gears shifting, wood scraping over wood, and the desk moved back, revealing stone steps.

Excitement tore through me and I quickly went to descend into the darkness. Torches stood flameless and I grabbed one and, with a flash of transmutation, it flared to life.

The stairs seemed to go on forever, my knees were begging me to rest for a moment. But I couldn't. Finally, my cold feet touched the even colder floor. Walking down a long hallway, I held the torch out in front of me, until the outline of a partially opened door came into view. Transmuting a sconce next to the door, I fixed the torch there. Gently, I pushed the door further open, stepping into a large cavern. There was nothing much to see in the darkness, except for the lone candle standing on the closed top of a stunning grand piano. The elements of mahogany and gold called to me but it was lost to the scene before me.

There was Alcaeus, hunched over the keys, his hair still wet. He was still naked.

Heartbreak seared through me and I bit my lip from letting out the sounds of my sorrow at the sight of my warrior. The once proud, wise gladiator was nowhere to be found; instead, there sat a broken shell of a man with the great weight of suffering and loss bearing down on him.

"Alcaeus?" I said his name tentatively, taking slow steps toward him.

"You should not be here. You cannot be here. You are just another one of Ragna's illusions. Her tricks." His response was hollow and empty. It broke me.

My steps continued, slowly but with surety. "Ragna has not the mental capabilities to imagine a single selfless thought, let alone create the likes of me. But I should be here. This is the only place I should be. With you."

Painstakingly slow, his head turned to me. Even sitting down, our height almost matched, my head only slightly above his.

Just when I thought my heart could not break more, I saw the look in his eyes. They were the eyes of a prisoner of war. Of one who had suffered at the hands of another for over a thousand years. It was the stare of someone who had had everything he cherished ripped from him.

"Are you truly real?" he asked, that rich baritone voice breaking slightly.

Upon reaching him, I took his face in my hands. My thumbs caressed his cheeks and I leaned down, placing a gentle kiss on his forehead. "Does this feel real?" Then I placed another on each cheek, and on each eye. His eyes remained closed and I took a moment to let my gaze roam over this breathtakingly handsome man before me, soaking up every aspect of his face. Leaning closer, I said, "I am real. The beat of your heart calls my name, remember?" Reaching down, I took his hand in mine and placed it over my heart. "This is real. Its beat is telling you that you are mine." He shuddered and, desperate to not let him be swallowed up in darkness, my lips pressed lightly against his. I made no move to deepen it, letting him just feel me.

For a moment, Alcaeus held still. With a swift intake of breath, he answered my kiss, swallowing my noise of surprise as he stood and pulled me into a back-breaking embrace. My arms quickly went around him, threading my fingers through his damp hair and then journeying across his shoulders and back.

His tongue plunged into my mouth with such veracity that all I could do was open wider, submitting myself to his kiss. Hands rushed up and down my body, one circling to the front and cupping my breast in a bruising hold. I cried out, but Alcaeus swallowed the sounds with his hot kiss. I welcomed the pleasure-pain. The darkness, the moment, demanded so much more than just simple desire. It needed both.

The hand on my back dipped low, squeezing and palming one cheek, hard. Rough fingers barely grazed inside as he spread my flesh wider. Whimpering, I pulled at him, needing more. Suddenly, he wrenched my head back, my eyes shooting open and meeting his fierce and wild gaze.

"I need you. Not like before. Not like in any way we have had. I need it to be my way," he growled out. "Please, *mikrós asvós*, let me have you... I will stop the moment our desires no longer match."

Let me have you how I want you. Help me gain control back over my own body. My own pleasure. That is what I really heard him say. The message he needed to convey.

Searching his eyes, I replied softly, "Then have me. I am yours. All I ask is that you do not hold back." His eyes widened at my last words, before being replaced with violent heat. Then, everything happened so fast.

I was whipped around and lifted; the front of my hips shoved against the piano. A force I couldn't see grabbed onto my wrists, yanking me forward so my chest was squished against the cold piano surface. The same force slid against my ankles before pulling my legs wide, to the point my limbs shook from the tension.

Both my nightgown and matching silk robe, that came up to midthigh, were now shoved above my derriere, and the cold draft of the cavern caused my skin to prickle and shiver. But warmth quickly came to the rescue as the feel of Alcaeus' large hands pressed and slid up my thighs. The tip of his nose tickled the sensitive skin there, the nearness of his face so close to my nether region causing me to clench in nervous anticipation. His deep inhale and whoosh of hot breath against my black panties had me releasing my own exhale. The sharp pull and the sound of fabric being torn from me forced a whimper but I said nothing. My excitement at what was about to happen was no doubt clear to Alcaeus, the evidence nearly dripping from my lower lips if the smell of my want didn't hit him first. I didn't need warming up; the anticipation for him and seeing this unknown, primal side to my Fated was enough to have me ready for him.

Without warning, he thrust his strong tongue between my folds and inside me. With a sharp gasp at the welcome intrusion, my nails slid uselessly against the varnish as I fisted my hands. Yet the warmth of his mouth did not last long, only long enough to confirm my readiness. Alcaeus only gave me a brief touch before shoving himself inside me until his hips were flush against mine. A cry ripped from my throat, and breathing seemed impossible in the single moment he gave me before he thrust hard again, demanding my body accept him. And accept him, it did.

His strong hands were like metal clamps on my hips, the bruising pain a delicious balance to the overwhelming pleasure each thrust of his cock brought. My prince took advantage of every inch the inside of me gave him, rutting into me like an animal. The combination of raw emotions and the physical neglect of not being able to see each other gave way to an explosive sensation I couldn't begin to describe.

Pounding away at me, the consistent slam against that most pleasurable spot had me screaming my release far sooner than I was prepared to. But Alcaeus refused to let me linger there.

"Not yet. More," he grunted, panting behind me. "Give me more of you!"

My arms were suddenly jerked above my head, forcing my spine to bow. My legs were still spread wide, several inches off the ground so my core met Alcaeus' groin perfectly. Hands reached around me, grasping my breasts before pinching and twisting my nipples, a pleasurable shout springing from my throat. Letting go of one, his hand slid down my stomach until the tips of his fingers brushed against my clit. One large finger covered it, then flicked it back and forth before settling on a circular pattern. My cries became louder, in tandem with his continued thrusts. My orgasm built quickly upon the intense stimulation of my nipple and clit, my toes curling before my body seized and I screamed my release.

Alcaeus moaned as my walls clenched hard around him, continuing his pace. When the stimulation became too much I cried, "Please, Alcaeus! I-It's too much! I can't—" A hand gripped me by the throat, the magic holding me, which allowed him to pull me so his mouth dragged against my ear.

"Yes, you can," he murmured, the command in his tone sparking a new wave of lust inside me. I moaned in answer, gasping and clenching as he squeezed my neck harder before slipping two fingers in my mouth. "Suck." My tongue ran over every line, every edge of his thick, rough fingers as they returned the massaging motion. "Make them wet. As wet as your prize. Good." They were suddenly ripped from my mouth with a wet *pop!* only for me to feel them sliding between my cheeks, right above where Alcaeus' cock had slowed his movement. Understanding what he was doing, anticipation and nervousness gripped me.

"Alcaeus..." I choked off his name when I felt the pads of his fingers circling my puckered hole before slowly pressing, patiently waiting for my flesh to give way. And when it did, his finger slipped deep before pulling back, only to push harder back in once more. This time, he added a second finger, letting out a husky groan as he pushed his hand inside me all the way to his knuckles.

My cry was primitive, my eyes fluttering back in my skull as he continued to play with my ass while still moving his cock inside me in short, quick thrusts.

"More," he groaned. I couldn't even begin to contemplate what that meant until he suddenly removed his fingers and I felt my cheeks being spread as wide as they could go. Then I felt it. *Magic.*

The darkness masked the black smoky power that both Ruarc and Alcaeus seemed to have but I felt it *there*. I felt it there, right where Alcaeus' fingers had been. A phallic shape pressing against my hole with slow but deliberate persistence.

The sensation was so overwhelming, I subconsciously struggled until Alcaeus grabbed me by the throat once more.

"Take it, Melisandre," was his guttural whisper into my ear, "Take all of me. Take the darkness and let me break you with it." His grip was tight enough I felt the rush from the pressure but I could still speak.

"Yes," I gasped, trying to relax my body against his penetration. My tender flesh gave way with stinging pleasure as both my holes were filled by him. Mouth wide in a scream, I couldn't even get the sound out, as the feel of another magic-shaped phallus filled the empty space between my teeth. There was no visibility but I felt every ridge, every inch of the velvet-smooth steel that was Alcaeus' cock in my mouth.

Hand still gripping my throat, his other grabbed my hip as an anchor, pulling slowly out before shoving back inside me. The ones in my mouth and ass mimicked his movements. As soon as he saw the one in my ass moved smoothly, he began thrusting inside me at an unforgettable speed and force.

My howls of pleasure were muted by the cock in my mouth, never engaging my gag-reflex but so close to pushing the limit. Alcaeus continued his onslaught. The pressure between my legs was immense, almost too overwhelming. Every minute or so, the hand wrapped firmly around my small neck squeezed, cutting off my air, only to release me just as the instinctual need for breath clawed at me. The rush of blood and oxygen sent wave after wave of pleasure through me and I came twice more, and yet my lover showed no signs of stopping.

Time was of no consequence here. The outside world didn't exist. The only reality was the one Alcaeus created within me and all around me. Every part of me was at his mercy, at his command. Tears of pleasure wet my face, drool dripping down into a lewd puddle on the piano as the cock in my mouth continued its savage thrusting.

Finally, the one in my mouth was ripped away. The hand around my neck slid up to grab my face, palm covering my mouth as my head was forced backward. Alcaeus' arm wrapped around my waist as he thrust into me deeply, holding me flush against his hips. I cried out against his palm, squeezing my eyes shut at the absolute fullness inside me. Pressing his cheek against the side of my head, the heat of his panting breath scorched my skin as his full lips teased my ear.

"You are everything to me, Melisandre," he said. "Every part of you was made for me, just as I was made for you. This," he pulled himself back only to thrust hard enough to elicit a cry from me, "is yours. Not hers. This is all. For. You." Then he released a volley of thrusts, faster and harder than before. My eyes watered at the pleasure-pain crashing into me, my mind breaking with the intensity. Screaming against his palm, I shattered just as he roared his own release, pumping into me with shorter thrusts before finally stilling. The warmth of his climax coated my inner walls and I went limp against him.

"I love you, light of mine," was the last thing I heard before the darkness stole my consciousness away.

CHAPTER 28

"Mm... oh," I groaned, flexing slightly as every part of me protested. My eyes were the last to move, cracking them open slowly. It was the lazy feel of fingers trailing over my body that had dragged me from sleep and it was the first thing that came into focus. Only a single candle burned by us, outlining Alcaeus' face gently.

We lay among a plethora of blankets and even a few furs on the stone ground. The initial inky blackness had shrouded this little resting area when I had come in. Alcaeus was propped on his elbow, his eyes roaming over my body. His expression was just as shadowed as the rest of the room as fingers continued to trace delicately over me.

Only the corner of the blanket covered me, just beneath my breast but the rest of me was exposed, but I was not cold in the slightest. No, the heat from Alcaeus' body was enough to keep me comfortably warm, the chill of the room a nice balance that prevented me from overheating.

My own finger reached up to trace the path of his cheek and jaw, the act drawing his eyes to my face. We shared a moment of intimacy, each enjoying the others' attention. Pulling back slightly, the tips of his fingers glided up and down my forearm, examining the finer details that made up my limb. I closed mine into a fist as his larger one engulfed it with ease before releasing me and going back to tracing the lines of me.

"So fragile. So delicate. A vast contradiction to my own physical attributes and yet," his delicate touches turned to a firm grip as his hand moulded with mine, "Haphaestus himself could not have crafted a more perfect fit." Alcaeus' voice was only slightly above a whisper but his deep tone still carried in the space. I could sink into the depths of it, the richness both comforting and arousing. Suddenly, his touch found my face, his gaze capturing mine as he tried to see beyond just my face. "I wondered what emotions would greet me when you awoke, now that you have seen this side of me." The fingers that had sought to memorise my body, now caressed my cheekbone. "I do not see any hate, nor resentment behind those beautiful eyes," he said softly, still searching my face, but he came to a stop when his gaze settled where his thumb slowly stroked my bottom lip. "Still, I must apologise—"

I cut him off with the finger that had been caressing his face, shaking my head. "No apologies. Never apologise for being who you are or expressing your needs with me," I said quietly. "Especially when it was more than welcomed. It's one more facet of you that I can enjoy."

Relief washed over his features, laying a kiss against the pad of my index finger. "How do you feel? I was not gentle."

I could barely suppress the devious giggle of satisfaction as the memory of being filled so deliciously came racing back. "Sore, most certainly. Yet, absolutely content," I smiled, turning my face to his. "Well...I am having a bit of a moral conundrum." At this, he stiffened but raised a curious brow at the mirth that danced across my face. "Alchemists and magic don't mix, remember? I cannot help but wonder if it is sacrilege for an Alchemist to be fucked by magic? Or do I have the excuse that it was merely a utilisation of the absence of light and that, truly, my own imagination is at fault?" A giggle escaped me at the theological chaos our activities had sprouted in my mind. "No matter. Just promise me that will not be the only time I get to experience your *darkness*."

His grin was full of promise as he smiled down at me. "Oh, the little badger likes it, does she? I would like to believe your Mother Nature would have you intimately acquainted with all aspects of her." Alcaeus stole a quick kiss in between smiles. "Now, if only you could have experienced my true glory when I was whole." Those teasing fingers turned into heady skin to skin exploration. "I would have you naked for weeks, addicted to my touch, wrapped in my magic and consumed by it."

Writhing, I slowly raised my arms above me and opened myself up to him. "I am already addicted to you," I let out a soft whimper as his hand hunted down my body before laying claim to my breast. "Rather, I am addicted to the unabashed version of you."

My words ended in a hitch when he leaned down to suck and swirl my nipple and tease the weight of my flesh there. But then Alcaeus' movement slowed and pulled back, dragging my own attention out of the heady fog he had teased me into. The pensive look taking over his face had chased away the rest of my lingering desire.

"We must go back." His words were so quiet, barely spoken.

I swallowed, waiting a moment to answer, as if my words themselves would rush the process. Pulling the blanket further over me, I shifted to my side to face him and snuggled closer.

"I know." I whispered back. The elbow he was perched on, extended for my head to lay on, while his other arm curled around my waist and held me. Wanting desperately to spend more time with him, I asked, "I remember the feel of your magic and the fear it brought with it. But I've never seen it so clearly. Alchemists cannot see magic nor manipulate it, so how can I suddenly experience it so vividly?"

"That is most likely the Mark manifesting itself," he answered. Alcaeus rested his chin on top of my head. "Although, my ability to call the Darkness has grown so much stronger since we completed the second bite. Only Ruarc and I have the ability to bend it to our will, as we were both created from it."

"That's right," I remembered. "When Ruarc took me away, he used the darkness to bind you. But how? If you can both control it wouldn't Ragna also be able to—"

"Because Ragna cannot," he interjected. "Many make the mistake that death and death magic are born of the dark but death is but an infant in the face of darkness, for the Dark came first."

No response came from me. Instead, I was mulling over his words, the feel of him, the blissful quiet of the cavern. Here, Ragna couldn't touch us. Couldn't take over Alcaeus and take him from me. Just the thought had the slithering feel of vengeful anger at her touching him crawling through me. My hand that had been petting his chest, curled into a fist and I hid my face away so I could deal with my anger privately.

"I'll kill her," I whispered. "I can't let you go back to her when I know she'll just.. She'll..." Swallowing hard, my teeth ground together as my voice grew stronger. "This facade Ruarc and I are playing at will not last much longer, Alcaeus. Not after what Ruarc did. Ragna will know and..." Sitting up now, my face still came below his, my nose nearly brushing his lips. "She will never touch you like that again. I refuse.

Toby is safe. Elis is safe. There is nothing stopping me from—"

"No, Melisandre, do not even think it! Even knowing you are the Philosopher's Stone, this castle is *filled* with Champions—" He tried to sit up with a jerk, only for me to put a hand to his shoulder and he let me shove him back down so his back met the blankets as I straddled him.

"I don't care," I pressed, my gaze boring into his. "I would take on every Champion in the Otherworld; render the earth silent if it meant giving you back what was wrongfully stolen." His face went slack at my confession, just as those beautiful dark eyes filled with a deeper emotion. "Tomorrow, I will fight. I am not a warrior. I am not many things that will be required to ensure victory against the Tengu. But I will not fail. Defeat will never know my name. Not when you are the prize."

In one motion, Alcaeus grabbed the back of my head, wrapped an arm around my waist and rolled us. His lips met mine in a manner that expressed his feelings deeper and more explicitly than any language could do justice. My inner thighs ran up and down his sides, gliding along his muscular legs, and the soles of my feet caressed his calves. I squeezed his body to mine as he consumed my mouth, losing myself in him.

Before, he was ruthless and demanding with his attention. Now, his touch worshipped me, drawing out my pleasure with masterful skill. Hips pressed against mine, I felt Alcaeus begin to harden against my slit, still very wet from our previous coupling. We rocked our hips together in a tantric rhythm, our lips still locked together in an intimate dance.

Then Alcaeus broke away from me, trailing kisses along my neck and shoulder, down the valley of my chest. Grabbing both of my breasts, he kneaded them in his large hands, nipping and licking at the hardened nipples and letting the heat of his breath caress my skin. Then he slid lower, his lips carving a path down my belly, kissing each rune there.

I watched him with heavy lids and rapt attention, my hands losing themselves in his thick chestnut hair. His midnight eyes watched me with just as much depth, a catalyst to the anticipation erupting within me. My heart raced as hot breath blanketed the top of my mons; the teasing temptation of his lips hovering over my flesh had me biting my own lip. When his mouth began exploring my folds, that built-up anticipation snapped, my body inundated with ecstasy.

"Alcaeus," I breathed, savouring his name. Threading through his silky, thick locks of hair, my hands moved with the motions of his head.

My own head rolled back and forth, still incredibly sensitive from our first lovemaking. His tongue slipped inside me, that perfect Greek nose brushing my clit over and over. The Champion between my legs moved with a confidence that one could only have if they'd lived as long as he had; none of the light, hesitant touches I'd experienced with human men. No, Alcaeus devoured every part of me like a starving man yet touched like a mastercraftsman.

My moans became frequent, my breathing coming in short gasps. I rolled my hips to meet his mouth but the hands that controlled the back of my thighs gripped me firmly. They then slid up behind my knees, pushing them closer to my chest. Alcaeus grabbed my hands from his head, placing them on the top of my knees.

"Hold them there," he commanded. "Don't move." I whimpered but complied as he laid a kiss on each inner thigh before turning his attention back to my needy core.

My nails dug into the skin of my knees as Alcaeus' movements became more rapid, my breathing matching his pace. Heart racing, my body began to tense. Head rolling, I focused on the velvet strength that searched my most intimate places. Jolts of electricity shot through me whenever the tip of his tongue swiped over my clit and my breath caught. But he didn't stop there. No place was safe from his adventurous search. It didn't take long for him to transform me into a quivering mess, ready for release. Alcaeus felt the change in my body, speeding up but then maintaining a consistent pace. Unable to hold onto my knees any longer, I threaded my hands through his hair once more, gripping him to me. His only response was a masculine grunt against me as my hold tightened, keeping his demanding, pressuring pace.

My teeth ground against the tidal wave that was my impending climax. Then I was nothing but a silent scream as my body bowed, shuddering as it hit me. Alcaeus held me down, riding the sensations with me. When I finally released the tension with a gasp, he released me, coming to a kneeling position and resting on his back heels. Watching me. The tender emotions on his face when our heady gazes collided was so intimate my heart swelled. With a look like that, I didn't feel exposed; quite the opposite. There was contentment to be found under his perusal. I felt...beautiful. Desired. Wanted.

Though our act had left him ready, the tip of him weeping with arousal, Alcaeus made no move to rectify it. Just soaked in the image of me splayed before him.

"If only time could stop for but a moment," I whispered, my voice still husky from pleasure.

A small smile crept along his face. "I would stop time for eternity just to capture this image of you." His wet lips captivated me, evidence that validated the afterglow in my body. He took a moment more; eyes flicked down and then climbed back up to my face before that sombre expression broke the spell. "But we must return. Ragna has woken and is searching for me. If she does not find you with Ruarc, I fear no tradition this Yalda will be honoured in the face of her wrath."

The chill of the room hit me with an ugly vengeance. Disappointment leaked into my veins just as my stomach dropped with the inevitable future looming over us. Fighting the urge to reach out and hold Alcaeus to me one last time, I nodded, schooling my features. My skin prickled and I sat up, seeking my nightie.

Then, suddenly Alcaeus was there, capturing my lips with a kiss that was filled with desperation, the key to breaking the fragile hold I had on my own emotions. He followed me back down to the ground, my arms and legs wrapping around his body as he settled into me. Rough, calloused hands dragged along my body as if to memorise every curve and crevice of me, my own movements matching with the same reckless abandon.

The tip of him grazed my entrance and I attempted to align my hips to it, a silent plea to have him fill me once more. We both knew we didn't have time. We both knew the right decision was to quickly disperse, continue this ridiculous charade if only to give Zhenbai more time to release the curse on Alcaeus' kingdom.

But hope was a fantasy in this darkness; the physical feel of one another was real.

Alcaeus gave in, the tip of his cock pressing harder and harder into me until my body gave way, where he sheathed himself to the hilt. Pressing even deeper still, just as I liked it, my lips broke away to a gasping moan. He swallowed it, demanding my tongue's attention while using the weight of his hips to continue dragging whimpers from me. When he began to move, it was with passionate purpose; not as hard or as punishing as earlier, no. But with sure and steady strokes.

Alcaeus made love to me. My body hugged and rocked with his in return, my hips moving in time with the intimate rhythm. This wasn't about reaching climax; this was an expression of all the words I dared not speak out loud. It was about accepting that this could be our last moment together in the unforeseeable future.

When we could hold on no longer, I did something so very unlike myself.

"Bite me, Alcaeus. I know she has sapped much of your strength so… take what you need," I offered, baring my neck to him.

Midnight black eyes dilated, flicking to my jumping pulse then back to my eyes. Licking his full lips, Alcaeus asked hoarsely, "Are you sure?"

Not trusting my voice, I simply nodded, remaining open for him. Closing my eyes, I afforded myself the heightened sensation of his nose skimming just underneath my earlobe before his lips continued the journey. My own lips parted as his hips dominated my own and his arms snaked underneath me; one weaving into my hair to anchor my head, the other coming to rest on the top of my scalp.

There was a frenzy of sensation and Alcaeus' hips worked in short but purposeful strokes. Then he struck, hips pinning mine with as much force at the same time. My mouth opened to scream but the hand on top of my head slid down, an iron force covering the noise. A muted whimper was all that could be heard as Alcaeus had me pinned in every way possible. The removal of his teeth and the long pull of blood was a shot of ecstasy through my veins and my eyes rolled. Buzzing heat scorched my neck and my core began to match the heat building within me. Long and steady but for only a few minutes, before the almost painful press of his tongue against the wound indicating enough blood had been consumed.

Releasing my head, Alcaeus pushed up on his fists and I almost mourned the loss of closeness but the vision of him above me, the look of pure desire on his face, took my breath away. I lifted my knees in order to shift my hips to better accommodate the increase of speed Alcaeus readied for. My hands glided up his arms only to end in cupping his face to bring him down for a quick kiss. I didn't care that there was a strong taste of metallic copper that was me upon his tongue. I was after the intimacy the kiss brought while his hips pounded into me, chasing release for both of us.

When it finally came, and my mental galaxy exploded from plea-sure, we collapsed together. For a moment more we held each other be-fore the cold bitterly reminded us our time was up. Both of us moved with a hint of lament; jerky actions portraying the mutual regret of our moments coming to an end.

"Are we really going to fight each other?" I asked, finding my silk nightie and slipping it on.

Alcaeus had summoned his own clothes, and was quickly tying his breeches when he simply answered, "Yes." Waiting for him to continue only brought more silence.

I paused, staring at him. "That's it? Just 'yes'? Is that all you have to say? Alcaeus, there has to be another way. I won't fight you." Suddenly I was staring at the Prince of Nightmares; not my lover.

"You will do whatever you can to survive, Melisandre." He stalked over to me, taking me by the shoulders. "Upon my word, I will never willingly lay a hand on you. But we both know Ragna will take control. When she does, and if you see an opening—strike, and strike true. Do not hesitate. We have not completed the mark, so the most damage you should take from my death will be... purely emotional, I should hope." He grazed a thumb over my cheek in a thoughtful manner; his tone, softening. "You once said that you were an Alchemist, that you were not made for love. Perhaps it is wise to embrace that ideology in the days to come." With that, he began to pull away but I caught his hands.

"No, how could you...? Please, no, don't say that," I replied earnest-ly. "It's not...it's not like that...any more." Swallowing hard, my words ended in a whisper. But before he could press me on that, I quickly con-tinued, "That is the worst-case scenario. We still have a bit longer; Zhen-bai could find a way—"

"We are out of time!" Alcaeus uncharacteristically snapped. Closing those midnight eyes, he took a long measured breath. "My love... Even one such as I, knows when to accept defeat. Let us do so with dignity."

A scowl overtook my features as I shoved his hands away to jab an angry finger into his chest. "If you think for one moment I came all this way, suffered the evils of portals, prevailed over every instinctive need in using Ruarc's body to create a supernova explosion to make for damn sure that Ragna gets her arse sent back to Hel in microscopic pieces, just for you to give up, then by the Mother—THINK AGAIN! !" My heart pounded with a prevailing fire I was determined to use to light a matching one in Alcaeus. "The words you spout are not the words of Alcaeus Pallas! Everything is possible until it is not! And even then, what is living if not to push the limits of the impossible until something is possible?" My scowl became even fiercer as I closed as much space between us as I could, taking his face in my hands. "You will not lose yourself to Ragna. I forbid it."

There, a glimmer of his old self peeked through at me; the dance of laughter in those eyes. With a gusty sigh, Alcaeus clinked his forehead against mine. "How could I, when it is you who has the true power over my heart and soul?" His lips replaced where our heads touched, bestowing a gentle kiss there. "Thank you, mikrós asvós. No light has burned brighter against my darkness than you."

Refusing to let me have the last word, Alcaeus' shadows consumed us. His lips found mine before releasing me abruptly enough I stumbled. The normally soft glow of sudden candlelight had me squinting around my new surroundings. The living quarters I shared with Ruarc. And speak of the devil—

"Where the HELL HAVE YOU BEEN?" A very angry Fae king was marching towards me at an alarming rate.

And Alcaeus was gone.

CHAPTER 29

16 Hours earlier...

Ruarc paced. He seemed to be doing that a lot since arriving at Fyrkat Castle. A glance back at the empty bed only ignited his simmering impatience. The Alchemist was as uncontrollable as her creator; a fact that made him both thirsty to find a way to subdue her and desperate for this entire fiasco to be at its end.

He stopped all motion abruptly. He could *smell* them. A raven cawed ominously outside; a warning to its master of the approach of the Queen's Guard.

Banging on the door. Ruarc sniffed. "About time."

Smoky darkness curled around him, caressing his body like an old lover. The glint of Fae blades, now present and strapped down by leather around the king's body, bounced against the blackness as Ruarc made his way to the door, swinging it open.

The queen's seneschal, Oweyn, greeted the Unseelie King with a stiff bow. "Your Highness, Queen Ragna formally requests proof of Lady Von Boden's presence in your rooms—"

Ruarc towered over the slimy minion before him, a predatory smile of sharpened teeth.

"I can do you one better, little cockroach: tell the queen, I shall be in her presence the moment I close this door. It's about time she dealt with me."

"Please! Your Highness, this would be a most inopportune moment—" The door slammed with finality.

Darkness swept around the Unseelie King, loose things around him fluttering and blowing away as he disappeared.

When the black smoke gave way, it was to an even darker room. Not an inconvenience for the King of the Darklings, who walked with confidence to the shrouded woman sitting silently in one of the stuffed chairs in her private sitting room.

The green fire of Ragna's emerald eyes glowed ominously as she acknowledged Ruarc's presence.

"Your audaciousness used to be something I was quite fond of, Ruarc." Ragna's tone was deceptively soft against the night. "For, surely, that boldness was well used in the uprising we claimed victory over. However," her voice became sharp with annoyance, "now it has become most vexing. How dare you use Unseelie magic against me? In my own home."

"Oh, don't be angry with me, Queen of Bones. You left me with little choice; you were causing great discomfort to my intended. Besides, my audacity is one of the most attractive things about me," Ruarc teased, seemingly unbothered by the queen's irritation. "If I remember correctly, it was that very trait you lusted after so beautifully, long ago. Out of all my past lovers, you were certainly one of the most memorable."

"Ah, but not enough to trump the seductive and mighty *Viviane*." Despite the aggressive annunciation of her words, there was no bitterness to be had in Ragna's voice. "If she had not caught your eye, perhaps I could have caged both the Raven and the Owl."

The Unseelie King put a hand on either side of the arm rest, trapping the queen. Their noses almost skimmed with how close he brought himself.

"Never," whispered Ruarc. "I would not make the same mistake that the Nightmare King made."

"Oh? And what mistake was that?" Ragna purred.

That playful smirk deepened. "Bringing life into this world while you still breathed."

The queen trailed a dagger-like nail down Ruarc's face. "Oh, but perhaps I would have slain Viviane. Your attachment to her could have brought me many things."

Snapping up her wrist, he gave her a *tsk tsk*, as if she were a child.

"No, my dear. Vivianne was still a goddess in her own right; she would have brought your body to the depths of a watery oblivion, where you would continuously drown for eternity. We both know this." Brushing a light kiss across her mouth, he pushed off, taking several steps backward, that smirk morphing into a full and mischievous grin. "And now you have the Alchemist to contend with. Oh, how that must drive you...*insane.*" The dark chuckle coming out of him saw Ragna come to a stand. Ruarc began to circle her. "Poor Ragna, always wanting what you can't have—"

"I already have him," she snapped, impatience coating her words. Suddenly, the room lit up as the necklace appeared. "Half of his soul is already mine. It is because of me he still gets to keep the other half; he should be grateful I've given him such freedom. Do not think me a blind fool, Ruarc: not for a moment do I believe that Melisandre has given up on him. But it matters not–Mage Ilirhun's spell and my own soul magic cannot be undone. The Alchemist fights a losing game. And oh, how I enjoy watching her squirm." Smiling, her white canines only seemed to emphasise the insidiousness of her words. "For how could their souls come together when he does not possess one?" A satisfied chuckle escaped. "I will merely claim the other half if she even so much as utters the word 'Fated'."

Ruarc stopped his stalking, stepping into her space once more. A long-tapered finger barely skimmed down her cheek, drawing a path to that luminescent orb resting just above her cleavage. His pupils constricted against the light as he toyed with the necklace.

"A conquered kingdom. Murdering his entire family and all of his men. Ripping his soul in two. Even with his soul in your possession, for over a thousand years Alcaeus has rejected you and continues to do so; is that not enough to tell you he does not love you, Ragna?" The words from the Unseelie King were so quiet, yet they rang out in the room like a thousand gongs, nevertheless. "Why do you continue to fight for him? Are you not tired of this weary one-sided dance?"

Stepping away from him, Ragna laughed. Loudly. She walked to the wall across from her, free of any decoration, and faced it. "I already have what I want from him. If he protests, well, there are ways to fix that, as you've already seen." She placed her hand on the wall and a huge rune lit up with a green glow. "Love did not save your Viviane from the Sickness nor will it save Alcaeus from my will. We are Champions, Ruarc. We are beyond such human attachments. For it is fickle and useless in the face of power and immortality. Come," the wall shimmered, disappearing and revealing a stone staircase, "let us observe the real reason you appeared before me. Unannounced."

Without hesitation, Ruarc followed the queen. His steps were sure-footed. Knowing.

After some travelling down the long staircase, they stepped into a large chamber. Dust and cobwebs indicated the room was untouched, but that was just an illusion. Great statues of Hel, Loki, and Fenris were positioned at three points in the room. At the base of the goddess' statue, stone bodies of rotting humans writhing in agony, were reaching up to Hel; some hopelessly gripping the ends of her dress as if to beg for mercy. Too many to count.

As soon as Ragna approached the goddess' statue, she extended a pale hand outward, and waited. Ruarc let out a huff, coming up behind her, black muscled arm extending beside hers. Razor sharp claws curled around her hand, engulfing it. A small gasp escaped the queen as the point of one of those spears pierced the delicate skin of her wrist. Blood welled until a small stream snaked down her forearm. Ruarc turned her wrist, holding it over the statues of the dead. The red against white stone was a stark offering to the goddess of death.

And she responded.

The dead parted in the middle, while the base of her statue moved back, revealing yet another staircase. Down into the depths.

Power, ancient and coated in a slimy viscosity that could only be interpreted as evil, snaked across the both of them. Ragna let out a gasp of pleasure. The flex of jaw muscles was the only reaction from the Unseelie king.

Emerging into a massive cavern, Ruarc halted at the familiar sight while Ragna continued further in. There were no torches or lighting. No, the green glow that served to highlight the massive chamber came from the thousands of magical runes that covered the walls, the floors, and the ceiling above.

"Welcome, my queen!" a cloaked figure greeted from a stone desk on the far side of the cavern. A stone slab with a few blankets several feet from it, indicated the man had been here for some time. "How may your humble servant assist you?"

Queen Ragna finally came to a stop at the large body strapped down by magical chains, spread-eagle at the centre of the room. Five other bodies lay similarly, one at each point of the massive pentagram on the floor. Underneath it were massive magic circles, so intricate and filled with ancient runes that even a novice could see that this was where the majority of power came from.

From a single glance, one could tell this had once been a mighty warrior of a man. Pale, long white hair around the head and a matching beard, impressive in its length, lay limp around the figure. But the colour of his hair wasn't due to age, for his skin, though shrunken, still had the smoothness of youth. No, it was as if his very essence had been sucked out.

His mouth was banded by black leather, magical lettering high-lighting it. Face slack, the eyes that gazed out were blank but for the green luminescence of Ragna's power. Her control.

"We have come to see how your progress goes, Mage Ilirhun, for the Unseelie King has yet to see the fruits of his labours."

"The great Oberon, King of the Seelie," said Ruarc, finally closing in the distance, "Champion of the goddess, Ériu. Oh, how the mighty have fallen." He crouched next to the body, his gaze flickering to the other bodies. "And here I thought the rest of the Vampire Champions were all snug in their mausoleums until the end of their thousand-year sleep. I see you've been hard at work with my end of our deal."

"*Yesss*, most hard at work," replied the mage. "I have finally finished attaching the runes to the ley lines. All the spells are in place. Now, it is but a matter of waiting for the planets to align for the summoning."

With a hand out, Ragna stepped over the body with disregard as she scanned the newly placed magic. Like she could touch it, assess it. "Very good, Ilirhun. Ah, this must be the circle enhancing my abilities; I am surprised Oberon had that much left in him. This would explain his current state, it seems."

"Yes, in part, Your Majesty. The other half of his soul is the main source, as you know. I have redirected the Sickness' hunger so that it does not touch you. This circle helps both feed and contain it." The mage noticed Ruarc stiffen. "Do not worry, King Ruarc, you are quite safe from us. The Sickness will not spread while it is contained. Queen Ragna's affinity for death magic very much prevents its spread. She should be immune, according to my findings but... Alas, I have not quite come to understand—"

"We do not need an account of your continuous failures, Ilirhun. The very act of reminding me should have prevented the loosening of that tongue," snapped Ragna.

"No need, I am pleased you have progressed as far as you have," said Ruarc, coming to his feet he took several steps away from Oberon. "Our deal is nearly at its end, it would seem."

"Once the moons have reached their zenith, together as one," replied Ragna, now moving towards him, "and the portal has been opened, then yes. Our deal will be completed. What shall the Unseelie King do, I wonder?" Instead of stepping over Oberon as she did before, her high-heeled foot stepped directly on his chest as she continued her path to Ruarc. No reaction came from the Seelie King.

"You know me, Ragna, I live for chaos. For the war that will ensue. Is that not motive enough?" he asked, watching the queen come closer. "To feel steel against steel and fill the air with smells of blood while ripping tortured screams from my enemies? To rend flesh from bone in the heat of battle? Do I need another reason beyond that which my very essence was created for?"

Now nose to nose, Ragna whispered, "There is always more than that."

Ruarc grinned. "And that is half the fun of it." They stared into each other's eyes, yet both revealed nothing.

Finally, the queen broke the stare. "Your *intended* is, no doubt, searching for mine. I'll allow it this once. Let her enjoy her soon to be slayer. But once and only once. I mean that, King of the Unseelie. Leash that whore or I will do it for you." Her voice hardened with the threat.

Ruarc snorted, crossing his arms. "Yes, because you have succeeded so well in that so far. Fine. I will try my best to reign her in but we both know we are not dealing with just anyone. Your biggest mistake has been underestimating her; which, I confess, I have enjoyed the consequences of that most thoroughly. But keep provoking her by playing with Alcaeus' body before I have had a chance to bypass their mark and this whole plan will erupt in our faces. Mostly yours."

Irritation flashed on Ragna's face. "If you insist, I will stop *right-*

fully playing with what is mine. Once the Alchemist is dead, no more complaints. Besides, with her gone and the Great Owl under my control, nothing will prevent the ritual from succeeding. Now, begone. We are concluded here." She waved a hand dismissively.

In a flash, Ruarc caught her wrist in a threatening grip, their eyes clashing as he invaded her space. "Careful, Queen of Bones. Do not forget your rise to power was because the Unseelie have deemed it so. Alcaeus is yours because of *me*. The ritual's success is because of *me*. I *will* get what I want in the end."

A tendril of fear crept into those emerald eyes, Ragna's gaze flicking between Ruarc's face and where he'd imprisoned her wrist. "I understand."

"Good." With that, darkness swarmed around him and he was gone.

CHAPTER 30

Sometimes, it's rather unfortunate being an Alchemist surrounded by magical creatures. Case in point: the firing of my fast glycolytic fibres is considerably slower than that of a demigod, which means that the firing of my neurons to command my limbs are always a touch behind. The Stone gives me the powers of creation and immortality but, Mother forbid it made me faster. Or taller.

Ruarc's hand merely blinked into existence; his claws curling around my forearm with a punishing hold as he jerked me against the wall of his body.

"Do you even have the slightest idea of the amount of damage I have had to mitigate in your absence?! Ragna has not let on publicly that her intended went *missing* for eighteen hours but her minions have been a pain in my ass!" He veritably shook me till my teeth rattled.

Jerking my arm but failing to break his hold, I snapped back, "You saw what happened! You saw what Ragna was doing to him! Are you really begrudging me for giving Alcaeus a semblance of comfort while you did exactly what we agreed for you to do!"

"Oh, I'm sure the Prince of Nightmares sucked up every ounce of comfort you provided while the rest of us managed the frontlines of that bitch's madness!" Ruarc was incensed, spit nearly flying from his mouth. Nostrils flaring, a darker look took over his face as I'm sure he caught a whiff of Alcaeus and our activities. The cruel grip around my arm twisted as he pulled me closer, ripping a cry from me. "You're drenched in his scent! Have you completely lost any sense or reason? What do you think Ragna will do when she smells that bastard Owl's seed all over you and not mine? Gods, why did I agree to this stupid, idiotic plan with this," he flicked my forehead enough I flinched, swiping at the empty space as he dodged my reaction, "walking political disaster!" The sudden release of my arm had me stumbling backward, glaring at his back as he began walking away.

The Unseelie King had this incredible ability to ignite my anger like it was an endless pit of kerosine. We were two rams on too small of a rock, always fighting to see who had the strongest bash or the biggest horns.

As much as I wanted nothing more than to drown in the watery depths of a bath, if only it meant escaping Ruarc's wrath, my pride had me invading the Fae king's space instead of running from it.

"The only thing due to you is perhaps my gratitude for holding the line until I came back. Nothing more, nothing less! I will not apologise for being there for Alcaeus when he needed me most! Never will I be shamed for being his guiding light! Would you not do the same for your precious Viviane?! If Ragna had her! Bound her! Raping her body and mind—"

"Silence!" he roared, magical darkness wrapping around my neck in a crushing hold before I could move out of the way.

But experience with these magical psychopaths has taught me to be prepared. The flash of a transmutation circle was all the time Ruarc was given before stone spikes from the floor kissed the skin of his own throat. Time stopped between us. Our stares unwavering, filled with all that was unsaid before our actions took over. The haunting pain of the past in his eyes, met the present suffering in mine. The raging intensity in the room started out as sharp as the points pressed against Ruarc, but was now fading into a deep and silent understanding that only those who have lost and suffered much can share.

Ruarc's shadow disintegrated and my transmutation reverted back at a simple mental command. He walked toward me. None of his demeanour indicated the threatening anger that possessed him just moments ago, so I stayed where I was. Lifting my chin so my face was easier to study, he searched me, the rough pad of his thumb gently swiping back and forth.

"You love him." The whisper of his words did nothing to soften the depth of meaning at his statement. Indeed, it wasn't a question. It was an observation. "You really love that silly, idealistic owl, don't you?"

Wonder, disbelief, shock coated those accusing words. "It's always him. They always want *him*. It was *his* name that the crowds roared for. Even Viviane's head turned in his presence..." Ruarc's eyes turned distant, words unveiling a new aspect that hadn't occurred to me; jealousy, maybe, but something deeper. More sinister. Coveting.

But to throw that in Ruarc's face would not only be a low blow, but put us down a path I was unwilling to take if it were true. Neither was he owed an answer in regards to my feelings with Alcaeus.

So instead, I attempted to pacify him by saying, "Heads may have turned, Ruarc, but she chose you. Right 'til the very end."

An arrogant sneer came to his defence, the haughty air of royalty slapping back into every line of his stance. "Of course she did. Only desperate fools who believe in wasting their time would ever succumb to the attentions of half a man, enslaved to another." With that low blow, he marched out the door like it was his own palace.

"I should have said it," I snapped at myself. "Man deserves every kick to the bollocks one could muster." Still grumbling, the bath came as an even greater welcome and escape than before.

The heady smells of cinnamon and clove oil and the splash of the vanilla and musk caressed my senses as I slipped into the hot water. My muscles ached with delicious memory, the ghost of Alcaeus' touch still hovering on my skin. The depths of his passions were just as deep as the sorrows that we both drowned in for hours. But, instead of enjoying the memory or the smells that were meant to be relaxing, my bout with Ruarc left me in an annoyingly depressive state.

Oh, how I wanted to go back to Alcaeus. Back to our hidden cavern with naught but a piano and warm blankets. Or to the cottage, where the birds were always singing in the morning and the setting sun's silence was more of a comforting serenity.

I gulped down the walnut of despair choking my throat and burned my eyes; to erase the pain in those midnight eyes and to live in a world devoid of Ragna was a fantasy indeed, from where we stood.

Pushing forward, I glided to the edge of the magnificent tub, my arms folded over the edge as I let my body float.

You love him.

Letting go of the sides, I slipped below the surface, curling into a ball as my body sunk to the bottom.

You love him.

Alcaeus' face, those tender lines and hidden laughter in that gaze, flashed across my mind. The way he would bend down only to lift me up for a kiss. And that kiss; the way every feeling is laid bare when his tongue dances with mine, beckoning, teasing, then conquering.

You know how this is going to end.

I curled in harder on myself, my need to breathe causing my heart to pound inside my ribs, but there was no desire to leave the water's embrace.

Did I love him? We had barely any time together, all things considering. Yet the time itself was under extreme circumstances; forced to be vulnerable for the sake of necessity. For survival. And yet... What little time we did have, not a moment goes by where I did not crave more. He was like a book that only left me with more questions, yet so captivating I couldn't put it down. Would that be considered love? For I certainly would propose there was no stronger emotion to be felt than when one finds a good book.

So, perhaps I was at love's door but... was I brave enough to open it? Did I have the courage to take that step, knowing that door might be about to close forever thanks to the scheming of Ragna?

Or, maybe... my feet had already crossed the threshold but my mind was still trying to catch up.

Alcaeus' speech of accepting defeat, the hopelessness that was so uncharacteristic of him, grated in the face of my determination. Perhaps I was an idealistic fool.

You once said that you were an Alchemist, that you were not made for love. Perhaps it is wise to embrace that ideology in the days to come. Unease and self-doubt were a poison, clawing and eating away my confidence.

The water suddenly felt cold and I shivered. Then hot, before finally settling on a perfect temperature. I shot up to the surface with a gasp.

And a scream.

"I was wondering when you would emerge," said Unatti, calm and serene as she watched me flail and cough, water violently splashing over the edge of the tub. "What burdens could keep the legendary Alchemist under so long?"

"What are you doing in here? How—" I snapped but a cough took over. "Why the hell are you here?!" Scrubbing the water from my face, I raised my knees to my chest for the sake of modesty.

She raised an eyebrow from her perch on the chair that was sitting flush against the end-side of the tub. "Whatever do you mean? You are in my bathing chamber, are you not?"

My head whipped around, noting the subtle changes in the room. The questioning of my sanity took hold of my thoughts. "W-what? H-how?"

The Queen of Were let out a hearty laugh. "Oh, the look on your face, my dear! Apologies, Melisandre; I transported us here. For privacy, of course. Your attempts at drowning yourself made it almost too easy."

Dumbfounded, I asked, "You mean to tell me you portaled the tub and me with it and I didn't feel a thing? How the hell did you even get into the room? Doesn't Ruarc have wards? Blasted fucking magic— Wait..." Then it dawned on me. The water vacillated between temperatures. That must be it. "The water...?"

"So, Alchemists can sense magic then?"

Shaking my head, my initial shock and anger morphed into irritated curiosity. "No..."

"Ah," Unatti leaned back, her posture perfectly straight, "that must be the effects of the Mark, then. I had heard rumours about Prince Alcaeus taking a Familiar but now I see it was far more than that."

We held each other's stare for a moment before I asked again, "What do you want, Unatti?"

Instead of answering me, she turned to the small table next to her. Bottles of perfumes and different oils stood out, along with several small towels and sponges. Several candles were placed decoratively around them.

She perused several of the items before selecting a bottle and pouring oil into her cupped palm. Placing it down, she extended her free hand towards me and beckoned, "Come, my dear. Let me wash that beautiful onyx mane—"

"I beg your pardon—"

"—and I shall tell you why I have brought you here." At my incredulous look, she said, "Let a woman take care of a fellow woman. What kind of queen would I be if I did not take care of my guest? Do not be shy. I do not bite." A playful smile showed snow-white pointed teeth. "At least, not too hard."

Hesitating, I stared warily at that outstretched hand. She waited patiently.

Ruarc did say she would make a good ally and, with my fight with the Tengu fast approaching, I will need one. Perhaps she may know something that would aid me in the battle to come.

Almost failing at overcoming my own logic and storming out of there naked as a babe, I crept forward. Getting to my knees, I twisted my body so my back was to her.

Though, my eyes never left hers.

She gave me another nod of encouragement before I finally turned fully away and leaned against the wall of the tub.

Unatti's oiled hands were confident but gentle as they deftly picked up and laid my hair over the edge, threading them through my locks and massaging my scalp.

Releasing a breath of begrudging satisfaction, I waited for her to speak.

"In nature, the owl and the raven are mortal enemies. Owls eat the ravens' young, attack them as they roost, and compete with them over food and territory."

"I am aware," I replied flatly, suspecting where she was going with this.

Warm spices and sweetness wafted through the air as she continued to massage my head, taking sections of locks and rubbing them gently between her fingers. Warm water sluiced the crown of my head, avoiding dipping into my ears and eyes.

"And yet, even knowing this, you still choose to roost with the Raven while your Fated, the Great Owl, lies trapped between the jaws of the hound."

Suspicion curled its tentacle around my gut, making me turn slightly to her so my eyes could meet hers. "How did you know about that? That Alcaeus is my Fated."

Like a mother speaking to a child, she replied, "My dear, Fated Mates may be a rare thing indeed among Vampires and Fae, but for a Were, it is everything. One could say we are the experts in such matters. Fated Mates are a little more common among my kind for our gods understood the importance of such things." With a gentle firmness from her hand, she encouraged me forward again as she picked up a new bottle, which I heard by the sound of glass on glass as she lifted the stopper off. "Hidden beneath the bite scars of my mate, I too share the same symbol. Once you have completed yours, the Mark will hide itself unless it is within the presence of your Fated. Now," I felt the oil seep into my scalp, a warm tingling spreading across the skin with a refreshing zest, "Would you tell me why the Alchemist leaves her Fated in the jaws of her enemy so she can fly with another?"

A scowl wrinkled my brow at her implication that I was somehow allowing this to happen. "I don't know you, Unatti. So far, your methods have been an unpleasant and unwelcomed shock. And, while I do not believe you have ill intentions towards me at this moment, that is merely me giving you the benefit of the doubt. Whether you deserved that from me or not, remains to be seen."

Her movements paused for a moment, as if she was thinking of how to respond. Then she laid her hand on my head, like a mother would a child.

"My creator, the great god Apedemak, was a god of war and conquest. His military prowess was unmatched among the gods of Egypt. But he had another name: the Lord of Life. With his blessings, so the land would prosper, for Apedemak's friendship with your Mother was exceptional; their connection ran deeper than the roots of the Baobab. He was her protector just as she was his provider. As I am now here extending the same, that it may be between us as it was between our creators."

Turning fully to her, I searched her face. There had to be more. "What do you really want? How do you benefit by allying yourself with me? What's your game?"

"No games." Amber eyes reflected nothing but sincerity, as pure as the golden flecks in her irises. "Hidden agendas and ulterior motives we leave to the Fae and Vampires. We Were-kind abide by a certain level of...a direct sense of integrity. You will know when you are the one we hunt."

Holding her gaze for a moment longer, I shook my head but said, "You saw what Ragna has done to him."

Disgust caused her brows to pull together and anger drew lines on her face. A dark growl shrouded her words. "Yes. It is blasphemy. Profane of the highest degree. I would have torn the spine right out of her body had it been my mate. That is why I ask—"

"It is all a lie. A guise." For once in my life, I wanted to be able to trust her. I had to. "A useless one now, I suppose, but Ruarc is pretending to be my potential mate in order to help us."

A warm scented hand cupped my cheek, drawing my attention. "Then why are you bathed in King Alcaeus' scent yet the mark remains incomplete? I do not understand. The need to bind your souls should be driving you into a frenzy by now. At first, I wondered if Ragna's hold on him prevented you from seeing each other but..." her nostrils flared. Sniffing. "I see that is not the case. You have coupled recently. Yet the Mark remains unchanged."

Shaking off the discomfort, I replied, "Alcaeus refused. He is waiting...for something." Suddenly, Alcaeus' truth felt too personal to share—

"*Paláti tou Efiálti,*" whispered Unatti, her eyes going distant for a moment. "Of course."

Unable to hold back my surprise I asked, "You know?"

She was present with me once more. "Yes. King Alcaeus and I have always been allies for Athena and my creator also shared friendship. My people are alive because of his agricultural genius when the Great Drought decimated our lands. He sent provisions and advised us until we were once again stable. We waited for his call when Ragna would march her undead armies upon his lands. Yet," her gloriously braided head bowed in shame, "King Ruarc's missive arrived too late when Queen Ragna had conquered the Messinia Kingdom. No one believed it at first. The power difference between Ragna and Alcaeus was too significant. It did not make any sense. But when word was received that King Alcaeus had accepted defeat... and stood alone, without his little owlet..." Unatti swallowed hard, looking back up to meet my gaze, sadness on her regal face. "I knew why he had laid down his sword. But not for a moment did I think Ragna was evil enough to take his soul. How he is still standing, still himself, I do not know—"

"She ripped his soul in two." Her mouth opened in shock, followed quickly by horror. "Ragna carries the other half of his soul around her neck," I said bitterly.

"By the gods! That's what that was?" she breathed. "And now Ragna has called for a fight to the death between you. Her cruelty knows no end." Then she shook her head, "But, you are Fated. The very fabric that binds you ensures that you cannot hurt each other."

I pulled my hair from her hands, letting it fall to the water as my fingers combed through it. "When Ruarc took me away from Castle Fyrkat the first time, Ragna's green-flamed necromancy seemed to possess him. With Nemesis, he came after me as if I was just another enemy. A stranger."

"I-I see. I will need to think on this. Consult my mate on how to help you." She took my face in my hands and, for some reason, I didn't feel so exposed. "You shall fight the Tengu soon. We shall first focus on your victory before concerning ourselves with your Fated. Unfortunately, unless you can fly, he will have the advantage over you. He is the master of the winds; the skies are his kingdom. But I can give you one bit of advice: he would make a worthy ally and it is allies you will need. Find a way to earn Tengu's loyalty and you will forever be guarded from above."

I pulled back gently and she released me. "Seems there is a simple solution then."

"Oh? And what is that?"

"I need to clip his wings."

CHAPTER 31

"It is time."

My fingers gently caressed the page I had been reading in the large book sitting in my lap. Sitting there for a moment more, I slowly closed the tome that held the histories of Japanese Yokai and the sound gave a sense of finality to Sage Kevyn's announcement. After being teleported back to my own bathroom, tub and all, I still had several hours before the fight began. According to Elis, many had departed for the arena already, enjoying the entertainment provided before the fighting would begin. I had opted for more research and, to my surprise, Elis didn't argue with me.

"You are most welcome to stay here," Kevyn suggested. "I am exceedingly creative and have an endless pool of excuses to draw from. Surely, one of them will suffice."

His offer had me giving him a tired grin. "You know there is nothing more I'd like to do than hide away from the world, especially in a place like this." Sliding off the top of his desk, I gently set the book down on top. "But there are allies to make and enemies to piss off. And a Tengu to catch."

The Sage looked down his nose and over the top of his spectacles at where I had been cross-legged just moments ago, hands behind his back just like a disapproving professor would. "Hmm, yes, well I can say that you and the Tengu share one odd and rather irking habit. Both of you seem to take great enjoyment in perching on furniture instead of using it for its intended purpose."

I bit my lip in embarrassment as blood rushed to my face and to the tips of my ears. "W-well, I...I just don't like being...confined."

"Yes, because sitting on plush chairs is positively suffocating," he chuckled, "silly goose. No mind. It is far more fun to tease you about it."

An urgent knock had both of us turning to the door. There was no break in the pounding and a tendril of alarm curled within me.

"Yes, yes! A moment!" Sage Kevyn hobbled quickly to the door, swinging it open. "What is so impor—"

"Ms. Melly! I need to talk to ya!" Toby, still glamoured as 'Ollie', rushed inside, signs of distress in every movement and in the wideness of his eyes. "Close the door! Please!" He moved closer to Kevyn, his voice a harsh whisper. "Is this safe from King Ruarc and Queen Ragna hearing us?"

Kevyn nodded. "Yes, my boy. Release your glamour; only truth in this room. Whatever is the matter?"

Toby looked around wildly though it was clear his mind was elsewhere, as if reliving some past memory. He ran a hand through his now thick brown curls, coming to a stop to grasp them in frustration. "I-I...I saw...well, no...more like 'eard something I...fuckin' 'ell!"

Quickly, I closed the space between us, trying to steal his focus. "Toby, calm down. You're safe. Tell me what is going on?"

Suddenly, he grabbed me by the shoulders, a wild desperation gleaming in those chocolate brown eyes. "Ms. Melly, I know King Ruarc is...he is my king, I know that. I-I'm loyal, truly! B-but you were there first for me and I-I don't..." He squeezed his eyes shut, inhaling sharply, breath coming out with a determined ***whoosh***. "No, you *have* to know. Ms. Melly," his grip on me was no longer crushing but still firm, "I saw King Ruarc with Queen Ragna."

Confused, I replied, "Uhhh, yes Toby, that would not be a strange thing, considering our current situation—"

Suddenly, Toby grabbed his hand and hissed in pain. I reached a hand out to his shoulder but he curled away from me, jaw clenched and his pallor going ashen.

"Damnit!" he snapped, frustration laced through the discomfort in his voice. Brown eyes faced both of our bewildered ones. "T-they...argh! I've gotta...tell ya! King Ruarc, he—ah!" Toby let out a growl of pain, a sound, then shook his head. "S-seems I can't tell you. He doesn't want me to." That's when I noticed the mark on his hand seemed almost... alive.

My scowl deepened at this display of ownership. Looking at Sage Kevyn, the look on his own face stopped my request of his assistance from being uttered.

"I know what you're going to ask and the answer is, unfortunately, no." Some strands of white slipped from the tie holding the rest of his hair back. "My authority only extends to the limits of this library and, as my position within this universe is to be a keeper of knowledge and protector of such, meddling in the politics of the rest of the world is forbidden. I am but a simple observer within the cosmos, I'm afraid."

With a nod, my attention turned back to Toby. "Can you tell me anything? Anything at all?"

He looked back, swallowing deeply. Sweat had broken out on his brow, enough to tell me he was in physical pain. "No."

I sighed. "The seed of doubt has been planted, Toby. That should be enough—"

"Not all is as it seems, Ms. Melly." The intensity in his eyes sent apprehension shooting through my veins. "Not all...is as it seems."

Holding his stare for a minute more, I slowly nodded. "I understand."

Then he turned and left.

"Are you sure you do not want to take me up on my offer now?" Sage Kevyn's question jolted me out of my thoughts and drew a chuckle out of me.

"Please, Kevyn, don't tempt me any more; after that, I want nothing more than to be rid of this entire debacle." Unease raced through me and I could tell the wise Sage could see right through my attempted humour. "But I should go. Wasting time will only delay the inevitable."

"Here," my Alchemist's staff slipped into my hold as he released it to me, "you'll need this." Kevyn's hands were warm as he grabbed hold of mine. "Now, tonight you will go into the arena, and you will be victorious!" Blue eyes shone with optimism and a wisdom I could only dream of having. "And when you're in there—"

Shouting outside, the angry words getting closer, was unmistakably Ruarc. The door had been left ajar slightly when Toby had left, just as the Unseelie King appeared, all fire and brimstone. Sage Kevyn flicked his wrist and the door slammed closed in the monarch's face. Gaeilge cursing ensued. I had to bite my lip to keep my composure.

"And when you're in there," Kevyn continued, as if he hadn't been interrupted, "remember that your mind is your greatest weapon. Tengu's are notorious tricksters and illusionists; do not believe everything you see."

With a nod, I gripped his hand back in a show of gratitude and we both turned to the door, which Kevyn slowly opened to face the furious Fae.

"Well, hello, Master Ruarc! Fancy seeing you here," greeted Kevyn, all smiles and innocence. "How might I help you? Still looking for information on the mating rituals of gorgons, is it?"

As if I thought Ruarc's face couldn't get any more ferocious, he let out a dark growl directly at me, ignoring the Sage. "You are LATE! You should have been at the fucking arena—"

"Ah, ah, ah, Master Ruarc," interrupted the Sage with utter calm, wiggling a reprimanding finger in his face. "Even kings must comport themselves with grace and serenity within the Library's domain. Especially in the company of a lady." He smiled, placing his hands behind his back. "If you'll pardon my departure, I have a lecture to give. Good luck my dear, and if you two will excuse me."

Ruarc growled again then whipped to me. "Where the FUCK HAVE YOU BE—"

"Grace and serenity!" called out Sage Kevyn as he walked away with his slight limp.

Ruarc raised his monstrous claws in the Sage's direction, curling them into a fist as if he was imagining squeezing the life out of him.

He probably was.

With a sharp breath through his nose, he grabbed my arm painfully, only for his hand to slide down and into mine as we neared Sage Kevyn, and began dragging me through the front door.

"You put the 'ass' in grace, you know that? Ow-Ruarc! Let go!" I snapped.

He kept going until we were outside of the Library's grounds. Black shadows swirled around us. Despite my ire, I clung to him, the magic around us making my stomach flip-flop.

As the blackness cleared, Ruarc shoved me off him as much as I pushed away. And gasped.

We were inside the Megálo Kolossaío.

Detailed stone archways led to endless corridors, smells of sand and earth both fresh and ancient at the same time, permeated the air around us. My eyes didn't feel big enough to take in the enormity of the place. Knowing we were ground level would be unbelievable if I judged the height of the ceilings but, if it was anything like the ancient Greek and Roman structures still seen in the human realm, this was just the beginning. What I knew of the place had more to do with the events that occurred within these walls, the blood that was spilled upon the sands.

As much as the architecture and history kept me captive, the roar of the crowds outside shook me out of my reverie. Guards were posted everywhere, and not just Ragna's; many of the Champions around me seemed to have their own personal retinue, some even being assisted in getting ready before their fights.

"Come." Was Ruarc's gruff command as he took me by the hand and began leading us through the middle corridor.

On either side, stations were set up for each champion fighting. Catching the eye of the current standing winner from last year's Divine Games, the beast of a man looked as though he could have been one of Alcaeus' former generals, just by his commanding presence alone. He was seated in a chair with the look of someone who was trying to sniff out weakness in those around him. Two beautiful and muscular women rubbed oil over his shirtless torso and arms; one behind him, the other kneeling beside the chair. Servants placed food and drink on small round tables, of which the large grey wolf laying at his feet took a sniffing interest.

"That is Siggeir, champion to one of the Kings of Were, King Managarmr, Champion of Fenrir," muttered Ruarc. "And before you even ponder it: he will not be your ally and is most certainly your enemy. His king has requested a special fight between the two of you."

"What?" I cried, "But...The Naming Ceremony—"

"I know!" he snapped and that was when I noticed his entire demeanour was as tight as a bow string, muscles straining, causing tendons to dance and veins to bulge. "I was...overruled. That's where I was before I came to get you. It seems that this is the year where tradition is what Ragna is using to wipe her own arse and rules are meant to be broken. Queen Unatti did not leave King Managarmr unscathed but, ultimately, she too was forced to accept it." Suddenly, he pulled me close to an archway that was just far enough away from prying ears. "Ragna has been not-so-secretly gathering her allies; she means war, Melisandre, and right now," his teeth clenched, breathing sharply through his nose, "you are the biggest threat that stands in her way."

Anger had already ignited at the simple mention of that tyrannical bitch's name but I saved my fury; I had expected this. Perhaps my over-active amygdala had finally matured, for instead of wanting to rage and blow the entire place up, I was almost... "When is the fight?" I simply asked.

Ruarc's stare was hard, as if trying to decipher my intentions, "Day after tomorrow... You're taking this rather well."

The suspicion was so poignant on his face, a smile cracked my normal perpetual glare. "Come, Ruarc, none of this should surprise either one of us. Ragna's lost her edge...I think that worries me more than her normal schemes. Which means..." My mind raced, swiftly coming to the only logical conclusion, "It means that her goals are nearly, if not already, reached. She believes she cannot lose."

Ruarc said nothing, just watched me with a shrouded expression.

Not everything is as it seems. Toby's words snaked back to me.

Without warning, I shoved Ruarc back against the pillar with my staff, my other hand clenching the back of his hair, bringing his head closer to mine. To anyone else, it looked like a passionate moment between two lovers; only the Unseelie King saw the violent fire in my eyes as my intense gaze clashed with his.

"I hope, for your sake," I whispered, our breaths lingering together at our proximity, "Ragna's successes do not contain even a whiff of Unseelie schemes."

We held each other's stares for a moment more; he gave me nothing so I let go of his hair. Suddenly, our places were switched and it was my back being slammed against the stone.

"And I, too, shall only say this once," growled the Unseelie King, lifting up the hand that bore his mark. "You swore to me your alliance; never again question my loyalties. Everything I have done was for you!" Movement to the side caught both of our attention and Ruarc used that moment to kiss me. Hard. Angrily.

But unlike with my Owl, this was empty. It was a point to be made.

The tension held an air of violence and it wasn't from the screaming and roaring from the arena. Suspicion sank in my stomach, dancing with Toby's words and all the facts of what I knew between him and Alcaeus. It was a hurricane in my mind, the web of information hiding their answers so close, yet too elusive.

Perhaps my past self would have angrily shoved him away but now, I let him kiss me. Let him believe what he wants, for the truth would surely come to the surface. And when it does, the Unseelie King would rue every forced kiss and unwanted touch.

He shoved away from me and turned without another word. I followed reluctantly, still consumed by the knowledge that there were roots deep and entangled all around me but I didn't know how deep they actually were.

Or how entwined I truly was.

"We're here."

Darkness, not of Ruarc, but of the great gate that held me in its shadow, loomed in front of me. My eyes slowly travelled up the majestic oak and gold doors; it was a giant scene of the primordial Greek god, Phanes, wrapped in a serpent. His left hand gripped the staff of Asclepius and his image was encased in an oval circle, with animals, people and other mythological creatures dancing around him.

We had arrived at the Gate of Life. The doors creaked loudly as light spilled through, the sands a golden ocean before me.

Gripping my staff, I gave one last measured look to Ruarc, who only gave me a nodding salute, before taking a step into the arena of the Megálo Kolossaío.

CHAPTER 32

Sand. Marble. Limestone. Travertine. As the sand crunched beneath the soles of my boots, my senses reached out to touch the elements around me. My materials. My tools.

The amphitheatre that was the Colosseum in the Human realm was a spectacular human feat. But it was just that—human. This place was created by the gods themselves and the size was mind-boggling. Made for Champions, monsters, and beasts to fight; which meant the arena was of a size to accommodate warring dragons the size of small cities. The crowds were far away, far enough for me to wonder how they could possibly see anything.

I walked. And walked. Still, I could not see the end.

Was I in the middle? Where was the Tengu?

My feet stopped moving. The breeze was cool against my skin, failing to conceal the subtle hints of elements it carried with it. But one thing was new and had me faltering in my movement.

Magic. I could see it. Couldn't do a damn thing about it but I could see it.

It was almost...plasmic. Transparent but filmy in visual texture. It covered the entire stadium; my guess would be to protect the audience from the violence about to ensue.

But one thing was for certain: I was done waiting.

"Tengu! Show yourself!"

The wind stirred but it was the only answer I received.

"Ladies and gentlemen! Kings and Queens! Champions of the

old gods! And all the creatures of Other whom are gathered with us today!" Unatti's voice boomed over the arena, commanding and regal. It had to be magic, for her voice was as clear as if she was three feet from me. **"We are here to witness the legendary battle between the mighty Tengu and the mythical Alchemist! This is a fight to submission! Warriors, prepare for battle!"**

The crowd's roar, though they were distant, reverberated through the stadium, causing granules of sand to vibrate and dance. Tiny hairs all over my body stood on end and a short rush of adrenaline answered the bloodthirsty screams of the audience.

Suddenly, the skies darkened. The wind picked up, whipping my hair around my face. My eyes struck forward. My attention hyper-focused on the dust-filled vortex which formed, only to dissipate quickly. In its place was a lone figure.

He wore the traditional garb of Yamabushi, the *kasa* on his head blocking his face. Two swords, a katana and wakizashi, were strapped to his left side where his hand casually rested.

The crowd went silent, a silence that was instead filled with trepidation, a tension so thick that I waited for the Tengu to draw his sword and slice it away.

"金術師か？　味深い(*You're the Alchemist? Interesting*)." The Tengu had bass to his voice that ran deeper than Alcaeus', making his presence more sinister than anything else. "It is said you command the elements, that you are truly nature incarnate. **名は何という**(*What is your name*)?"

"You know my name."

His head lifted, the protuberant nose being the first thing that caught my attention, it being the common Tengu trait.

"知っているさ Melisandre Von Boden.**自然の娘、だろう?"**(*I do. Daughter of Nature, right*)?"

The wind blew. Our gazes measured the other. His left thumb flexed, shifting the blade loose as he prepared for nukitsuke: the initial draw of the katana, followed by the first cut.

My body tensed. My stance shifted, readying for him to make the first move. Tengu were incredible swordsmen; my staff, combined with my inexperience in fighting meant I stood little chance in hand-to-hand combat. Yet, even as adrenaline crashed through me, so too did ideas.

He remained still.

Suddenly, Unatti's voice was back. **"Whoever can force the other to submit will be named victor! Death is forbidden! Bloodshed,"** she gave a rich throaty chuckle, "**is expected! Nay, demanded!**" The crowd screamed wildly. "Let the fighting commence!"

Neither of us took our eyes off the other. Waiting.

Suddenly, the Tengu drew his sword in one smooth, swift motion, pointing it right at me. My back stiffened.

"我が名はアタゴリョウボウ。覚えておけ (*Remember this! My name is Ryobo Atago*)!"

Ryobo Atago. I pointed my staff, mirroring him. "Then give me something to remember—show me the might of a Karasu-tengu!"

He laughed. A deep, resonating, echoing belt of a laugh. "面白い！いいだろう(*Fascinating! I will*)!"

Shifting his stance into *Chūdan no Kamae*: one of the most basic but effective sword stances. "I will have you on your knees; I can already taste your tears of defeat, smell your sweet submission. さぁ始めようか、錬金術師よ (*Then, Alchemist, let us begin*)!"

The katana gleamed in the light before it was drawn down, only to slice upwards. A wall of wind mixed with sand came at me. I threw my arm up, blocking my eyes as I tucked my head away.

Snapping back to where the Tengu had been, my eyes frantically searched the empty space. A sting on my cheek stopped me, my fingertips grazing it before pulling away.

Blood.

Another gust of wind flew at me and, this time, I transmuted the sand within to a ceramic cup and it dropped to the ground, the breeze passing me harmlessly. But just then, a gust hit me on my back, rushing my side.

I didn't have time to even see it or react, and this one felt more powerful than the last. It pulled me forward and my footing wavered. Looking down at my side, small rips glared up at me in my clothing where the sandpaper wind had rubbed against it.

"Ah, yes," I said loudly, "I do remember reading how much Tengu love to play games. Is this truly your idea of fun? You're no better than a child."

A flickering to my right. With a thought, the sand transmuted into a pike. In a blink, Ryobo sliced his katana and the pike was nothing more than a dull stub, like a tree trunk protruding from the ground. I took several steps, and pikes of ceramic continued to shoot out of the air.

His steps matched mine perfectly, like a dance; his sword making quick work of my alchemy.

"If that is all you can do—じゃ錬金術師も子供だ! (*Then you are a child as well*)!" Ryobo sliced his katana right at me, a huge gust of wind coming at me faster than I could blink.

The tiny tornado bowled into me, my body thrown to the ground. My death-grip on my staff kept it from rolling away. Sharp and immediate pain stung enough to have me hissing between clenched teeth as my hand instinctively came over my right side.

Warm blood greeted my palm.

Quickly getting to my feet, I inspected my hand again. My entire palm was red. His wind had cut through leather and fabric, down to the bone of my ribs. The crowd's cheering became louder.

""見えるか (*See that*)?" the demon asked, a hand leaving his sword to sweep wide in a gesture of grandeur. "個天狗だ (*I am a bird-demon*)! I command the north, south, east, and west winds!" He raised his arm heavenward. "I am the master of the skies! And you will submit to me!"

I smirked. Blood was quickly congealing from my wound and I knew it would be healed in several minutes. But my humour wasn't at the healing wound, no. It was how true the literature was on how cocky Tengu actually were. My smirk morphed into a grin and my head cocked in challenge.

"Let's make a bet, Oh Great One."

Now it was his turn to give me a questioning look and, although his face gave away nothing, I just knew I held his interest. "かける (*A bet*)?"

"If I can make you submit to me, you give me something."

"何欲しい? (*What do you want*)?" His response was suspiciously quiet, as if he was almost afraid of my answer.

"Your alliance."

"なるほどな (*I see*). And if I win?"

"What do you want?"

His demon red eyes gleamed with mischievousness and he gave a show of thinking over it. But we both knew he had already decided. "You belong to 烏さま (*The Raven*) so I cannot take you for myself. One night; for one night you are mine."

I didn't hesitate. "Done."

There were no visuals of his sword moving but blasts of wind came at me from all directions and the flash of transmutations became a solid light for several minutes, ceramic pieces flying everywhere. Calling upon my Alchemist's Vision, what I saw had my brows crawling to my hairline. The shimmer of magic, shaped like a blade, was woven within the wind.

But my discovery caused me to hesitate, my surprise coming at a price.

Another gust came at my back and my body turned just as it hit me. The immediate pain to my abdomen and thigh seared through me, igniting my nervous system and I cried out, hitting the ground, this time dropping my staff. Blood poured from my belly and leg. My fingers sunk into the sand, curling angrily as I stubbornly pushed myself to all fours but did not stand.

"You have already lost, 錬金術師 (*Alchemist*)! 諦める (*Give up*)!" Ryobo growled.

With a grunt, I swiped my staff and pushed myself up to face him. "Never."

A low growl emanated from his throat. Good. Now we were truly fighting. Those massive gusts, swirling with magic blades and sand, came at me at blinding speed.

This time only a single transmutation happened. All around me was a sandstorm. I stayed still.

When it finally cleared, the Tengu was livid with how he found me. "あり得ない! 何それ! 答え (*Impossible! What is this? Answer me*)!"

"Laminated glass," I said with a smile, my staff tapping against it. My voice was muffled but I knew he could hear me just fine. "All your commotion gave me exactly the amount of energy I needed to create it. Glass layered with polymers made up of PVB, ionomers, EVA and TPU and a bit of heat and the lovely pressure you provided... You are so very helpful, Ryobo," I goaded.

Fury and wrath exploded from the demon. His physical appearance suddenly morphed as he sprouted huge black wings. That long nose was replaced with a massive, sharp beak that covered the lower half of his face and those red eyes glowed so bright they looked like flames dancing in his skull.

Raising his sword to the heavens, the clouds darkened further, the chorus of thunder answering his rage. Temperatures shifted. Tails of clouds swirled, reaching for the ground below. North. South. East. West. When those tails finally hit the ground, it got thicker and thicker until four massive tornadoes surrounded us. The power and pull of them rattled the glass box I was in; laminated glass was tornado resistant but not proofed; and my Alchemist's vision confirmed the thousands of magic blades that swirled within.

I closed my eyes. Strangely, a human man from my memory struck my thoughts. Strong posture. Handsome. Striking grey eyes filled with intelligence. A gentle voice. Him making me laugh in a cafe as we poured over schematics, formulas, and innovative ideas. Brief was our friendship yet a lifetime of memories.

"Nicola," I whispered fondly.

But that brief recollection had given me my solution.

Ryobo the Kotengu once more pointed his sword at me.

"俺は王様の風!！ 決して勝てない! 諦める! (*I am the King of Wind! You cannot win! Give up*)!"

"No."

With a swipe of his katana, the tornadoes slowly began to move and he took to the skies. His kingdom. How foolish he was.

The power of the Philosopher's Stone rippled and I let it fill me, feeling the buzz of creation, of change, of destruction igniting every single nerve of my body.

Laminated glass disappeared and my staff slammed into the sand. A flash of purple that covered the entire inside of the stadium was accompanied by circles underneath the tornadoes, matching their circumference. I searched deep below the earth.

There. Bauxite and a huge vein of copper chimed out at me.

Transmuting the bauxite through three different stages until it formed massive aluminium rings, I pulled the copper from the earth and it came to me like a clean melody. Together I moulded them into Tesla Coils the scale of building-sized towers.

A roar stole my attention skyward, only to see the Tengu fighting against the colossal glass dome I had erected to keep our fight contained.

Like a birdcage.

"You call yourself the king of skies!" I shouted up at him. "But I am the last daughter of Mother Nature! The earth is my sword!" I began transmuting the tornadoes into pure energy, drawing it into myself. "The sky is my anvil!" Electricity danced chaotically all around as the tornadoes disappeared. "The earth's core: my forge!" The moment all of the energy was transmuted, I released it into the Tesla Coils and a lightning storm exploded all around us. "And you are in MY HOUSE!"

I held my arms wide, letting the power of the Stone flow. My eyes closed against the blinding light but my vision wasn't needed; my Alchemist senses told me everything.

The Tengu's body fell, cutting through the molecules that I could see. My runes lit up as I transmuted the energy back into the ground, the glass case around us dissipated, raining sand. The Tesla Coils followed suit. As Ryobo's body hit the ground, an alchemical circle flashed underneath him, trapping him in a copper cell shaped like a birdcage.

Letting out a pained groan, his scorched feathered wings receded and then disappeared. The fall wasn't enough to kill him for he was truly a demi-god in his own right, but he would feel that shock for some time.

Blackened hands grasped the bars as he pulled himself up, his face once more that standard Tengu visage, with the long nose and demon-esque face. Surprisingly, a rough smirk greeted me.

"You want my submission, 錬金術師 (*Alchemist*)?" That deep voice was hoarse but no longer threatening.

Taking confident slow steps towards the cage, I replied, "I don't want your submission; I want your loyalty. I want your alliance. To watch my back as much as I will watch yours."

I came to a stop a mere inch from the bars, the Tengu regarding me though his face was overall unreadable.

Then he drew his katana and my heart dropped. But, to my shock, he presented it to me as he dropped to both knees, head bowed.

"I submit to you, Melisandre Von Boden. Claim your victory. Solidify our alliance!"

Transmuting the cage away, I gently placed my hand on the blade but did not take it.

"The Alchemist, Melisandre Von Boden, Champion of King Ruarc Ó Ceallaigh, has claimed victory over the Tengu, Atago Ryobo!"

Suddenly, the arena seemed to magically get smaller and the crowd was visible all around, cheering and roaring. Slowly, I turned in a circle. With staff in hand, I raised it before slamming it onto the ground.

The crowd roared.

As my eyes travelled, they stopped at the only person whose presence could make thousands upon thousands of living beings disappear.

Love and pride filled Alcaeus' face and my Mark burned to be near him. So much so I took a step toward him but stopped.

Next to him was Ragna. But it wasn't anger or fury that I had been so sure would greet me.

No.

She was smiling so wide, all her teeth were showing, the whites of her eyes clear even from here.

Like it was she who had truly claimed victory.

CHAPTER 33

The Great Owl looked down at his Fated, her chin high, eyes blazing with a fierceness that sent goosebumps racing across his skin. His own Mark matched the fire of desire he had for her, which he was grateful for. Before her overwhelming display of power, the threads that bound them and those waiting to be tied, screamed at him to protect her. It took the discipline of every single year of his life not to interfere, to slay the Tengu for even touching his sword in her presence.

But Melisandre needed to do this. She had to show the Otherworld the power she possessed if only to ensure that her enemies acknowledged the absolute contender that she was.

And how she had blossomed this day. This grumpy little badger of a woman had let go of her fear and was beginning to embrace herself; a truly terrifying and wondrous sight.

Doubts of her losing to him in their inevitable battle were beginning to crumble and Alcaeus' fear of hurting her grew less.

She would be fine. She had to be.

He met her gaze, surging with pride and love for his beautiful warrior staring back. The entire Otherworld seemed to be here and yet, no one existed for him at that moment. This was the woman he had waited centuries for. His Fated. His Equal.

"Such a shame she has to die," said Ragna, jerking his attention away. "She would have been such a powerful toy. Had you done as I had commanded..." The queen stood, so too did her subjects around her. She stopped right in front of Alcaeus, an intimate distance between

251

them as she continued, "Then she would not only get to live but would have been by your side as we speak.

Ragna's expression snapped, her face rapidly morphing from annoyance to seductively sweet as she kissed her Consort's unresponsive lips. "The rest of the prophecy cannot come to pass if she is dead, however. And in three days," her hand trailed down his neck and rested on his chest, hovering over his Mark, "she will be. The time for life and love is at an end, *ástin mín*." Walking around him, she disappeared with the rest of her entourage.

Alcaeus stayed, eyes never leaving Melisandre. No word from Zhenbai on his progress in breaking the magical curse that enshrouded his kingdom. What was left of his armies remained in a petrified state, awaiting the return of their king.

Yet, even if the curse was lifted, he knew that he would not be returning. For there was a darker secret Alcaeus had failed to reveal to his love.

No one saw the muscles ticking in his jaw. No one saw the slight flare of that strong nose nor the slight twitch of his hand. No one saw how glassy their king's eyes became for only a moment.

No one saw the last bit of hope going out like the last candle in the night.

☿☽♃ℏΨⅤ♒

"Oh, my goodness, my victorious Melisandre! Come here—Get out of my way, you peasants! Oh, my darling!" Elis elbowed his way through the crowd that had gathered at the Porta Triumphalis, reaching out to me. Llyr was behind him, making apologies while placing a guiding hand alongside his mate to keep others from bumping into him.

There was no helping the full grin on my face at seeing them, returning my best friend's embrace.

"Why am I not surprised you're the first person I see," I teased, only then noticing the redness around his eyes and nose. "Elis, were you crying?"

"Crying? Pish posh, I would never be so undignified," he retorted, the hand that waved me away still holding his scrunched up lavender handkerchief. "The dust is rather irritating on my delicate and supple skin; horrid place."

Llyr's eyeroll behind him nearly undid me as he reached past Elis to take my hand and place a delicate kiss. "He was absolutely beside himself, a veritable sobbing mess; the sight of your blood had everyone around us scrambling to get away lest their derrieres become impaled with the thorns that grew around him." A charming and teasing smirk was upon the Fae noble's lips and Elis gave him a playful smack on his arms, gasping dramatically.

"My love is not in his right mind; all this excitement is positively befuddling," sniffed Elis.

Llyr's face settled into sincere admiration. "Never would I have guessed our little grumpy bookworm held such magnificent power. To watch you was spectacular; to celebrate you, an honour, my lady. Your victory is truly deserved."

A small tendril of happiness wound its way through the embarrassment from his adoration.

"Wielding that silver tongue of yours as always. Thank you, Llyr," I replied.

"Who better to receive it this day?" he smiled and Elis' eyes nearly rolled out of his socket.

My best friend shoved in front of his mate, taking my hand. "Come my dear, you must be utterly exhausted. You must come sit with us in our section—"

"Melisandre is my intended, and so she shall watch the rest of the games with me, as suits her station. Lord Llyr, your queen requires your presence."

We all turned to the Unseelie King, standing tall and with one hand resting on the hilt of his sheathed sword. There was no visible threat, but perhaps it was due to the bloody screams coming from the arena or the tension of those around us waiting for their turn to shed blood, but arguing with the battle-ready king in front of us seemed unwise even to me.

Giving my hand a quick squeeze, Elis withdrew his touch as he stiffened away from me. "Then we shall see each other after the games, my dear, in the Twilight Gardens for the Midnight Tea Party. Come, my love, let us get back to our seating, *appropriate to our station*," replied Elis. Though his tone exhibited utmost respect, I could not help biting my lip as my best friend served back Ruarc's words.

Both Vampire and Fae bowed stiffly to the Unseelie King and, with a wink to me, left us standing in the corridor. I wanted to go with them so badly; I missed Elis, and Toby's warning in the Library had left me itching to tell him about it.

My glare rested on the pushy monarch. "Must you always piss on every good moment I have?"

The bastard had the nerve to look taken aback.

"Whatever could you mean?" With a splayed hand over his heart, Ruarc's mouth curved with mischievousness. "I merely wanted to celebrate with my beloved fiancée, her smashing victory over the mighty Tengu. You were breathtaking, Melisandre." His gaze switched to the receding backs of my friends. "It is truly a wonder Queen Ragna has not snipped that facetious little Vampire in the bud yet."

I huffed, leaning on my staff. "She tried and failed. So don't even think about it. Elis is under my protection."

There was a curious look behind those bi-coloured eyes that I didn't quite like but couldn't interpret. "Yes, bringing the dead back to life just to spite the Queen of Bones. Oh, how that must have irked her pride." Stretching out his hand, he said, "Come, love. You must be exhausted after such a fight. My box is far more comfortable than a fighter's lounge."

I stared at that proffered hand begrudgingly. All of me wanted to slap it away and tell him he had no idea the endurance the Stone gave me but I would only be setting myself up for a bawdy retort, no doubt.

So, I took his hand.

When we arrived at his personal box, it was indeed far more comfortable than the standard stone seats given to the rest of the crowd. This particular section was the only covered part of the Kolossaío, at a perfect height to see all that was happening. The cushioned seats were high enough so the ledge did not block your vision, and there were plenty of titbits of food laid out on the small tables.

Ruarc sat down, resting a booted foot on one knee as he gestured to the seat beside him. I, instead, chose to perch upon the wide stone ledge overlooking the arena, crossing my legs as I laid my staff across my lap.

Almost immediately, my attention was drawn to several boxes down, where an arrestingly handsome face stared back at me.

Alcaeus. Our eyes locked and the general buzz of the mob faded away.

"My love." His words were a whisper, barely a touch on my thoughts.

The sensation of his arms wrapping around me, sliding down my body, his lips trailing a path down my neck, was so visceral I stopped breathing for a moment. Images of our time in the cavern below the library flooded my mind, just as the tendrils of desire gripped me in response.

A masculine chuckle answered psychically, the rich tone rubbed against me like velvet. Suddenly, flashes of a path outside our box leading down the corridor. Owls staring down, as if guiding the way. A door.

"Meet me there."

"I have missed that look," said Ruarc, shattering the intimate moment. He moved to lean a hip against the half-wall I sat on, crossing his arms as he studied my face. "Viviane had the most beautiful blue eyes; they put Mab's to shame. They were radiant whenever we were together." Blood-red hair fluttered along my knees as he leaned closer. "Remember that look, Melisandre, for our façade is not yet over."

A high-pitched hollow hoot, followed by a rustling of feathers interrupted us as Maximus called out, landing with delicate grace on my shoulder. My attention flickered to where I had seen Alcaeus but there was only an empty space.

"Perhaps, but it seems like the King of Nightmares does not agree," I replied with a soft smile. "By all means, we will continue this charade if you want. But Ragna certainly knows by now. There is little reason to pretend any more, beyond satisfying your own sadism."

"She knows I desire you, that is not a falsehood. And," Ruarc picked up my hand, stroking the top of it with his thumb, "it is not due to my own amusement that we've continued this. I would handfast with you, truly, if you agreed."

I froze.

How unexpected. Not for a single moment did I ever believe the Unseelie King had any other motive with me but to serve his own ends. I still didn't.

Maximus took off through the exit and my gaze trailed after him. Pulling away from Ruarc's grasp, I got to my feet.

"Do not make this something that will never be, Ruarc. Neither of us have the time to play that game."

I was almost out the door when he called out, "Do not waste your hopes on a dead man, Melisandre. He belongs to Ragna. Not you."

My jaw clenched just as my fist gave an angry squeeze around my staff. "If you'll excuse me."

Now, more than ever, Toby's warning resounded like an alarm bell through my head. Ruarc had promised to help me free Alcaeus but he spoke only of defeat. In what way had he ever truly helped? Instead, all my attempts have been met with how 'futile' it is and to 'let Alcaeus go'.

There was more to this and I needed to find out exactly what he gained from Alcaeus' fall or his possession of me.

Little Maximus led the way, landing on small surfaces until I caught up. The corridors were pretty empty, as many were too busy watching the bloodshed.

Just as it was shown in my mind, the path to the dark wooden door became clearer. When it came into view, Maximus flew off out of sight. My steps slowed as I watched the tiny owl disappear.

Carefully turning the knob, the hinges creaked as I opened it further and stepped inside.

Darkness swept around me like a cloud, engulfing me in the same way as Alcaeus' arms gathered me. I let go of my staff as he buried his face in my hair, but his shadows must have caught it for only silence and our mingling breaths resounded in the room.

"Ah, you were magnificent, *mikrós asvós*." His voice was husky, vibrating with the same desire that scorched through me. "To not only have defeated Ryobo, but to have earned his respect, is an impressive feat."

A wry smile danced on my lips. "I once told you that you didn't know what I was capable of."

Sharp teeth grazed me, his body tightening around mine. "True, but never did I believe you were incapable. Far from it. To see you unleashed was a reality I have long waited for."

"I—Ah! Oh god!" Were the only words ripped from me when my clothes vanished and my cold lower back was suddenly rubbing against his very hard and throbbing groin. Both hands snaked up to cup my breasts with a confident grasp, kneading, rolling and pinching them as his tongue left a burning trail down the outline of my ear.

"And you are worth," he growled those succulent words between hot breaths, "every," a groan ripped from me, "single," his hands kneading me into his body, "agonising moment." Alcaeus' fingers delved deep while his other continued to play with my breasts.

The whimper that escaped me was needy and desperate. "Please, Alcaeus...I want—"

"We only have moments, my love, so let's make the most of it," he growled, groaning deep as I reached a hand back to pull him closer just as I pushed my hips back into him. A scorching slide of tongue along my neck and shoulder sent shivers running across my sensitive skin.

Suddenly I was lifted, enough that my feet came off the floor, my toes finding purchase on the tops of his booted ones. The hand that was buried between my thighs reached further back as Alcaeus guided himself to my entrance. My hips pushed back in response, eager to be filled by him.

Both of us moaned as my body stretched to accommodate him, his shaft sliding in until my backside was flush against his hips.

The strength with which he held me was mouthwatering.

Firmly in his embrace, he began to slowly pull back then thrust forward, my arms clutching onto his. I was drowning in him, the sensations he was invoking, drawing out my pleasure with passionate expertise. He began to increase his tempo which, in turn, elicited further cries from me. Two strong fingers slipped between my lips, effectively muffling me as I ran my tongue along the lines of them. Alcaeus used his hold on my mouth and chin to tilt my head away.

He increased his speed even more, my body tightening like a bowstring being pulled back. A rush of hot, wet breath was all the warning I had before Alcaeus' fangs punctured my neck. I cried out against his hand, for the drug in his saliva sent a wave of pleasure through me, ripping an unexpected orgasm from me. He shuddered and groaned deeply, taking a long pull from my neck after relieving his teeth from my flesh. As he had bitten me, his hips had thrust deep, holding himself there, only resuming his gruelling pace when he began to drink from me.

My body was a ragdoll in his arms, barely clutching to him as waves of pleasure rolled through me like a hurricane. Yet, in the midst of this storm, flashes of memory sucked my attention away.

Endless courtyards. Massive stone fountain structures, no water flowing from its spouts. Dead leaves rustling across the way, bumping into stone figures with screaming faces. Gardens filled with only the skeletons of the plants that had once been. The last glimpse flashed in my mind, a magnificent castle rose above it all, situated perfectly atop a mountain of rock with sheer cliffs. Angry dark clouds of green fire swirled above it in a vortex, leading me to only one conclusion.

Paláti tou Efiálti.

Yet, what I was not prepared for, was the rush of sorrow that flooded me before quickly shutting off like a valve.

The moment of Alcaeus' sharing of memory was over as quickly as it had begun, my body on the edge of completion that my mind wasn't ready for. But as soon as his fingers brushed across my folds, seeking, I was swept back into the flames of his desire.

He was close. I could feel it in the speed, the desperation of his movements.

I never wanted this moment to end.

But end it did, as Alcaeus' hold on me constricted, his hand turning my face so his full lips captured mine and we moaned our releases together, as our tongues entwined. We held each other for a moment, consumed in darkness and the feel of the other, the roar of the crowd only caressing the edges of our little reality away from it.

"I don't want you to let go," I whispered.

He nuzzled my hair and kissed my cheek, giving me an affectionate squeeze. "Then make time stop, my little Alchemist. Stop the hands that steal these moments away from us."

If only I could. Being held against him like this, the way his massive frame engulfed mine, felt like the safest place in the world. Nothing could touch us.

"I would," I admitted, my fingers making small circles over his forearms, that still held me. "Then I would drag you back to my home, make you explain yourself for hiding away from me."

"There would be no dragging," chuckled Alcaeus, "If I had my wings, we would soar over the mountains, guided by the stars. But, *mikrós asvós*, it is you who could take the guilty verdict on hiding." When I attempted to wiggle out of his arms at the tease, he held me tighter. "But you could never hide from me; I will always be in the shadows watching over you."

The reminder of that poignant sorrow had me turning in his arms so that we faced each other.

"Don't give up, Alcaeus. Promise me. Ragna will not have her ending."

He kissed me gently. "I must go. Dress quickly; our absence cannot be noted." His lips captured mine once more before the chill of the room washed over me and he was gone.

CHAPTER 34

"Alright, Ms. Melly?" The tentative voice of 'Ollie' sucked me back into reality, my mind having been a hundred miles away.

I turned away from the mirror, straightening my black silk button-up blouse.

"Ah, Tob-Ollie, you came to see me," I replied warmly. I'd missed my little ward and feelings of guilt were trying to sneak past my happiness in seeing him.

His glamour fell, and rich brown eyes looked back at me. "Of course! And you can call me Toby when we're alone. I'm sorry I haven't been back but I've been trying to gather more information for ya. King Ruarc has me doing a few other things as well, mostly spying on Queen Ragna. But her spies are a pain in the arse to avoid!"

Together we went and sat on the small bench that was flush against the bed.

Tousling his hair, I said, "Well, knowing you, I bet you gave them a run for their money, eh?"

With a cheeky grin, he replied, "Every time."

"Good boy." I gave him a loving chuck under the chin. "How are you?"

"Ah, I'm alright, Ms. Melly. I'd ask how you are but after watching you in the arena! Ms. Melly you didn't tell me you were such a feckin' badass!"

"Language, child," I laughed, but knew he'd take no heed. He was among adults too much for that kind of censoring. "I still don't like making such a scene but it's inevitable I suppose. So, what has you seeking me out this time, hmm? Anything else on what we discussed in the library?"

His brows furrowed. "No...but I did ask Sage Kevyn for help."
"Oh?"

"Yeah, after I met with you, I wanted to learn more about that Mark on your shoulder since my gut tells me I should. Sage Kevyn agreed so we were reading and talking. You should finish the Mark, Ms. Melly; Sage Kevyn insists on it."

There was a time I would have hushed him, for children had no business being in my business but... Taking in those big brown eyes that held so much suffering and, from it, a depth of wisdom no pre-teen should have, perhaps I needed to let him grow up.

With a sigh, I replied, "Trust me, Toby, Alcaeus and I have had that talk and he does not want to complete it until his kingdom has been released from the curse that holds it." Chewing my lower lip, I confessed my theories. "From everything I have read and gathered, what is left of Alcaeus' armies are frozen in time. If he were to regain his soul, Ragna would wage war because his freedom would cause a revolution. Especially now, thousands would die; how else do you think she builds her armies of undead? And her allies are here as well. Without a place to escape to, I fear for Elis. Llyr would no doubt be called to battle. It's all a mess, really."

Toby's hand dove into his thick curls, scratching furiously. "I'll keep trying Ms. Melly. There's got to be an answer there. If you taught me anything, it's that there's always a solution—you just have to find it."

Whisking a fly-away curl away from his face, I said, "Very true, my boy. Now, off with you; I need to meet Llyr and Elis at the Garden Party."

In a posh and mocking voice, Toby repeated 'garden party', mimicking raising a teacup with his pinky-finger out, that had both of us laughing. Then his glamour took hold, like it was second nature already to him, and now Ollie stood before me.

"Best get to it then," he said, making his way to the door. "And don't forget, Ms. Melly: pinky up!"

I laughed, calling out after him, "We are too far past the Middle Ages for any of that nonsense!"

Turning back to the mirror, I smoothed my blouse out again,

more out of procrastination than anything else. An adorable ***hoot hoot*** caught my attention and Maximus flew silently from the balcony right up to my outstretched hand. He landed on the fingers, his little clawed feet careful not to cut my skin.

Giving his little head a single-finger scratch, he closed those large round eyes in pleasure.

"That damned thing is still here?" Ruarc's voice was gruff, annoyed. "We must go. We are already late."

"His name is Maximus and he is welcome to spend time with me at his leisure," I retorted, still giving the tiny owl scratches.

"Maximus? Ridiculous oxymoron for a creature that should be plucked and boiled."

Ah, the Raven and his hatred for owls.

I gave the owl a nudge and he flew off into the night. "Omit the 'oxy' and you would be aptly describing yourself, Ruarc."

Darkness swirled around us as he stomped closer, coming nose to nose with me. "Watch. That. Sharp. Tongue," he growled. "It's growing ever sharper at your own demise."

My eyes narrowed just as the darkness released us, the smell of fresh, fragrant air confirming our location had changed.

"All the more to cut through the layers of deceit that drench this damn place; perhaps you would be wise not to get in the way of its sharpness, Fae."

Now it was Ruarc narrowing his eyes.

"Ah! There you are, my dove. Looking splendid in funeral attire, I see." Elis was a vision in pastels as he flounced up to us. With an obligatory bow and greeting to the Unseelie King, he grabbed my hand and tucked it into the crook of his elbow, but followed royal protocol by waiting for Ruarc's dismissal.

Said royal held my gaze for another heartbeat, his holding a thousand things unsaid before dismissing us without another glance, disappearing down the path.

"Perfect timing as always, Elis," I whispered.

"I would be a very rich man if I had a penny for every time I've saved you from your own impertinence."

"He deserves every bit of it. Besides, how did you know—"

Elis tugged me forward and we began walking. "My darling, the look of murder and violent lust has been a permanent expression on King Ruarc's face whenever you two are around. Knowing you, I can only imagine why."

My grin was almost painfully wide. "He's a lot of bark and very little bite. Besides, he deserves a good tongue lashing; he's hiding something, Elis, I just know it."

Elis stopped us for a moment, looking me up and down. "If anything, he deserves it for not allowing me to dress you properly. Honestly, Mels, you couldn't manage a single colour in this monotonous outfit for a bloody *Garden Party*?" He gave a dramatic sigh. "Your preferences are positively quotidian if I'm not involved."

"I have no intention of being seen tonight," I replied. "I want to get this done and over with as soon as possible."

"This is our first time in ages we've been able to enjoy each other's company without that damn Unseelie breathing down your neck like an Alpha-Were in rut. Can't you just enjoy my company and only mine for once?" Elis' annoyance was tinged with hurt that prompted a defeated sigh from me.

I wrapped my other hand around his arm and gave it a squeeze. "You're right, Elis. We are certainly due."

He gasped dramatically, those lavender eyes sparkling like jewels. "You said I was right!"

"For once," I teased. "Wait, how would you know what an Alpha-Were is like in rut?"

"I-I don't-whatevercouldyoubepossiblyimplying," scrambled Elis, only to have Llyr come to his rescue. "My love! Look who I found! And she said I was right!"

Llyr's perfect brow raised at the same time my eyes rolled. The Fae Ambassador greeted me with kisses to both cheeks. "Hello, my dear. You look lovely this evening, although I'm sure my dearest had something to say about it." He looked pointedly at Elis who was all innocence.

"What? It's a royal garden party and she chose to appear as the grim reaper! Honestly, Llyr, I know you're on my side with this."

"At least it's silk!" I replied.

"Oh! Yes, silk because that makes it so much better. Except when you finish your executions, as reapers do, wearing the blood of your victims: you'll come running to me to help with the stains; which I will not help you with, by the way."

"Alright you two," cut in Llyr, who managed to slip between us and tucked our hands around his elbows, "put your adult faces on; we have royalty to greet and nobility to endure. Come, come." He went on to inform Elis of some political gossip, boring me immediately.

Without conversation to distract me, I was free to take in the scenery.

The royal gardens were breathtaking. There was a large lake that settled in the middle, the expansive gardens surrounding it. It was also plain to see that they were sectioned off to represent different cultures; horticulture from around the world, all in this estate. An elaborate large arched bridge connected one side to the other. Wooden walkways branched off from it, leading to floating gazebos that were filled with softly lit lanterns and vined flowers along the railings. Far off in the distance, stood a massive glass conservatory that looked like it belonged next to the Taj Mahal.

Flickering lights stole my attention from the botanical paradise we were approaching.

"Fireflies?" I mumbled, only to realise they were, in fact, not a living thing at all but pure magic.

All around were little glowing yellow and white lights. Romantic and soft, they floated around perfectly, somehow never blocking the view. With the moons reflected on the mirrored surface of the water, it was an ethereal view.

In my moment of awe, my steps slowed.

"What is it, Mels?"

"I'm just realising how little I saw of this place, last time I was here. The Nightmare Court it may be but, if one were to see only this, they'd think it a dream." My reply ended in a whisper, as I was leary of admitting that anything of Ragna's could be enjoyable.

"Oh, this is all the Prince Consort's doing," replied Elis, Llyr nodding in agreement. "Queen Ragna's glory would be the castle itself."

Surprised, words escaped me for a moment.

"Alcaeus did all of this? I didn't really take him for..." My words trailed off, unsure of the proper word to describe my thoughts.

"You don't know him very well, do you?" asked Llyr, not maliciously but in an almost empathetic response. "I suppose your time together has been unfairly short. Prince Alcaeus is renowned for his creations, said to be formed from dreams themselves. Must be the blood of Morpheus in him."

My heart clenched at the truth of his words. At that moment, I wanted to walk these gardens with Alcaeus, hear from his own mouth their history and see the pride and fondness in his eyes.

Elis swung around so that I was now between the pair of them, as we continued to stroll towards where the main party was.

"Then all the more to learn about your dearest!" Elis said excitedly. "He called upon me once to assist in its design; the English and French gardens were done by yours truly." It appeared we were heading there now. "Of course, there are all of my favourite roses..."

As Elis chatted, I searched the large courtyard we were approaching. Tea tables were tastefully placed on the outside, with an elegant buffet sporting a feast of various types of finger-foods. From the smell, anyone could find a dish that would remind them of home. Of course, there was a fountain of wine as the centrepiece; because what would a garden party be without alcohol.

Tea party, indeed.

Marble statues and fountains could be gazed upon and many did, small groups laughing and drinking. A much larger and more ornate table stood out in the area; no doubt for royalty.

"I see an empty table just there," said Llyr, "Why don't you two get settled and I'll get us something to eat. The servants will be by with the tea, no doubt."

"Oh, good heavens, my darling," cut in Elis, "this is a *social event*. Give me wine and lots of it." A quick glance at my glowering face and he added, "They aren't doing a whiskey fountain by chance, hmm?"

Llyr let out a delicate snort, his only answer a quick kiss on Elis' upturned cheek and headed toward the food. A few looks our way and hushed whispers followed us but we were otherwise ignored.

"It's wonderful to be around my flowers again," said Elis as we took our seats facing the courtyard. Thankfully, the table was far away in the corner, so it was unlikely our conversation would be heard. "After everything that's happened, it's easy to forget how relaxing the small things can be." The tinge of weary sadness in his voice turned me introspective. "I miss the days where my problems consisted of getting stains out of

Toby's clothes and luring you out of that cave you call a library."

A small smile crept up my face. "It was rather nice."

Elis' brows shot up. "Nice? You nearly bit my head off the last time I interrupted your precious research."

"Oh, I meant the stains. Terrible nuisance and you're so much more domestically inclined than I." His deadpan stare nearly pulled a giggle out of me.

Elis shook his head. "You wouldn't have deserved me as a wife."

"And I would have made a horrible husband," I retorted and we both laughed.

Then he took my hand that was resting on the table into both of his and said with dramatic seriousness, "My darling, it was never meant to be."

I placed my other hand over both of his, "I don't know how I'll go on without you."

"Finally airing out your repressed love underneath all that bickering? About time. Is there room for a third?" teased Llyr, setting down two plates loaded with food.

"We were just reminiscing over simpler times, dear," replied Elis. "And how dare you call yourself third; you will always be my number one." Llyr leaned down and they gave each other a kiss appropriate for public but there was naked love in it.

"Can I ask you two something?" The question on the tip of my tongue had my stomach in knots for how uncharacteristic it was of me but I felt compelled. When Llyr took his seat and at Elis' welcoming gesture I continued, "How..." I cleared my throat, "How did you know? That you loved each other enough to choose each other for life."

Both their shocked expressions filled me with regret instantly but Elis recovered quickly, smacking Llyr on the shoulder, "Llyr, she asked a question, don't look so surprised." Putting a finger to his chin he said, "It certainly didn't start out that way, did it?"

"Hardly not," agreed Llyr. "Elis wanted nothing to do with me. When my Queen sent me to the Nightmare Court at an attempted parlay, those lavender eyes bewitched me; as if they looked right into the heart of me."

"My father commanded me to spy on you," Elis retorted, crossing his legs as he swirled his wine, "and you know how well I took to his commands. But I will admit that Llyr was...far more appealing than the rest of the Fae consul."

"You would never have believed he found me even remotely tasteful."

"I would never be so plebeian as to make my interest so obvious." Elis took a graceful sip, eyes teasing over the rim of his glass.

Llyr gently shook his copper locks. "Well, when I *finally* convinced him I was at least worth looking at, there was a mountain of impossibility between us. Negotiations took 10 years, going back and forth to each other's realms. We went months doing nothing more than stealing glances. I would whisper my affections to the trees, their leaves and roots would carry my words to him when we were apart. Then his flowers responded, appearing in places whenever I was alone."

"You're straying, Llyr, but I will say: he has a marvellous way with words," Elis said to me. "My father forbade me, threatening to disown me if I so much as thought about betraying House LeGervase by mating with a Fae, even a duke of The Wood. But I knew; Llyr was the only one who saw every flaw and wanted more of me. I could be...imperfect, and still he stayed. When we were together, there was no Vampire or Fae; it was just Llyr and Elis." The tears that had begun to gather midway through his speech, spilled over. He dabbed at them delicately as Llyr reached across the table to take his hand. "So yes, that is how we knew."

"I could not have worded it better myself, my love," Llyr said gently.

A cup of tea and a glass of wine sat before me untouched; all I could see was Alcaeus.

"Do you think...being Fated means that my attachment to Alcaeus is...premeditated? That it's not real by my own design but rather by our creators?" My biggest fear unravelled in front them and in that moment, I wanted it to be wrong.

"I do not know enough about Fated Mates, my dear; none really do," answered Llyr. "That is something that you and Alcaeus must decide for yourselves. What I can say is that even when all the stars seem to align against you, when hope is a distant dream, real love remains true. It is not a fleeting feeling but the burning coals that ignite every action towards that person. And it is stronger than we know it."

He didn't look at me while he said it, but at Elis.

A fluttering of wings distracted us and Maximus landed on the table with a plant in his mouth. He hopped toward me, wobbling a bit from the size.

"That's an olive branch," said Llyr.

A knowing smile crawled across Elis' face. "It appears our Greek King calls upon his Queen. You've been summoned, my dear."

CHAPTER 35

Maximus led us toward the boardwalk, flying to one object until I caught up, then flying to the next. Part of me wanted to stop and enjoy the scenery but my little owl was clearly impatient, chirping and fluttering at my attempts to do so. There was no getting enough of the smells of fresh water, cedar, and plant life; the elements sang to me. Happiness seeped into me, all the way to my very bones.

"My lady, the beauty of your smile puts my own creations to shame." Alcaeus stood before me, stopping me in my tracks.

My face went slack.

The lights flitted around him, illuminating the bronze in his rich chestnut hair. It was loose instead of being tied back, and my fingers craved the feel of it. There was a pleasing softness around his eyes; one that gave the sharp angles of his face a gentleness that beckoned me closer.

What truly stole my breath away was his traditional Greek garb. He wore a deep royal blue *chiton* with sparkling silver embroidery that no doubt told a story. A matching *himation* hung over his left shoulder, leaving his right arm exposed. Though, not entirely. Bands of silver wrapped intimately around his bicep, emphasising its physique and matching the rings he wore on his hand. The delicate platinum wreath was a crown on his head and, finally unable to resist, I reached out to touch it.

Alcaeus stepped closer and bent slightly so my fingers could run along the beautiful craftsmanship. It wasn't just a laurel, but tiny flowers that peeked out from the leaves, with even smaller diamonds in the middle of the petals.

"Beautiful," I whispered, my eyes trailing down to meet his. He was so close, our breaths mingled. We studied each other then, in both adoration and admiration. "You clean up quite well."

He grinned. "If I knew wearing traditional clothing would turn your head, I would have worn it sooner."

I drew even closer; any more movement and our lips would have met.

"Now you know." Alcaeus' eyes dilated at my husky tone.

The call between us buzzed with warm energy.

He pulled away, offering his hand instead. "Come, my love. Walk with me."

A pang of disappointment was quickly washed away at my eagerness to see more of his creations.

Tucking my hand into the crook of his elbow, we walked at a leisurely pace, neither of us eager to break the silence. His smooth warm skin felt wonderful and I couldn't resist squeezing where my hand was affectionately.

Alcaeus smiled down at me. "You look lovely, Melisandre."

"I'm underdressed and you know it," I teased. "Not that I don't enjoy looking nice when the occasion calls for it but I had hoped to slip away before anyone noticed tonight."

He chuckled, "Then allow me to fix that for you, my little hermit."

We stopped and he turned to face me. Cocking his head for a moment, Alcaeus pondered my form.

Perhaps this was a mistake...

Shutting his eyes and, in the span of a heartbeat, opened them. Now that shining geometric pattern stared at me and the feel of fabric changed. My hands grasped the buttery soft, white wool of the *peplos* that hung around my shoulders. Looking down, I gasped in awe at the beautiful embroidered scene of amber owls flying amongst gold tiger lilies. As I leaned forward, my hair fell and I realised Alcaeus had modified that too. Reaching up, I felt for the gold hair net that held half of my wild curls away from my face. Little white flowers were woven in, cascading down my hair like a delicate waterfall.

When I finally looked at the Prince of Nightmares, his expression brought a full blush to my face.

"Well," I said, turning in a circle, "How do I look? Could I have fit into Ancient Greek society?"

The hard swallow and the slight shake of his head was enough to stroke my feminine pride. "Let me only say that I am even more grateful for your reclusive nature."

"Oh? Perhaps, I should change—"

"Because I would have to hide you away from the gods themselves from your beauty alone. Surely, my sword would never rest."

I stepped into him, smiling as my hands ran up his chest. "I would hope not, my owl." My heated look did not go unnoticed and Alcaeus pressed his forehead against mine.

"I would kiss you, *mikrós asvós*, but I would not stop. And I would prefer not to share the sight; it is for me and me alone." The smell of fresh skin, cedarwood, apple, and that hint of leather made my mouth water.

"Then take me somewhere away from prying eyes."

"As my lady commands." My breath caught as he placed a gentle kiss on my forehead.

Crossing the long boardwalk was quiet; perhaps neither of us wanted to ruin the moment with our impending fight looming ahead. Or maybe it was the simple fact we were together and it was enough.

As soon as our feet touched the stone path, it opened up into a Japanese-style garden; complete with a koi pond with blooming water lilies, a huge Japanese Maple and many Sakura trees. A traditional gazebo in the middle was opened up and there sat Ryobo with several others. As we walked by, he raised his teacup to us with a polite bow of his head and we returned the gesture before continuing on.

"Ryobo is an old ally. Gaining his favour was a wise move. He will be loyal as long as you are," said Alcaeus.

"What is the saying? Ah, 'birds of a feather', as it were," I replied.

"Birds of prey may not always get along but we certainly respect one another."

"As you do with Ruarc?" His face tightened, much to my curiosity. Their history ran deep and what was not said between them when they were together, weighed heavily in the air.

"Though an alliance has existed between us before, do not mistake it for the same understanding that Ryobo and Zhenbai and I have. Ruarc and I had a common enemy. My brief ties to his court benefited him at the time. Nothing more."

The recent events with the Unseelie King swirled in my mind. "He's up to something, Alcaeus," I confessed. "I feel it. Toby came to me, trying to tell me something and Ruarc's mark prevented him." We had come to a quieter part of the Japanese garden and I pulled away, needing room to think. "At first, I believed Ruarc would help us because of the deal we made but... Something isn't right."

"Fae can be just as self-serving as Vampires; they merely scheme in different ways. Of course he's up to something. He would not have helped you if there was not something he wanted out of it first."

"I'm not so naive to believe he made our deal out of the goodness of his heart," I retorted. "But neither do I believe he has any intention of upholding his part of our agreement."

Alcaeus' presence behind me was comforting, as was the warmth of his hands as they gently slid down my shoulders and arms, laying a kiss upon my right shoulder. "He certainly made it clear to me how much he desires you." Though his words were soft, there was an underlying menace to it. Not jealousy. Something more protective.

Nevertheless, the idea alone had my eyes rolling. "We both know that is just a distraction to keep me from discovering his true intentions."

"Perhaps," said Alcaeus, "or perhaps both can be true at the same time."

"Ruarc desires me the same way humans desire gold; it's shiny and a valuable material. It is not romantic in nature but stems from greed. In that, Ragna and he are no different."

Alcaeus turned me to face him, tucking a finger under my chin to lift my face, searching it. "You underestimate the effect you have on those around you, my love. For as much as you would have the world believe you are a termagant, that is but your defence. There is a comfort about you that is foreign to creatures of magic." He gestured to the plants around us, "Just as nature brings a sense of peace to the soul, you bring a sense of home and belonging. That is something every Otherworld creature desires but will not find."

I wanted to snort in disbelief. "Don't be nonsensical. That is our Fated Bond speaking, Alcaeus."

"Accuse me of being a romantic but illogical I am not," he shot back. "Our bond merely draws us together and amplifies the feelings that already exist. It does not manufacture it." He took my hands in his. "You are a woman like no other here in the Otherworld and Ruarc knows this."

"True, I am the only Alchemist in existence," I teased, deflecting.

Not rising to the bait, Alcaeus replied, "You are the only creature here not driven by ambition or greed. There is no ulterior motive. But there is a pureness in you that was eradicated by the gods when they first arrived and has not been seen in this realm since."

This time I did pull away, following the path we were on, unseeing. Irritation bubbled within. Alcaeus painted a pretty picture of me but it was the kind that a man does when he places a woman on a pedestal.

"I have upset you." His statement came from close behind as he followed me.

The plant life around us changed slowly, introducing an entirely new area as we rounded the bend in the path.

My head shook as I whipped around, "The blood of my people coats my hands and mine alone and yet you call me pure. Even now, something tells me my time for taking life away is not yet at an end. And you call me 'pure'." A bitter laugh escaped me before letting out a ragged sigh. "You don't know me at all, Alcaeus." Sadness dug its claws into my heart and doubt overcame me.

The silence that followed worsened what I was feeling so I continued to walk, disregarding whether Alcaeus followed or not.

Marble statues began emerging, the white stone stark against the colourful foliage. The plants were all native to Greece, their symbolism eliciting my inner knowledge of them and I ran my hands along petals, leaves, and branches as I continued further in.

A beautiful fountain was the centrepiece to this little piece of serenity and its sounds of trickling water beckoned me closer, soothing me.

"Bright Diamond lilies are your favourite flower." I didn't turn to Alcaeus' voice behind me but his words froze me. "Out of the 117 species of plants you grew in your garden, those you nurtured the most. Then the begonias." His voice changed direction, though still from behind. I wrapped my arms around myself. "You drink coffee as if it was water and you are dying of thirst. Warm smells; cinnamon, vanilla, patchouli, and sandalwood are your preferred scents. There are not enough pillows or blankets in the world when it comes to your bed." The truth of his words tugged a small smile at the corner of my mouth.

"Though you bluster and grumble when people interrupt your research, it is only because you make it a point to give them your full attention. In this way, you are utterly genuine. You actively listen, careful to consider what is said and what is not." Alcaeus stopped once more behind me, yet still I did not turn. "You were strict with Toby, but you were fair. The diversity of your friendships, the loyalty you've incurred, and the sacrifices you have made, are a testament to the integrity of your character."

A gentle tug at the back of my *peplos* finally convinced me to face him. My breath caught.

Alcaeus held a single Bright Diamond lily in his hand. "If I was to begrudge our creators anything, it would be how long it took before you came into this world. Yet, when I first saw you, the length of time I waited was gone in an instant. Over a thousand years of waiting and, suddenly, it had become inconsequential. All that matters to me, from now until the time I draw my last breath, is having the privilege of loving you." He dropped to one knee, extending the flower out to me. "I would slay the Fates themselves if it could buy us even minutes more, just to learn the most minor detail about you. Yet, what I know of you, I love unequivocally."

The moisture that had pooled in my eyes at his words spilled over and my fingers tentatively touched the hand that held the flower out to me. I didn't take it. Instead, I stepped into him and cupped his face. Cherishing every line, every scar, every facet of his face, I hoped he could see what I felt because words had failed me. So, I showed him. Leaning down, my lips captured his firmly. Not out of lustful passion but of something that burned deeper and truer than anything I had ever felt.

His arms came around me, firm without squeezing, a large splayed hand running up my back. My fingers gave into temptation and dove into his thick locks as our mouths opened to each other. The heat and taste of him was intimate and perfect. Kissing him always felt that way.

Slowly, I pulled away, taking in his full lips, wet from my kiss. His gaze was naked with emotion.

The confession trembled on my lips but went unsaid.

He stood and I stepped back, giving room.

"Come," he said, holding out his hand once more, "We have a bit more time before sunrise."

Taking it, we began to meander through the Greek Grove, as Alcaeus referred to it. All of me did not want to ruin this perfect moment with talk of our upcoming fight, but who knew if we'd have another chance?

"Whatever is bothering you, let it go, if just for tonight," said Alcaeus, ripping me from my thoughts. He stopped only to put a hand gently against my cheek. "When the time comes, you will know what to do. Our fight is inevitable. Remember what I told you: with desperate reliance on your intuition and intellectual fortitude, I ask you to continue searching for the truth. Tonight, we shall fill it with only the memory of each other. Please."

"Alright," I conceded, all my bluster deflating though my frown perpetuated. "How do you do that?"

"What?"

"Overcome my own logic." As much as I tried to hold my frown, a relenting smile took its place.

"Our Fated balances us like no one else can; that is their gift." Unatti stood ahead of us in the path, her hand tucked in the crook of her mate's arm. "And he is right: cherish these precious moments as you have been afforded so little."

I smiled at her. "Good evening, Unatti."

Before she could respond, Alcaeus held out his hands to them. "Queen Unatti. Prince Tambal. What good company to keep this evening." Unatti's strikingly handsome mate stepped forward and the two men embraced forearms. When he bowed his head, Alcaeus responded, "No, Tambal. You are amongst friends here. We can forego royal protocol."

Tambal's handsome face brightened. He was as tall as Alcaeus and looked just as naturally battle-ready.

"Of course. It's good to see you, old friend." A look passed between them that spoke of sincere friendship...and concern. But Tambal looked past him. "So, this is the woman who conquered the heart of *The Great Owl*. The one Athena fated you to." His smile was so warm and welcoming, so sincere, my blush scaled my body. "Greetings, Alchemist. I am most honoured to meet you. Unatti speaks highly of you and your fight with Ryobo only showed us how worthy you are to be queen to the King of Nightmares."

"There is no *King* of Nightmares. That title was lost long ago." All of us turned to the Champion with the sharp Irish brogue. When Alcaeus stepped forward, blocking me from the view of the Unseelie King, he held his hands up. "Calm yourself, *Great Owl*. Tonight is not the night for old quarrels." When I emerged from behind Alcaeus, Ruarc's gaze ran me up and down, a glimpse of heat before the mask of mysteriousness slipped over his face.

"Greetings to the Unseelie King," Tambal's voice was a rich distraction to the tension, his cadence holding a royal edge. "What brings the Morrigan's Raven to dwell among the flowers with us?"

"I'm sure you know I have a façade to play," teased Ruarc, looking sharp in his plaid. "I am merely keeping up appearances."

There was a current of danger in the atmosphere, despite his attempts at elevating the mood. For the first time in a long time, I felt... young. To be surrounded by kings and queens of some of the most ancient cultures this world has known, by walking legends, left me feeling tentative. Careful. This situation was not for me to take the lead but rather, to observe and watch how this game was played.

A warm hand slipped into mine and I looked up to see Unatti by my side. Her presence chased away my discomfort. Until she lifted my hand to her face, the one that held the mark of agreement between Ruarc and me.

The deep growl that came from her raised the hairs on my skin, my body stiffening.

"You *dare* mark a Fated with your own," she said through clenched, sharp teeth. "It is forbidden! You know this, Raven."

The man in question took on a bored look, an edge of annoyance in the way his shoulders dropped. "It's merely a formality; she and I have a deal. A simple mark of transaction. You Were and your piousness with mates is downright insufferable."

"It is sacrilege," Unatti snapped back. "I know you still ache with the loss of your own Fated. Viviane was a great loss to us all. But this gives you no right to—"

"That is not why and you know it!" Finally, Ruarc's true feelings spilled out. "This has nothing to do with her," he pointed an accusing finger at the Were-Queen, "so don't you even utter a syllable of her name to me!"

Another deep, guttural growl emitted, sending shivers along my skin and fear racing through my veins as Tambal took a step toward Ruarc. "Careful, King of the Unseelie. It is known how much you enjoy bending rules to suit your needs. Unatti is right; the Alchemist is new to our way of life and you have clearly utilised her ignorance to benefit whatever plans you have."

"Plans?" Ruarc scoffed before pointing a finger at me, "She was the one who came to me for a deal. A deal made for *him*." He glared at Alcaeus, who remained steadfast; his face gave nothing away. "And yet you treat me as though I am a viper in your midsts!"

Unatti opened her mouth only to close it when Alcaeus lifted a hand to silence them all. "Enough. If Ruarc is guilty for marking Melisandre then I am just as responsible in allowing him to do it. My Fated made her choices, as did the Raven. It's useless to bicker over it now." Unatti narrowed her eyes at him, seeing something that I did not. Alcaeus shared a look with her. "I fear our time together this night is at an end." He took my hand from Unatti's, his thumb tracing the mark Ruarc had left before slowly raising it to his lips. My other hand cupped his face but he released me, urging me to the Unseelie King's side. "It is in all of our best interests not to risk drawing Ragna's attention."

"Alcaeus," I began but he shook his head.

Unatti now stood beside Tambal, who had his arm around her waist. Their expression of frustration and disapproval said everything words could not.

"Go." Hurt snuck its slimy tendrils around my chest yet there were no words to change the course of the situation. Glaring at the smirking Unseelie King, I took several angry steps toward him but then I felt a tug.

Alcaeus pulled me back to him, twirling me to face him so his lips came crashing down to mine. His kiss was consuming, branding me. Our tongues danced but he commanded our steps. I wanted to absorb every sensation, every smell, every taste. My hands wound their way around his neck and chest as he pulled me closer just to kiss me deeper.

And then he let go. Dark sensuality burned in his eyes, and something else. Pain.

The strong arm that wrapped around my middle was not enough to tear my eyes away from Alcaeus. Only the darkness that began to swirl around us was what finally broke our connection.

ቖᚖ𐐼ħΨⅤ⅗⅗

When the darkness faded away, we stood in a quiet gazebo which appeared to be far away from the Greek area of the gardens. The distant sounds of chatter told me we were much closer to the party which only fuelled my irritation.

Yanking myself away from Ruarc's hold, I moved away just to get some space between us.

"What? No snappy remark? No accusation for ruining your precious moments with Alcaeus?"

Pulling in a long breath and taking the time to release it was exactly what I needed at that moment. My emotions cooled and rationale took over.

"Ruarc," I replied simply, "You always have a reason for your presence. I merely want to know what it is."

He cocked his head at me, as if I had done something unpredictable. Maybe I had.

"Interesting," he said, "very interesting. The Alchemist is learning." When I didn't feed into his response, he continued, "Tomorrow you fight the reigning champion. He is a true Lycan; a Werewolf above Werewolves. The Tengu prefers trickery, waiting for the right moment before striking. But a Were? He will come at you with such force, your tender flesh will be shredded in an instant. His magic is in his ability to shift at will, to multiply his image into a full pack that is capable of replicating the damage his main form does. So, the fight must be quick. And," Ruarc stalked over to me until he was all I could see, "I may know something about him you do not."

He met my deadpan stare with a grin. "You know everything about him I do not, Ruarc, don't be coy. Why are you helping me?"

Red hair grazed the side of my face, mingling with my own as he whispered in my ear, "Because it benefits me to do so." Swiping my hand, he tucked it into the crook of his arm. "Now, come. Use those legendary senses I've heard all about and find his weakness. Ah, but one moment."

He stepped back and whispered something.

The feel of my outfit changed and instantly I felt the loss of the beautiful outfit Alcaeus had conjured on me. But I also knew I could not approach the Champions wearing Alcaeus' traditional clothing. Instead, a supple black cocktail dress flowed around me. My ears felt heavy and I touched the pear-shaped rubies that dangled from them.

"Half of me expected you to put me in a *léine*," I mumbled, flexing my hand as his ring reappeared. It had taken a spot on my bedside table and stayed there, until now.

"As much as I would love to see you clothed in the tradition of the Éire, that is one lie I will not condone. Out of respect, you understand. But if you do change your mind about my proposal…" Ruarc's teasing grin widened at the 'not on your life' look I gave him. Especially after witnessing the kiss Alcaeus gave me.

We approached the main area of the party and it was clear from the leisurely positions that it had reached the end of the festivities. There were still a few groups of people standing and talking, but those sitting held the posture of many hours of drinking and merriment. Across the main table where Ragna was seated were several smaller, though no less decorated, tables. It was here that Ruarc led us. As I went to take a seat beside him, he made a tsk tsk sound, pulling me into his lap. Trying not to stiffen, my attempts at only sitting at the very edge of his lap failed when his arm wrapped around my middle and tucked me into his chest.

But I knew why as his voice resonated next to my ear. "Now, I'm going to feed you and you will sit there and look like you're enjoying my attention. But observe. See without seeing." My hair waved in our faces at the gentle breeze and he pushed it back, looking to all like a loving gesture.

The smell of olives and cheese awakened my hunger and I didn't protest when he lifted a stuffed olive to my lips. As the oily and salty goodness exploded on my tastebuds, I did as he commanded.

I observed.

The woman Elis had chastised at the welcoming feast was bent over laughing across from me with several others, whispering gossip between giggles. A bit further away, the Seelie queen lounged on a gold chaise among the flowers, surrounded by her court. They, too, looked merry, though flickering glances made it very clear all were under surveillance.

As my gaze landed upon my truest enemy, I glowered instinctively but Ruarc took advantage, kissing me right underneath my ear. My breath hitched in surprise and as I opened my mouth to tell him off, a plump raspberry plopped inside and stopped my words.

"Easy. Observe," he whispered against my skin. Grumbling inwardly, I did so once more. Siggeir, the former champion, sat next to Ragna. My eyebrows hit my hairline.

The Lycan leaned in and kissed her and she kissed him back with equal vigour. When they broke apart, he trailed kisses up her jawline and she smiled indulgently. They looked like two lovers, lost in each other's gaze.

"I thought relations between Vampire and Were were prohibited?" I whispered, confused.

"Highly discouraged because of the creature that can be born from the two species but it is well known Ragna need not worry of breeding. Hel had no intention of letting her pet multiply." Ruarc said it so matter of fact but I believe it went without saying we agreed it was for the best.

Looking at them, realisation hit me.

"Ragna is behind our fight, isn't she?"

Ruarc nuzzled my ear. "Very good, Alchemist."

"She wants me dead. She wants me out of the way, so she's seduced Siggeir to do her dirty work."

"Look closer."

I frowned, but after searching Ruarc's face, it dawned on me. Switching to my inner sight, I saw them on a molecular level. My eyes chased the geometry of the molecules that made up Siggeir's body, many parts coated in an oily sheen; magic. But then I saw it. My eyes widened as I looked back at Ruarc's knowing smirk.

CHAPTER 36

"Too slow! Your enemy will see the second you show vulnerability and will strike! You must know your weaknesses before they do. Again!" Athena slammed down her spear, and the spar continued.

Sweat dripped from Alcaeus' brow, his muscles shaking from exertion. Yet his focus was unbroken as he faced off against the Champion of Jiutian Xuannü. Zhenbai's wings burned with heavenly light in his phoenix-like form, chasing away Alcaeus' darkness that was attempting to envelop them.

The left side of Alcaeus' body was scorched and a sharp wound from Zhenbai's biting beak oozed. Athena would not allow him to heal until the training session was done. To rise above physical adversity was a fundamental principle in her training; it was also a painful reminder of his mistakes.

The phoenix dove for him and Alcaeus attempted to dodge but Zhenbai's talons snatched his ankle with a powerful crunch, yet made no move for a killing blow. Letting slip a growling curse, Alcaeus used his momentum to swing himself upwards. The steel sword in his right hand thrust against Zhenbai's leg, its razor edge finding its mark.

The Fènghuáng released him with a cry. But instead of flying away, Alcaeus saw an opportunity and took it. His sword swiped at Zhenbai's left wing, scoring it. A piercing shriek escaped from his sparring partner, and he fell to the ground below. As soon as Zhenbai hit the ground, his body was once more a man's.

"當你的敵人唯一目標是想毀滅你時，表現出寬大的態度，就是把自己的刀刃對準自己，真白．反思這一點，我的創造物 *(To show leniency when your enemy seeks only your destruction, is to turn your own blade on yourself, Zhenbai. Reflect upon this, my creation)."Jiutian Xuannü leaned back in her seat, her pale fingers grazing cherry-red lips in consternation. Her other hand caressed the glimmering pearls against her chest.*

Alcaeus glided to the landing that overlooked the arena where their goddess observed them. As his feet touched the ground, his wounds began to heal rapidly.

"Your Champion shows great promise, Athena," said Jiutian Xuannü, her eyes roving over him in admiration.

Athena bowed her head in acknowledgement. "As does Zhenbai; his soul magic was clever of you."

The Chinese goddess gave a sultry smile, "I fear he would make a better lover than a fighter. Regardless, he and Alcaeus will be one another's sharpening stones." Then her beautiful face pulled together in focus as if seeing beyond just him. In an otherworldly tone she said, "A storm is coming. Together, their bond will be as strong as spider's silk in the hurricane."

Alcaeus fiddled with the jade pendant Zhenbai had given to him after his first victory in the Divine Games so many years ago. In a time where creations like him were naturally born to be enemies with each other, the friendships he developed went beyond political necessity.

The Chinese goddess of war was as wise as she was beautiful and he would be a liar if he said he hadn't admired her in his youth, when she and Athena would meet. Champions are not born but created in their full image; however, their minds are new at the beginning, like a small child's.

He chuckled to himself at many of the verbal blunders he'd made in the presence of Athena, several times pulling laughter from her at his antics. Or how he would sometimes hide away to read instead of going to the practice yard for hours of gruelling combat drills. To his surprise, his mistress did not reprimand him but adjusted his schedule; *"A warrior's training begins in the mind, Alcaeus–it would be counterproductive to punish you for training your most invaluable weapon. But do not shirk one for the other; we must find balance."*

Those days seemed far more simple and, for the first time in a long time, Alcaeus wished he could seek her wisdom. He clenched the necklace, touching his forehead to his fist as he shut his eyes.

Without his wings, the battle between himself and the giant Scottish serpent was going to be exceedingly difficult. Aerial combat was his specialty as was the ability to bring his opponent's greatest fears alive in the fight. Weak minds would crumble in terror. But a Beithir was not an intelligent creature, acting on pure instincts of ravenous hunger. It had no fears he could wield against it.

"Sire, we must make for the arena; the games are about to begin." Tomwyl's calming voice broke through his rumination and Alcaeus stood from his seat at his desk.

A large owl suddenly flew in to perch on his outstretched arm. The bird hooted before taking the necklace from Alcaeus' hand. "See that Melisandre gets this."

With a quick scratch to its feathered head, it took off. He watched its departure for a moment before magic swirled his body, changing his attire into armour. Tomwyll walked over to him, adjusting the joints and checking to make sure all was in its proper place.

"You will win this, Sire," said Tomwyll, "a Beithir is no match for Athena's warrior, even with your weakened magic."

Alcaeus adjusted his gloves and cuffs, frowning in thought. "Under any other circumstance, I would agree. Yet, I have the mind to allow it the upper hand. Perhaps it is time for me to accept my fate. Put an end to Ragna's manipulation."

Tomwyl paused. "Why would you possibly consider such a thing, Sire? It is not like you to accept defeat. Especially in regards to the queen."

Rubbing a hand against his Fated Mark, Alcaeus replied, "Truthfully, because I cannot live in a world where I could hurt Melisandre. There is no reality in which I would readily raise my blade to her nor force her to do the same. The time I did, even under Ragna's control, still haunts and sickens me."

The steward finished his fussing and walked to the front of his liege. His arms went behind him as he visibly contemplated his answer.

"My king, I am but a simple Vampire, a lowly servant. So, my words may hold little importance, but might I be frank with you?" Alcaeus nodded and Tomwyl continued. "You are a most noble warrior, a fine protector. You have spent years protecting Lady Von Boden, shielding her from the horrors of the Otherworld. As any mate would do for his lady love. But the lady in question has shown you, on numerous occasions, that she is very capable of handling herself."

Alcaeus slowly nodded. "That is a very accurate observation, yes, she has."

"I think, if I may be so bold, that your overprotective nature prevents you from trusting her to have answers when you do not, especially to your current predicament. Have faith, my king, that Lady Von Boden might come up with a solution. Responsibility to rule does not lie on the king alone; that is why he has a queen. Allow her the opportunity to do so."

Giving his steward a firm squeeze on the shoulder, Alcaeus replied, "You are anything but a lowly servant, Tomwyl. You are a wise advisor. And you are a true friend. Thank you."

The greying Vampire gave a bow of his head. "Thank you, Sire. It is my honour to serve you." Then, a teasing smile lit the corners of his mouth. "Besides, tonight is the Yule Ball; how could I allow my king to miss the opportunity to have his first dance with his beloved?"

Alcaeus gave a masculine chuckle, patting Tomwyl on the shoulder before making his way to the door. "True, although trying to get her to dance with me in front of everyone will be a feat even greater than defeating the Beithir, I think."

The steward smiled and with a regal bow, replied, "The Champion of Athena will persevere, as he always has."

☿☽⌇ℏΨ♈︎♈︎

Clinging to my pendant, I surveyed the arena from where I sat on my perch in Ruarc's box. This time, there were cushions awaiting my spot on the wide stone bannister that I had turned into my bench. The Unseelie king's consideration was always cause for concern but I wasn't so impolite as to not offer thanks. Of course, I was met with a teasing remark on the many ways I could show my gratitude. My biting reply gave me the silence I desired as well as the satisfaction of shutting him down. Again.

The sudden fluttering of wings had me sitting up straight as a large owl descended, landing in front of me. Dangling from its sharp beak was a silver necklace with a jade medallion. When I did not reach for it right away, the owl bobbed its head and flared its wings before hopping as close as it could without touching my crossed legs.

As soon as the cool metal reached my hands, the bird hooted several times and flew off. My thumbs ran over the ornate carved stone; a phoenix with its wings spread. There was an intricate silver dragon wrapped around the top half, as if guarding the magnificent bird. It was a bit large in size, covering a sizable part of my palm. But on a man, it would be perfectly sized, and not too gaudy.

Concern bloomed inside me. Yet, my stomach sank at the implications of what this gift could mean. Alcaeus was losing hope, this I knew well.

But could it mean more? Is there a hidden meaning behind this gift?

I glanced over at Ruarc, who was in deep conversation with Cú and Fionn. They were seated amongst a small coffee table of food and drink. Occasionally, a small Brownie servant would stop by to refresh things and, to my surprise, Láeg was always quick to show gratitude and to help them while the others ignored the servant's existence.

He caught me watching him and came to join me.

"What sparks your interest so, Alchemist?" He leaned his hip against the stone, surveying the noisy crowd around us before those gentle eyes settled on me.

"Just observing a trait that is usually foreign in this kind of company."

"Oh? And what is that?"

"Kindness."

Láeg smiled, tucking his hands underneath his arms. "That is a beautiful necklace; does it hold any special meaning to you?"

His deflection didn't bother me as I looked down at the piece of jewellery fit for a king.

"It is from Alcaeus," I said quietly. "As to its meaning, I have yet to discover it. But...I think it might have belonged to Lord Zhenbai. The phoenix is similar."

"Well, either way, you may not have to wait long."

We both looked down to see the lone figure walking in the sand toward the middle. Suddenly, the arena expanded, yet our view encompassed everything. Magic.

Alcaeus was dressed in the same clothes as when I first met him; all leather, metal, and black fabric. Nemesis hung at his side, swinging gently with each confident step he took.

Unatti's booming voice resounded around the arena, the richness of her alto sending shivers over my skin.

"Ladies and Gentlemen! Many of you have never seen a true Champion fight! But today is a most fortunate day! You will be witnessing the undefeated winner of all the Divine Games! Queen Ragna Valdis Heldottir, the Nightmare Queen and Champion of Hel, gives you: The Godslayer—Alcaeus Pallas, Champion of Athena!"

To say the crowd roared was an understatement; this was their Prince of Nightmares. For many, it was their king. Dishes and furniture veritably shook from the applause. Alcaeus made no other move once he stood in the middle. When he should look small from here, instead, his presence matched the magnanimity of the arena.

"He shall face none other than the proxy of the Champion of Aine! Queen Mab, The Shining Sun of the Seelie Court, brings you: THE BEITHIR!"

Suddenly the sand on the other side of the arena began swirling, like the tornadoes that Ryobo had conjured. The ground opened and the monster's head slithered through, followed by its serpentine body. No words were adequate to describe quite what I was seeing.

Yet, this serpent had four legs, equipped with large, thick claws. It reared its massive head, flaring out its hood the way the king cobra does. The term 'snake' would be so inadequate to describe it. Blue-green iridescent scales glittered in the light of the arena. Its forked-tongue tasted the air, instantly zoning in on Alcaeus, who had yet to move. Waves of screams and shouts resounded from the mob, the sheer size of the Beithir causing instinctive panic.

"There is a reason you should always burn the body of a snake after cutting off its head," murmured Láeg, possessing a calm demeanour in the face of chaos. "Otherwise, that is what you get."

I sat up, taking in a sharp breath only to hold it in, trying to comprehend the beast before me. It was as breathtaking as it was terrifying.

"This is a fight to THE DEATH!" The crowd roared at the declaration. **"Warriors, prepare for battle!"**

The Beithir slithered to the middle but I gasped at the sheer speed with which it moved. Alcaeus simply drew his sword in one long, slow movement. A deep hood came over his head, his face now masked in shadow.

A silent tension fell over the arena. My heart was a pounding drum awaiting the one who would make the first move.

"BEGIN!"

The serpent struck. Alcaeus leapt into the air, away from the deadly poisonous swords thrusting towards him. The move was seamless and the two began a dance of death.

Gasps and screams erupted as the Beithir raced past him, cutting off his escape. But Alcaeus merely jumped over its tail, slicing through its shining hide, separating flesh from bone. The decapitated tail continued to writhe and the great serpent gave a roaring scream, chasing him with a vengeance.

Sand kicked up so badly that it blinded onlookers, and I got up on my knees, my fingers digging into the stone pillar my back had been resting against. Rapid and chaotic movement had me switching to my Alchemist's vision; I regretted it in an instant.

Alcaeus had been snagged in the thick coils of the Beithir, its muscles constricting in hypnotising movements. His arms were trapped – Nemesis useless at his side.

Green-gold slitted eyes burned with a predator's gaze as it lifted up its prey. White fangs flashed in the light and I reflexively jerked forward as the monster's open jaws hit where Alcaeus was.

An arm came around me as Láeg whispered, "Easy, now. Look."

Inky blackness exploded from the centre of its coils. Then a large black sphere appeared, high above the Beithir's hooded head. A gleaming light, like a falling star, pierced through the sphere as Alcaeus flew down from it. Straight towards the head of the snake. Like a bullet cutting through the air. Bright light sliced at the base of the Beithir's head, before Alcaeus exploded through it. Blood sprayed with the pulse of its heart and the arena rained red.

With a swift thrust, he stabbed Nemesis into the meaty flesh of the fallen beast. As he absorbed its power, I eased back onto my heels. Láeg had let me go, moving back to stand next to me. But the fluttering of blood-red hair saw me looking past him to Ruarc, who stood with his arms crossed. His brows were drawn together hard, his profile filled with tension. But not with concern or pure concentration, no, but with rage. Pure, unadulterated rage.

As the Beithir disintegrated, its body now a dry husk to become one with the sands of the Megálo Kolossaío, only its open-jawed head remained. The crowd watched the Prince of Nightmares.

Suddenly, tendrils of shadow burst forth from Alcaeus, swirling around until it flared out as massive black wings. They expanded, and he thrust his glowing sword to the sky.

All of the Otherworld roared. They chanted his name. They stomped their feet with arms raised. Chills broke out from my whole body, the adrenaline and soundwaves of the entire arena reverberating through me.

When the magic of the stadium condensed in size and Alcaeus turned towards our box, we locked eyes. I kissed my fingers and reached out to him. Placing a black-gloved hand over his heart, my Fated bowed his head to me. Emotion consumed me, dominated by relief and some deeper affection.

"Come, Alchemist," Ruarc's growling voice shattered the moment. "You must get ready, for your fight with the reigning champion is next."

Clutching the jade necklace, I took one last look at Alcaeus before heading off to face Ragna's assassin.

CHAPTER 37

What I was about to do was insane. It was a complete gamble, where one mistake would cost me everything. Today would be the day that I tested the theory of my immortality.

Gripping my staff with both hands, I leaned against the wall. The gates to the arena were to my left, and I waited with bated breath for the sound of those hinges groaning when it opened.

The noisy crowd was an incessant buzzing of sound. I closed my eyes. Sweat trickled through my hair and down my neck. Dusty air scraped through my nose. A low whine breaking through it all.

I looked down to see those golden eyes of Ares staring up at me from where he sat. A grin of relief and gratitude washed over me and I kneeled down to him.

"Ares! Where have you been, my black wolf?" My fingers scratched through his fur deeply.

His pink tongue licked my forearm and then my cheek. I leaned down and gave him a kiss on the head. My forehead replaced where my lips had been and Ares and I stayed there for a moment, happy to be together once more.

Pulling back, I said, "I'm glad I got to see you, Ares. You've been sorely missed." He gave a desperate whiny, growly bark, as if desperately wanting to tell me something. I gave him a bittersweet smile. "I know, boy. I wish you could tell me too. But this is enough."

My pendants came free from where they were hiding underneath my shirt and he did a curious thing: first, teeth clamped around the jade, giving it a gentle tug before letting go and nudging his large black nose into them.

"Have you…? Were you with Zhenbai? Is that what you're saying?" He gave a definite nod and, in that moment, I so desperately wished I could read minds. "Has he succeeded? Did he find a way to free Alcaeus' kingdom?" With another nod, my excitement lifted. "Was he able to do it?"

Ares stared at me. No nod or shake of his big head. Just a slight tilt to the side, telling me nothing.

Chewing the inside of my cheek in thought, I came to a stand but not before giving him one last kiss and a scratch behind his ears. That large groaning of the hinges caused me to turn, watching the gate open. Yet, one thought, one about completing my Mark with Alcaeus, bugged me.

"Ares, is it safe to complete—" When I turned back around, Ares was gone.

Unspoken thoughts weighed heavily on me. I stared out into the waiting stands and boisterous crowd. For a moment, I tried to imagine what it would have been like if my only purpose was to put my life on the line out there, just for the whim of others. To settle quarrels that were not my own. To slay another if for no other reason than because some spiteful god or goddess said so.

"Alcaeus…" The whisper of his name on my lips was the afterthought of the anguish at what he'd been subjected to. What we'd both been subjected to.

No. Today, I was going to make Ragna regret crossing me. This was the moment I would put fear into those twisted and psychotic emerald eyes. And I would only raise a single hand to do it.

Shouts erupted, the buzzing sounds of everyone going from a steady rhythm to a crescendo as I walked deeper into the sands. Walking the same path as Alcaeus just moments ago.

What surprised me was that the yelling of the crowd towards me was angry, full of insults and mockery. Things were thrown in my direction but the magic of the arena saw them dissolved before even hitting the ground.

Ah, I was going against their reigning champion after all. Perhaps it's not surprising their competitive nature came out in full force now. Though, I did have some cheering for me.

It wasn't hard to spot Elis and Llyr; their entire row and the one above and below it was covered in flowers. And there stood my best friend, waving his hands at me. Llyr was seated, and looked to be pulling fallen flowers out of his hair. Failing to completely hide my smile, I gave him an acknowledging nod as I came to a stop in the middle of the arena.

A lone figure was sauntering towards me, his confident swagger only strengthening my resolve at what I was about to do.

Pride doth come before the fall, they say, and oh, how far you shall plummet, Siggeir.

He was classically handsome. Strong. But I wasn't Ragna. I would not delight in the consequences of my future actions. In fact, guilt tried to barge its way in, causing me to second guess myself in more ways than one. I shut it down.

No. A wise man once told me: *Therefore, let him who desires peace, prepare for war.* If peace is what I desired, then Siggeir must become a casualty of the war that Ragna had waged.

Unatti's announcement boomed, but I barely heard it. Time seemed to slow as the Lycan Were drew closer, eventually coming to a stop. He was still quite far from me, at least 100 metres. Siggeir squared his broad, naked shoulders. Only linen pants covered his lower half but barely.

The tension in the arena mounted as Unatti finished introducing us and stating the terms. My mind raced with equations, replaying what I was about to do over, and over again. I had to get this right. One wrong symbol, number, could cost me everything. My palms began to sweat and I squeezed the metal of my staff harder.

"BEGIN!"

☿☧♄Ψ∨ϟϟ

Alcaeus looked out over the arena to where his Fated stood once more. His strong arms were crossed firmly over his chest in his spread-legged stance, hard consternation all over his face. Melisandre had beaten the Tengu because the demon had given her the time to do it; all for his love of mind games. But Weres were a different fight entirely. Worry ate at him, wondering how Melisandre would handle the incoming assault that was the equivalent of taking on an entire battalion.

He had once fought against Managarmr, Fenrir's Champion. Alcaeus' throat was nearly torn out and he almost lost a wing. It was one of the hardest battles in his career as a gladiator.

That proud jaw ticked in worried frenzy but a deep part of him knew not to underestimate his beloved.

At Unatti's announcement to commence the fighting, Alcaeus stepped closer to the open window.

"Perhaps, Milord would prefer sitting next to his queen? It would be far more comfortable—" attempted a black-robed advisor but Ragna cut in.

"No, let him watch. I have been waiting too long for this moment. I want to see his face when Melisandre falls." She sat back, crossing one leg over the other as a servant poured more blood into her chalice. Blood slaves hung on the back walls of the royal box, knicks from their necks dripping into bowls below them.

Alcaeus ignored her. Paid no heed to the rich metallic taint in the air that a lesser Vampire would have been tempted by.

He was consumed with the scene in front of him. At first, nothing happened. Melisandre stood there, her brilliant silver staff firmly in her right hand. She wore no armour, no kind of protection against the sword-sharp claws and teeth Siggeir would attempt to shred her with. His lover was a tiny thing in this massive arena. Vulnerable. Prey.

Then it happened. Siggeir let out a roar that turned into a chilling howl, thrusting his arms out as black fur rippled over his shoulders, cascading down his back and over his body. Every part of him grew, muscles bursting as joints and tendons snapped into place. The pants he wore ripped off as his thighs morphed and elongated. The Norse Were now stood over 9 ft tall, his arm span terrifyingly wide. He continued to howl through his wolf face, jaws so visibility powerful they could break bones without a thought.

Melisandre simply stood there and watched. Alcaeus leaned down, putting both palms against the stone bannister.

What are you doing, my heart? What are you planning? He thought to himself, not attempting to connect their minds, for the ancient magic of the Megálo Kolossaío prevented anyone or anything from interfering as soon as the battle began.

Siggeir swiped his left arm out, holding it there. Mirror copies of him flickered into existence. They mimicked his every move for a moment, before flickering again and becoming autonomous.

She continued to stand there, doing nothing.

Nervousness was a growing fire in Alcaeus' chest. Only for the feeling to explode at the same rate as the Lycan who now bolted for Melisandre.

His little badger still had not reacted. But when she finally moved, it was only just. She raised her staff, only to smack it into the sand. Nothing else.

Purple light flashed underneath the copies of Siggeir, and each one began to methodically shatter, like glass. As if she was deconstructing them mid-step. They tried to dodge, but to no avail. The Lycan only briefly took notice, running harder as each of his wolves disappeared until only he was left.

Siggeir was now just a few paces from Melisandre. In mere moments he'd be on her, and yet, still she didn't move.

Alcaeus could hold back no longer. "Move!" he shouted, only to reach out with his hand and scream "No!" His heart plummeted as he watched the massive Lycan hit Melisandre full force.

The Werewolf brought his beloved to the ground, dust swirling around them from the impact. The kind of impact that could kill her instantly.

Jerking away, Alcaeus rushed to the huge bowl that stood on a pedestal in front of the seating, where its magic water gave them a close-up view of the contestants. Helplessly, desperately trying to connect their minds, knowing it would end in failure.

"No, no, no," he chanted desperately, the Fated Mark on his chest burning in anguish. In pain. He dared not breathe.

Siggeir remained above her, his claw still posed for a fatal strike. Yet, he appeared frozen.

Locked in time.

That's when Alcaeus saw why: Melisandre had a hand against Siggeir's chest, right above his heart. Blood trickled from the side of her mouth but her eyes glowed molten metals. Through them, he assumed what could only be bright purple transmutation circles, ticked in her eyes.

The scene triggered a memory. *Never let an Alchemist touch your heart*, she had said. Back then, he had thought it was merely a romantic gesture, a tease.

Alcaeus' eyes widened. Siggeir's face looked as if he was choking, eyes bugging out of his head. He suddenly ripped himself away from her, stumbling with a shrieking, painful whine. His claws grasped at his chest and throat, throwing himself to the ground, writhing. Fur began rapidly falling out in clumps. Drool and fluids ran like waterfalls from every orifice.

Melisandre moved then, dragging her staff to her, she used it to push herself to her knees. Her left arm hung broken at her side; her shoulder oddly contorted. But she showed no pain. Just watched the scene unfold.

Shock filled Alcaeus as his attention turned back to the Lycan. Open sores appeared all over his body, only to become wider until the white of his bones shone through. His flesh was actively rotting off him. He howled in agony, a scream that became more human as his body decayed before the entire crowd. There was only one thing that had caused the same exact effect.

The Sickness.

"By the gods..." said someone in a horrified whisper beside him.

"The Alchemist... S-she...she wielded the Sickness?"

"The proxy was infected!?"

Alcaeus stood, returning to the window.

Siggeir, proxy of King Managarm, was dead. His body looked as if he'd been dead for days.

The entirety of the arena was silent. Horror wrapped around that silence in the same manner the Sickness had taken their reigning champion.

Melisandre got to her feet, leaning heavily on her staff. She doubled over for a moment, blood rushing out of her mouth. Alcaeus' hands became fists, clenching in worry.

Yet, she simply wiped her mouth and proceeded to stand tall. Proud. Then she looked up to their box as the arena closed in. Past him and straight to Ragna, whose face was tight and pale. And filled with her usual psychotic rage. But there was a deeper wariness that was quickly turning into fear.

Then, his little Alchemist pointed her staff at their mutual enemy. Her message was clear for all the world to see.

See me and know your days are numbered.

In the eyes of all the Otherworld, Melisandre had just become an equal power to the Queen of Bones.

CHAPTER 38

My legs gave out the moment I passed the Gates of Victory. My body was in shock. Eyes watering at the pain, I struggled to breathe. Siggeir had collapsed one of my lungs, my ribs were broken. My spine was thankfully intact but there was bone bruising. Based on my hematemesis, I had also sustained injury to my stomach and esophagus. My left arm was a constant throb, from fingertip all the way to collarbone. I dared not look at my shoulder. I felt it well enough.

Stone hit my knees, my pain so great it muted what I felt in my fall.

"Melly! Oh my god, Mels!" Elis' voice barely registered but his tear-covered face filled my vision. A white linen kerchief dabbed at my face as he called over his shoulder, "Llyr, come quick!"

Even with my regenerative abilities, the damage was causing my whole body to shake, teeth rattling my skull. I squeezed my eyes shut against the eye-watering pain, taking an unsteady hand to my shattered shoulder.

"E-Elis," I rasped, "I need you to push down on top of m-my hand, on my shoulder when I s-say. I have t-to—"

"Sh, shh, don't speak, just nod when you're ready," he replied, placing his warm hand over mine.

Taking a ragged inhale, I gave the nod.

"Stop!" Llyr was suddenly beside us on my other side. That's when I took notice of the small crowd of onlookers. "Cease and desist whatever you were about to do and let me take a look at you."

299

"My s-shoulder needs to be reset...before we—"

"Heal the break, yes, however," his hand hovered above my body, assessing as those olive-green eyes met mine with a firm look, "perhaps let the healer of over a thousand years of experience do the healing, hmm? Just relax, Melisandre, and let us take care of you."

He would get no argument from me. Just as he hovered his hands over me, a sharp command of move! had both men quickly coming to a stand, only to have Ruarc scoop me up in his arms as the air around us turned black. Blackness gave way to our shared room and he quickly laid me on the bed.

Not saying a word, the king backed up as Llyr was once more beside me.

"I am going to have you sleep while I do this, so it won't be so painful."

"No, please, I'd rather not...in such a weakened state...too vulnerable..." Concern deepened the lines of his face and I could tell he didn't want to but gave a quick nod anyway.

"How long will this take? I need her ready for the ball after the games. Her presence is expected." Ruarc's voice was curt. Impatient.

For the first time, Llyr's diplomatic demeanour slipped as angry annoyance passed over his face.

"She will be ready, Your Highness." The pound of leather boots on hardwood and the slam of the door was the only answer Llyr received. He gave a laborious sigh, opening his mouth to say something only for Elis to cut in.

"The nerve of that pompous, heartless Fae! Why are they always so self-serving, such entitled pieces of shi—"

"I am Fae, my darling..."

"—and I cannot fathom how he can ask such a question when his intended lies broken and bleeding on the bed—"

"Elis," I croaked. "Please let your mate work his healing wonders."

Deflated amethyst eyes took me in and he nodded, "Quite right, my dear."

The bed dipped and, to my surprise, Elis cuddled up next to me but still gave Llyr room to work. Taking my right hand in both of his, he tucked our hands by his face, looking at me through glassy eyes of emotion.

"I realised a most terrible thing today, Mels," whispered Elis. "I could have lost you. When he...struck you down, I really believed my best friend had just been murdered in front of me and I just stood by and watched..."

I didn't turn to look at him, instead my eyes stayed closed as I sighed, "You're not going to lose me, Elis. The Stone gives me immortality, from what I have concluded. Besides, I had it all in hand."

"Mmm, I see. Is that what you call this then?"

"The plan wasn't without risk," I retorted. "But I'm here. Siggeir is not. I'd consider that a success, all things considering."

"It *was* a fight to the death, my love," piped in Llyr.

Elis sat up. "Key word being 'fight'! She just stood there! You didn't even try to protect yourself!"

It took everything in me not to snap grumpily back, between the eye-watering pain and exhaustion settling over me; I just wanted to be left alone. But admittedly, what my friends must have witnessed was no doubt horrifying. They were owed an answer, at the very least.

"I am very capable of transmutation at a distance but...Siggeir being a Were, means he has a considerable amount of magic surrounding his form when he transitions. The Sickness had barely taken hold; the virus had only just made its way to his nervous system. But magic that surrounded him was a barrier, impenetrable by distance transmutation. There was no way I could outrun him, which left only one solution: I had to touch him directly in centre mass; then I would have complete control over his physical makeup, bypassing any limitations the magic would have given me. Thankfully, his copies were merely projected reflections; I suspected he would use magic to solidify them once they reached their target. So, I had to disrupt the waves of light before they could become corporeal."

"I see," said Elis, looking down at our linked hands. "That certainly makes sense."

"It was foolish," Llyr snapped and both of us turned to him, mixing several things in a glass. Shock was evident on both of our faces at his response. "Reckless to the point of stupidity. Elis was right: you could have died.

"I am always right, but what Mels just said makes sense—"

"Judge me if you must—"

Llyr cut us both off by pulling a surprised gasp from me when warmth cascaded over my body like a warm bath, the throbbing pain easing instantly. The hands hovering over me were the culprit of my ease, no doubt. A long breath released from me. He cupped my face with his slender hand.

"But it was *necessary*." Combing his fingers through my hair, his green eyes softened and the glow of candlelight gave his copper locks a beautiful shine. "You slayed the reigning winner, a known ally to Ragna, in such a manner that no one will challenge you without just cause. You were once a potential prize to be won, to be conquered. Now, all the Champions will see you as an equal they must contend with."

"They will see me as a threat."

"They will see you as an equal *because* you are a threat," corrected Llyr. "The Sickness does not discriminate; it devours all who come in contact with it, Champion or lesser. You did something no one else can do, Melisandre: you controlled it. Wielded it. And that terrified them."

"That's our girl," smiled Elis, squeezing my hand to his chest.

My eyes watered but I could no longer claim it was from the pain. "Thank you. Both of you."

Leaning down, Llyr gave me a gentle kiss on my forehead. "As soon as I am done, you can get some rest. The ball is in several hours so you have time. And you *will* rest." He closed his eyes as his hands found my wounded parts, whispering unknown words. A pinching discomfort was all that I felt and for that I was most grateful.

Once he had finished and my body no longer felt like it had been run over by a raging rhinoceros, Llyr handed me the glass with the mysterious mixture. "Drink this. It will ease any other lasting pain." At my look of suspicion, he gave me an exasperated look. "It's not drugs, Melisandre, just a tonic."

Easing up with the help of Elis, I drank the bitter liquid quickly, then laid back down. Elis released my hand and placed a kiss on my cheek.

"I will come back to wake you and help you dress. I...actually made you a gown for tonight. I was hoping you might..."

A smile lit up my face. "I'll wear it, of course. But you didn't have to, Elis."

He scoffed. "King Ruarc would only turn you into a backdoor, brothel-stinking strumpet. Tonight, of all nights, I refuse to let that happen."

"Thank you, Elis."

He smiled back and said, "Rest." Then quietly followed Llyr to the door, only for it to burst open as Toby barged in.

"Ms. Melly!" My former ward whipped around the bed to my side, skidding to a halt. Shoving his hands in his hair, his brown eyes raced over me, glistening from the tears that hovered in them. "Oh my god, a-are you? Is s-she gonna be alright? A-re y-you...I-I saw you get hit..." He was so close to breaking that I did the only thing I could.

I held my arms out to him. He collapsed against me. Thankfully, most of me was healed, thanks to Llyr, but my soreness was still present and I had to swallow my grunt of discomfort. Wrapping my arms around his back and neck, I held him close as he cried.

Toby was still a child and it was moments like these that reminded me of it. He pulled back slightly, tears and snot flowing freely now.

"W-when you went down, I couldn't watch, Ms. Melly. It was shameful, I know but," Toby hugged me close again, "Please don't make me lose you. P-please."

Rubbing his back I urged, "Look at me, Toby." When he did, I continued, "You won't lose me. It must have been brutal to watch, I'm sorry. But it would take a lot more than a Were to kill me."

Giving a slight smile in an attempt to lighten the mood, Toby gave me a leaky grin in return, only to hug me once more, saying, "I love you, Ms. Melly. So don't die, okay?"

Squeezing him harder, I replied softly against his brown curls, "Alright."

Letting go, we shared one more meaningful look before he joined Elis and Llyr who were equally teary-eyed.

When the door finally shut, the sigh of release was like a pressure valve releasing. Weariness crept along both body and mind. No matter how grateful I was for my friends, my little put-together family, there was only one person I wanted to see.

One person I desperately needed to be held by. Because what I would never admit to a single living soul was just how much I drowned in fear. Perhaps it was the rush of post battle, for during the fight I was numb, but what could only be described as a landslide of emotions hit me.

Throwing an arm over my eyes to stem the tears, I took deep breaths through my nose. But they continued to come and no amount of shoving down my feelings seemed to be working.

Thoughts of singing birds curiously came to mind, then. Running water. Dusty books. The warm fingers of the evening sun touching my skin through old glass windows. Fresh linens on the bed. Silky skin, dusted with hair, muscles rippling underneath as he moved above me. Rough, warrior hands cupping me. Caressing me.

Warm lips descended upon mine. I didn't panic because I knew who it was.

The kiss was deliciously deep, every sensation seemingly spurred by an anxiousness he carried.

"Alcaeus," I gasped as his hand slid my arm away from my face, a firm hand around my wrist to pin it above me. He kissed me again and again and I responded just as fervently. Aggressively. Today, I had looked death in the face. Slammed to the ground by it.

Alcaeus' kiss was proof of life.

Opening my legs, I pulled his big body to me. He settled his hips into mine, pressing as his tongue plunged deep inside, massaging. The sensations, the realness of him, were so overwhelming that my tears began flowing again, hysteria creeping its way between desire and frustration.

Jerking my head away, I covered my face with my arms, shaking as a sob wracked my body.

"Oh, my heart," whispered Alcaeus, "You are safe now. I am here." He shifted off me, wrapping me up in his arms and pulled me against that wonderfully broad chest of his. He was careful, avoiding squeezing me too hard.

But I wanted to *feel*. So, I snuggled up to his body until my arms wrapped around his neck like the anchor of safety his presence promised me. My tears were silent, my body shuddering with each sob. Warm, soothing patterns of touch ran up and down my back as Alcaeus continued to comfort me.

"I-I'm sorry I don't know what's come over me," I choked out, my breathing becoming erratic. "Adrenaline, no doubt."

Alcaeus slid his hand over my Fated Mark, and a soothing warmth came over me.

"Your mind still believes in its mortality; today, it tasted its inevitability. Breathe easy and remind yourself that tomorrow is promised."

"Tomorrow is never promised."

He eased my arms from around him, so my back met the mattress. Putting a large hand over my eyes, his hot breath kissed my lips as he whispered, "For you, it is. Rest."

The kiss he left stayed with me as fatigue finally won out.

♀♂♃♄♅♆♇

The kisses that pulled me from slumber were not the sensual, silken press of Alcaeus' lips. No. Far from it. These were sloppy, slobbery, and stinky.

"Keep at it, old boy, she's bound to wake from your rancid breath alone."

My eyes shot open. Golden eyes and a panting, open-mouthed Ares stared back at me.

"Get off!" I snapped but Ares got a few good licks in before I successfully shoved him off. "I hate you," slipping off the bed and making a beeline for the basin with fresh water and dunking my slimy face in, "and I hate you for allowing him to do that."

Elis was grinning from ear to ear, holding up a towel as I finished washing my face. "If you think I am going to risk any part of me to wake you, then you've learned nothing during the time of our friendship. Now, why you're bothering with that when your bath calls—"

"Bath...?" looking at him through bleary eyes, it dawned on me what event was happening. "Oh, Elis, can I just skip it?"

His elegant features were suddenly smacked with horror. "Miss the—you want to skip the YULE BALL? Are you insane? Did Siggeir hit you that hard? Absolutely not." Like a mother with her disobedient child, Elis took me by the upper arm and marched me to the bathing chamber, shoving me inside. "Now, get in there and scrub every nook and cranny or so help me—"

I crossed my arms. "I could transmute that door..."

"And I could..." he hesitated, because we both know his threats were empty, which only drew a smirk from me, "do some very unpleasant things in retaliation that we can discuss at a later date, but right now," he pointed to the bath with steaming, scented water, "get in. I will not allow even a speck of dirt to touch my masterpiece. Get. In."

As the door closed, the steam from the heavily scented water beckoned me. Temptation was too great and I relented. This was Elis' time to shine, after all; he is a true artist and tonight, I was to be the canvas for his creative prowess.

CHAPTER 39

"My goodness, Elis... This gown is stunning," I said breathlessly, for surely this gown took my breath away. "I don't even recognize myself."

"No, *you* are stunning, my dear," My friend's face beamed with pride as we both stared back at the mirror. "Never could I have imagined..." He shook himself, "Well, as much as I'd love to give you the fawning we both deserve, this is one event we mustn't be late for. Come, King Ruarc is waiting."

Tucking my arm into his, we made our way to the ballroom. Elis looked beautiful in his shimmering lavender tailcoat with cream shirt. Truly dressed to the nines, I was eager to see what Llyr looked like.

Thankfully, Elis knew the way and I only had to focus on not breaking my ankle in these diamond and gold heels. So focused on the floor and a few feet in front of me, I nearly stumbled when Elis brought us to a stop.

Ruarc stood before us, mouth falling open. Half expecting him to be in his usual shirtless attire, or maybe even traditional, I was surprised to see him looking sharp in a black and red suit and waistcoat. Upon his head was that infamous raven-feathered crown and a beautiful gold and ruby Collar of Esses-styled chain across his chest that indicated his high prestige. The monstrous half I'd grown so accustomed to was concealed impeccably by glamour.

Personally, I think he would have been more striking revealing his true self.

He cleared his throat loudly. "Well... You have certainly accomplished what would be otherwise impossible, Lord LeGervase."

A cool look passed Elis' face as he raised the back of my hand to his lips. "I only expounded upon the original canvas, Sire. She naturally does the rest."

Everything Ruarc wanted to say but did not, was clear in those roaming eyes. "Indeed."

My jaw clenched in irritation; so rarely did I take the time to look my best that doing so often left me in a state of vulnerability. Perhaps I should utilise it for the armour it was.

"Let's get this over with," I snapped.

Just as I began to walk forward to Ruarc's outstretched hand, Elis pulled me back.

"I would claim your first dance—"

"You absolutely will not, my flower," Llyr appeared behind him, an admonishing look on his polished face. "That is for me and me alone."

Elis rolled his eyes but could not hide the pink blush brightening the tops of his pointed ears.

"Then your second is mine."

"And your third is mine." Llyr grinned a grin so infectious I almost caved.

"I don't dance."

"Yes. You do." Ruarc tugged me to him, then motioned for Llyr and Elis to go ahead of us to be announced first. A beleaguered sigh escaped the Fae king, his thumb and forefinger pinching the bridge of his nose. "Please, for the love of the Slough, tell me you know how to dance..."

My eyes rolled skyward. "I know how, you silly man. But the act itself is annoying since the enjoyability is completely reliant on the competency of one's partner."

He tucked my arm into his arm, smirking down at me. "If that is your fear, then you can rest easy."

"When my second dance comes, you're right, I will be," I retorted in a bored voice.

Instead of a snappy remark, Ruarc just let out a laugh. When the rumble of his humour naturally died down and silence continued to greet me, my discomfort increased when realising that Ruarc was looking down at me, observing. As much as it bothered me to do it, I did take note of how soft his features were, instead of the dangerous severity they normally held. A true Celtic beauty stared back at me, with all the wildness and mysticism that came with the ancient culture.

"I am about to prove you wrong, Alchemist," he began in a hushed tone with a gleaming challenge twinkling in those aquamarine eyes. "Besides, as you've dressed to impress, only the most skilful dancer should have the right to show you off."

Biting back my snappy reply, the Master of Ceremonies announced Elis and Llyr, and Ruarc led us forward.

"Lord Ruarc Ó Ceallaigh, King of the Unseelie and Master of the Wild Hunt, joined by Lady Melisandre von Boden, the Alchemist."

Panic gripped me as we came to a stand at the top of the staircase leading down to the ballroom. The sheer size of the area and all those in it was a shock to my introverted system. While royal balls and any other type of large social event were things I stayed quite clear from, nothing could have prepared me for the hundreds of eyes that stared back at us.

At least, for once, I was dressed for it.

The mermaid-style ball gown Elis had crafted was a glittering starlight silver, lit by swirling gold that intricately climbed up the skirt. My bodice displayed a beautiful handsewn golden paisley pattern that shone against the background of silver. It flared out at mid-thigh into an appropriate ballroom skirt, the fabric swimming like pools of liquid metals. The sweetheart neckline unabashedly showed, not just the abundance of what the good Mother blessed me with, but my many runes. Silver snakes danced with gold ones around my upper arms to form arm cuffs, which gave way to long silver sleeves that hugged my arms, only to flare out past my hands when I held them at my side.

Tiny diamonds sparkled among the strands of my hair, which had been pulled back gently, only to billow out and cascade down my back. Golden threads were woven amongst my black locks as well, all leading to the diamond and platinum tiara that rested securely on my head.

But the best part was when Llyr whispered magic into the dress and it came to life; the gold moved like gentle rivers, the silver twinkling brighter than the clearest starry skies. My eyes had never stood out more.

When the Unseelie King had given the diamond tiara to Elis, knowing I would protest, his message was simply this: I am a king. Thus, it is only proper for you to look like my queen.

"One would think I would be used to all this staring by now," I mumbled under my breath. Yet deep down, the truth glowed so warm there was little doubt the tips of my ears burned red.

Just as I was about to give into the desire to flee the scene, Ruarc reached across my body to take my hand in his, raising it up.

"It is only natural for people to gaze at the most captivating creature in the room." He raised my hand closer to his face, running the pad of his thumb over the top. Quite the show of intimacy, despite my subtle attempts at pulling away.

"I'm not a 'creature'. And that's not why they're staring."

"Perhaps," warm lips pressed firmly against my skin, overstaying their welcome by far when those ethereal blue eyes looked back into mine, "but that is most certainly why I am."

Oh, how badly I wanted that cheeky grin to replace the utter seriousness on his face just to negate the blush forming on my cheeks. This hot and cold game he played was sending my stomach into knots and I wanted no part in it.

This was all for show but, blast it all, why must he be so... the way he is?

"Come, let us do our formal greetings to our hosts and then I can finally have you in my arms." At the frown ripening on my face, he leaned down and whispered, "The room's hearing is sensitive, my dear."

My attempted smile probably came across as a pained grimace but I relaxed, giving a nod and saying, "After you, then."

As we made our way down the steps and onto the floor, people moved away quickly, giving us a wide berth. My suspicions were confirmed with every fearful and wary glance, groups quickly relocating as we drew near.

They feared me.

Unexpectedly, memories of my own people looking at me with those same eyes, that same fearful disgust. That... same question, the accusations, haunting their eyes...

Why must you exist?

Monster!

Abomination!

My shoulders stiffened as I reflexively schooled my features into the frown that was natural to the lines of my face. But unlike my youth, I would not hide in the shadows in a desperate attempt to try and avoid their assaults. This time, I would hold the eyes of my persecutors and there would be no hiding.

"Look at them," whispered Ruarc, whose own posture was drenched in royal arrogance, "the absolute terror there." He took a deep inhale, the air whistling through his nose. "Taste the power that fear gives. Exquisite." Ruarc leaned closer. "Before the Sickness, that look was reserved for the gods and their creations alone. You are truly one of us now."

There was no hiding my curling lip of disdain; that was the last thing I had wanted.

As the waves of people parted, steps leading up to the two thrones beheld the lone monarch of the Nightmare Court. Other Champions stood speaking, mainly with Ragna, who was an impressive sight to behold. The emerald ball gown hugged her body and flowed to the ground, the depths of green fading to black. It was sleeveless, the bodice so tight it gave the illusion of an impossibly tiny waist even sitting.

However, disappointment struck me hard at seeing the throne beside her empty.

Next to me, Ruarc gave a polite but quick nod of his head as Ragna turned her attention towards us.

"Queen Ragna," he began, "Lady Von Boden and I bid you good evening. The grandeur of festivities has no limits. We commend you on your marvellous sense of decor."

Her red lips lifted slightly in a smile and with a graceful nod in return, replied, "Greetings, King Ruarc. Always the silver-tongued flatterer. You clean up well when you try." Though her eyes flickered to me, she blatantly ignored my presence.

To everyone else, it was a public display of disrespect. To me, I merely returned it by lifting my chin a little higher, looking bored.

"Rarely do I get the chance to dance with the beautiful Queen of Bones and such an event demands my finest display of fashion. The King of the Slaugh would never disappoint."

At this, her grin bloomed. "Sly little Raven. Fine. A dance you shall have." Ragna leaned back, her posture still straight as an arrow. "Off with you now, lest your sugared tongue manages to convince me of a second dance." With that we were dismissed as she turned back to the people sneering down at us.

It was moments like this that those ignorant of Ragna's madness would never believe the depths of her insanity. But I knew.

As Ruarc led us away, the need to search for Alcaeus became too much and my neck craned to see into the depths of the crowd, the twirling partners swaying to the orchestra. But even with six-inch heels, the view proved empty of my objective.

Coming to an abrupt halt as Ruarc swivelled to face me, he raised our joined hands and said, "My lady," he bent gracefully at the waist, "may I have the honour of leading you in the first dance?" Just as the question took flight in the air, a lovely waltz joined it.

Anxiety crawled up my spine but the twinkling aquamarine eyes staring back at me, promising nothing short of a fun time, proved too much.

With a gentle curtsy, I acquiesced. His arms slid around me as he closed the distance and away we went. It was a lively waltz and the King of the Unseelie did indeed prove to be a most skilled dancer.

Even so, my attention wandered. Faces blurred. In all the exuberant colours that painted the room, they all dulled compared to the empty spaces within.

"Etiquette would argue that ignoring your dance partner is considered one of the highest offences one can commit." Despite the admonishment, Ruarc didn't seem fazed in the slightest, only a sardonic raise of his brow.

My snort was far from delicate. "You speaking of etiquette is the funniest thing you've ever said to me."

He let out a hearty laugh, proving my point. "True. I prefer to take it as more of a suggestion."

"If only to ignore it," I shot back and this time we both laughed.

Ruarc spun me and as he tugged me back to him, our eyes locked in merriment. For a moment, I took the opportunity to appreciate the wild and handsome Fae in front of me. A bittersweetness filled my heart at realising that in another life, another realm, Ruarc Ó Ceallaigh would have captivated me. Or driven me to murder. Always pushing and shattering my boundaries, it was enough to tear my hair out but...that endless charm and that very persistence had forced me to grow.

The lines of his face softened as he spoke, his tone dropping to a husky timbre, "You are very beautiful, Melisandre." Fingers pressed firmer against my waist, pressing me closer. "But tonight, you've become the very definition of the word."

Never one to handle compliments well, I merely cleared my throat and said, "Elis is a genius when it comes to fashion; this was all his doing."

Warm breath trailed against my temple as the Unseelie King drew ever closer and discomfort hit me like a splash of cold water. I pulled back but it only brought me close to his face.

"Take the compliment, Melisandre," he whispered, those silky words crawling over my skin. "Nay, take the truth and bask in the attention for once. Tonight, of all nights, is meant for enjoyment." That straight nose brushed the tip of mine. "For pleasure."

The music slowed but my attempts to pull away seemed impossible with how tightly Ruarc held me.

"The pleasure of dancing with the best dancer in all of Khaviel." Elis' voice was the epitome of my salvation and I turned to grin at him in relief. "Pardon my interruption, Your Highness, but I do believe it is my turn to steal this lovely lady away."

Ruarc gave Elis a measured look but my friend was steadfast in his demeanour that dripped with politeness.

"Indeed. My lady." The king gave me a short nod and released me, taking my hand and placing it in Elis' waiting one.

As the music picked up once again and we were free of the presence of royalty, both Elis and I let out a collective sigh as he took me into his arms.

"Just in time, I see," he said.

"Your timing is always impeccable."

"Kind of you to recognise one of my many, many talents, my dear. By the by, King Ruarc seemed to be getting awfully cosy with you," Elis grinned as my eyes rolled, pushing me out for a twirl. "From what I could see, King Ruarc just might actually be genuine in his feelings for you," he commented.

"Perhaps, but I get this feeling there is a deeper desire there that has little to do with attraction and everything to do with what he believes I can do for him."

"Of course he does, he's Fae. That is their very nature."

"Don't let Llyr hear you say that."

"Llyr would agree. Even my love had something to gain when feelings between us developed. As did I. But a romance with King Ruarc would not end well."

"Fear not, I have no intentions of ever letting it begin," I stated, finding myself looking around the room for Alcaeus.

Elis lifted me for two beats then twirled me around. That's when I saw him.

There, in a black and silver ensemble, he stood tall and commanding. A group of people stood around him. The silver filigree from the vest and coat arms brought out his bronze colouring. The outfit was fit for royalty. A military jacket hung across his shoulders and even from where I stood, it was lavish and pristine. My Mark warmed and pulsated. Alcaeus looked up, seeking. But before I could see more, Elis pulled me back to him.

"Careful, my dove," my friend whispered, "that couple behind us almost tumbled."

"But Alcaeus—"

"Shh, don't fret; you'll have plenty of time with him." A quick glance at Elis confirmed the mischievousness in his voice matched the twinkle in his eye. "The night is young and Llyr and I have it all in hand. Now, at least try to enjoy our first dance together."

He was right and I grinned, replying, "Yes, show me this magnificent Lord of the Dance you have deemed yourself."

The music changed at that moment to a lively tune and Elis said, "Say no more!" and we spun and twisted, proving him to be incredibly light of foot.

For the first time in a long time, I lost myself in the merriment, laughter flowing easily from my lips. Violins and cellos created the colours of festivities just as the piano's dancing keys dictated our steps. The woodwind and brass instruments gave depth to each dip and twirl that Elis led me in.

He was a vision in creams and lilacs with a hint of gold that made his own honey curls shine in the candlelight. It was no wonder Llyr had been so taken with him.

As we came to a graceful stop, I complimented him, saying, "You have, indeed, lived up to your boasting of being an excellent dancer."

"I do believe I said I was the 'best' my dear, but your elderly memory is forgiven," he teased back.

My eyes rolled at the jibe but said, "The very fact that my ankles are still intact despite wearing these ridiculous heels is a testament to your skill, I'll give you that."

A happy tune commenced indicating it was time for a quadrille. Llyr came to our side and, with a flourishing bow asked, "My lord, my lady, shall we?"

Together, we lined up with other dancers, Llyr directly across from me and Elis beside me. We worked in pairs, each taking turns, sometimes four of us split into groups, our hands in the middle as we twirled. Faces blurred. All too fast the song ended and we gave the orchestra a hearty cheer. Llyr and Elis led me away, all of us eager for refreshments.

As we reached the table, Elis handed us all glasses filled with sparkling champagne that was refreshingly chilled as I gulped it down.

Draining my glass like a sailor taking a hearty swig of ale, I let out a loud sigh ending with an indelicate hiccup.

"Well," said Elis, giving me a dry look, "You can take the woman out of the barn but you can't take the barn out of the woman." Llyr gave him a smack on the shoulder and took my empty glass from me.

"And clearly you haven't danced enough if your sass is still so sharp. Come, Elis," Llyr held his hand out to his mate. "Allow me to render your legs to exhaustion and your tongue beyond distraction."

Crimson stole Elis' pale complexion away as he blushed, but a wicked gleam met Llyr's own as he slipped his hand into the waiting one.

"Have fun you two," I called out as they slipped through the crowd. Moving towards the outside of the room, I watched the pair of them get lost in a Viennese Waltz. Their movements were so graceful, so perfectly in tune. But it was how they looked at each other, as if they were the only ones in the room. As if the sun rose and set in the other's eyes.

My arms slid around my torso, hugging myself.

There was only one man I had any desire to be with tonight. I searched the crowd for him but only found fearful glares and wary glances.

Suddenly the room felt cold. Alone.

It hit me that *that* was all I wanted, really.

Eyeing the doors that led to the exit, temptation proved too great as I made a beeline for them. Just as I passed the large glass doors that opened to the courtyard, a hand caught mine.

"Alchemist? Where are you going?" Ruarc asked, brows drawing together in concern as he took in my face. "What's wrong?"

I pulled at my hand. "Just let me go."

"Come." His command left no room for argument and I allowed him to tug me outside into the night. We walked past multiple couples who had sought refuge from the festivities, going down stone steps that led to a gazebo overlooking a lake and I realised it was the same one from the Tea Party but from the opposite side from where we had been.

Ruarc turned to face me. "Tell me what had you running as if the Wild Hunt was after you?"

For once, I had no glib response. With a sigh, I walked to the edge of the wooden railing, resting my arms on it. "It all became too much for me. I'm not used to all of..." I waved back at the festivities, "this."

He came to stand beside me, leaning a hip against the railing. "I sometimes forget how much of a solitary creature you are. But I am to blame for leaving you alone; I meant to come back to you as soon as you had finished your dancing with—"

I shook my head, cutting him off. "No, really Ruarc. You are right; I prefer being alone."

A measured silence rested between us before, "You do not have to be, Melisandre." Fingers trailed against my bare shoulder, making their way up my neck slowly.

I stiffened but turned my head to look up at the Fae king. His hand continued to gently follow the line of my jaw until they rested along my chin, his thumb caressing my lower lip. That piercing gaze followed the motions hungrily, and my heart began to pick up speed.

"A woman like you was meant to be with a man who will never leave her in the biting cold of darkness. Someone who will slay any and all who would even think to bring sorrow to your doorstep." His other hand came to cup the side of my face. "Who embraces all that you are and all that you were. Who is not bound to another woman and even now, holds her in his arms instead of you." Following his line of sight, I turned and, even from where we stood, I could see a blonde crowned head being led in dance with a man whose chestnut hair I had memorised the feel of.

My heart clenched as a slimy tendril of a darker emotion twisted within and moisture gathered in the corner of my eyes.

"You deserved to be worshipped," whispered Ruarc, his hot breath tickling the shell of my ear. "To be wanted." Images of people kicking and spitting at me assaulted my memory, as I desperately tried to dodge their hatred. "You deserve..." lips kissed my skin, "to be loved." I closed my eyes.

A tear rolled down my cheek and my Mark began to ache. Visions of the man who had come to occupy the confines of my heart flashed in my mind's eye. Everything I had come to love about him. Yes. I said it.

Love.

A faint, crawling and filmy sensation covered my body ever so slightly and with it, the images in my mind took a turn; Alcaeus attacking me. Nemesis covered in my blood. Ragna shoving her tongue down his throat as he groaned in pleasure.

"Let me be the man that you know you crave," Ruarc's voice was a tempting oasis amidst the painful and bitter images so real in my head. "Let me love you, Melisandre." That sensation grew stronger and now the images morphed into a scene where it was Alcaeus laying down, holding onto the naked hips of Ragna, grinding and riding—

"No!" I screamed, shoving away from Ruarc. "Get away from me!" As much as I should have expected it, the feeling of betrayal sat heavy in my gut. "Don't you ever do that again!" I pointed an accusing finger at him and Ruarc's face filled with anger. "You manipulative—"

"Damn you, woman!" He shouted back, arms wide as he said, "A king offers you the world and you reject him and for what? For a man who has always been destined for death and the author of your demise! Alcaeus can never be yours! Can you not see that I am trying to help you?!"

"You have offered me nothing but lies and deceit, reneging on your oath to help me at every turn!" I countered. "Manipulating my thoughts and feelings with magic is not love!"

"And what would you know of love?" he sneered. "You have been hated since the beginning of your own existence. Alone all your life! Only to allow those close to you to meet their end at the blade of your enemy before you cared enough to do anything! What have you ever truly sacrificed? Tell me, Alchemist: What would you know of love?!" His last words ended in a shout and hurt was clear in his eyes. Bitterness. Haunting pain. "You. Know. Nothing!"

The memory of Alcaeus' confession to me in his study, the look in his eyes as he pressed my hand against his chest. The feeling of his heart beating against my palm. The way he would play for me when my heart was in turmoil. The knowledge that for years, he kept the Otherworld at bay so I might know peace. Our walk in the garden of his creation, and how he had noticed all the little things about me that no one else ever had.

His words.

Though my soul may be in pieces, my heart in its entirety is yours, always. I love you... I would slay the Fates themselves if it could buy us even minutes more, just to learn the most minor detail about you. Yet, what I know of you, I love unequivocally.

My eyes filled with tears again and I choked out, "Maybe I don't know what love is. But I sure as hell know what it isn't. And this is *not* it!" With that, I stomped towards the doors leading to the ballroom.

Ruarc's voice chased after me but I didn't stop. "Run to him, little Alchemist! For tonight will be your last together!"

The reminder only sped up my steps, blind to everyone and everything around me except getting to the doors. Ugly whispers chased me and I cursed these blasted heels. Suddenly, my shoulder collided with another, causing me to stumble.

"I-I'm so sorry, excuse me—"

"Melisandre? My dear child, are you alright?" Unatti's warm voice and gentle hands stopped me in my tracks, the genuine concern on her beautiful face and that of her mate's almost too much to bear. "I have been looking for you. I have been tasked to bring you to Alcaeus—"

I pulled away, stuttering, "I m-must...I... Go..." My emotions were proving too torrential, painfully aware of the attention we were drawing.

Unatti's elaborate headdress swivelled as she turned to see Ruarc coming through the doors after me. She growled low but I was already rushing away. "Melisandre, wait!"

But I couldn't. I just wanted to be alone.

Yet fate was cruel and, this time, someone else bumped into me hard enough that I stumbled and collided with the ground. Snickers and laughs at my humiliated fall resounded around me. A green and black gown filled my vision.

Ragna.

"Ah, Alchemist. You are exactly where you should be." She looked down her nose at me, a haughty brow raised. Then she leaned to the person closest to her and said loudly, "Call a servant to clean this refuse off the floor." The crowd laughed.

Before I could even open my mouth or transmute her dress to ribbons, strong arms lifted me against a solid chest. My Mark told me who it was the moment he touched me.

Alcaeus hugged me to him as I buried my face into his neck. He kissed my forehead and everyone around us went silent.

He faced down the Nightmare Queen. "Enough." That commanding yet soft tone reverberated throughout the room and gasps echoed throughout. "Too long have I remained silent. No longer. There will be no wedding!" Now shouts and questions rang out, only to go instantly silent as the Royal Consort, once king, continued his outcry. "Let it be known that Melisandre Von Boden is my Fated Mate!" More gasps and outraged cries followed, and several people close to the queen, backed away with horror on their faces. "Athena, together with Gaia, bound her to me! My heart beats for her and her alone! Which means her union with King Ruarc is a falsehood!" He turned to where Ruarc stood, a thunderous look on his face. "She will *never* be yours. Not in this life or the next."

Before Ragna could respond, Alcaeus walked us away from the crowd. The moment we were clear of everyone, his shadows engulfed us and the room shifted.

The last thing I saw was Ragna's rage-filled face promising revenge, and the Unseelie King letting his glamour fall.

CHAPTER 40

Alcaeus set me down as the darkness gave way to the gentle candle-light of his secret cavern.

"Why did you do that?" My question sounded hollow in the dead silence of the space. So many emotions ran through me that I feared they would swallow me whole with every breath that left my body. There was so much to process. "You shouldn't...have.

"It needed to be done."

"No," I shook, my hands coming to hold my face, "T-that was prob-ably...the repercussions..."

"You cannot ask me to stand by and allow you to be humiliated—"

"It's nothing I have not had to contend with before," I shot back with a bit more bite than I had intended. My pace quickened. "It's not new. I was leaving anyway, had you just let me go–"

His large, warm hands came around my own, stopping my erratic walking and forcing me to look up into eyes full of certainty. Unswayed.

"It *needed* to happen. The people must know what Ragna has done. This may be our very last night together; it is my will that we spend it in truth. *You* are my truth."

I pulled away, trying to intellectualise the possible outcomes of what he just did. My pacing continued. "Then it's only a matter of time before Ragna takes complete control of you, isn't it?" A sickening thought hit me. "There is nothing stopping her from swallowing the rest of your soul, is there? She has what she wants, after all." My errat-ic thoughts came to a screeching halt since the answer was so simple. "Then we complete the Mark. Right now. There is no other solution."

Alcaeus let out a tired breath. "*Mikrós asvós...*"

"We must! Why have we waited so long to do something when, collectively, we are more than a match for her? We can limit casualties...I know that's why you're worried. Yes, there would be a terrible battle but you have equally powerful allies. Surely—"

"We cannot."

"Yes, we can!" My voice rose in desperation, frustration at his repeated obstinance grating on my every nerve. "You cannot ask me to fight you! I couldn't even stop you last time because the Mark prevented me! Even if it did not, I won't hurt you. Did you not just show the world you would not be her puppet any longer?" Only exasperating silence answered me. "Damnit Alcaeus! Stop being so obstinate! Why won't you work with me? Fucking hell, say something!" I cried, twirling to face him.

The look on his face was one I instantly hated—a resolute sorrow, as if he knew of something I did not and had accepted the outcome before it had even come to pass.

"I...cannot." Alarm raced through me as his eyes became glassy. "I physically cannot finish the Mark, my love."

Swallowing became ten times harder. "What? W-why not?"

Muscles worked in his jaw as he held my gaze unflinchingly for several moments. Then he spoke.

"Melisandre Von Boden, To thee I—Argh!" Suddenly his whole body seized, his hands straining towards his neck. Green light shaped like barbed wire flashed around his throat, green flame suddenly flaring from his eyes and mouth. Then it was gone. Alcaeus fell to his knees.

Rushing to his side, my hands hovered over his neck. "No..." My words came out in a horrified sob, "No, Alcaeus, please no..."

"She," the tears in his eyes were painfully real and cut into the depths of my soul, "had Illirhun place a curse upon me so that I may never utter the words which would complete our Mark. That would bind us in every way." His beard was rough against my hands as I held his face and Alcaeus closed the distance, resting his forehead against mine. "I would marry you, Melisandre." That strong baritone voice broke with loss and my soul echoed the grief. He pulled back just enough to cup my face.

"W-when? When did she do this?"

"The second night after you left with King Ruarc."

"Why did you not tell me? Why make it about your kingdom?"

He looked down in shame. "It was the main reason for the delay initially, that was the truth but...then it became about the release giving us more time. Stupidly, it occurred to me that perhaps you...staying with Ruarc would have been for the best, as much as I hated it. I am sorry. I should have told you sooner, even though it would have changed nothing."

Pain was an unforgiving lance through my heart, shattering what little hope had been left within. Ragna had officially stolen the only way to free Alcaeus. No words existed to describe the depth of despair that consumed me.

Suddenly, Ruarc's words came rushing back to me: *He belongs to Ragna... A man who has always been destined for death and the author of your demise! Alcaeus can never be yours!*

Hopelessness warped into a sickening realisation.

"He knew," was my broken whisper.

"What is it?" Alcaeus rose with me, letting me go as I pulled away to think.

"That bastard...knew. He knew we couldn't...yet he still made a deal with me." My runes began to glow as anger's turbulent form flooded me. "He never intended on helping me with you. No, instead he has been actively trying to seduce me, manipulating my body with magic—"

"He did what?" It was a low growl that matched the menacing rumble of the WereLioness queen we were both fond of.

"Oh yes, Ruarc is a tenacious one, I'll give him that," I scoffed, my anger only rooting itself deeper within me. "Though, tonight was the worst; I'm sure his words were coated in magic and, as you danced with Ragna, Ruarc was filling my head with images of you and her. He filled my ears with all. The. Right. Words." My gaze went distant, lost in the memory that made me wish I had given that slimy, backstabbing man exactly as he deserved instead of walking away.

"Ragna and I never danced. The Raven was manipulating your perception of reality. It is something he has always excelled at." Strong arms flexed visibly through his black jacket as his fingers tensed like spears curling inward. "I would kill him for this."

My hand covered his straining one. "I always knew Ruarc had ulterior motives. I even said as much to you the night of the Garden Party." Coaxing his hand open, my fingers traced the map of lines there. "But now, I believe those motives run far deeper than seeing his old rival fall or trying to take me as his Chosen. Far deeper than either of us ever thought. I just don't know why. Or what." When he lifted his hand to my face, cupping my cheek, I closed my eyes, sinking into the feel of his warmth. That strong hand.

Would I ever feel it again after this night?

As if reading my sorrow, Alcaeus pulled me suddenly closer and his lips found mine. Our kiss was one of grief and anger, of longing and loss. We each consumed the other, pulling and pushing.

His hands began to wander. I tugged at his cravat, his buttons, briefly wondering how upset he might be if I reduced his clothing to their pre-production state.

"Wait," said Alcaeus, breathing heavily as he captured my hands, "We have the rest of the night to enjoy each other, that I can guarantee. My apologies, but," he pulled away from me, raising my arms away from us as his eyes took in all of me, "it would be a crime against Aphrodite herself if I did not worship the beauty that is before me and that, my dear, requires a certain level of ceremony." Not a hint of sadness was in his eyes now, just masculine appreciation and something deeper.

Though a smile crept up my face, sadness still played along the lines of it. Alcaeus kissed my forehead.

"If tonight is our last, then let us make it one where neither Ruarc nor Ragna occupies the slightest bit of thought. Instead, let it be a night of passion," he kissed my temple, "one of truth," my chin was lifted to meet his gaze, "One of love." His kiss was so light, so gentle.

After a moment, I nodded and then said, "Are you sure it was not Aphrodite that created you?"

He laughed and the tension melted away. "Not that I am aware. Though, Eros no doubt snuck in a drop of blood or two, I am sure of it."

"As am I. You are far too romantic."

His voice dropped an octave as he stepped around me until his chest pressed against my back. "Mmm, is that a complaint?"

Chuckling, I replied, "No."

"Good, because that is only the beginning. We cannot leave this room lest Ragna gets her way early but that does not mean I cannot still take you somewhere."

My brows raised. "Oh?"

"Close your eyes."

Biting my lip, I complied. There was a shift in the air. Even the smell changed. Jasmine. Fresh spring night. Gentle and warm light tempting me to crack my lids open. Gentle stringed music. It became too much and so my vision sharpened at the change of scenery around me.

My jaw dropped open.

It was a completely open ballroom, as if we had been plucked, castle floor and all, straight into a fantasy of nature. Three majestic waterfalls behind provided the background, the rush of water oddly gentle instead of the roar that the reality of physics would demand. Triple moons, with hints of blue and purple lorded over us, the bright stars twinkling in the bed of the night sky.

Marble flooring was a pristine black with white, with deliberate Greek patterns that turned it into nothing short of a work of art. Faceless beings played in a quartet on several stone steps at the end of the ballroom; the sounds of frogs and crickets joining in. Elegant standing candelabras were placed at the edge of the floor, except where the side opened to a small path that led to a crystal-clear spring that the waterfalls fed into below. The trees and thick brush brought smells of the forest while providing a sense of intimacy despite the open space.

"This is," I was breathless at its beauty, "magnificent, Alcaeus. Where are we?"

Walking towards the middle of the floor, he held out his arms, "Lady Von Boden, I bid you welcome to the ballroom of *Paláti tou Efiálti*."

I scoffed. "This is no nightmare—this is a dream."

"The heart of the castle was certainly a place of terror, where I could feed on the fear of all those who stepped foot there. But alas, dancing requires joviality. And so, here we are." Nostalgia was thick in his voice; pride clear in the way he held himself.

"It's perfect."

He looked back at me, his eyes softening. "It pales in comparison to the vision standing before me."

I smiled. "Only to match the handsomeness of the man in front of me."

The volume of music increased slightly with the beginnings of a waltz. With a regal bow, he asked, "My lady, may this 'handsome' and 'dashing' man have the honour of dancing with you?"

Unable to contain my laughter, I curtsied back, saying, "Taking liberty with my compliments already, I see." I slid my hand into his, "I thought you'd never ask."

Never would I have believed I'd be grateful for six-inch heels but it made dancing with Alcaeus far easier with his considerable height. Yet, perhaps it was his many years of combat, but he glided with such grace that I was captivated. Unlike my dance with Elis, or even Ruarc for that matter, a leashed strength lay just under his movements. It reminded me of the time in the meadow, when it was only his sword in hand.

Losing myself in his midnight gaze, he twirled me, my skirt flaring out beautifully. His hair had been styled back but several pieces refused to be caged, falling over his brow in a debonair way.

Pleasure snaked its way along my core as my attraction to this man began to burn.

Alcaeus saw it and the flame of desire lit up in his eyes. His hands held me a little tighter. The arm around my waist, a little firmer.

Our gazes teased each other for several more songs until the music became slower, less of a waltz and more instrumental. He moved me in front of him, our bodies still swaying together. One hand trailed up the front of me, fingertips grazing over my cleavage, coming to wrap gently around my neck. My arm came up to grasp his own as his lips found the shell of my ear and his tongue darted out for a moment. I shivered as my Mark pulsated with the growing heat between us.

But he pushed me back out, spinning me to face him. This time I didn't come back when he tried to tug me back. Instead, the desire to memorise everything about him, about this night, dominated my priorities.

"What is it?" he asked.

It took me a moment before I answered. "My mind can't reconcile the idea of this being our last. But if it is, I want to remember every detail, down to the last molecule. I want to remember the view of you with waterfalls behind you. The way you look at me—"

"Like a man dying of thirst and you are the one to alleviate it?" he teased.

Giggling, I replied, "Perhaps." My mirth died quickly, my need to be vulnerable with Alcaeus far too strong. "But there is a sincerity there that cannot be debated with." Blinking rapidly to keep my emotion from spilling over, I confessed, "Never has a man looked at me the way you do, Alcaeus. No one has. Hatred, absolutely. Lust, more often than I care for. Friendly affection, at most. Yet, all of Ruarc's shiny words pale in comparison to the sincere love that stares back at me now." His face filled with bittersweet tenderness and I knew it was time for me to meet his honesty with my own. "Alcaeus, I love—"

Suddenly he was there and all I could do was open to him, his mouth conquering the words I had never uttered to another. I barely noticed the shift around us. It wasn't until the chill breeze caused me to shiver against my naked skin that gave me clear indications that we were once more back in Alcaeus' cavern.

As if we'd never left.

The who, what, where, why, and how needed to be left for later, because he had already lifted me in his arms and laid me upon the makeshift bed. Taking the crown from my head, he tossed it away.

My knees were raised up, but as his eyes began to travel downwards, I slowly opened them wide to his gaze. He swallowed hard and the action ignited me.

Taking his hand, I guided his fingers to my lips, never breaking eye contact. Sucking the tip, I took his finger deeper into my mouth, swirling my tongue around it the way I have done to his cock. Teasing him. He groaned as my lips reached all the way to his last knuckle before sliding back just to take a second one.

Slipping his fingers from my mouth, I pushed his hand down my chest, over my breast and down my abdomen. Alcaeus turned his palm, taking over as he brushed against my lower lips before pushing them into me.

I gasped, rolling my hips into him. His other hand hooked behind my knee, pushing my leg up to my chest just as he curled his fingers inside of me, walking them along my wall.

"Oh, yes," I breathed, and he nipped at the inside of my thigh, continuing to play with me.

Removing his hand from me, those fingers glistened in the dim light. I reached for him but suddenly Alcaeus said, "Oh, this will simply not do." Grabbing my hand that had Ruarc's engagement ring on it, I felt his magic engulf it.

Rubies turned to sapphire, the metals morphing into platinum. Tiny metal feathers danced around the band and a large tear-drop sapphire rested amongst delicate leaves. It wasn't gaudy but shone with elegance.

"That is the ring I would see my Fated wear."

My breath escaped me. "It's beautiful, Alcaeus. I love it."

We smiled at each other and, snaking my hand around his neck, I pulled him to me and we sank down together. Those muscular arms came around me, cocooning us in, just as his hips fit into the cradle between my legs. The tip of his nose gently nuzzled mine, eliciting mutual smiles. Alcaeus studied my face as my fingers trailed up and down his sides.

There was nothing to say; words would do nothing but ruin our closeness.

Chestnut hair was a curtain around us as he leaned in to kiss me. It was lazy but thorough, stoking the fires of desire gently.

I never wanted it to end.

As our tongues curled around each other, he shifted his hips and instinctively I moved mine, aligning him to me. Even the way he pressed into me was subtle but unhesitating. He pulled his face away just enough our noses touched and our breaths mingled. But mine quickly turned to small pants as he pushed in farther still, my body adjusting. All the way until even my cervix felt the fullness of him. My fingers dug into his back when he pushed my knees up and down, creating an even deeper angle.

Now I was gasping as Alcaeus kissed and nipped at my mouth and neck. When he began to move, he said, "Look at me, Melisandre."

When I did, our minds connected. His breath hitched, and I knew he could feel my pleasure also.

Never before had I experienced such intimacy, such closeness. It was so much. To my horror, tears gathered in my eyes, slipping down my cheeks. I tried to wipe them away but Alcaeus grabbed my wrists in one hand, pinning them above my head.

"Don't wipe them away, my love. Let me see every part of you." This time, his thrust hit harder. Deeper. "Let me feel all of you."

I could only moan as he picked up his rhythm.

"Kiss me," I demanded, desperately needing distraction from the hurricane of pleasure throbbing between us.

Oh, and what a kiss it was. His hand came around my neck firmly as his mouth plundered mine, only to move to the back of my head as he buried his face in my neck. The pace was vigorous now but steady, and I clawed him as my orgasm embarrassingly drew near.

As my body tensed, shuddering when my climax took over, Alcaeus bit down. My mouth opened in a silent scream.

Through the shattering pleasure, I could taste the coppery flavour of blood but it was so faint, in favour of the robust, sweet richness that Alcaeus was experiencing. Energy filled me and I had this strange sensation, like I was starving, finally eating for the first time.

Alcaeus' pace slowed for only a moment, then picked up again. The combined feelings of everything already had my body tightening once more. Squeezing my eyes shut, all I could do was hold on.

"Alcaeus," I gasped, "Please! I-It's too much!" My nerves were on fire with ecstasy, our syncing mental pleasures almost breaking me.

Judging by the sweat already at his brow, I was not alone.

"I'm close," he grunted but there was no need to tell me. I felt it.

It hit us both and I came a second time, screaming. Alcaeus roared. Our bodies strained against each other until he finally collapsed against me.

As he went to slip off, I used what little strength I had to squeeze him to me.

"No, stay. Stay." Was all I could manage to say.

With a gentle kiss, he did so, snuggling his face into my neck. My walls continued to squeeze around him, relishing the throbbing heartbeat.

Darkness beckoned me, coaxing my consciousness to sleep.

ỻᎧᎵ♄Ψ∨ӡӡ

We made love several more times that night. But when I awoke, it was the lonely cold of the cavern that greeted me.

Alcaeus was gone.

As I reached for my dress, I noticed a piece of parchment resting on a linen-wrapped object. Opening it, it read:

My dearest mikrós asvós,

I would have hidden away with you for eternity but it would have only delayed the inevitable. Today is the day we must say goodbye. I will not waste words expressing how much I wish it were not so. Instead, let this broken Vampire, this weary Champion, fill the lines with the words that have been carved into the walls of my heart since the moment I first saw you: I love you. More than every star that shines in the night, so is my love for you, yet a thousand times greater.

Today, in the arena, know that it is not me but a corpse you fight. So, when the moment arrives, strike true. I die at peace, knowing the best part of us will go on to become the most fearsome Champion the Otherworld has ever seen. And through you, my heart will continue to beat alongside yours.

Take my gift and know that I will be with you, always.

Yours eternally, my dearest heart,

Alcaeus

The letter fell from my fingers, tears racing down my cheeks. Carefully, I unwrapped the linen from the oblong object. With a sob, my knees buckled and I began to cry harder. There it lay, the only weapon that could truly kill him.

Nemesis.

CHAPTER 41

For the third and final time, I stood at the great entry gates of the Megálo Kolossaío. Gone were the tears of grief and loss. In its place was a hollow coldness. The same one that had filled me as Ragna attempted to reanimate the bodies of my then-dead loved ones. A quiet rage that had slowly built in the last year bubbled just below the surface.

My staff gleamed bright against the shadows of the darkened interior. No sword hung at my side.

After taking the stairs back to Sage Kevyn's study, he found the mess of me. Giving me one of the warmest and tightest hugs I'd ever received, those gentle blue eyes looked at me with such hope it almost made me angry. Then he had said to me, "Prince Alcaeus told me this once and I think you need to hear it: 'The elements of love cannot be determined when happiness is at its peak, but in its selflessness when faced with great sacrifice'. Many years have I lived, Melisandre, long enough to know truer words have never been spoken."

With a heavy heart I bid him goodbye and, with his help, I was transported to Elis and Llyr's living quarters. I could not be near Ruarc because I did not trust what I would do.

For once, my time with my best friend was a quiet and forlorn one. He fussed over me until he became distraught, at which point Llyr took over, sitting Elis down while I dressed.

When I came out, there was only one thing left to do.

"Take this. Keep it safe." I had said to Elis, handing over Nemesis. He, too, cried at the sight of it.

Elis crying was nothing new to me but this time, it wasn't theatrics. His broken sob nearly undid me as the door closed between us.

Reality was a cold and biting thing.

The crowd roared again, bringing me back from my disassociation. Several fights had already taken place. Ours had been saved for last. Naturally.

Drums boomed and my own heart jumped at the suddenness. That was the signal to clear the arena of anything or anyone dead.

Staring at the doors so hard that I could burn holes right through it, I clenched my grip around my staff harder. Soon they would open. In moments, I would be forced to face the truth that even now my brain refused to believe. I was about to—

"Ms. Melly?"

I whipped around, coming face to face with those chocolate brown eyes and wayward curls of my former ward. Metal clanked loudly as I let go of my staff, my arms going around Toby wordlessly. He hugged me back with equal strength and we stood there for a long moment.

Regretfully, I stepped back, but not before shoving a few curls out of his eyes.

"You need a haircut," I mumbled.

His face cracked into a smile. "Y-yeah... 'bout that time, I suppose." But then seriousness took over. "Ms. Melly, I've done a lot of looking into your situation." He leaned in to whisper his next words. "You have to complete that mark!"

His words stabbed the already open and raw wound that was my heart. "We can't, Toby." Before he could argue, I quickly filled him in. "Ragna and her sorcerer cursed him so that he can't speak the words of the ritual."

Toby looked at me in shock. "What?" I could only nod back. But then, a strange look came over his face. "Wait, Ms. Melly, didn't he already—"

"Out of your glamour and in full sight, speaking to Lady Von Boden without my permission. Begone!" Ruarc's command held power and Toby vanished.

There was no thought. Just reaction. My staff swung towards Ruarc's face. With lightning reflexes, he snagged it.

"What the hell are you—"

My fist connected with his jaw with a crack. He stumbled backwards as I yanked my staff back, only to point it at him again.

"You lying, scheming, slimy piece of shit!" I screamed. "You knew! You knew that Alcaeus could not complete the Mark and you kept it from me! You made a deal with me that could never be fulfilled!" The creaking of the doors behind me signalled they began to open and I turned towards them but then turned back to say, "I never trusted you. I always knew you had something else up your fucking sleeve. But there were points where I thought we had reached an understanding—"

"Come away with me, Melisandre." At the look of outrage on my face, he stepped closer but I gave him a warning look. "I had suspected from visions I had seen but it was only confirmed once we arrived. Truly, I had thought Alcaeus would have told you—Wait!" I had turned and began walking, my foot just about to touch the sands when a steel hand grabbed my forearms, jerking me back to face Ruarc.

"Let go of me!"

He grabbed my arm. "Marry me. Or don't. But come with me. You don't have to do this. Your purpose is better than this! I need you!"

That rage that had been simmering, boiled over. With all the power I could, I shoved him away from me, transmuting a stone gate between us.

I glared at him with all the hate burning within me. "Don't you ever, and I mean ever, touch me again. And if you ever are stupid enough to show your face to me, I will kill you. That. Is. A. Promise."

The Unseelie King's face morphed from pleading to sorrow and then...nothing but coldness.

As my boots crunched against sand, his voice echoed behind me.

"I could have loved you. Instead, you chose death."

CHAPTER 42

The man that stood across from me no longer held the straightened posture of a well-seasoned fighter. That graceful poise of the man I had danced with just hours ago. Instead, those same strong shoulders I had just held in the epitome of pleasure, now slumped with lifelessness. Even that beautiful mane of hair hung without the golden-brown sheen it once had. Green fire danced around him with flames that licked the air.

My Mark ached with loss. Tears brimmed along my eyes at the crippling sight of Alcaeus. But I let my devastation feed my will to see this through. The plan was to find a way to contain him and then...

Then what? No... You know exactly what.

Unatti's rich voice resounded throughout but this time, it held much of the same emotions I was feeling.

"People of the Otherworld. Champions. Those who call themselves kings and queens. Today is a day that should never have come to pass. We shall all bear witness to sacrilege. To the very destruction of our most sacred traditions. Two Fated Mates have been called to fight! It is against everything we stand for and I, for one, will have it be known that Queen Unatti will never condone this. So, challengers, begin as you will. And shame upon those responsible!"

The Arena was silent. Ragna stood in the window of her booth; her eyes were closed in concentration as that same green fire danced around her.

I had a feeling the Arena would not let me attack her. Only Alcaeus.

335

There was no warning. Suddenly, he was just…there. A booted foot straight into my solar plexus catapulted me. I hit the ground rolling, my staff flying out of my hands.

Steel chimed as a sword was pulled from its scabbard. I jumped to my feet, racing to my fallen staff. The shift in the air told me Alcaeus was mere seconds from me. I dove.

The moment my hands touched metal, I rolled, swinging my staff up just in time to block the sword slamming down.

Twisting to my feet, I transmuted the sand into the laminated glass container I had contained myself in when fighting against the Tengu. Except this time, it was a prison for Alcaeus. He beat against it, though no expression could be had on his face.

I gripped my staff to me, desperately racing through what I could do and how I could end it for him.

My face fell in horror. The fire around him burned brighter, just as a circle of flame appeared in front of me.

I ran.

A shift in the air again. Swinging my staff around, metal collided with metal as I barely blocked his slice at me. Shoving his blade away, I hit him in the face with the butt of my weapon, hard enough to snap his head back.

My Mark became like ice and fire at war on my skin. As much as I wanted to cry out in agony, comprehension of what it meant hit me like a wall: his half-soul was still there. Ragna had not swallowed it.

"Alcaeus, stop!" I cried, even though there was little hope of breaking through to him.

He came at me with robotic swiftness. ***Clang! Clang! Clang!*** The symphony of our parrying steel filled the arena. My muscles shook. The sword swiped at my side and I dodged but stumbled. It cost me. The blade pierced my shoulder.

"Ahh!" I screamed, attempting to transmute it only to find it dripping with a magical layer.

Alcaeus yanked the sword from me. My runes lit up, and a shockwave blasted him a good distance away.

I struggled to stay standing. For a moment, my gaze drifted to the crowd. So many. Even children.

Toby. His words came back to me: *Ms. Melly! You need to complete the Mark! Wait, didn't he already...*

"Didn't he...? Oh my god," I breathed out as my mind finished what he hadn't been able to finish. "Didn't he already say the words?"

Memories bolted through my mind in quick succession. Ragna's loud lament at seeing our Fated Marks and then...

"Yes! Yes, he did!" I let out a hysterical laugh. "Oh Toby! I am going to owe you the biggest damn bridie Scotland ere' did see-ssshit!"

Alcaeus was on me. I blasted him back again, trying to remember.

I just have to say the words and then we exchange blood. I have to live long enough for that.

"Alcaeus Pallas! To thee, I give my mark," I twisted just as the point-ed blade thrust towards me, "the last of three—ah!"

Yelping at the river of blood now flowing down my side, I quickly transmuted the sand into laminated glass that surrounded me. I let out a sigh, leaning heavily against it. Alcaeus just continued to smack his sword against it.

"That which was once unmade, made whole again. Together our blood doth flow. Thine in mine, mine in thine." It was quiet. He had stopped smacking the glass. His hand smacked against it and green flame engulfed my little casing, growing brighter.

Hotter.

"Goddammit, Ragna!" I roared.

Shifting to my Alchemist's Sight, I sought the magnetic field lines running all around me. Executing a three-part transmutation chain, the magnetic lines pulled together, broke apart, only to rejoin. Just before the lines combined upon the rejoin, I released my glass cage. Fire began to reach for me. I snapped the line away as hard as I could, successfully completing a magnetic reconnection. The energy such a process releases caused both of us to fly yards backward from the explosion. As if we'd been thrown from a train going 300 miles an hour.

My body rolled and rolled until I did not know if the earth had an axis anymore. The pain of my Mark tore at me like knives and I let out an ugly keening sound when I finally came to a stop.

But I could not give up. "T-the t-thread in which our—ah! S-souls thus bind." My breath came in short gasps, my ribs surely having been broken again. "As...was proclaimed at the breath of first light."

I heard running.

Though every part of me complained about moving, I forced my-self to. My staff was so far from me. Unusable.

Thinking quickly, purple light flashed just as a laminated glass short staff appeared in my hand, just in time to block Alcaeus' next attack.

"Return unto me," *block, parry, dodge,* "as the stars align. One chord," *dodge, stumble, block,* "one soul." His attacks suddenly became harder, faster, the fire around him blazing brighter. "To thee, I claim ye bound for all eternity!" My makeshift weapon vaulted out of my hand from one brutal swing of his sword. I scrambled back.

So close.

"Beginning to end, in darkness and in light—argh!" The tip of the sword sliced across my cheek and hot blood poured down my face. I held my palm tight against it. "Death nor life shall tear asunder that which— ach!" His sword found my bicep and he kicked me to the ground. I crawled away. "Death nor life shall tear asunder that which was made for none other." I stood.

Suddenly, Alcaeus was there, his face almost nose to nose with me. I didn't have to look down to see that his blade had gone right through my chest, its end sticking out my back. Blood rushed into my mouth as I let out a violent cough. Tears pricked my eyes from the unbelievable pain.

Yet, my will remained.

"Thusly...to...thee...I...bind." I grabbed the back of his neck, push-ing the sword farther in as I kissed him, dipping my bloodied tongue into his mouth. My teeth found the plump flesh of his lip and bit. His own blood gushed between us.

Letting go, I whispered into those dead eyes filled with Ragna's magic, hoping my words would reach the man inside.

"Because I love you."

The sword slipped from my body as I hit the ground. My vision darkened quickly, my heart twitching as it failed to pump; seeing only the retreating black boots of the man I'd just given my life for. His sword dropped to the sand.

My eyes closed.

Tha-Thump... Tha-Thump...Tha-Thump...

Pain turned to numbness. My thoughts quieted.

Silence.

CHAPTER 43

As darkness became my reality, there was a sudden pulling at my consciousness. Then light. A summer's light. A man. A woman. Together they stood in front of the great Tree of Life. Man and woman joined hands, only to suddenly become half of the other. It spoke with the voices of both. Masculine and feminine.

"Melisandre, mine child. My Chosen. My Champion. Seek me upon thy completion, for the seedling must grasp on to the roots of its elder. In death thou hath cometh full circle. So back in life shall ye return. Go. Seek me."

My mind was ripped away from the scene, back into the darkness.

Choking. Gasping. Breathing burned and my hands shook. Purple light crackled all around me and I became aware I was floating between two massive circles, electricity racing through.

The Philosopher's Stone.

As I came to rest back on the ground, a violent cry came from Ragna's box.

"Noooooo!" She screamed in rage, her flames burning brighter. "She dies!" Ragna poured her magic into whatever connection she had but Alcaeus did not move.

In fact, no flames raced around him. He dropped to his knees. Black tendrils of inky magic began crawling up and out of the sand. Reaching for him. A low whine came as he sunk his head into his hands. I looked up just in time to see the necklace around Ragna's neck floating away from her. She tried to clamp it to her. Her body trembled.

Suddenly, white light flashed, blinding all who looked upon it. A woman's blood-curdling scream cut the air. After a second, the light died down only slightly, but enough for me to see that it now surrounded Alcaeus' hunched form.

That haunting whine turned into a guttural growl. I got to my knees, slowly coming to a stand. My hand paused its outward stretch.

"A-Alcaeus?" The question barely left my lips before I gasped.

He threw his arms out and roared. Great wings exploded from his back. They billowed out, the light bouncing off the gold and copper that gleamed from each feather. The tips were dipped in black.

Like an avenging angel, they flexed high before he flapped several times. That's when he swerved around to face me. Tears streamed down his face.

"M-my heart?" With a cry, I ran to him, stumbling along the way.

His arms captured me and my body melted against him.

"Your soul! It's back!" I cried.

"Are you alright?!" Alcaeus asked desperately, pushing me away to inspect the rest of me. He froze at the sight of blood and the massive hole his sword had ripped through my shirt. Tears fell from his eyes. "Oh...M-Melisandre," his fingers shook as they hovered above it, "I-I..."

I took his hand and pressed it against my perfectly healed chest. "I am the Stone. You can't kill me." We smiled at each other through our tears.

But our joy was cut short when I saw an ancient look in Alcaeus' eyes. It also made me see the changes in him. There was so much magic around him. So much power. There was a darkness in those already midnight eyes that wasn't there before.

"Go. Take your revenge," I said, my own grudge flaring to life. "Slay her, Alcaeus!"

His face turned feral. Blackness raced around him like the snakes of Medusa. He raised his clenched fists in front of him, sliding them slowly apart. A glowing white sword emerged. Holding the hilt of Nemesis, his other fingers trailed along the flat portion of the glowing steel.

"Her reign ends today." He sheathed his sword, then grasped my chin, "But you will come with me. Together, my queen, we shall see her fall."

A glance in the direction of her box confirmed what I suspected: she had fled.

"We have to find her!" I said, running to grab my staff. No reply came as I trotted back over to him.

His eyes were closed. Through our completed Mark, I knew exactly what he was doing: racing through the psyches of his owls stationed throughout the castle. Thousands of them.

Silver geometric lines littered his eyes, far more elaborate than I had ever seen.

"I know where she is."

CHAPTER 44

Footsteps slapping against stone. The first sounds I heard before Alcaeus' shadows gave way to an almost equally darkened room. No. More like a cave.

Three gigantic statues stood alone in this massive area under ground. Only several torches lit the room, two at the base of each figure.

A large wolf. Fenris. The trickster god, Loki. And there, in the middle stood a woman surrounded by the dead. Hel.

Ragna stood in front of the statue of her primary creator. Her arms opened as if in welcome.

"So, the beloved Fated Mates believe they have claimed victory," she sneered. "How precious." Battle-axes appeared, one in each hand. "Either way, you're too late." With a war cry, Ragna flashed out of existence.

Nemesis came down onto her crossed blades as Alcaeus predicted her exact relocation. My eyes could barely keep track with the rapid exchange of blows. But I did not intervene. Deep down, I knew how badly Alcaeus needed this. Needed to be the one to sever the head from the spine of the snake.

A low growling caught my attention, just as two hellhounds lunged for Alcaeus, but transmutations were quicker. Spikes impaled them, their bodies violently spasming before twitching in death.

Ragna swung at Alcaeus with the ferocity of the deadliest Berserker but with the precision of a surgeon. Her fighting cries rung out, green flame dancing around her. They flashed in and out of existence, each trying to get behind the other and catch them off guard.

But their battle did not last long.

The clattering of a dropped weapon stalled both warriors from their teleportation. Ragna had lost an axe. Blood ran in spatters on the ground. And a hand.

Seemingly unfazed, she swung her other axe but Alcaeus blocked it easily, only to come back with an efficient swipe. The other axe fell to the ground, along with the hand that held it.

Ragna stumbled backwards but stayed standing, her bloody stumps squirting all over the marble floor.

"That was for Sotiris." His voice was the coldest point in the night.

To my shock, she laughed, her emerald gaze coming to rest on me. "Oh yes, get your revenge, Alcaeus. How you have longed for this moment! Take it! But know this: I am not alone in the plotting of your downfall. There is another."

Too fast to comprehend, Nemesis blinked from the front of Ragna to the back of her. Emerald eyes bulged in shock. Then, her torso slid from her pelvis and legs. Blood ran in rivers.

My jaw dropped as Ragna began using her bloody stumps to crawl towards her goddess, dragging her innards behind her. A wet cackle erupted from her.

"Oh yes. And with his help, we have completed the gate."

"What have you done?" asked Alcaeus, his voice low and menacing.

"I only did what we agreed to: I opened the gate to the Realms of the Gods so that he might free his creator and in exchange he gave me you. Or rather, he gave me your wife and son so I could have you." Ragna had managed to drag herself close to her idol.

"You will name this traitor!" demanded Alcaeus, as black shadows began to gather around him. White fire began dancing on the blade of Nemesis.

Ragna's wet laugher grew followed by a bout of violent coughing

"NAME HIM!" he roared.

"I name thy traitor: Champion of The Mórrígan: Ruarc Ó Ceallaigh!" she screamed back maniacally.

My stomach dropped as fast as my knees did. "What...?"

Another roar came from Alcaeus and he grabbed Ragna by the neck, vaulting her against the Hel statue. With preternatural speed, his sword slammed into her lower ribcage, pinning her against the stone.

Finally, she cried out.

But my thoughts were still consumed with Ruarc.

You don't have to do this. Your purpose is better than this! I need you! It dawned on me then.

"That is why he wanted me, isn't it? To use the Stone to bring back... Viviane." Suddenly, the room shook with a vengeance and stone began falling from the ceiling. Ragna cackled again.

"You're already too late! The magic from the remaining Vampire Champions and of King Oberon has opened the gate! My armies are already awakening, awaiting their real master." Her eyes narrowed as she looked at Alcaeus, her voice dropping to an ominous quiet. "You are already dead! She is here!"

There was no warning. Alcaeus' hand punched through her ribs, yanking out her still beating heart. Black flames burned the flesh away until ash fell from his fingers.

He leaned close to her but I could still hear his words. "That was for Aleksei. But before you die, allow me to give back the suffering you have forced me to endure for over a thousand years." He squared up with her, forcing her eyes open.

Ragna began to scream.

My own eyes slammed shut just as my curiosity caused me to reach out mentally to Alcaeus. Images of such violence, such gore...unbelievable suffering through torture, hit my mind like a stampede. So real, I immediately yanked my mind away, eager to grasp onto reality instead of the live nightmare happening before me.

Perhaps I should have felt bad. And maybe the sight of such pure suffering did not sit well with me but...In the Otherworld, this was justice. And Alcaeus and all those she had murdered in cold blood, all those she had tortured, deserved this revenge.

The room shook again. Yet still she screamed.

Suddenly it was over. I could not see her face but I heard Alcaeus say, "This last one is for me. For Melisandre." Yanking on the sword, it flashed again in the darkness. Her headless torso hit the ground. Blonde tresses dipped in blood rolled a few paces before coming to a stop. Alcaeus' black boot came down with a vengeance, smashing her head like an egg.

The fire in those emerald eyes was gone.

Alcaeus and I stared at her remains for a moment longer before the room shook again.

"We need to go. If what she said was true, more than a war is about to be upon us." His arms came around me and he teleported us right outside the library.

Sage Kevyn was there to greet us. "My King! Praise this day! But look, look!" We followed his erratic pointing at the sky. Green fiery beams hit the sky from Castle Fyrkat. Stones fell from the parapets.

At the same time, a portal opened up in the sky. A fiery phoenix flew through it, circling around. Two winged steeds followed him.

"Zhenbai!" Alcaeus cried out and elation filled me. But so did worry.

"Toby? Elis?" I asked. "I need to get them to safety!"

"Don't worry, Melisandre," piped in Sage Kevyn, "Llyr and Elis have fled to the Summer Court as soon as you two completed the Mark, as was commanded by Queen Mab to Llyr. They told me to tell you that Toby is with the Unseelie King."

My heart dropped but great flames pulled my attention to Zhenbai landing and morphing into human form. He dropped to one knee as I ran to Zephyr, who whinnied and pranced at the sight of me. Ares appeared as well, jumping all over me with kisses and happy whining.

"King Alcaeus, I bring great news!" He looked up, a beaming smile on his handsome face. "The curse is broken! We're able to safely continue the evacuation of Khaviel! Cillian is overseeing it as we speak!" Alcaeus pulled him to his feet, embracing him.

"As much as I want nothing more than to celebrate our victory, we must go there now." The Great Owl's face was taut with seriousness. "Ragna has reopened the Gate of Divinity. The gods will come. And when they do, they will want their revenge."

Zhenbai's face fell in shock but he quickly pulled himself together. "Sage Kevyn, will you need assistance in relocating the library?"

Kevyn waved him off, "No, no. But thank you. Not even the gods would dare touch a place protected by the Cosmos itself."

"Then we make haste!" Hands suddenly lifted me onto Zephyr's back, who danced a bit at the sudden presence of me on his back. Alcaeus helped me adjust the reins before hopping on his Pegasus.

As if reading the question in my mind, he said, "I have not had wings for thousands of years and we must get to my kingdom as fast as possible; we cannot do that if I fall from the sky with exhaustion."

I nodded in agreement. The ground rumbled. Suddenly skeletal hands, then arms and legs pushed through the ground.

"Go!" commanded Alcaeus. We all took to the air as Sage Kevyn rushed back inside. The building shimmered suddenly and then disappeared into thin air.

"Oh my god," I gasped. As we climbed further in the air, the more of the castle grounds I could see. Thousands of corpses emerged from the ground. A wave of them. More of the city came into view. Zombies pushed through the cobbled stones, through buildings and houses alike.

Ragna's dead army lay beneath her castle.

As we flew farther and farther away, her words haunted my mind.

You are already dead! She is here! The Queen of Bones must have meant the goddess, Hel. My heart clenched.

Looking at Alcaeus' stiff back, his wings no longer visible, my heart ached for him. More of Ragna's words echoed in my mind. Like a broken record, those words spun around, rage climbing its way up my spine.

I name thy traitor: Champion of The Mórrígan: Ruarc Ó Ceallaigh!

THE END

Thank you for reading **The Soul of a Champion**! I sincerely hope you enjoyed it! If you did, feel free to:

- Help others experience the same by writing a review on Amazon, Bookbub, or Goodreads!
- Head over to my website, armorganbooks.com, to catch up on the latest news and extra content!
- Like and FOLLOW my Socials:
  https://www.facebook.com/armorganbooksandnarration
  https://www.instagram.com/armorganbooks/

Read on to see a SNEAK PEEK of the next in the series:

THE BODY OF GODS

PREVIEW

THE BODY OF GODS
Coming soon

An elegant foot stepped through the Gate of Divinity. It had been centuries upon centuries since she had breathed the crisp air of the Otherworld. She took in the drained bodies around her, impressed with the craftsmanship of the spell-worker.

A puny man; a sickened walking, talking corpse lay prostrate before her. She ignored him and all of his fumbling praises. Instead, she continued towards the call of flesh she herself moulded. Ascending the stairs, they finally gave way to a marbled surface. Looking around, she admired her surroundings for a moment. Most especially the body ripped and crushed to pieces, strewn about the floor.

"Oh my," she drawled, green fire beginning to leak from her fingertips. "I left you in one piece even after you betrayed me, and this is what I return to. Shame." Tendons, ligaments, and bone stitched, convulsing. "I have returned, my pet." Hel picked up the reconstructed head of her Champion and smiled into Ragna's dead eyes. "And this time, there is no escaping me."

END OF PREVIEW

ACKNOWLEDGEMENTS

I would like to thank everyone who made this book possible; I could not have done it without you. But I would like to give a special thanks to my beautiful daughter, for being the reason I wake up every day and give it my all. Thank you for being so patient with me.

To my parents who have just been the absolute best in cheering me on and supporting me in everything they do. I could not have been blessed with better parents and a the most excellent example of parental love and family values.

To Mel, Misty, and Stephanie: you guys are my circle of power. I cannot fail with you three by my side. Thanks for cheering me on the loudest when I wanted to throw in the towel.

To my street-team and ARC readers: without you, I would be lost. Your feedback and the time and energy you've spent into helping make both my book and writing possible are invaluable and I thank God for you guys.

To Joe: Your insights and feedbacks have no only strengthened the backbone of the story but also have continued to turn me into a better writer. I don't know what I'd do without your magnificent brain.

To Anther: what a journey we have been through! Words cannot describe how grateful for your presence in my life once more. You have been my rock for so many years. I can't wait to see what the future holds for us, dear soul-friend!

To Mel, Misty, and Stephanie: you guys are my circle of power. I cannot fail with you three by my side. Thanks for cheering me on the loudest when I wanted to throw in the towel.

Last, but most certainly not least: To you, my dear reader. Thank you for trusting me enough to take you on a journey once more. See you next book!

ABOUT THE AUTHOR

A R Morgan can be found in the wilds of the Pacific Northwest, surrounded by her many fur-babies. She is a lone mama bear to a smart and courageous cub, who has been her biggest cheerleader and reason for pursuing her own dreams. When she is not writing three different stories at a time, or sticking her nose into twelve different books, you will probably find her playing her 134th run through of Baldur's Gate 3. A collector of curio and relic firearms, she can also be found finding peace at the local range.

Ms. Morgan has a background in Criminology and Psychology from Washington State University.

From the age of five, she began writing her own stories, her overactive imagination desperately needing an outlet. Once in adulthood, authors like Laurell K. Hamilton, Keri Lake, J. R. R. Tolkien, George R. Martin, and Brandon Sanderson only fuelled her desire to pursue her own creative path of writing epic romances filled with fantasy, folklore, myths, and legends.